TOWN IN A BLUEBERRY JAM

Town in a
Blueberry Jam

B. B. Haywood

WHEELER PUBLISHING
A part of Gale, Cengage Learning

GALE
CENGAGE Learning

Detroit • New York • San Francisco • New Haven, Conn • Waterville, Maine • London

GALE
CENGAGE Learning

LIBRARY OF CONGRESS CATALOGING-IN-PUBLICATION DATA

Haywood, B. B.
    Town in a blueberry jam / by B.B. Haywood.
        p. cm. — (Wheeler Publishing large print cozy mystery)
    "A Candy Holliday murder mystery."
    ISBN-13: 978-1-4104-2609-3 (alk. paper)
    ISBN-10: 1-4104-2609-2 (alk. paper)
    1. Murder—Investigation—Fiction. 2. Maine—Fiction. 3.
Large type books. I. Title.
PS3608.A9874T69 2010
813'.6—dc22   2010003200

Published in 2010 by arrangement with The Berkley Publishing Group,
a member of Penguin Group (USA) Inc.

Printed in the United States of America
1 2 3 4 5 6 7 14 13 12 11 10

To Sarah for her Ode, and Matthew for
his Melody

ACKNOWLEDGMENTS

Warmest thanks to Kae Tienstra for believing in the book, Leis Pederson for making it happen, George Feeman for his encouragement from the very beginning, and Officer Paul Gasper and Chief Neil R. Williams of the Cape Elizabeth (Maine) Police Department for the tour and invaluable information. Also, a special acknowledgment to Todd Merrill and Jen Dyer at Merrill Blueberry Farms, Ellsworth, Maine, for answering endless questions about blueberry farming. As always, big hugs for Sarah and Matthew for help with the manuscript and the website. For updates about Candy and Doc Holliday, Holliday's Blueberry Acres, and Cape Wellington, Maine, as well as details about upcoming books, visit www.hollidaysblueberryacres.com.

PROLOGUE

He was falling.

A moment earlier he had been standing on solid ground, near the edge of the seaside cliff that dropped sharply to wet black rocks below. Now here he was, his face turned toward the night sky and nothing beneath him but open air. His arms windmilled back and his legs pumped wildly as the memories of a life well lived flashed before his eyes with such speed and vividness it made him gasp.

It really did happen like that, in the moments right before death. He could attest to the fact, if he lived long enough. But he knew he'd never get the chance.

He could still feel the spot on his chest, like a hollow wound, where the hand had struck him hard, coming out of nowhere in a stab of anger. It had caught him so suddenly, so unexpectedly that he'd lost his footing and stumbled to the edge of the cliff, where he'd teetered as a terrifying surge of panic swept through him. An instant later his feet lost contact with solid ground. Now, as he fell, his mind exploded with disbelief and regret, and his face tightened as his mouth pulled back in a death grimace. And underneath it all he cursed himself. He should have seen it coming. All the signs were there. He should have been more attentive. He shouldn't have been standing so close to the edge. But he'd lost his bearings in the argument. He'd let his emotions drive the wits from him — a fatal mistake, he realized now, and his whole body shuddered at the hard, horrifying realization:

I have just been murdered!

How could this be happening? The surrealism of the moment threatened to overwhelm him, to send him into deep shock. His eyes rolled back, his fingers tingled unnaturally, and his chest felt cold, colder than he would have thought possible. His breath was pulled from him by the rushing air as he felt death closing in on him all too quickly.

In those last moments anger spewed forth from him, a hot blast of furor, and he tried to fling curse words back up at the shadowed figure that stood at the edge of the cliff above, watching him with a shocked expression, eyes wide, hands out, grasping at emptiness. But he could bring nothing forth — not a curse, not a scream, nor a grunt or even a spasm of sound. His throat constricted with preternatural fear, all words and sounds choked off, for death was racing toward him at an incalculable speed. How much time did he have left? A heartbeat? Two? Was his heart even still beating? He heard a roaring in his ears as he considered the question within the space of a milli-second. He decided to measure the remainder of his life not in heartbeats, nor in seconds, nor in the blinks of a watery eye, but in the beats of a hummingbird's wings. Surely he had a few dozen of those left, perhaps even a hundred. It would give him a small bit of time to ponder his life before it was crushed achingly from him.

And there was much to ponder, for the memories were coming lightning fast now, like rapid bursts of fire from an automatic weapon. His first remembered glimpse of his parents' faces, younger than he'd ever remembered them before. Touching tiny toes in a retreating wave at the beach. Seagulls whirling overhead. Skipping rocks on a quiet stream, fishing with his father, hockey on the ice pond, his first moments underwater in a wading pool. Then the passion that consumed him, compelled him through life, a life as a professional swimmer. Racing with his friends in the ocean's rough surf — and always winning. Indoor pools at the YMCA, his earliest lessons, and soon after, his first formal swim meet. The cheers of the crowd and the odor of chlorine in his nostrils like the breath of life. The faces of coaches and trainers and myriad competitors, every face remembered. Endless meetings and practices, the tension and excitement of race day, followed by powerful surges of adrenaline for bare moments in the water that became his sole reason for existence. Controlling his rhythm and holding back just a bit of extra energy for the finish. The roars of the crowds growing louder as the crowds themselves grew. Awards and honors, "Oh Say Can You See," feeling the tug of heavy medals draped around his neck, the way they gleamed in the spotlights. Sitting around the kitchen table, talking to his folks about the greater goal. The worry but determination on their faces as they considered the costs, the struggles, the uncertainty of such an unimaginable future. Driving in his dad's old truck to statewide meets, his first time on a plane as he flew off to Nationals, then his first trip overseas with his father, to Europe. Where he won. And continued winning, so many meets, so many wins, so many steps along the way, all laid out like pages of an aged scrapbook that flipped rapidly across his vision. Then to Tokyo and the Olympic Village and the Parade of Nations, all passing by him with such detail, such clarity that he could remember the sounds and the smells as if he stood there now. And his eyes watered as he wondered where it had all gone, how it had slipped away too fast, too fast . . .

Back home, with the parades and speeches, the handshakes and hugs, the looks of pride, admiration, and often jealousy — those last looks were the ones he came to love the most, for they empowered him, gave him a sense of worth and accomplishment.

And the women. Lots of women. They had always come easily to him, attracted by his confidence, his skills, his lean body, his good looks, and that burst of unruly, always uncombed red hair that became his trademark. Even cut short for swim meets it was noticeable, but after his retirement he let it grow out again, and the women couldn't keep their hands off it. Through all the years of traveling, of broadcasting and commentating, of commercials and special appearances, milking his celebrity for every cent he could get out of it, his hair was his calling card.

But in the end it had not saved him. In fact, more than likely it had, in some not-so-small way, led to this moment, his literal downfall.

That almost made him laugh as the hummingbird's wings beat a few more times, and the hard black rocks raced toward him with astonishing swiftness.

He'd heard the rumors around town, the whispers, the surreptitious nods in his direction, the looks askance, and the occasional finger-pointing when they thought he wasn't watching. Folks liked to talk about the plethora of redheaded children around town, though no one ever said anything to him directly about it. And what problem was it to him anyway? Just because he never married, and made little distinction between married and unmarried women — were any of those kids his fault? But that hadn't stopped the threats, the lawsuits, the angry husbands, and sullen stares from jilted lovers. The worst were the clingy ones, who expected more from him than he ever wanted to give. Their emotions spun on a dime, moving from adoration to terrifying

14

rage with a speed that always left him cold and confused, cautious, and ultimately uninterested in any form of intimacy and attachment.

But again, that had been part of his attractiveness, what drew the women to him. There were many who accepted him for what he was, of course, and those were the ones who figured most prominently in his final thoughts. He recalled them all fondly as he fell back, his head below his feet now, his gaze rolling up. The stars in the black sky above glowed brightly before him, so close, so distinctively sharp, elegant pinpricks in a restless infinity. Its beauty struck him with such force that he was distracted from the memories, and in the last moments those memories were lost to him, fading away like a foamy wave rolling off a sandy beach, drawn back into the greater ocean.

The ocean. Water. It had always been his sustenance, his greatest love, his only mistress. It would accept him for a final time now, and he would give himself fully to it.

But still, he had regrets. Too much left undone, too much life still left to be lived. And again, he wondered — how had this happened? How had he come to this moment?

His mind raced in those final few flutters

of the hummingbird's wings, and it was only then, in the last milliseconds of his life, as his body broke on the rocks, crushing the air from his lungs and stealing away his life, that the final flash of memory and realization shot through his screaming brain. The clarity of it was striking, and he knew in that last instant who had driven him to his death. No, she hadn't pushed him off the cliff herself. Her hand wasn't the one that had struck him in the chest, ending his life. But she'd been there in spirit, in the dark shadows of motivation. Hers was the hand behind the hand, her words the whispers in the ear, her thoughts the seeds that led to this tragic end. Scheming and manipulating behind the scenes, she'd driven the killer to murder, flicking domino-block events out to this final, inexorable moment.

It had been her, he was certain of it.

His last thought was of Sapphire Vine.

From *The Cape Crier*
Cape Willington, Maine
July 23rd Edition

THE WEEKLY GRAPEVINE
by Sapphire Vine
Special Correspondent

Blueberries For Everyone!
Are you ready to par-tay? Of course you are! Once again, good citizens, it's time for Cape Willington's world-famous Blueberry Festival! As I'm sure you well know, the fabulously fruity festival is an all-day event scheduled for Saturday, July 27, and it's usually the town's busiest day of the year. (Tourists are *everywhere!*) Festivities kick off at 7:30 A.M. at Legion Hall, with other events taking place around Cape throughout the day. The Blueberry Parade begins at 3 P.M., with Olympic Gold Medal winner Jock Larson serving as the Grand Marshal (again!). Most important, the Blueberry Queen Pageant will take place at 6 P.M. at Town Hall. There are many lovely contestants taking part this year, including Yours Truly — *moi!* Do wish me luck!

17

Don't forget to check out the many wonderful booths that will be lined up along Main Street and Ocean Avenue during the festival. There will be plenty of goodies for everyone. See you there!

Celebrities Abound

Seems like our attractive little town has been a celebrity magnet lately. A few weeks ago we reported sightings of big-time chunky-hunky TV and movie star Patrick Dempsey (he's sooooo McDreamy!) and the lovely missus, who toddled about town with their brood and sampled the wares at a local restaurant. (Patrick was born in Lewiston, you know.) Now a more literary celeb is gracing the starstruck streets of our village — none other than Sebastian J. Quinn, he of the revered poetic tome, *The Bell of Chaos.* And we're thrilled to report that the esteemed Mr. Quinn has consented to serve as a judge at this week's prestigious Blueberry Queen Pageant. Remember, you read it here first!

Engagements

Little Kimmy Whitebridge is all grown up

and planning to marry D. Douglas Douglass III of Cape Willington. Both are graduates of CWHS. Kimmy is currently working in hotel management at the Motel 6 up on Route 1. Douglas is employed at D. D. Douglass & Son Realtors. (I wonder how he got that job?) A September wedding is planned. Happy honeymoon, kids! Do they have heart-shaped beds at the Motel 6?

Kudos

Once again we have to thank the amazing (and seemingly tireless) Wanda Boyle for her committee work at our local schools. In the last year, Wanda planned the teacher luncheons, the Soccer Extravaganza, and the Music Club Money-Makers Fair; worked on the planning committee for reading evaluation of our gifted children; made costumes for the third-grade play; baked cookies for the Halloween and Valentine's Day parties; chaired the PTO — and didn't miss a single meeting. (I think she even cleaned the classrooms a few times.) Wow! Have you seen your own kids lately, Wanda? Ha! Just kidding!

Attention All Gardeners!

Get out your trowels and dig your way to the Cape Garden Club's First Annual Flower Festival, to be held at the Cove Inn on Sunday, August 2. The theme of this very merry special event will be "Tea in the Garden." (Make mine Earl Grey, please!) You can call Lily Verte for all the flowery details. We hope this turns out to be a blossoming event for them.

The Theatre

Apparently Lyra Graveton can carry more than buckets of ice cream. She can carry a tune as well! We normally see Lyra at the Ice Cream Shack scooping up gobs of delicious homemade ice cream. (Have you seen those ice cream cones? They're humongous!) Starting next weekend, you can see (and hear) Lyra belting out tunes in Cape Summer Theatre's musical version of everyone's favorite cowboy show, *Oklahoma!* Tickets are still available at the box office (though they're sure to go fast with Lyra up there on stage!). The show runs through August 12 at the Pruitt Opera House. See it, and Oh! we guarantee you'll have a beautiful, beautiful morning!

Tasty Tidbits

Rumors that Town Council Chairwoman Bertha Grayfire will wear her outrageous Dolly Parton costume (a favorite with the kids at Halloween) when she emcees the annual Blueberry Queen Pageant Saturday night are completely FALSE! (We have heard, however, that the costume has fallen into disrepair lately. You should take better care of your assets, Bertha!). . . . My spy tells me that Melody's Café, that new restaurant up on River Road, is doing a booming business. The lobster rolls are supposed to be absolutely scrumptious! (Don't tell the tourists, though, or I'll never be able to get a seat!) My spy's only request — better desserts, please! . . . Official Judicious F. P. Bosworth sightings for the first two weeks of July — Visible: 9 days — Invisible: 5 days. Sounds like Judicious has been out enjoying this glorious Maine summer weather! Be sure to pass on Judicious sightings to the Grapevine for future publication!

ONE

Candy Holliday was standing at the kitchen sink, cleaning up after making another batch of blueberry pies, when she looked out the window and saw Doc's old pickup truck rattling up the dirt driveway way too early. Curious, she glanced at the clock on the wall over the kitchen table. Usually he wasn't back home until ten thirty or eleven, preferring to linger over his coffee cup as long as possible. But here he was at a little past nine.

She knew right away something was up.

The kitchen wasn't Candy's favorite place to be; she had never considered herself much of a domestic sort. She would rather be outside, tending to her chickens, fiddling around in the barn, taking care of the gardens, or walking the fields behind the house. But when you had a blueberry festival to prepare for, you did what you had to do.

So to stay out of her way (or perhaps just to avoid the chores that always seemed to need doing around the farm), her father, Henry "Doc" Holliday, had gone into town that morning for coffee and donuts with "the boys" — William "Bumpy" Brigham, a barrel-chested semiretired attorney with a deep passion for antique cars; Artie Groves, a retired civil engineer who now ran a bustling eBay business out of a cluttered office over his garage; and Finn Woodbury, a former big-city cop who had segued into small-town show business, serving as producer for three or four community theater projects each year, including the annual musical staged at the Pruitt Opera House on Ocean Avenue. They were golfin' and jawin' buddies, all in their mid- to late sixties, who spent their Friday nights playing poker as though it were a religion and could be found most weekday mornings holding court in the corner booth at Duffy's Main Street Diner. These freewheeling breakfast gatherings, where the latest headlines, rumors, gossip, and sports stories were chewed over like well-cooked bacon, were as addictive as coffee and salt air to Doc, who, despite his retirement, still had an unquenchable thirst for knowledge of any kind and liked to keep his finger tight to the pulse of his adopted village.

So it wasn't surprising he heard the latest shocker before Candy did.

The story had been on the front page of the morning paper, of course, but Doc always took that with him to the diner. Candy only got it around lunchtime, after it had been well pored over and thumbed through, and smartly decorated with coffee rings and swaths of smeared donut icing. And she could have switched on the TV and gotten the story that way, but for the past few days she had been too busy to waste time sitting in front of the tube. Anyway, TV watching was a winter activity around Cape Willington, Maine, where the Downeast summers were short and glorious, and so had to be enjoyed to their fullest. That meant being outside as much as possible, letting the sensual warmth squeeze the chill completely out of one's bones before winter set in again with its unrelenting timeliness.

Candy wasn't outside today, though. It was the day before Cape Willington's much-anticipated Forty-First Annual Blueberry Festival, and she had been in the kitchen since six thirty that morning, making last-minute preparations. She still had way too much to do, and now here was Doc, distracting her when she had no time for distractions.

He pulled the truck to a stop in a cloud of roiling dust; it had been a wet spring but a dry summer so far, causing them both to worry, what with the crop and all. But the upper atmosphere patterns were changing, according to the weatherman, who promised rain in the next week or so, possibly as early as next Tuesday, which could salvage this season's harvest. But she guessed Doc wasn't here to talk about the weather.

He jumped out of the truck, slamming the door hard behind him, and walked with a determined gait into the house, his limp barely slowing him down. He managed to find his way into the kitchen without tripping over any of the baskets and boxes that littered the floor. With a dramatic flourish he laid the paper out on the countertop, front page up. "Have you heard?"

She gave him a confused look and shook her head. "Heard what?"

Doc jabbed with a crooked finger at the paper's front page. "They announced it this morning. It's all over the TV and newspapers." He paused, then said in a low breath, "It's Jock Larson. He's dead."

Two

"Dead?" At first Candy wasn't sure she had heard what she thought she had heard. Maybe her ears weren't working right. She almost smiled, thinking Doc was just playing with her, as he sometimes did. "You're kidding."

He shook his head. " 'Fraid not, pumpkin." His face was stern; there was no trace of a smile to indicate a joke. "Jock's gone, that's for sure."

Candy felt a chill go through her that made her think of winter's coldest day. Suddenly hushed, she asked, "What happened?"

Doc started to speak, but his voice was low and hoarse. He paused, took a moment to clear his throat. Obviously the conversation at the diner that morning had been more spirited than usual. It must have been quite an event. *The boys are probably in a frenzy,* Candy thought. *The whole town probably is.*

Her next thought was, *This is big news. I've got to call Maggie.*

Gathering himself, his voice grave, Doc said, "Well, the information's still pretty sketchy. But what's clear is that sometime late last night, Jock took a nosedive off a cliff up on Mount Desert Island —"

"Oh my God." Candy's hand went to her mouth.

"— and fell to the rocks below, or at least that's the official version. He must have landed hard. Probably killed him instantly." Doc paused. "I've seen those rocks. I was up there just a few weeks ago." He took a deep breath. "Anyway, at some point during the night, his body must have rolled into the water and drifted out to sea. But the tides brought it back in this morning. He washed up on Sand Beach sometime around daybreak. Some elderly tourist up from Maryland found the body. Gave her quite a shock, too, or so I've heard."

"Dad, that's awful."

Doc Holliday nodded. "Yeah it is." He shook his gray-haired head. "This whole thing seems so unreal. I guess it's just hard to believe he's really gone. It sure is going to shake up this town, though."

Falling into silence, he leaned back against the counter, arms crossed and head bowed, and for the first time in a while Candy took a good look at her father. The crags on his face seemed deeper, his dark brown eyes more guarded. His clothes were as rumpled as ever, though, hanging loosely on his frame. He had never been a burly man, but he seemed thinner these days, though not frail. He was getting stronger again, she realized, after years when it seemed he would never fully recover. Despite his efforts to conceal the truth with his humor, the death a few years ago of Holly, Doc's wife and Candy's mother, had hit him hard, and it had taken him a good while to recover from the loss. In the end it had taken a major change — retirement from the university and the purchase of a blueberry farm in a small Maine coastal village, at the strong urging of his daughter — to help him start his recovery. The farm, his life's dream, had become his raison d'etre, keeping him busy and giving him purpose. He started writing again, beginning to fill the hollowness inside him with books and research and activity and friends. And he had quickly adopted this community as his own, taken its people into his heart, its history into his bones.

Now the town's loss was his loss. And it seemed to draw him back just a little into the funk he had worked so hard to pull himself out of.

Still, Candy thought, he and Jock had never been good friends. Come to think of it, they had disliked each other. A lot.

It was all because of that parking spot, Candy recalled. She hadn't lived here then, hadn't yet pulled herself out of the downward spiral in which she had, for a time, floundered herself. But she had heard the story from Maggie Tremont, her best friend in town.

Jock (Maggie had told her) was like a god around Cape Willington. That might have been an overstatement, but it was hard to deny that Jock had put the place on the map, given it a face to the rest of the world. If nothing else, he had been for decades the town's adventurous soul, its favorite son — though a somewhat immoral and often arrogant one, filled with the juice of life. He was not shy to claim his privilege, whatever that might be. For the past few years, that privilege extended to a primo parking spot in front of Duffy's Diner every weekday morning and at around noontime, when Jock stopped in for a cheeseburger and a bowl of homemade chicken noodle soup. New in town and unaware of the etiquette that followed Jock around, Doc parked in that spot one morning and had promptly been warned by both Dolores, the waitress, and Juanita, who worked the counter. Doc listened but hadn't moved his car; he wasn't about to play that game.

When Jock walked in, stomping about and complaining loudly that his parking spot had been taken by some blasted out-of-towner, and that he had been forced to park almost a half block away — an inconceivable affront to his quasi-celebrity status — Doc calmly assumed responsibility and then proceeded to tell Jock, to the horror of all in listening range, that the parking spots in town were for the general public, available on a first-come-first-served basis, and that it was foolish and downright undemocratic to assume they could be reserved for any one individual. With that, he paid his check and left, leaving stunned diners and a sputtering, disbelieving Jock in his wake.

Once they got off on the wrong foot, it had never been set right. Jock took to getting up extra early so he could get to the diner before anyone else to claim his spot, and Doc let him have it, ambling in at his usual time, around eight. Jock usually sat at the counter, so Doc opted for the corner booth. Jock had his friends, so Doc found others. After that first meeting there had been few words between the two, and there had never been any overt confrontation, but it was clear they rubbed each other the wrong way.

So why was Doc so upset now?

With a start, Candy realized there was more to the story, something he hadn't told her yet. She could see it in his eyes now; somehow she had missed it earlier, or misinterpreted it. Her mind lurched off in a different direction as she thought back over what Doc had said . . .

He took a nosedive off a cliff and fell to the rocks below . . . or at least that's the official version . . .

She shuddered as she was struck by a horrendous thought.

"Dad . . . was it an accident or . . . did he jump?"

Doc's gaze shifted toward her. "Suicide?"

Candy had the impression he was ready for the question but still held something back. She pressed on. "Well, it's possible, isn't it? Unless he was just trying to dive in. You know — doing something crazy. Maybe he had a few drinks in him and took it as a challenge."

Doc shook his head. "Jock pushed the limits, but he wasn't crazy."

"Well, then he either fell by accident . . . or he jumped."

32

But Doc wasn't buying it. "That doesn't make any sense. Jock was treated like a god around here. He never had a care in the world — got everything he wanted. No, pumpkin, I don't think he jumped. I think the real question is, did he fall . . . or was he pushed?"

THREE

"Pushed? You mean he was . . . murdered?"

Even as the words left her mouth, Candy realized she wasn't completely surprised. For years Jock had gotten away with murder — of an entirely different kind, of course. He had been a fifty-five-year-old "bad boy," tooling around town in an old Cadillac convertible in the summer, chasing women with little discretion, and behaving more like a teenager than a mature adult. That made Candy smile inwardly, for *maturity* was not a word one would have used to describe Jock Larson. Everyone in town knew he pushed his luck too far — and now luck had pushed back.

Doc reacted to her question with an arched eyebrow and a scowl, a look he had perfected over the years with his students. "When you put it like that, it sounds absurd, doesn't it?" He dug into his back pocket for a handkerchief and dabbed at his face, then blew his nose. "Blast, it's getting humid again. Too damn warm for Maine, that's for sure."

He crossed to the cupboard with a slight limp — a remnant of a biking accident long ago that still hitched up once in a while and bothered him — took out a glass, and walked to the fridge, a thoughtful expression on his face. "As crazy as it might sound, though," he said as he opened the freezer and scooped up a handful of ice, which clinked noisily into the glass, "it makes the most sense."

"More sense than an accident . . . or suicide?"

Doc closed the freezer door with his elbow and opened the lower door, then stood staring into the fridge for a moment. "What happened to the lemonade?" he asked finally.

"You drank it last night."

"You didn't make up a new batch?"

Candy raised her arms to the room. "Look around, Dad. I've been kinda busy today." She paused, letting out a huff. "Besides, we're out. I've got it on the grocery list."

Doc sighed audibly, closed the fridge door, and walked to the sink, filling the glass with water. The cubes cracked and popped loudly.

People who didn't know much about Doc assumed that, because of his nickname, he was a medical doctor, and he rarely corrected that misconception. "Let them think what they want," he often said with a shrug. Truth was, he had taught ancient history for more than thirty years at the University of Maine at Orono, up near Bangor, after receiving his doctorate from the University of Pennsylvania. He was a careful, thoughtful, studious man who loved nothing more than to close himself up in his office and delve into the mysteries of history to try to understand the motivations of those who had shaped the world centuries ago, for better or worse. And though he often said he would have been better off had he been born into one of those ancient eras he loved so much, he was no less fascinated by the motivations of those who went about their lives in the modern age. "Technology changes," he often said, "but people don't."

He took a long drink of water, then tilted his head thoughtfully, as if he had just heard Candy's question. "Suicide doesn't make any sense," he said after a moment. "Not when you think about it. It just doesn't seem like something Jock would do, does it? He wasn't the suicide type." Doc shook his head as he swirled the glass lazily, mixing the tap water and ice cubes. "No, it just doesn't seem like something Jock would do."

"Why? Because he was too arrogant to kill himself?"

"Bingo." Doc's finger shot out to emphasize the point. "No one believed the hype about Jock more than Jock himself. He was a cult figure around here — though I'll admit he turned into a caricature of himself long ago. But no one seemed to notice — or mind much if they did — so Jock went about his life and milked his never-ending fame for all it was worth. He was good at it too. This was Jock's town, and he was having his way with it. No, Jock had too much going on and too big an ego to throw himself off that cliff. So suicide's out of the question — I'm sure of that."

Candy muttered a quizzical "Hmm" and tapped at her pursed lips with her fingers — subtle actions she knew would egg her father on. This was getting interesting. "An accident then?"

Doc took another drink of water as he considered this. "Could be," he admitted as he worked an ice cube around his mouth, "though unlikely. For that to happen we'd have to assume that, for whatever reason, Jock — who despite his age was an accomplished athlete who still exercised regularly — was out taking a midnight stroll along an island cliff forty-five minutes from his home, got careless, stepped too close to the edge, and took a tumble." Doc shrugged, bit into the cube, and chewed it noisily. "It just seems to go against his training and abilities."

"But it's possible that's exactly what happened," Candy pointed out.

Doc gave a nod. "Sure, it's possible. Jock was a loose cannon who'd been known to do stupid things. Let's assume he went hiking alone up on that cliff in the middle of the night — no one would put that past him. But what would cause him to wander too close to the edge in the first place, let alone lose his footing and fall over the side? The sky was clear last night and the moon was half-full, so there was some light up there. And he must have had a flashlight with him — he wasn't foolish enough to take a hike in the dark. So we can probably assume he didn't just walk off the edge of the cliff."

"Alcohol?" Candy suggested.

"Jock drank but he wasn't a drunk — and he wasn't stupid."

"Maybe he had a stroke, or maybe he was startled by a badger or porcupine that caused him to lose his footing."

"Maybe . . . but that's stretching the boundaries of logic, isn't it?"

"Murder, though?" Candy shook her head skeptically. "Is that any more logical?"

Doc's response was adamant. "Damn straight it is! Jock had plenty of admirers around here — mostly of the female persuasion — but he also had plenty of enemies — mostly the *husbands* of those female admirers. It's easy to imagine someone following him up to that cliff or luring him there under certain pretenses. Perhaps an argument ensued, a fight broke out, punches were thrown, someone got careless, and Jock went over the edge."

"Or perhaps, like you said, it wasn't an accident," Candy said softly. Doc gave her a satisfied look. "Now you're thinking my way."

Despite the warmth of the morning, Candy shivered. "So what's the official word? Has Finn heard anything?" Being an ex-cop, Finn Woodbury, one of Doc's diner buddies, had a few contacts inside the Cape Willington police force.

"So far they've been tight as a clam. But Finn's been sniffing around. Something's up, or so he says. The word he's heard on the street is that the death looks 'suspicious.' They've brought the crime lab van over from Augusta, and the medical examiner will probably perform an autopsy. But the investigation's just getting started. Far as I know, they're on the island right now, combing the place for evidence."

"Suspicious, huh?" Candy shuddered again involuntarily. "It's just so strange to think something like that can happen around here — especially to someone like Jock. It's so . . . so unexpected."

"Unexpected death can take place in the most unexpected places. But that's not such a bad thing. Caesar once said an unexpected death is preferable to an expected one."

"I guess he should know. So speaking of the unexpected . . . what are they going to do about the parade?"

"Parade?"

"You know. The Blueberry Festival? Tomorrow? Jock's supposed to be the grand marshal this year, isn't he?"

"Oh, that." Doc shrugged. "Jock's the grand marshal *every* year — or at least he was. I'm not sure what they'll do, but his death is sure going to cast a pall over the whole weekend."

"You got that right." Candy started as a thought shot through her. "But everything's still on schedule, right? Nothing's been canceled?" She had invested a lot of time

40

and effort in her preparations for the festival; it would be disastrous if it had all been in vain.

But Doc just waved a hand. "No, course not. Everything will go on as planned, with or without Jock, you can be sure of that. Too many people are involved, and too many tourists are coming into town to change things now. Hotel rooms are booked all up and down the coast. Every merchant in town is counting on the money they'll make this weekend."

"Including us." Candy eyed the fruits of her labor piled on the counter and floor.

"Right. Including us." Doc's gaze followed Candy's. "So what'd we wind up with?"

"Oh, you know, the usual," Candy said, nonchalantly tossing aside a few strands of thick honey blonde hair. After keeping it short for years to give herself a more professional appearance, she had decided to let it grow out. It was one more concession to the here and now, one more step in leaving her previous life behind. Her expensive suits had been hung in garment bags at the back of the closet, makeup was reserved for only the most special occasions now, and her hair, normally straight, was starting to curl as it reached her jawline. It was a good look for her, she decided, a more comfortable, earthier look, fitting in well with the jeans, T-shirts, and work boots she found herself wearing more often than not these days.

Doc surveyed the items piled around the kitchen. "A lot more than usual, I'd say. Looks like you've been cooking yourself into a frenzy."

"You got that right," Candy agreed, for even she had to admit it was an impressive array of goodies. Ready for sale at the Blueberry Festival the following day were a dozen large blueberry pies, three dozen mini pies, half a hundred blueberry scones, and an equal number of oversized blueberry cookies — a popular seller with the kids. There were jars upon jars of blueberry jam, blueberry honey, and blueberry syrup, lined up in neat rows like soldiers on parade. Toward the end of the counter were stacks of balsam wreaths and garlands interspersed with sprigs of fresh blueberries, which had taken her days to make. There were twenty squat jars of blueberry butter, an experiment this year, and more blueberry muffins than she cared to count, neatly packed into battered tins that had once belonged to her mother.

On the floor by the back door were two large cardboard boxes stuffed with a hundred blueberry tie-dyed T-shirts of various sizes, another favorite with festival-goers. She had made those herself too, with pastel-colored T-shirts she had ordered wholesale from a company in upstate New York.

Next to those was a smaller box filled with bars of blueberry soap, also a hot seller. Then there were the empty baskets she still had to fill with a variety of carefully arranged homemade products — the Blueberry Acres gift baskets were her most profitable items.

She also had a few dozen pints of fresh blueberries ready to go, though there would be so many of those available at the festival tomorrow that she wasn't counting on selling too many of them. Most tourists preferred something a little more exotic than the pure and simple fruit itself.

And, of course, there was the last batch of pies, still warming on the stovetop. And the chocolate-covered blueberries, which had to be packed into small cellophane packages and tied up with blue and green ribbons. Some of the items still had to be labeled. She had to pack everything up for transport into town in the morning.

And she still had to finish the booth . . .

She felt exhausted just looking at it all. She had spent the better part of three weeks getting it all together, and there was still so much to do.

"You've done a heck of a job, that's for sure," Doc said, hitching up his trousers, "but it should get easier for you this afternoon. Ray's coming over to help out with the booth."

It was like someone had set off a bomb. Candy looked up at her father, thunderstruck. "What?"

"I saw him at the diner," Doc continued, unaware of the reaction he had just drawn from his daughter. "He said he'd be glad to help out. He wasn't doing much this afternoon anyway."

"Ray? But . . . no, Dad, tell me you didn't."

"Didn't what?" Doc looked confused.

"You didn't invite Ray over."

For a moment, Doc hesitated. "Sure I did. We can use his help with the booth, can't we?"

Candy groaned. "No, Dad, not Ray. Not today. He gets in the way more than he helps." Her shoulders dropped as she leaned back against the counter, crossing her arms in frustration. "Besides, I thought *you* were going to help me."

"Me?" Doc didn't seem to know how to respond to his daughter's disappointment. "I'm a scholar. You know that. I'm no good with a hammer. I'd just screw things up. Ray's the guy you need. He'll do a good job."

"But Dad . . ."

"Oh, don't worry, it'll be okay. Ray'll build you a fine booth," Doc said, and he winked and gave her a smile. "Besides, he's got a thing for you, you know."

"Dad! Don't you dare . . ."

But Doc went on, sensing a way out of the doghouse. "Well, he does. Anyone can tell that. I realize he might not be the right fellow for you, but you can't stay single forever, pumpkin. It's been how long — three years — since the divorce? Time to get back into the scene."

Candy glowered at him and lowered her voice to a threatening level. "It's only been two and a half years, thank you very much. And I'll decide when it's time to get back into the *scene,* as you call it." She gave him a solid harrumph. "And don't call me *pumpkin.* You know how much I hate that name."

A twinkle came to Doc's eyes. "What else do you want me to call my favorite Halloween-born daughter?"

"Dad, I'm your *only* Halloween-born daughter. And my actual name would be nice for a change."

He chuckled. "Sure thing, pumpkin," he

said, checking his watch. "Oops. Got to go. I should be home by dinner. I'll bring something. Chinese okay?" He started for the door.

"What? Where are you going?"

But before Doc could answer, the phone rang. It was Maggie, calling to talk about Jock. "Candy! It's me. Have you heard? It's unbelievable, isn't it? There are rumors flying around town like bats on Halloween night."

"Hang on," Candy told Maggie, putting her hand over the phone as she called after her father. "Dad!"

Doc paused at the door. His eyes looked contrite, but his body was ready to go. "Sorry, honey, but I promised the right reverend I'd help the church folks with some of the setup. They're putting up three booths, you know. We'll pack everything up when I get back, okay?" He gave her a wave, and then he was gone.

A few moments later, Candy heard the old Ford pickup truck sputter to life and watched out the window as her father drove down the dirt lane toward town.

"Ohh," she muttered to herself as she lifted the phone back to her ear, "I'm gonna kill him."

"Kill who?" Maggie said. "What did I

miss? Tell me everything — and don't leave out a single word."

FOUR

Half an hour later Candy was out in the rickety old barn, cursing loudly as she struggled with a four-by-eight sheet of plywood, when she heard a truck in the driveway.

"Dad, you're back!" she blurted as she poked her head out the barn door.

But it wasn't her father.

"Oh, Ray, it's you," she said as the local handyman climbed out of his tan Toyota pickup, which was nearly as old and beat up as her father's Ford.

"Howdy, Miss Candy." Ray Hutchins greeted her with a tip of his well-worn Red Sox baseball cap, revealing a mop of un-combed dark hair that was starting to go gray. "Doc said I should stop by to help you out." He pronounced it *hep*. "Says yer building somethin'. What are ya up to?"

Trying hard to hide her disappointment, Candy waved him into the barn. "It's a new booth for the festival tomorrow. Might as well come on in, long as you're here."

Ray's head bobbed happily. "Sure, Miss Candy, be glad to," and he grabbed his toolbox from the back of the truck and ambled over to the barn with that odd gait of his. It was as if the bones in his shoulders and legs had been fitted together all wrong, making his body seem disjointed. The way he walked reminded Candy of a marionette.

Ray was about ten years older than she was, tall and lean, with an innocent smile and droopy eyes that seemed ready to slide off the sides of his face. Thirty years ago he would have been called something cruel and unfortunate, but these days when folks around town talked about Ray, they often referred to him as being "special" or "mentally challenged." Even that was hardly accurate, though. Ray would never be considered an intellectual giant, true, but he'd finished high school, and he had more common sense and life knowledge than many gave him credit for. More important, he was a gentle, kind soul who made his living with his hands as a talented carpenter, capable plumber and electrician, and overall handyman.

Doc had him out to Blueberry Acres every few weeks or so, fixing one thing or another

— building shelves in the den or putting in a few extra electrical outlets in the basement or repairing some of the outbuildings. Ray didn't seem to have a problem doing any of those things when he was working for Doc. But when he got around Candy, all his carefully honed skills seemed to leach right out of him, and he often was reduced to the level of a shy, awkward schoolboy.

Which was one problem Candy didn't need today.

"Have you heard about Jock?" Ray asked as he followed her into the barn.

Perhaps a bit too distractedly, she said, "I've heard. It's a terrible tragedy, really."

"Sure is. Terrible, terrible." Ray pronounced it *turrible*. He shook his head sadly. "Jock and me was related, you know."

Candy stopped and looked at him curiously. "No, I didn't know that. Were you two cousins?"

Ray blinked shyly and his face reddened just a bit. "Sort of. His mama's husband was my mama's second cousin."

"Oh. I see." Candy had to think about that a moment. "So he was, what, your second or third cousin-in-law?"

"Um, yeah, I guess."

"So did you and Jock see each other much? You guys talk a lot?"

50

"Oh no. He was a real busy person, you know. Real famous. We didn't get together much. But when we was younger we used to hang out sometimes at the diner. He tried to fix me up with a girl once."

"I bet you're going to miss him."

"Yup. Yup I am. He was a real good man."

"He sure was." Candy fought an urge to glance at her watch. "So, you ready to get started?"

"Yup, sure am."

Candy clapped her hands together. "Okay, here's what we've got," she said as she walked farther into the barn, pointing to a pile of wood near the back. "It's a simple project — a three-sided booth with a wide counter in the front for displaying items for sale. I thought I'd hinge the sides so I can fold them in and load the whole thing into Doc's truck." She picked up the brass hinges that sat on a swaybacked bench along the back wall, then indicated a pile of raw wood nearby.

"Doc's already got all the wood we need. There are extra two-by-fours to use as crossbeams across the top of the booth to stabilize it. And I'm working on the banner I'll hang across the front."

She pointed to the five-foot-long swath of canvas nearby, with the words HOLLIDAY'S

51

BLUEBERRY ACRES, CAPE WILLINGTON, MAINE sketched out in pencil along its length.

"I'd also like to build some shelves into the back side of the front display section," Candy continued, "and maybe we can put some hooks in the crossbeams so I can hang up a few of the gift baskets for show."

Ray listened to her carefully, surveyed the materials and what she'd done so far, and set to work without a word. Doc had already cut some of the two-by-fours and marked the quarter-inch sheets of plywood for cutting. Ray walked back to his truck to get a cordless circular saw, and for the next half hour or so the summer air was filled with the smells of sawdust and the shriek of metal teeth cutting into raw wood, mixing in with the buzzing of honeybees, the chirps and trills of sparrows and terns, and the earthy smells coming off the blueberry barrens and surrounding woods.

For the most part Ray worked silently, his mouth drawn into a tight thoughtful line, his hands fumbling about a bit more than usual. Candy regularly caught him glancing her way. She was used to glances like that. She knew that, at thirty-six, she still looked pretty good in a pair of jeans — not because she exercised a lot (which she hated to do) but because she did lots of farmwork. ("Who needs a gym," Doc often said, "when you've got a blueberry farm?") The sun had added some color to her high, full cheekbones this summer and a touch of rosemary honey to the tips of her hair. It contrasted nicely with her eyes, which were a light shade of blue but bright — "the color of forget-me-nots in the spring," her mother used to tell her. And that morning she'd slipped on a faded red T-shirt, which clung to her a little more than she would have liked on this hot, humid July afternoon.

Thank God she'd remembered to wear a bra.

After awhile Ray settled down to business, his eyes focused on the work in front of him more than on Candy's figure, and the booth began to take shape.

At around three thirty they took a break. Candy invited Ray into the kitchen for some fresh-baked blueberry pie. Ray's nervousness made him fidgety and restless. In a moment of carelessness he knocked his water glass to the floor, shattering it, and tipped over a chair when he turned around too fast. Sweat began to break out on his forehead. He mumbled a lot, shifted his eyes this way and that, and even had to ask directions to the bathroom.

"Ray, you've been here plenty of times before. You know where it's at," Candy said, a note of frustration creeping into her voice. Struggling to hold back a sigh, she pointed him to the proper door. She didn't want to hurt his feelings but she had too much to do today, and didn't have time to deal with these kinds of delays.

Chastised, Ray dropped his head as he walked down the hall and closed the bathroom door behind him.

Once they were back outside, Candy decided Ray needed a few minutes alone to settle down, so she left him in the barn while she went out back to check on her chickens.

Ray had helped her build the chicken coop last fall, right after she purchased the "girls," as she called them. She'd opted for bantam hens — mostly because she had been so taken with the small, squat black and white birds as she walked past them in the poultry shed at the Common Ground Country Fair up in Unity. She'd bought six hens on impulse that very day. Doc had grumbled a bit as he loaded the cage into the back of the truck, but he soon warmed to the idea.

Back home, Candy had been surprised to find that in short order she developed a strange affection for her little flock. She discovered that each hen had a distinctive personality and a little routine, and they seemed to listen to her when she talked to them, which amused her to no end. They were also surprisingly good egg producers. She had quickly increased her flock to a baker's dozen and since then added two more — perhaps because having thirteen hens seemed to be tempting fate. Now they had more than enough eggs, which Candy gave away to friends or dropped off at a local bakery where she worked part-time. Lord knew Herr Georg, the baker, went through plenty of eggs, and he clucked over them almost as much as the chickens did.

The girls chattered and gathered curiously about her as she fed and watered them and collected their eggs in a wire basket — seven today so far.

Before she headed back to the barn to check on Ray, she walked out past the chicken coop and looked out over the blueberry fields that rolled like a choppy blue green sea back to a ridge of trees in the distance. A few years ago she would have been greatly amused to see herself standing here on a farm holding a basketful of eggs. She had been an urban girl, an up-and-comer working for a busy marketing firm that served the top high-tech companies in Boston. She'd had a killer wardrobe, a tight group of friends, a solid, happy marriage with a smart, handsome guy. . . . And then it unraveled so fast she'd barely had time to come to grips with it all. Clark, her husband, lost his lucrative job as a software engineer when the company he worked for lost its financing and had to make cutbacks. When he had trouble finding another job, he invested a big chunk of their savings in a start-up venture, which went under in six months, making household finances even tighter. After that he became despondent, which seemed natural to Candy, who assumed it was because of his work situation. But she had the whole thing all wrong. He left her shortly after that, telling her he had fallen in love with someone else. He was out in California now, remarried with a child and a second one on the way. Even the thought of that still gave Candy pain; she and Clark tried for years to have children but had never been successful.

But that was not the worst of it. A few weeks after Clark left her, she had gone out to dinner with her best friend Zoe. They'd met in college, dated some of the same boys, and stayed friends after Candy and Clark married. Zoe married also, but it hadn't lasted long; she'd been divorced for years. The dinner had been a time for them to commiserate with each other, and they even shared a tiramisu. They parted on what Candy thought was a positive note. But not more than a few hours later Zoe committed suicide, alone in her apartment. According to police reports, she had taken an overdose of pills.

Candy was devastated, not only because she'd lost her best friend but also because she, Candy, hadn't even been aware of Zoe's depression and had done nothing to save her friend.

After that the bottom fell out of her life. She became physically ill, took to bed for weeks, neglected her work, and stopped eating. She turned away from her other friends, unable to face them. She started drinking heavily. She wound up in the hospital and eventually lost her job. Officially she'd been fired, but in her heart she never had any intention of going back. She simply gave up on her old life.

That's when Doc called, one dreary morning when she was feeling particularly down. He told her he was at the coffee shop around the corner and was coming by to pick her up and take her up to Blueberry Acres for the weekend. Five minutes later he knocked on her front door. She tried to put on a brave face but quickly fell into his arms, sobbing, and let him take her home.

Doc had discovered Blueberry Acres, a twenty-five-acre farm off the Coastal Loop just outside of Cape Willington, during one of his long drives along the coast a few weeks after Holly died. He and Holly had looked for a place just like this for years, and he knew as soon as he saw it that this was exactly what he had sought for so long. At first he had hesitated in making such a big change, which involved leaving teaching and taking up a career as a gentleman farmer. He questioned whether it was wise to make a decision of that magnitude when he was in such an emotional state. But in the end Candy had convinced him that it was the right way to go. He loved the farming life immensely — but he realized only after he moved in just how much work the place needed, and had been picking at it as best he could ever since. Still, at times it seemed to overwhelm him.

Candy had visited the farm many times before, but during that weekend stay after Doc had come down and rescued her, she began to see the place in a new light, and the idea of a permanent change for her as well took shape quickly in her mind. She knew Doc could use her help. She knew she could use a change. It hadn't been a difficult decision.

So Doc drove her back to Boston, they cleaned out her apartment, and without looking back, she moved to a blueberry farm in Downeast Maine.

Now they had just over fifteen acres of the lowbush wild blueberries that were native only to this far-northeastern corner of the country, and they were planning, in the next year or so, to push back the thin piney woods that edged their property even farther to open up a few more acres. They also had half an acre of vegetables, a small herb garden, and various flower beds around the property, as well as the chicken coop behind the barn. They had talked about adding more — a few farm animals, a larger vegetable garden — but decided to keep things manageable, at least for the time being.

It was a good life, a simple life, and it had been her salvation, Candy thought as she headed back to the barn to check on Ray. She and Doc had been through a lot, but the farm had healed them both. Right now, she couldn't imagine living any other place on earth than right here, on Blueberry Acres in Cape Willington in Downeast Maine, just a mile or so from the sea.

FIVE

When she walked back into the barn, Ray was cursing.

"What's wrong?" Candy asked.

But he didn't have to answer. She saw the problem instantly — he had put the hinges on backwards, so the sides of the booth folded the wrong way.

"I'm sorry, Miss Candy," he said, his eyes bright with held-back tears and his hands trembling. "I just got ahead of myself and wasn't thinking."

Candy sighed and set the basket of eggs on a sideboard. "It's okay, Ray. Come on, I'll help you fix it."

Working together, they unscrewed the hinges and got the sides on the right way. Then, while Ray set to work on the shelves on the back of the front piece, Candy took up Ray's hammer to nail brackets onto the ends of the crossbeams, so they could be easily attached to the tops of the side pieces.

Candy wasn't the handiest person on the planet, and she swung the hammer wildly at the nails, missing the flat heads more than a few times and swearing under her breath as she pounded away. But she got the damned nails down into the damned wood without hitting herself on the thumb or fingers, which was good enough for her.

She had two of the brackets on and was reaching for a third when she realized Ray wasn't doing anything. Looking up, she saw that he was frozen, staring at her.

Her brows knitted together in annoyance. "What's wrong now?" she asked crossly.

Ray pointed. "M-myy . . . m-myy . . . my hammer."

Not understanding, Candy looked down at the tool she held in her hand. "Yeah, what about it?"

It took Ray a moment to speak. "It's . . . it's brand new."

He was right about that. He must have just bought it at Gumm's Hardware Store in town. It had a red fiberglass handle with a black cushion grip and a polished claw head that looked as if it had never been used — except by her just now. She noticed that she had scarred the head in a few places and nicked the handle.

"Oh," she said as understanding dawned

on her. "Guess I am being a little rough with it, huh?" She rose, crossed to Ray, and held it out to him. "Here."

He took the hammer gingerly in his fingers, practically cradling it, as if he were afraid it would snap in half if he held it too tightly.

Candy looked around the barn. "I think Doc's got an old hammer around here I can use." It took her a few moments to find it, but soon she was back at work. As she nailed on the last few brackets, she looked up to see that Ray had wrapped the red-handled hammer in a white cloth, placed it back in his toolbox, and had taken out another one, older and well used. He apparently had no intention of using his shiny new hammer any more that day.

In another twenty minutes or so they were done. Candy stepped back to admire their handiwork. "Thanks, Ray," she said, hands on her hips. "I couldn't have done it without you."

After that, things got really awkward. With the booth done, Candy tried to shoo Ray on his way so she could finish up the banner and the other things that needed to be done. But he seemed reluctant to leave.

It took him a full ten minutes to pack up his tools while Candy paced about impatiently. After that he hemmed and hawed in the driveway, talking about the weather, about the folks in town, about fishing, about anything he could think of to delay the inevitable.

Candy couldn't help glancing at her watch, feeling the press of time. Finally, as gently as she could, she said, "Ray, I've got a lot to finish up to get ready for the festival tomorrow. Thanks again for helping with the booth."

"Um, sure thing, Miss Candy." He paused a moment, his gray eyes shifting. "Can I help you with anything else? I got some spare time today."

"Today's not a good day. Maybe next week when things calm down, okay?"

"Doc said something this morning about fixing the banister. He said some of the spindles were loose."

"I'll have him give you a call and we'll set something up. You'll send us the bill for today, right? And, um, I'll buy you a new hammer if you want. I didn't mean to nick up that one with the red handle."

He nodded absently but still he hesitated, looking down at his steel-toed boots, kicking at a stone. Finally he set his jaw firm, as if he had made up his mind about something. He looked up at her.

"Miss Candy," he said with great seriousness, "would you go out with me some day?"

"What?" The word came out as sort of a bark, surprising even Candy. She was a little embarrassed by her outburst, but the look on Ray's face never wavered. He had put the question out there. Now she had to answer it.

"Ray," she began softly, "you're a wonderful person and all, and one of these days you're going to meet some lucky woman . . ."

She came to an abrupt stop when she saw the look in his eyes change. The sense of hopefulness that had been there a moment before turned wary, protective, as if he were bracing for the rejection he knew was to come.

Candy hesitated. What could she say to him without hurting his feelings? Her body relaxed a little as the tension seemed to leak out of her. She hadn't realized she had been holding herself so stiffly.

"Oh, Ray . . ." Finally, impulsively, she took a step toward him and kissed him lightly on the cheek. "I'll think about it, okay?" she said as she heard a car horn beep.

They both turned. Coming up the lane was an old red Volvo, driven by a balding, distinguished-looking gentleman with a white handlebar moustache.

"Oh, it's Herr Georg!" Candy called happily, waving. She pronounced his name the German way, the way he liked it pronounced — *gay-org.*

Georg Wolfsburger was a German immigrant who had lived in Cape Willington for nearly three decades — and, in truth, he helped put the sleepy coastal town on the culinary map with his Black Forest Bakery, a quaint little shop nestled between a bookstore and a coffee shop on Main Street. Though patrons could always find scrumptious breads and cookies at Georg's bakery, they came mostly for his specialties — cakes and pastries baked from old German recipes.

His blueberry strudel was to die for, and the cherry, blueberry, and especially chocolate cheesecakes were heavenly. Brides-to-be and their mothers came from as far away as Boston and Connecticut to purchase Herr Georg's towering wedding cakes, and cars with license plates from such distant and exotic places as New York, New Jersey, Ohio, and Pennsylvania, even Colorado and California could be found parked in front of Georg's shop throughout the summer and well into the fall.

Georg and Candy had struck up a friendship soon after she moved to Blueberry Acres. In season, Georg bought pounds and pounds of fresh blueberries from her, and she often helped out in his shop during busy periods. He had even helped her perfect the recipes for her muffins, scones, and pies, offering up a secret ingredient for each one — olive oil in the muffins, for instance, or a touch of vanilla in the scones. She still would not reveal these secret ingredients to anyone else, including (or perhaps *especially*) her father. Doc had many positive traits, but discretion was not one of them.

Herr Georg brought the old Volvo to a stop in a roiling cloud of dust and climbed out of the car, carrying a pink pastry box. "*Guten tag,* Candy!" he called with a wave as he joined them. "Hullo, Ray," he added with a polite nod.

"Afternoon, Mr. George," Ray responded in a guarded fashion. He followed the lead of many of the locals, who refused to use the German pronunciation of Herr Georg's name, believing that if he lived in America, he should be referred to as an American would be.

Georg appeared not to notice, though he immediately turned his back to Ray, focusing his attention on Candy. "I've brought

something special I just took out of the
oven, and I couldn't wait to show it to you,"
he said in an accented voice as he held up
the pastry box. "Could I perhaps tempt you
with a little afternoon delight?"

Herr Georg's innuendo was not lost on
Candy, but she knew his insinuations were
harmless and usually didn't let them bother
her. In fact, at times she even thought them
charming in an Old European sort of way.

"Ray and I just had some pie," she said
with a teasing smile.

"Oh, but you must try this," the baker
coaxed, tapping the box with a well-
manicured finger. "It's quite decadent." The
way he wiggled his eyebrows, trying to
entice her, reminded her of Groucho Marx.

"Herr Georg, if I didn't know better, I'd
say you were trying to fatten me up."

"I promise you, it will be worth your
while."

Candy grinned. "Promise?"

"Of course!" said the baker heartily.

"Then how could I possibly refuse?" Her
gaze shifted. She nodded at the handyman.
"Ray's been helping me out with the booth
today, but we're all finished. Right?"

Ray seemed to finally get the hint. He let
out a breath of resignation through his nose
as his whole body slouched. "Um, yeah.

Yeah, we are." Forlornly he tossed the tool-box into the back of his truck, climbed into the cab, and drove off with a halfhearted wave.

"Nice fellow," Herr Georg observed as Ray's truck disappeared down the lane. "A bit slow but friendly enough. I'm having him over to the shop on Monday to put up some shelves."

"Oh, Ray's great," Candy agreed as she watched the truck drive away. Then she turned and took the baker by the arm, steering him toward the house. "So, tell me, what have you got in the box?"

"Oh, well, as I said, it's quite special. It's a German pastry called a *linzerschnitten.*"

Inside the kitchen, he dramatically opened the box and let her smell the aroma first, then with a flair lifted out a plate that held the layered torte pastry.

"It looks delicious," Candy said. "What's in it?"

"Three thin layers of spicy dough made with ground almonds, hazelnuts, cinnamon, and lemon zest. There's a delightful butter-cream between each layer. And on top, a layer of almond paste, followed by a layer of fresh blueberries, topped with a crosshatch of dough, all delicately baked to a crispy brown. In Germany, raspberries, apricots, or cranberries are usually used for the fruit topping, but of course blueberries are a must here."

"Of course." Candy nudged the still-warm, golden brown crosshatching with her pinky. "Herr Georg, no one makes pastries as flaky as yours."

He grinned at the compliment, showing off the gap between his two front teeth. "Would you like a bite?"

"More than one, I hope. I'll put on the tea."

Herr Georg's *linzerschnitten* was like nothing Candy had ever tasted before, but she'd come to expect only the best from him. They ate two small pieces each, washing them down with cinnamon-orange tea. Herr Georg left the rest for Doc and Candy to enjoy as dessert that evening.

The baker carefully surveyed Candy's preparations for the festival, pronouncing her pies and scones among the best looking he had ever seen. Then, late in the warm afternoon, she walked him out to his car.

"I've made several batches of *linzerschnitten* for sale at the festival tomorrow," he said as he climbed into the driver's seat.

"Guess I'd better bring along my checkbook then."

"Ah, Candy, *meine liebchen,* your money

is no good with me. You know that." He winked at her as he started the car. "I'll save one for you."

After he drove off, Candy walked back into the kitchen and began to pack up the baked goods and gifts for the festival in the morning.

Doc called just before dinnertime. "Sorry I'm late, pumpkin, but I got sidetracked. I stopped in at the diner to check the news about Jock, and it looks like something's up. Rumor is they've found some incriminating evidence at the scene, but we don't know what yet. Finn's checking it out now, so I thought I'd hang around in case he needs any backup. I probably won't be home for dinner. You want to join me here?"

She was tempted but, in the end, decided she still had too much to do. "What about the festival and the booth? We still have to load up the truck."

"Don't worry. I'll take care of it when I get back. We'll do Chinese another night, okay?"

Candy couldn't help feeling disappointed as she hung up. "Another Friday night alone," she muttered to herself as she dropped into a chair, surrounded by silence.

On an impulse she called Maggie, just to find someone to talk to, but all she got was an answering machine.

She hung up without leaving a message.

In a moment of weakness she thought of calling Ray but quickly decided that was crazy.

"Well, guess it's time to get back to work," she said as she rose. And then she spotted Herr Georg's *linzerschnitten* sitting on the counter where he had left it.

She finished off the whole thing right then and there, washed down with half a bottle of white wine.

Doc would just have to find his own damned dessert.

SIX

By seven thirty the following morning Candy and Doc had set up their booth on Cape Willington's Main Street, which was blocked off to traffic for the festival. They had a prime spot — at the northeast end of the street in front of McGuire's Travel Agency, just across from Duffy's Main Street Diner — so they'd get plenty of foot traffic all day.

By eight o'clock Candy had set out her items for sale, all arranged neatly on the booth's display counter, which she'd covered with a blueberry tablecloth she'd bought at the L.L.Bean store in Freeport.

She attached the banner she'd made to the tops of the front posts and wove blue and white crepe paper streamers around the posts to add some color. Finally, she hung gift baskets from hooks in the crossbeams above her head. The baskets swayed gently in the sea breeze that always seemed to be coming in from the ocean.

When she was done, she stepped out into the street to have a look at it all. She was pleased with what she saw. This was her third year selling homemade items at the festival but her first time with a booth; the last two years she had gone the novice route, setting up a card table near the park. This year she'd decided to put a professional spin on the blueberry-selling business, purchasing booth space along Main Street and significantly increasing the variety of items she offered.

Now all she had to do was sell it all, and she'd provide a much-needed boost to the Holliday household finances.

By eight thirty the crowds began to arrive, and by nine the streets of Cape Willington were swarming with festival-goers. Events had kicked off at seven thirty that morning with a pancake breakfast at the American Legion Hall. The Fun Run at eight thirty was followed by 5K and 15K races. The flea market at the First Congregational Church was about to open, a pet parade was scheduled for noon, a local folk band would start playing in Town Park at one, a blueberry pie–eating contest would take place at three, and other events would follow throughout the afternoon.

Things would really get rolling with the Blueberry Festival Parade at five. Featuring the Blueberry Queen contestants, it would wind its way around the Coastal Loop and end up at the Pruitt Opera House, where the Blueberry Queen would be crowned after a pageant that started at six. The day would culminate with a dance at the Cape Willington Community Center at eight, presided over by the Blueberry Queen and her court.

There was no doubt about it — it was going to be a long but fun, and most certainly fruitful, day.

The weather cooperated nicely. A bright late July sun rose through a nearly cloudless sky. The heat and humidity of the previous day had broken overnight. Today was cooler and crisper, a perfect festival day.

Still, by midmorning the temperature had risen into the seventies and threatened to approach eighty. Main Street was well shaded, so Candy didn't have to worry too much about her chocolate-covered blueberries melting in the heat, although she did keep the bulk of them in coolers she had brought along to prevent just that. With any luck, she'd have them all sold by noon.

The large pies went quickly (at twelve dollars apiece), and she sold the T-shirts, soap, and cookies at a good clip, as she knew she would.

Doc helped out in the booth for a while, until the boys showed up. They were in an anxious mood. Bumpy's wide ruddy face was ruddier than usual as he finished off a doughnut, brushing crumbs down the front of his wrinkled Hawaiian shirt, which he always dragged out of the closet on holidays and special events like the festival. Artie, looking disheveled as he pushed horn-rim glasses up his blade-thin nose, carried a clipboard, on which he jotted notes about the items he had purchased that day and planned to resell on eBay. Finn wore an exquisitely serious expression on his bearded face and, despite the heat, was dressed in an ever-present tweed jacket, patched at the elbows and fraying at the ends of the sleeves. "Got more news," he announced to Doc as they approached the booth.

Doc was instantly drawn in. "About Jock?" Finn nodded. "That evidence they found? It's a flashlight."

"Ha! I knew it!" Doc announced proudly, pounding a fist into an open hand.

"They found it on the rocks below," Finn went on, sounding not unlike Joe Friday in *Dragnet.* "It's got someone's initials on it."

75

He lowered his voice to a gruff whisper as he leaned in closer. "Not Jock's, though."

Doc's eyes narrowed. "Whose?"

Finn leaned back, hitched up his trousers, and shook his head. "Haven't found that out yet. I'm on it, though."

"You headed to the diner?"

The boys nodded. For a strange moment they reminded Candy of the Three Stooges, especially Bumpy, who with his crew cut and generous proportions bore more than a passing resemblance to Curly. And now that she thought about it, Artie Groves, with his straight black hair, could pass for a much taller Moe. She almost expected them to start slapping each other around. Doc rubbed at his hip before he turned to her, looking like a little boy about to ask if he could go outside and play. "Leg's starting to bother me a little. Mind if I take a break?"

Candy gave him a gentle push, letting him know he wasn't fooling anyone. She was surprised he had lasted as long as he did. "Go ahead, get off your feet for a while. I've got help coming."

He gave her a grateful smile. "I'll be right across the street if you need me," he said, and off he went with his crew.

Fortunately, Candy had arranged for Maggie's daughter to stop by to help out in the booth. Tall, dark haired, and serious, Amanda Tremont was soon to be a senior at Cape Willington High School, with dreams of becoming an architect. Candy knew she was always looking to make a little extra cash, so it hadn't been difficult to persuade her to help out at the booth for a couple of hours.

With Amanda working beside her, Candy was able to handle all her customers during the busiest part of the day — mid to late morning — and the battered gray cash box behind the front counter began to fill up with tens and twenties, and even a few fifties and hundreds.

As midday approached, Candy found that, rather than feeling tired or stressed, she was energized and actually enjoying herself. Main Street, lined with colorful booths and banners, and crowded with chattering tourists, families with little children, elderly couples strolling along, and groups of excited teens huddled together like seagulls against the wind, had taken on a festive atmosphere.

Blueberry pies and T-shirts and garlands were everywhere. Peppy music drifted from loudspeakers attached to lampposts. Sounds of laughter could be heard up and down the street. Everyone seemed to be in a good mood, yet there was an underlying melancholy that lay just beneath the surface, Candy noticed, though for the most part folks avoided talking about Jock's passing. It was whispered about here and there, yes, but it was still too shocking, too unbelievable, to bring out into the open on such a sunny festival day.

Just after noon, Herr Georg stopped by to pay his respects and purchase one of Candy's mini pies. Ray made an appearance and walked away with a dozen large muffins — probably eleven more than he'd originally intended to purchase. Candy gently tried to talk him out of buying that many — she knew he lived alone and couldn't eat them all by himself — but he insisted, telling her they were his favorite.

Other townspeople passed by or stopped to say hello. One was Judicious F. P. Bosworth, a fortyish gentleman whose father and grandfather had both been judges, hence the lofty name. But rather than following in the family business, Judicious had skipped out on his senior year of high school and backpacked his way through Europe and Asia, winding up years later at a Buddhist monastery on a mountaintop in Tibet. He had been close to thirty when he had finally returned to Cape Willington a decade ago, firmly convinced he had mystical powers and could make himself invisible at will.

At first, when told of Judicious's peculiarity, Candy had found it endlessly odd and amusing, but eventually she had warmed to the idea of having an invisible man about town, and accepted Judicious as just another townie. She had also rather easily fallen into the town-wide practice of inquiring about Judicious's status whenever she encountered him around town. "Are you being seen this morning, Judicious?" she would ask him, or "Mr. Bosworth, are you here?" If he responded, then clearly he was visible and a conversation could ensue, during which Judicious usually revealed himself to be well informed and erudite. But if he declined to answer or simply walked away, then he was considered to be invisible, and Candy would think nothing more of it and go about her business. Following accepted practice around town, she would always inform others whom she encountered that day as to the visibility — or lack of it — of Judicious. And Sapphire Vine, the gossip columnist for the local paper, kept a running count of Judicious's days of visibility and invisibility.

Today, Judicious waved and mouthed a pleasant "Good morning" to Candy as he passed by. Obviously he was being seen on this fine day.

Another visitor to the booth was Bertha Grayfire, the fifty-something chairwoman of the town council, who stopped by to say hello. Bertha was dressed nicely in a lime green frock and a large floppy hat — a distinctive change from the Dolly Parton outfit she liked to wear to Halloween parties or to amuse trick-or-treaters. The outfit had been a hit for years, and Bertha usually tried to one-up herself each time she wore it, coming up with ever more elaborate hairdos and overdone makeup. She had also been known to warble a few tunes made famous by her country-singer idol. Today, she chatted briefly with Candy before walking off with a couple of T-shirts for her grandchildren and a few bars of soap for herself.

All in all, it was turning out to be a very good day.

During one of the lulls in the action, while the pet parade was making its way down Ocean Street to the delight of the large crowd that had gathered, Candy had a few minutes to talk with Amanda. "So, are you all ready for the big night tonight?" she asked. Amanda was to be one of the contestants in the Blueberry Queen Pageant that evening.

But instead of being excited about it, Amanda shrugged and picked absently at a broken fingernail. "I guess so. I really don't want to do it."

That took Candy by surprise. "Why not? I thought you were looking forward to it. It sounds like a lot of fun."

Amanda tilted her head a little but kept her gaze cast downward. "I just don't want to, that's all."

"Well," Candy said after a moment, "maybe you're just a little nervous about it."

Amanda shrugged. "Maybe. It doesn't really make any difference if I'm there or not. Everyone knows Haley Pruitt is going to win."

Candy tried to temper the flash of anger that shot through her. "No she's not! Who told you that?"

Haley Pruitt was the granddaughter of Helen Ross Pruitt, the town's wealthiest citizen and owner of Pruitt Manor, an English Tudor-style "summer cottage" that sat out on the point near Kimball Light.

Amanda seemed completely disinterested by the conversation. "No one told me. I just know. She always wins everything."

Candy let out a breath of exasperation. "Amanda, she doesn't win everything. You

can't think like that. You have as good a
chance to win as anyone. Besides, you're
much prettier than Haley."

Amanda looked up, her soft brown eyes
hopeful. "You really think so?"

Candy smiled reassuringly. "I know so.
You just have to go up there and do
your . . ."

She was interrupted when Amanda's serious demeanor suddenly brightened and her
eyes flashed with excitement. "Oh, hi, Cameron!" Amanda said with more energy than
she had mustered the entire morning.

Candy's gaze shifted. A tall, shaggy-haired
teenage boy with a lopsided grin and intelligent green eyes stood in front of the booth.

"Oh, hi, Cameron," Candy echoed.

"Hi," said Cameron, barely looking at her.
Then, more shyly, he added, "Hi, Amanda."

"Hi."

There was an awkward silence in which
both teens looked at each other and then
looked over at Candy. When neither of them
spoke, apparently tongue-tied, Candy asked,
"Having a good time today, Cam?"

The boy shrugged. "Not really. Working,"
he said in a voice surprisingly deep for
someone his age.

"Oh, that's right. How are things at
Gumm's?" Cameron worked at the town's

hardware store during the summer.

"Busy." He paused. "How are things going here?"

"Just great," said Candy cheerily. "Amanda's helping out a lot. She's doing a great job."

"Hmm." Cameron's eyes flicked from Amanda to Candy and back as he fidgeted and chewed his lip. He seemed to want to say something but didn't quite know how to say it. Or maybe something — or someone — was preventing him from saying it. Candy guessed that "someone" was her. The kids probably wanted a few minutes by themselves, she realized. Young love and all that.

Leaning over, she dug a twenty-dollar bill out of the cash box. "Tell you what," she said to Amanda. "Why don't you and Cam run over to Duffy's and get some lunch? And you can bring me back something."

Amanda snatched the bill from Candy's hand almost before the words were out of her mouth. " 'Kay. What do you want?"

Candy's first thought was to ask for the usual — a salad and a Diet Coke — but what the hey, it was a festival day, right? Why not celebrate a little? "How about a cheeseburger, extra pickles and mustard, fries with lots of ketchup, and an extra thick chocolate shake," she said quickly before she changed her mind.

"You got it!" Amanda dashed around the back of the booth, grabbed Cameron by the hand, and pulled him away with her. He flashed a silly grin at Candy before he turned and followed his girlfriend. "Back in twenty minutes," Amanda called over her shoulder, waving.

Candy chuckled. "Yeah, right. Twenty minutes. Like that'll happen."

Turning her attention back to her booth, she started rearranging the items on the front counter. As she did, she noticed a large, bearded man standing to one side, surreptitiously watching her as he pretended to read the label on one of her pies. Catching her glance, he shot her a tight smile. "You're pretty good with teenagers," he observed.

Candy laughed. "I don't know about that. But we get along pretty well together. They're good kids."

The bearded man squinted in thought as he turned to glance back over his shoulder. "She looks familiar. Do I know her?"

Candy gave him the once over. "Who wants to know?" she said protectively. She wasn't about to discuss Amanda with a stranger.

He pointed a finger at his chest. "You want to know who I am?"

"That's right."

It wasn't much of a clarification, but he seemed to get it. His mouth formed the tight smile again. Could be it was constricted by all that facial hair? "Oh, I see. I thought you knew."

"Why would I know?"

"Well, it's just that . . . my name's been in the . . ." A bit flustered, he finally stuck out a hand. "Sebastian J. Quinn."

"Oh. Hello." She shook his hand, which dwarfed hers.

Now, as she took a closer look at him, she realized he did look vaguely familiar. His size was imposing. He was tall and a bit heavy, though not overweight. He wore dark gray slacks, a crisply pressed khaki shirt, and a shiny green and rose cravat, the likes of which had gone out of style thirty years ago. Okay, fifty. Truthfully, it had never been in style. He cradled a newspaper under one arm and held four or five small burgundy-colored books in his meaty left hand.

It took her a few moments, but it finally dawned on her. "I *have* seen you in the paper. You're the poet, right?"

His smile genuinely widened. He bowed slightly. "The very same. I'm honored you've heard of me."

"Well, just about everybody in town has heard of you, haven't they? You're here for the pageant, right? One of the judges?"

"Actually, I'm vacationing in the area. I must admit, I'm quite taken with your lovely little town. I've rented a cottage on the coast for a month. Acting as a judge for the pageant is a last-minute arrangement."

"So I've heard." It had been front-page news in the local paper. The organizers of the Blueberry Queen Pageant liked to have at least one celebrity judge every year, in addition to the regulars. The frenetic search for this year's celebrity judge had been widely reported by Sapphire Vine in her column. According to her reports, Stephen King, who lived up in Bangor, had been asked (for the fifth year in a row) to be a judge but had graciously declined. Other offers had gone out, but none had been accepted. For a while the search had seemed destined to failure. Then, when someone found out Sebastian J. Quinn was vacationing in the area, he had been asked and had ultimately agreed to become this year's celebrity judge.

"It's quite an honor for us to have a poet of your stature as a judge," Candy continued.

"Oh, well, that's a very nice thing to say. Tell me, are you a fan of poetry?" Sebastian asked.

"I guess you could say that. I've read Robert Frost, Walt Whitman, that sort of thing."

"Any of my works?"

Candy hesitated. She knew he was fishing for a compliment. "Of course."

"Oh? Which ones?"

"One of the early ones." She thought a moment, trying to recall the title. "Something about chaos," was all she could remember.

"Mm. Yes, that one. *The Bell of Chaos,* it's called."

"That's right! *The Bell of Chaos.* I enjoyed it a lot."

"Yes, you and many others." Sebastian looked quite unimpressed. "I won the Pulitzer for that, although I think my later works are much better." He held out one of the burgundy-colored books he was carrying. "Here's my latest. *A Drop of Peace.*"

"Oh." Candy gingerly took the book that had been thrust at her and flipped through the pages. "It looks wonderful," she said, closing the cover and handing it back. But Sebastian waved it away. "Keep it. My gift to you. Here, I'll sign it for you, though I'm afraid I don't know your first name."

"Oh, I'm sorry. I guess I neglected to introduce myself. It's Candy. Candy Holliday."

He looked at her curiously, glanced up at the sign over the booth, then back at her. "Of course. Holliday's Blueberry Acres. Candy, though? That name is quite . . . unique."

"It's sort of an inside joke. I was born on Halloween." After a moment she added, "My parents had a warped sense of humor, I guess."

That tight smile returned. He seemed to have practiced it a lot. "Hmm, yes, I see." He scribbled something hastily on the book's front page, signed his name, starting with a large swooping S, then slapped the cover closed and shoved the book toward her. "There you go. Do enjoy. Now, I must confess, I've heard you make the best blueberry pies in town. That's why I came over, to check out your wares . . ."

What could she do? The man had just given her a free book. Fortunately, she had sold out of her larger pies, but he still walked away with a mini pie, a couple of cookies, and four blueberry scones, plus an extra-large T-shirt, all free of charge.

"You know, sweetie, I think you've just been taken."

"Huh?" Candy twisted around. Standing behind her, arms crossed and wearing a suspicious smile, was her best friend Maggie Tremont, Amanda's mother.

"Oh, hi, Mags. What was that you said?"

Maggie tilted her head toward the huge bulk of Sebastian J. Quinn as he made his way down the street, stopping at various booths along the way. "I think he just ripped you off for some free goodies."

"Wasn't the first time today." Candy smiled bleakly and held up the book. "Besides, he gave me this. It was sort of an exchange . . . I think."

Maggie looked unimpressed. "No one wants to buy his moldy old books of sappy poetry. He probably can't sell the damn things. I bet he gets them for nothing and uses them to get free stuff from suckers like you."

"Go ahead, rub it in."

"I'm telling you," Maggie went on, "you've got to protect yourself. There are vultures everywhere."

Candy gave her friend an appraising look. "You're sounding a bit cynical. Been a rough day?"

Maggie waved a hand at her. "Honey, you don't know the half of it. That pet parade almost did me in. Got attacked by a goat with a tennis-shoe fetish."

Candy couldn't help but laugh. "You're making that up."

Maggie's dark eyes twinkled as she made an *X* across her chest. "Cross my heart. Couldn't keep him from chewing on my shoestrings." She held out her left shoe as proof. The shoestrings had obviously been chewed on.

"It wasn't one of Sally Ann Longfellow's goats, was it?"

"The very one. She was all dressed up, with an old cowbell and a beat-up hat with a plastic flower in it, but she still looked raggedy, like she's been sleeping outside all summer."

"The goat?"

"No, Sally Ann. The goat actually looked in pretty good shape."

They both laughed at that. Maggie could always make Candy laugh, no matter what. They had met shortly after Candy moved into town. She'd gone to the local insurance office to check on Doc's homeowner's policy, and there Maggie had been behind the front desk. They hit it off immediately and had been close friends ever since.

Maggie checked her watch, then flicked her eyes left and right. "So where's that daughter of mine? I've got to get her to the hairdresser's."

"I sent her and Cameron over to Duffy's to get some lunch. My treat."

Maggie eyed her with horror. "What? Are you mad, girl? Do you know how much food that boy can pack in? He was born with a bottomless pit instead of a stomach. He practically lives at our place. He's eating us out of house and home."

"They're growing up all right," Candy agreed, then added subtly, "Amanda seems quiet today."

Maggie rolled her eyes. "She's convinced Haley Pruitt's going to win the pageant. But I told her that's crazy talk, that she has as good a chance to win as anyone. She just has to go up there and do her best, no matter what the competition does."

"That's what I told her," Candy said, and then grabbed Maggie's forearm as she saw a woman approaching the booth. She lowered her voice. "Speaking of the competition . . ."

"Oh my God," Maggie muttered under her breath as a thirtyish, dark-haired woman wearing a cherry red, low-cut dress and white spiked heels stopped to talk to someone two booths away. "It's Sapphire Vine, the queen of Cape Willington herself."

"She's looking all prettied up today,"

Candy commented.

"Yeah, like an apple that's waiting to be plucked off a tree."

"Or stuffed into a pig's mouth. I'm surprised she's not wearing blue. You know, with her name and the festival and all."

"Just wait 'til you see her outfit tonight."

"You've seen it?"

Maggie shook her head. "No one has. Top secret, she says. Won't even rehearse with the other girls. But she says she's pulling out all the stops. From the rumors going around town, she's got a presentation guaranteed to have you rolling in the aisles."

"Or win that crown for herself."

"Don't even think that," Maggie said, nearly seething. She tilted her head toward the oncoming woman in red. "You know what she's doing, don't you?"

"No, what?"

"She's campaigning."

It took Candy a moment to realize what Maggie was saying. "You mean she's trying to influence the judges?"

"Wouldn't put it past her. She's been following that poet character around all morning." Maggie's gaze narrowed. "Just look at her. You'd think she was a teenager instead of a thirty-seven-year-old woman."

"I thought she was thirty-two."

"Thirty-seven if she's a day. I guarantee it."

"Well, anyone can run for Blueberry Queen. She sure proved that."

"Yes, but just because you *can* do something doesn't mean you *should* do it. Everyone knows that traditionally only high school girls . . ."

But she broke off as Sapphire Vine walked up to Candy's booth and happily slapped the display counter to announce her arrival.

"Good afternoon, ladies!" she chirped with barely contained glee, then reached into a large basket she carried on one arm. "You ladies are looking so pretty today. You deserve something special!" She pulled out two pale blue silk roses on long wire stems

"Beautiful, aren't they?" she asked, handing one to each of them. "I found them on eBay. Got them for a song. That color is called ice blue. And if I do say so, Candy, it brings out the color of your eyes. Though we have to do something about your hair. There's a wonderful color rinse you should try. Honey Sunrise. Isn't that a lovely name? It'll add a little shine to your hair and hide some of that gray."

Candy took the proffered rose, uncertain how to respond. "Um, well, er, okay, I might give that a try. Thank you . . . I think." She held up the rose. "That's . . . that's very nice of you."

"Just my way of spreading a little joy in our wonderful little town!" Sapphire Vine bubbled as she cast a wary glance at Maggie. When she saw nothing but a scowl, she turned her attention back to Candy. "And would you tell Amanda I wish her the best of luck. I saw her here at the booth earlier, but I didn't get a chance to stop by and chat with her. I'm sure she'll do wonderfully. She's such a sturdy girl, and I hear she's been working so hard on her talent — once she found one, of course."

Candy almost had to hold Maggie back, but Sapphire had already turned away, her gaze searching. "You haven't seen that nice poet fellow, have you?" she asked, glancing back.

Candy pointed down the street with the rose. "He went that-a-way."

Sapphire beamed at them. "Then I must be off. I'll call next week to see how things are going on the farm." Her eyes shifted quickly to Maggie. "I'd ask how the diet's going, but I guess you're off it already," she said without a hint of meanness. "Toodles!"

As she scurried away, Maggie clenched a fist and muttered with amazement, "Did she just call me fat?"

"Did she just say *toodles?*"

"That woman knows no shame."

"She's out of control."

"She's more than that. She's a menace to society." Maggie's glare nearly burned a hole in the disappearing back of Sapphire Vine. "I swear," she said quietly, "if she wins that pageant tonight, I'll kill her. I mean I'll kill her." She shot a dark glance at Candy. "You're with me on this one, right?"

Candy fingered a few strands of her hair, pulling them in front of her face so she could check them for gray. There was none that she could see, but that didn't mean they weren't there. Her brow lowered. "I can't let you do it alone and have all the fun, can I? Tell you what — if she wins, you hold the gun and I'll pull the trigger."

SEVEN

Cape Willington's most famous landmark, aside from the twin lighthouses at Pruitt Point and Kimball Point, was the Pruitt Opera House, which occupied a prime spot on Ocean Avenue, just a half block from the rocky shoreline. Completed in 1881, it was one of the first such facilities in Downeast Maine, and its patrons agreed it was one of the most impressive built in the state before or since. Horace Roberts Pruitt, the building's namesake and primary benefactor, had brought a team of architects up from Boston to design the structure, because he knew they were experienced in the emerging Colonial Revival style, with which Horace was particularly enamored, given his love of Georgian architecture that had been popular a century earlier. The result was an instantly classic building, with a symmetry and elegance that, in its earliest years, had seemed wildly out of place among the surrounding ramshackle buildings that tumbled down the wide, dusty street to the waterfront.

In the intervening years, those ramshackle wooden buildings had been replaced with more sturdy brick-and-stone affairs. Though in their early years some had been summer residences for the town's wealthier citizens, most by now had been converted into storefronts (with apartments on the upper floors). The street had been paved, first with cobblestones and then with asphalt, and oil lamps had given way to electric streetlights. But despite all the changes that had taken place on Ocean Avenue over the past century, the Pruitt Opera House remained, a testimony to one man's cultural vision, a Georgian queen among architectural commoners.

Visitors to the Pruitt (as it was called around town) were particularly enamored with its two most prominent architectural features: the stately columned portico that fronted the building and the elaborate widow's walk that sat atop the structure "like a crown," as Horace noted at the building's dedication on July 4, 1881. That latter feature had been a point of great contention during the building's construction. The architects had specified a copper-capped cupola to grace the building's roof, but Horace, who dabbled in architecture, made some adjustments to the design, insisting on a domed, open-sided, octagonal stone structure accessed from below by a simple steel ladder. It was an homage, he insisted, to all the long-suffering sea widows who had stood for countless hours, days, weeks, and years, gazing out to the sea for the first sight of sails on the horizon, searching earnestly for any sign of the return of their loved ones.

Horace's own grandmother had paced just such a widow's walk for years upon end at the family's primary home in nearby Searsport, awaiting her husband, an esteemed sea captain, who had set off on a three-year voyage and never returned, lost somewhere at sea on a journey that was to have taken him and his crew to Africa and the Far East. It was told that she had fretted away and eventually died there on her widow's walk, wrapped in a frayed black shawl, grieving 'til death for her beloved husband.

Unable to persuade Horace otherwise, the Boston architects had relented, and the widow's walk atop the Pruitt was still the tallest point in Cape Willington, affording a spectacular panoramic view of the town and the far-reaching sea for those privileged enough to see it.

The Pruitt had a third unique feature: In the late 1970s, when the aged Town Hall on Main Street had burned down due to faulty wiring, the town offices had been temporarily relocated to a series of rooms in the Pruitt's basement. These rooms had once been rehearsal halls and storage rooms, but once properly renovated and lighted, they served their new purpose so well that the town never moved out. It had proved to be a mutually beneficial relationship, for the town had the entire building at its disposal for whatever purpose presented itself, and the Pruitt's operating committee had a continual flow of income from the town that proved immensely useful with repairs and upkeep. So the Pruitt Opera House now served as not only the cultural and social center of the town but also its governmental center.

Over the years, the stage of the Pruitt had been graced by performers of nearly every ilk, some truly gifted, but for the past twenty years or so it had been taken over annually for one night a year in mid-summer by a different troupe of performers — the young contestants in the town's Blueberry Queen Pageant.

This year, like every other in recent memory, a full house was expected for this greatly anticipated event, and the turnout did not disappoint. The place was packed to its gilded rafters. The main hall's maximum capacity was posted at three hundred and fifty, but Candy could have sworn there were more people than that stuffed into the auditorium, its wide balcony, and its half dozen viewing boxes, making the fire marshal scowl nervously as he paced the side hallway at the outer edges of the crowd.

The noisy crowd assembled there was crackling with anticipation as the clock in the foyer pronounced six o'clock, and Bertha Grayfire, the town council's chairwoman for nearly a decade, and tonight's mistress of ceremonies, bounced up a set of well-worn wooden stairs and took the stage with a wave and a smile. She was dressed in a pale yellow flowered dress with a high collar and a low hemline, giving her an appearance that was at once festive yet conservative, which was appropriate, considering her station in town.

Bertha was well-known around town as a good listener and a friendly sort, witty, approachable, and socially savvy. But what the townspeople most admired about her was how she could be tough and focused when necessary — say, during the annual budget process — and light and personable at other times. So it was not unfitting that she was greeted by a warm round of applause as she strode to center stage.

"Good evening, everyone!" she said into the microphone, "and welcome to the Forty-First Annual Cape Willington Blueberry Queen Pageant!"

Applause erupted again, louder and more energetic this time, accompanied by a few whoops and whistles, which were quickly buffered and absorbed by the Pruitt's excellent acoustics.

For those unable to snag a ticket to the event, the pageant was being broadcast live over community-access cable. Candy would have preferred to watch it on TV at home with Doc, her feet propped up and a glass of white wine in her hand, but a week ago Maggie had thrust a ticket at her and insisted she come.

"I need you there for moral support," Maggie had told her. "Ed's going to be traveling — another damned business trip that he says he can't postpone — and I need someone there to hug if Amanda wins, and a shoulder to cry on if she doesn't."

So here she was, sitting in the middle of a row of padded seats halfway back the auditorium, wedged between Maggie on the right and an older, overweight gentleman with a bad cough on the left, trying to remember why she had come.

Maggie leaned in close. "Isn't this exciting?" She had to practically shout into Candy's ear to be heard over the applause.

"More fun than baking a blueberry pie," Candy said with a sarcastic edge that was lost on her friend. She'd had a long day at the booth, spending nearly eight hours straight on her feet dealing with demanding customers, so it was not surprising that she was finding it hard to match Maggie's enthusiasm.

Maggie gave her a nudge and pointed into the crowd. "Oh look, there's Mrs. Pruitt!"

Candy craned her neck to peek around the heads in front of her. Sure enough, sitting in the front row was a dangerously thin older woman wearing an impeccably tailored mauve business suit with a lavender-colored scarf. Her steel gray hair was pulled up into a tight swirl; a string of large pearls adorned her thin neck.

"How'd she get such a good seat?" Candy wondered.

Maggie waved a hand and twitched nervously in her seat. "Connections. Everything's about connections these days, especially in this town."

"Looks like she's got her brute with her."

"Who? That butler or chauffeur or whatever she calls him? Looks like a pug dog, doesn't he? She never goes anywhere without him."

"I saw the Bentley parked in front of the drugstore the other day, and there he was in the driver's seat, reading a comic book and waiting patiently for her while she ran her errands."

"They're probably lovers," Maggie mused, but before Candy could scoff at the idea, Bertha Grayfire continued from the stage, her voice booming through the hall.

"We have an exciting show for you tonight, but before we get started, I would be remiss if I didn't take a moment to thank Wendy Bassett for her wonderful set decoration and Ned Winetrop, Ray Hutchins, and their crew for set construction. We also should recognize the generous contributions of Zeke's General Store and Gumm's Hardware Store."

The audience joined her in polite applause.

Bertha's expression turned suddenly serious. "Of course," she continued, her voice falling to a near hush, "I would be remiss if I didn't acknowledge the sudden and shocking departure of one of our town's favorite sons, Jonathan 'Jock' Larson. We all knew Jock well, and we all loved him dearly. He was a great supporter not only of this pageant but also of this town and all its citizens. I'm sure you'll all agree that he will be sorely missed."

The hall had fallen into deep silence as Bertha reached for her reading glasses, which hung from a thin silver chain around her neck. She slipped them on, paused for an appropriate period of time, then raised a hand holding a sheaf of five-by-eight-inch index cards, which she waved excitedly in the air. "Now on with the show!"

EIGHT

"First, I'd like to introduce our esteemed judges, who will determine the winner of tonight's competition . . ."

Bertha swept a hand toward the five pageant judges who sat at an angled cloth-draped table at the foot of the stage and to the audience's right, directly in front of the first row of seats. As Bertha read their names, each judge stood briefly and acknowledged the crowd with a bow or a wave.

"Starting at the far end . . . Mrs. Jane Chapman, director of the Downeast Maine Summer Theater program. Next to her, Mr. Oliver LaForce, proprietor of the renowned Lightkeeper's Inn, located right here in beautiful Cape Willington. Next, Ms. Sheila Watson, music director at Cape Willington High School. And, of course, Mr. Georg Wolfsburger, baker extraordinaire and owner of the world-famous Black Forest Bakery." The applause was a bit louder for

Herr Georg as Bertha added, "This is Herr Georg's tenth year as a pageant judge!" The baker, wearing an elegant navy blue evening jacket and a crisply pressed striped shirt open at the collar, put on a strained smile and waved halfheartedly at the crowd.

Bertha waited until the applause died out before she continued. "Finally, I am very pleased to introduce our fifth judge. He graciously stepped in at the last moment to fill a vacant slot, and we couldn't be happier to have him with us. He's the author of numerous books of poetry, including *The Bell of Chaos,* for which he won the Pulitzer Prize, as well as *Tap Dancing on the Volcano, In the Steps of Kings,* and his latest, *A Drop of Peace,* which, he tells me, is available in bookstores everywhere. Currently an adjunct professor at the University of Massachusetts at Amherst, he's also taught at New England College in New Hampshire and at the University of Southern Maine. Ladies and gentlemen, fellow Capers, please give a warm Downeast Maine welcome to . . . Mr. Sebastian J. Quinn!"

The crowd responded enthusiastically as Sebastian rose and bowed elegantly, first to Bertha, then to the audience. He was dressed resplendently in a white shirt, checkered vest, dark gray slacks, burgundy sports jacket, and yellow bow tie. He seemed to bask in the audience's applause and twirled his upheld hand in small circles in the air, as a Roman emperor might have done before a particularly bloody gladiator battle at the Coliseum. He milked the moment for all it was worth before he finally took his seat, smoothing his beard as he settled himself.

"And now," Bertha continued, "on with the introductions of the contestants!"

As she read the names of the six contestants, they emerged one by one from stage right, all wearing broad smiles and carefully chosen outfits.

To rousing cheers, dark-haired Jennifer Croft came out first, wearing an iridescent pink knee-length taffeta dress with spaghetti straps. She crossed to the far end of the stage, taking up her predesignated spot with a smile and a wave.

Emily Fitzsimmons was next, dressed in a black and white skirt-and-top ensemble that had been tailored to show off her youthful figure. She was followed by Mollie MacKay, in a calf-length denim skirt and butter yellow mid-sleeved top with a lace-up plunging neckline.

Haley Pruitt came next, looking radiant in a trim-fitting, off-the-shoulder powder blue number that perfectly set off her honey-colored hair.

"Amanda's next," Maggie whispered to Candy, clutching her arm tightly. "I don't think I can stand it. I'm afraid to look."

"Breathe, girl, breathe," Candy urged.

A moment later, Amanda walked out looking prettier than Candy had ever seen her. In a charming sleeveless pink and yellow flower-print dress complemented by pale pink pumps with thin ankle straps, Amanda Tremont strode onto the stage, smiling nervously as she gazed out at the assembled crowd and took her place beside the other contestants. Her long dark hair hung loose about her shoulders and had been brushed out so much that it shone in the spotlight. A single pink rose was tucked behind one ear.

"She looks absolutely gorgeous," Candy breathed.

Maggie sniffed back tears and tightened her grip on Candy's arm. "My little baby is growing up."

Candy patted her hand. "I hate to tell you this, dear, but I think she's already all grown up."

"Oh my," was all Maggie could say.

"Our final contestant," Bertha Grayfire continued dramatically, "is someone you all know, someone who has made quite a name for herself in our little community —"

"Oh no," groaned Maggie. "Here comes She-Who-Must-Not-Be-Named."

"— Miss Sapphire Vine!"

"Oops, I think they named her," Candy whispered.

Maggie snorted as Sapphire pranced onto the stage wearing a cowgirl costume, complete with rhinestones, long leather fringes, red boots, a cowgirl hat, and a holster with a wooden gun.

Candy almost burst out laughing. "That's not Sapphire Vine. It's Annie Oakley!"

"Looks like Lord Voldemort to me," Maggie muttered.

"You've been reading too many Harry Potter books."

"I know. I've got a Hogwarts headache right now. Wish I were a wizard so I could make her disappear. She doesn't belong here."

The crowd, though, appeared to love Sapphire and her costume, as did the judges, who applauded approvingly.

With that, the competition began.

"By tradition," Bertha explained, "we'll begin with a contest designed to test each girl's knowledge of our world-famous wild blueberries. During this portion of the competition, which will account for thirty percent of each contestant's final score, judges will not only be listening carefully to each contestant's answer but also will be watching to see how the contestant acts under pressure, handles her stage presence, and thinks on her feet."

And so the questioning began. In an order predetermined by draw, the contestants were asked about the nutritional value of blueberries, how the berries were grown and picked, about their history and popularity, and even about cooking with blueberries. Candy was surprised to find she knew many of the answers, which she mouthed to herself, as if she were standing on stage — or watching *Jeopardy!* At one point she felt Maggie nudge her side. "You know, you should be up there," her friend said with a grin.

Candy almost blushed. "Not for all the tea in Boston Harbor."

Amanda handled herself well, to Maggie's delight, but so did most of the other girls. Haley Pruitt obviously had been studying up on blueberries. But the surprise of the evening was Sapphire Vine, who not only answered each question properly but also did so in a way that clearly distinguished her from the other contestants.

"Ooh, I *hate* that woman," Maggie seethed as Sapphire answered one question concerning acid rain's effect on blueberries in a particularly canny way.

"She's overdoing it," Candy whispered. "Don't worry — the judges notice things like that."

"They do?"

"Sure, I think so."

Maggie looked mildly relieved. "You're a good friend."

Then came the talent portion of the show. "Rather than appearing in alphabetical order, as they were introduced," Bertha announced, "our contestants have drawn numbers to determine the order in which they will perform. This portion of the pageant will account for thirty percent of each contestant's final score. First up is" — she paused as she glanced down at her index cards — "Amanda Tremont!"

Maggie's hands flew to her mouth. "I think I'm going to faint."

"Hang in there," said Candy, patting her friend on the back.

"She's been practicing this for weeks. I just hope . . ."

Her words faded as piped-in music blared from speakers at the front of the auditorium. Amanda appeared onstage wearing a workout outfit — snug-fitting white polyester-and-spandex pants with navy stripes down the sides and a matching cotton tank top. She launched into an athletic routine that included moves she had learned as a cheerleader, gymnast, and dancer. She bounced and tumbled about, did handstands and splits, and even worked a few hip-hop moves into the three-minute routine. An appreciative ovation rewarded her as she finished.

The music struck up again, a different tune this time, for Mollie MacKay, who sang a heartfelt if slightly off-key version of "Memories" from the musical *Cats*. Jennifer Croft came next, playing an acoustic guitar and singing a familiar old tune by Simon and Garfunkel. Emily Fitzsimmons followed, twirling batons.

Then came Haley Pruitt. She walked down off the stage to a piano at the left side of the main floor, opposite the judges' table, and sat gracefully on the bench. Turning toward the audience, she said in a soft, lilting voice, "I'd like to perform for you now the Prelude in C Sharp, opus three, number two, by Sergey Rachmaninoff."

"Sergey who?" Maggie whispered hoarsely.

"Rachmaninoff."

"So she's playing a rock song?"

"It's a classical piece, silly. Shut up and listen."

As Haley took a moment to breathe deeply and compose herself, a buzz of whispers arose from the audience. Many of them seemed as confused as Maggie by Haley's introduction, but once she played the first few commanding chords of the piece — *dumm, da, dumm, da, dummmm* — recognition dawned on many of the faces in the audience.

As Haley moved through the piece, Maggie leaned over. "Hey, I've heard this before," she whispered. "I think that Sergey guy wrote it for a Chevy car commercial."

Candy gave her a quieting glance. "Shh."

The hall hushed as Haley moved into the intricate fingerings that made up the middle portion of the piece, the notes sounding sharp and clear, played with a practiced hand. The audience sat mesmerized, transfixed by Haley's skill and the grandeur and beauty of her performance. As she neared the end, echoing the majestic opening chords, the audience held its collective breath, hands poised to applause, anticipating the ending.

Not being familiar with the piece, some clapped prematurely at awkward silent places, but Haley ignored those, playing the piece as it was meant to be played, until the final quiet notes.

When she rested her fingers upon the keys, bowed her head forward, and finally rose with a slight smile, the hall erupted in applause.

"Lovely, just lovely," Bertha said into the microphone. "My, we have such a talented group of contestants here tonight! I don't envy the judges their job one bit. It will be a very difficult task to select a winner from these remarkable girls, I can tell you that. Now, for our final performance of the evening . . . the moment you've all been waiting for . . . Miss Sapphire Vine."

As the lights went down and the hall quieted, Candy whispered, "Do you think she'll do a striptease?"

"That's about the only talent she has, honey. Unless she plans to drag a typewriter onstage and write a newspaper column right before our very eyes."

"Now that would be exciting."

"About as exciting as painting toenails."

"Hey, careful. That's the highlight of my week."

"Mine too."

"Shh. Here she comes."

A pause. Then, "Oh . . . my . . . God. She looks like . . . a giant blueberry?"

A wave of gasps, chuckles, and whispered conversations swept through the audience as Sapphire Vine appeared on stage wearing one of the most outlandish outfits Candy had ever seen. It looked as though it could have been a Halloween costume, except it was worn by a woman in her midthirties instead of a six-year-old child. It was blue — lots and lots of blue — and bulged widely in the middle, approximating the look of a giant blueberry. She wore shimmering blue tights on her arms and legs, and had woven blueberry stems into her hair, many of them bearing clumps of the small blue fruit.

Oblivious to the crowd's reaction, Sapphire stepped up to the microphone as the spotlight centered on her. She nodded at the judges and then addressed the audience.

"I would like to begin by telling you," she said, "what an honor it is for me to be here on this stage tonight. I know my decision to appear in this pageant with these other wonderful girls has been controversial and that many of you believe I shouldn't be here at all. But there is one reason I'm here: I love this community, I love the people who live here, and I love this country. But most of all, I love the blueberry."

"That's about four reasons," Maggie hissed. "Shh!"

"So tonight," Sapphire continued, "I would like to perform an original poem that I've written expressly for this momentous occasion. It's called 'Ode to Blueberries.' " She lowered her head and took a deep breath to center herself, standing still and silent until the brief applause and scattered whispers died down. Then, raising her right arm and curling it inward in a dramatic pose, she began to recite in a loud, clear tone:

The blueness of a blueberry, a beautiful
    fruit
That hangs from a stem throughout the
    times of warmth,
A wonderful love.
And we cherish this fruit, lying on a hill, in
    the grass,
Eating the delicious berries,
Tasting the sweetness in our mouths,
Devouring all of the berry at once,
Enjoying it so that it lasts forever.
Then, eating yet another again,
And still more, so that you seem to spend
    all eternity
Resting lazily in the succulence of a
    blueberry.
Loved are these summer fruits,
And, indeed, they are the season's best.

She paused, her gaze sweeping over the audience before alighting on the judges. When she continued, her voice took on a deeper, darker tone:

But too soon the love for the berries is
    betrayed.
The summer grasses in which you once
    ate
To your heart's content are frosted over in
    cold hate.
The one you have loved hits you hard,
And, all at once, it is gone from you.
And you are alone.

Her gaze turned skyward, and anger crept into her voice as the next words came out hurried, sharp, and accusatory, her tone rising in volume and intensity:

It is then when I feel a deep hatred for
    this time,
The sweetness gone away.
All that is left is bitterness.
The love and kindness are gone,
Replaced with agony and anger,
Something you regret but cannot erase.
A love, lost.
The blueberries, gone.

Speaking the final words almost in a

whisper, Sapphire Vine closed her eyes, let her arms fall limp at her sides, and dropped her chin to her chest.

For a moment the audience sat in stunned silence, uncertain of how to react, uncertain if she had finished. But when several long seconds had passed, and Sapphire still stood unmoving with eyes closed and hands clenched, the audience sensed that she was indeed done.

Someone near the front clapped tentatively. Others followed hesitantly, politely.

It was far from the ovation Haley Pruitt had received, or even Mollie McKay, for that matter. But when she heard the applause, Sapphire opened her eyes and lifted her head. Her face was radiant.

"Did you like it? I wrote it myself!" she bubbled, hopping up and down like a two-year-old.

Most of the judges sat with their heads bowed to the table before them, scribbling on their judging forms. None was able to meet her gaze. Sapphire apparently took this as a good sign, for she waved frenetically toward the audience, blew a few kisses toward the judges, and bounced off the stage.

Maggie shook her head in disbelief. "Did I just see what I just saw, or did I black out and have some sort of dreadful dream?"

"That was no dream. It was a disaster."

"What could the poor girl have been thinking?"

"That was the worst thing I've ever seen in my life. It was like watching a train wreck happen right in front of your eyes."

Both of them burst out in high-pitched giggles but quickly slapped their hands over their mouths as a few audience members shot questioning looks their way.

"Oops! We'd better be good," Maggie whispered, "or they'll throw us out of here." Both struggled to contain their giggling, but it seemed like a lost cause.

After a brief interlude, the contestants gathered onstage for the final portion of the pageant. They all wore formal dresses and stood nervously with clenched hands as they faced the judges.

"Now comes our final event of the evening: the Q and A. Each contestant will be asked a question chosen at random," Bertha Grayfire explained. "Contestants will be judged on their speaking skills, ability to think on their feet, and stage presence. This portion of the pageant will account for forty percent of each contestant's final score. Let us begin."

A pretty young girl wearing yellow chiffon

walked onto the stage carrying a basket. From it, Bertha withdrew a length of paper, upon which was written the first question. She turned to the contestants. "Jennifer, you're first. Here is your question." And she read, "If there is one feature you could change about yourself, what would it be, and why?"

Jennifer Croft thought a moment, lips pressed tightly together. "I wouldn't change a thing about myself," she began tentatively, "because I'm happy with who I am. Many people feel they need to change something about themselves to be happy, but I believe it's best to just accept yourself as you are. Each one of us is unique, and each one of us has a special place in this world. It's best for us to accept that rather than dwell on what's good or bad about ourselves. If we can accept who we are, that is the first step on the road to personal happiness."

Jennifer smiled and let out a breath of relief as she finished, and the audience applauded politely.

"Very nice," Bertha said. "Emily, you're next. Here's your question: If you could invite any person or persons, living or dead, to have dinner with you, whom would you choose, and why?"

As she announced that Helen of Troy,

Abraham Lincoln, and Justin Timberlake were her preferred dinner guests, and explained why, the audience smiled appreciatively.

Amanda Tremont, looking nervous, fielded the next question, "What is your definition of success?" and seemed to answer it well, using her mother as an example, which caused tears to well up in Maggie's eyes.

Sapphire Vine was asked, "What do you believe is the greatest crisis facing our world today, and how would you fix it?" Her answers: intolerance, and loving each other more.

After the other two girls had answered their questions, Bertha brought the competition to a close. "We'll have another short intermission now," she announced, "while we total the scores and determine the winner. We'll see you in ten minutes."

She stepped down off the stage to collect the judging forms, shaking hands with each judge as she did so. Then she disappeared out a side door with two assistants.

"Now we wait," Candy said, easing back into her chair. "Pretty good show so far, though, huh?"

"Oh my, that was wonderful," Maggie managed to say, her voice still cracking with emotion. "She did such a good job."

"Nice answer on that question about success, huh? How does it feel to be so highly thought of by your daughter?"

Maggie's smile said it all. "It feels more wonderful than you can imagine," she admitted, tears nearly welling up in her reddened eyes again. "I have to go and give her a hug. I'll be right back."

After she had gone, Candy checked her watch. It was nearly seven thirty. She had been up since six that morning. A sudden wave of exhaustion swept through her, and her eyes stung with tiredness as she crossed her arms and let her gaze wander aimlessly around the hall.

Mrs. Pruitt was whispering furiously to her butler — what was his name? Hopkins or something like that? His face had gone bright red. Apparently Mrs. Pruitt was not happy about something and was taking it out on the paid help.

Candy's gaze drifted.

At the judge's table, Herr Georg looked particularly subdued — not his usual buoyant self at all. Sheila Watson, the high school's music director, was leaning sideways in a relaxed manner and chatting with him, but he seemed to be having a difficult time focusing on her. Sebastian J. Quinn also seemed strangely quiet — not at all the pushy, self-assured man who had stopped by her booth earlier in the day.

Candy's eyes moved on. Ray Hutchins was in the room, leaning against a wall toward the back of the hall, his hands stuffed deep into his pockets, eyes focused on someone at the front of the hall. Candy followed his gaze. Who was he looking at? One of the contestants, maybe? Or one of the judges? She couldn't tell.

She turned her head, surveying the crowd. Lots of couples, she noticed, middle-aged and elderly. Families with small children. A few teens mixed in here and there. But surprisingly few single people like her, and almost no single men her age.

Candy sighed. Cape Willington was not the best place to be if you were a single woman of dating age. The pickin's here were mighty slim — which was a depressing thought.

She was contemplating a future spent in spinsterhood when Maggie slipped back into the seat beside her. "Here we go. Keep your fingers crossed."

Sure enough, Bertha Grayfire crossed the stage to the microphone. Her face looking a shade paler in the harsh stage lighting than it had earlier in the day, she stood with tightly drawn lips, holding up a hand, as she waited for the crowd to settle. Finally she spoke.

"Before I announce the winners," she began, almost too quietly, "I think we once more should express our appreciation to all of our contestants and acknowledge the hard work they've put in this evening. Won't you join me in a warm round of applause for our Blueberry Queen contestants."

After the applause had died down, Bertha continued. "As is the tradition in our little pageant, I'll begin by announcing the specialty awards. The winners of these awards will each receive a fifty-dollar gift certificate, good at most stores in Cape Willington, as well as a wonderful gift basket from the Cape Willington Merchants' Association. First up is our Ms. Spirit Award, which is presented to the contestant the judges believe best exemplifies the spirit of life here in Cape Willington. And the winner is . . ." She paused momentarily for dramatic effect, then announced, "Mollie McKay!"

The audience applauded heartily as two young girls emerged to present Mollie with a bouquet of roses and a white satin sash with red lettering, which was placed over her head and draped from her right shoulder across her body.

"Next is our Ms. Charm and Personality

Award," Bertha continued, "presented to the contestant whom the judges believe best fulfills those qualities. And the winner is . . . Emily Fitzsimmons!"

Again, presentations of roses and a satin sash were made, as they were to the winner of the third specialty award, Jennifer Croft, who won for Ms. Photogenic.

"From our final three contestants," Bertha Grayfire announced, "the judges have chosen two runners-up, as well as this year's Blueberry Queen. I should mention that the queen and her court will preside over the Blueberry Queen Dance, which will kick off in about half an hour. I hope you'll all attend. And now it's time to announce our winners."

As the audience sat in hushed expectation, Maggie reached over, took Candy's hand, and pressed it to her chest. "Feel my beating heart," she said, her voice trembling. "I'm so nervous."

"Hang in there," Candy whispered supportively. "We're almost at the end."

"The second runner-up," Bertha said as she glanced down at the card in her hand, "will receive a two-hundred-fifty-dollar scholarship award, as well as a one-hundred-dollar gift certificate and a gift basket. And the second runner-up is . . . Amanda Tremont!"

"Oh!" was all Maggie could say in a surprised voice as she joined the audience in applause. "She came in third place."

Candy nudged her friend. "That's pretty good. Look, she's happy."

With a wide smile Amanda stepped forward to accept her bouquet of roses, her white satin sash, and a small silver tiara. She bent down so the two young girls could place it securely on her head.

"Amanda Tremont, our second runner-up!" Bertha called out to the crowd as the applause welled up again.

As Amanda stepped to one side, Bertha gathered the two remaining contestants to her side. "Ladies and gentlemen," she said dramatically, "we've come down to our final two contestants — Haley Pruitt and Sapphire Vine. As you know, the first runner-up plays a vitally important role. Should the Blueberry Queen not be able to fulfill her duties, for whatever reason, the first runner-up will assume those duties. And now, the moment you've all been waiting for."

Bertha took a moment to place her reading glasses on the end of her nose and check her card a final time. Candy noticed her hand was shaking. Finally, she lowered her glasses and stepped up to the microphone.

"It's got to be Haley Pruitt," Candy hissed, leaning close to Maggie's ear.

Maggie gripped her arm. "Pray to God you're right. I hate to think what will happen if the Blueberry Blob wins."

"The first runner-up will receive a five-hundred-dollar scholarship award, as well as a one-hundred-dollar gift certificate and a gift basket," Bertha said. "The Blueberry Queen will receive a one-thousand-dollar scholarship award, as well as a one-hundred-dollar gift certificate and a gift basket."

Bertha paused and looked out over the audience. "There's nothing more to say, except to announce the winners. And so, without further adieu, the first runner-up is . . . Haley Pruitt!"

A wave of shock and gasps swept through the audience, and Mrs. Pruitt appeared to faint, as Bertha Grayfire announced over the tumult, "That means this year's Blueberry Queen is Sapphire Vine!"

NINE

So Sapphire Vine is the Blueberry Queen.

Candy shook her head. She still couldn't believe it.

Hell has definitely frozen over — and has become a skating rink for the Sapphire Vines of the world.

It was Monday morning, two days after the festival and the pageant that had ended so dramatically. Candy was in her ten-year-old teal Jeep Cherokee, headed into town to run a few errands. She had a lot to do before she met Maggie at noon for lunch. But for some reason she just couldn't get Sapphire Vine out of her mind.

Twice yesterday, the video of the Blueberry Queen Pageant had been rebroadcast on the local cable-access channel. Candy watched it both times, from start to finish, with a mixture of horror, fascination, and outright glee.

There were so many parts of it she loved,

like when Sapphire came prancing out on stage in her cowgirl outfit, or when she recited that wacky poem of hers while dressed as a giant ripe blueberry. But Candy also liked watching Amanda go through her athletic routine, and she especially enjoyed hearing Haley Pruitt play the Rachmaninoff piece.

Her favorite part, though, was what had happened *after* Sapphire Vine had been crowned the Blueberry Queen. Whenever that part came on the TV, Candy leaned forward, rested her elbows on her knees and her chin in her palms, and scrutinized every delicious moment.

As Bertha Grayfire announced the winner, Sapphire Vine had overreacted wildly, squealing like a teenager at a sixties Beatles concert. She had bounced up and down shouting "Oh! Oh! Oh!" and flailed her arms about so wildly she actually came close to pummeling the other contestants on stage.

At the same moment, Helen Ross Pruitt, Haley's sour-faced grandmother, rose quickly to her feet, much to the surprise of her butler Hopkins (or whatever his name was). He reached out to perhaps comfort Mrs. Pruitt, or perhaps to restrain her, but she forcefully shoved him aside and charged the judges' table like a bull on the streets of Pamplona, her long bony finger leveled at them as she spat out her displeasure, her face dark with rage.

The judges had risen uneasily to their feet in defense, and the shouting had begun. Wild accusations and vehement denials had flown back and forth. Mrs. Pruitt actually came close to blows with one of the judges, Oliver LaForce, who ran the Lightkeeper's Inn. He had vehemently denied any wrongdoing and accused her of overreacting and, worse, bad sportsmanship. Candy had watched as Mrs. Pruitt flourished her tightly clenched fists in rage. She looked ready to swing out but had finally been restrained by her long-suffering butler.

It was a surrealistic moment straight out of the movies but something rarely seen in real life.

Candy loved every moment of it.

The entire hall erupted then as the camera lens swung erratically about, trying to record the ensuing chaos for posterity. The audience members were on their feet; some clapped politely, but most just stood in shock, and a few — perhaps supporters of Haley Pruitt and some of the other contestants — stormed from the hall in disbelief or disgust.

And though she stood in the middle of the firestorm, Sapphire Vine had been strangely oblivious to what was going on around her. Instead, she acted every bit the Blueberry Queen — probably because, Candy suspected, Sapphire had been anticipating and practicing that moment for weeks, more than likely in front of a mirror. It was almost as if she had known she was going to win — or at the very least, thought it her destiny.

With great dignity she accepted the bouquet and sash from the two little girls and bent forward regally so Bertha Grayfire could place a crown on the queen's head. Sapphire then responded to the muted congratulations of the other contestants by pulling each of them to her in tight, glorious hugs.

At this point, Candy had squinted closely at the TV to watch the barely controlled expressions of distaste on the faces of the other girls. Amanda stiffened as she allowed Sapphire to give her a hug, but she did a good job of forcing a smile. The other girls reacted similarly, trying to be good sports in a difficult situation. Still, the shock they felt was as plain on their faces, as it was on most of those in the audience.

As for Haley Pruitt, she had not waited

around to congratulate the winner. In tears, she dashed off the stage to be with her grandmother, who finally allowed herself to be escorted away from the judges' table by Hopkins the butler. It was clear from his grim expression that he knew he was on shaky ground even touching his mistress, but she finally turned to him and gave him a hard nod. At that point, he released her, and with Haley in tow, the three of them had stormed from the building.

Meanwhile, Sapphire Vine stepped to the front of the stage, where she flashed a radiant, obviously well-practiced smile and waved out at the audience, tears of joy streaming down her face. (Whether those tears were real or carefully and purposefully leaked was yet to be determined, Candy decided.)

But Sapphire hadn't stopped there. Caught up in the grandeur of the moment, she stepped down from the stage and marched out into the audience, hugging anyone and everyone she came to — grandmothers and schoolteachers and bankers and burly lobstermen and little girls, whom she lifted off the ground and twirled happily about.

She's really into this, Candy had thought as she watched the rebroadcast for the second time on Sunday. *She must have been really desperate to win this . . . but why? Has her life been that empty? Did she need this positive affirmation that badly?*

Eventually the images on the TV had faded, to be followed by rebroadcasts of the previous week's town council meeting or committee meeting or some such thing, and Candy had reluctantly flicked off the set.

She thought that, if it were broadcast again, she would tape the pageant so she and Maggie could watch it whenever they wanted, perhaps accompanied by a pitcher of blueberry daiquiris (a specialty of Candy's, made with fresh blueberries, natch, plus blueberry schnapps and white rum). She knew that taping the pageant for perennial mocking might be crass, but hey, when you lived on a blueberry farm on the outskirts of a sleepy seaside village in Maine, you had to get your pleasures where you could.

In fact, Candy thought as she turned off the Coastal Loop onto Main Street and looked around for a place to park, she could hardly wait for lunchtime so she could talk more with Maggie about it. They'd already had three or four phone conversations that had descended rapidly into tear-filled bouts of uncontrollable laughter, but there was no doubt they would be talking about the Blueberry Queen Pageant, and the new Blueberry Queen herself, for months, perhaps years, to come.

Life, as they say, was good.

But it wouldn't stay that way for long.

TEN

Candy's first stop was the Black Forest Bakery. She had promised Herr Georg she would drop off a few pounds of blueberries she'd raked the day before. The larger harvest would take place in the next couple of weeks, but in the meantime she was harvesting small batches for herself and a few others like Herr Georg, who loved to bake with fresh blueberries.

She and Doc were pleased with their crop this year and were expecting a good yield, though they would harvest only about seven acres — half their fields — this season. As was common when growing wild blueberries, the fields were harvested in two-year cycles. Half of the fields were in the sprout year. The plants would produce bud sets by the fall, and the following spring those bud sets would flower and produce blueberries in July and August. The other half was ready for harvesting this year.

The system worked well, producing an abundance of long, unbranched shoots that made for easy harvesting of the fruit. It also helped control pests and diseases, since after the field was fully harvested, it was burned, or sometimes mowed, to take the plants back to their roots, and the two-year cycle began again.

In a single day, working by herself and using a short-handled metal rake, Candy could harvest several hundred pounds of blueberries, though that was admittedly backbreaking work. So far she had gone easy and was delivering only about sixty pounds to Herr Georg today.

He was thrilled with what he saw. "Oh, they are beautiful!" he enthused as he grasped one of the eight-quart buckets in his hands and shook it gently. He leaned forward and inhaled deeply, taking in the scent of the ripe succulent berries. "I can do wonderful things with these!

"Ah, Candy," he continued as they settled into chairs at one of the small round tables near his shop's front window, "this is my favorite time of year. I love it so! Surrounded by all this freshness, all this goodness and healthiness! Blueberries straight from the fields, delivered right to my door just hours after harvest by a beautiful woman! It is like giving new paints to an artist or a new instrument to a musician. How could a baker ask for more?"

"Well, you know me — I love to keep my customers happy. Just let me know when you need more." Candy paused and leaned forward a little. "By the way," she continued conspiratorially, her voice dropping just a notch in volume, "I'm dying to ask you about the pageant on Saturday night. You must have been stunned when Mrs. Pruitt charged the judges like that and started yelling at you."

At this sudden change in subject, Herr Georg's expression became guarded, and he drew back in his chair. His gaze shifted back and forth. "Oh, that? Well, yes, yes, it was a very strange night, wasn't it?" Absently he licked his lips. "I mean, that Vine woman winning? How odd that was. It surprised us all, I think. Very shocking."

"Yes, it *was*, wasn't it?" Suddenly enthralled, Candy shifted her chair a bit closer to him. "So tell me *everything*. What did you think about that cowgirl outfit of hers? Wasn't that *odd*? And that poem? It certainly was creative, yes, but you couldn't have given her very high marks for that dreadful performance, could you? So how did she win anyway?"

Herr Georg looked at her nervously. "Candy, *meine liebchen,* you should know I can't talk about those things. I'm sworn to secrecy."

"Just a hint. A little tidbit. Please? For your old friend Candy." She made goo-goo eyes at him, egging him on.

Herr Georg hesitated for the longest time, glancing this way and that, then allowed himself a small smile as he leaned in close. "Well," he said quietly, obviously unable to resist Candy's charms, "I suppose it won't hurt to talk about this just between the two of us. As long as the conversation goes no further than this table."

Candy made a gesture of locking her lips with a key and tossing the key away.

Herr Georg laughed, then continued in a tone barely above a whisper. "Just as you say, I was horrified, simply horrified, when Mrs. Pruitt charged us like that! It was so unexpected and so *frightening!* Such fury from such a small, thin woman! I thought she was going to slay each of us right there!"

"I know! Wasn't she *wretched?*"

"Shocking. Quite shocking — and most inappropriate," Herr Georg agreed.

"I can't believe she just flew off the handle like that. I mean, I was as surprised as anyone that Haley didn't win. But I guess you were surprised about that too."

"I, um, yes, ah, yes, yes, as I said before, of course I was."

"And who can believe Sapphire Vine actually won? I was thinking about it this morning, and the only reason I can come up with — the only way she could have won — is if one of the judges marked the scoring form wrong, or something like that. You know, got the contestants mixed up and put the wrong scores in the wrong place. But that's crazy, isn't it? I mean, I can't imagine that sort of thing happening. But it seems like the only explanation."

"Hmm," mused Herr Georg. "Do you really think so? It doesn't seem possible, does it?"

"Well, no, I suppose not. I mean, these things *are* carefully monitored, right? It wouldn't be possible for a judge to screw up like that, would it?"

"Oh no, of course not, of course not!" Herr Georg replied emphatically.

"And if one of the judges made a huge mistake like that and threw the vote to Sapphire, the rest of you would know about it, wouldn't you?"

"Hmm." Herr Georg shifted uneasily in his seat and tugged at the end of his white moustache. Clearly he was uncomfortable with this line of questioning. "Well, not necessarily," he said cautiously. "I mean, we scored the contestants independently, and we didn't review each other's scores, so *theoretically* it's possible, I suppose, that one of the judges could have been a little, um, mixed up, as you say. But it doesn't seem likely, does it? Perhaps, as strange as it may sound, Ms. Vine really did win, fair and square. It *is* possible, I suppose. Don't you think? Would you like some tea?"

"I'd love some but I can't. I have to stop at the bank and post office, and then I'm off to meet Maggie for lunch."

"Ah, yes, I suppose I must press on as well. Ray is due by at any moment. I should get ready for him."

"Ray's coming?" Candy rose and looked around. "Are you remodeling?"

"Putting in some shelves along the wall here." The baker pointed to the far side of the room. "Expanding my offerings. I've decided to import German-made candies and cookies and sell them here in the store. Here, I'll show you."

He darted behind the counter and pulled a package from a large cardboard box. "You must try these. They are called Waffeletten. Wafer rolls dipped in chocolate. Straight from Germany. Absolutely delicious!"

He opened the bag and held it out to her. "Here, take one."

"Herr Georg, I just can't." Candy patted her stomach. "I ate way too much this weekend. I'm going to be on a diet for the next month, at least."

Georg nodded, closed up the bag, and passed it to her. "Take them with you then. Doc will enjoy them. Ah, here comes Ray now . . ."

Candy grabbed the bag from him, mumbled a quick "thank you," and headed out the back door so she wouldn't have to spend the next fifteen minutes making small talk with Ray.

The morning raced by, and before she knew it she was pulling up in front of the Stone & Milbury Insurance Agency, where Maggie worked as an office manager.

"We have to hurry," Maggie said, grabbing her purse and dragging Candy out the front door with her. "I have to be back by one sharp."

"Where are we going?"

"There's that new café that just opened up on River Road."

"Oh yeah. Melody's, right?"

"I've heard good things about it. Let's check it out."

Melody's Café was a soup, salad, and

sandwich bistro with only eight or ten tables crammed into a small wood-floored space, but it was cool inside and tastefully decorated and smelled wonderful. And it was almost full. Candy and Maggie managed to snag the last open table in the back corner and settled gratefully into their cane chairs. Crisp white linen covered the tabletop, fresh flowers added an elegant touch, and fine china and fresh-baked rolls were placed in front of them the moment they sat down.

"Yummy," Candy said as she and Maggie tore into the bread like wolves into a fresh kill. Their waitress was a pleasant young woman named Stephanie. Maggie ordered a teriyaki chicken salad, and though it seemed a bit decadent and she was seriously trying to cut back on her food intake, Candy opted for the lobster roll and chips. Both ordered a glass of Chateau Ste. Michelle Chardonnay from Washington State, which was recommended by Stephanie.

"So," Maggie said as she sipped her wine and nibbled at a fresh-baked roll oozing butter, "before we get distracted, you never told me how you did at the festival. Did you make out okay?"

"I had an *amazing* day. Made almost twelve hundred dollars."

"Wow! I'm impressed." Maggie patted her

friend's hand. "I'm so proud of you! You're so resourceful."

Candy sighed. "I need every penny. I just had to pay a killer property tax bill and make a quarterly payment to the IRS. It looks like Doc's going to need some dental work. Registration on the Jeep is due next month — I just hope to God it doesn't need any work to pass inspection. And I have to pay the harvest help. With all these bills I feel like I got the sword of Damocles hanging over my head."

Maggie's mouth twisted in thought. "Hmm. Damocles? He's not that good-looking UPS driver, is he?"

They both had a good laugh as their food arrived. Candy nibbled at her lobster roll while Maggie speared a forkful of salad.

"So tell me," Candy said between mouthfuls, "how is Amanda doing after her big night onstage?"

Maggie shrugged. "You know teenage girls. One minute she's bouncing off the ceiling because she won second runner-up, and the next she's down in the dumps because she lost to Sapphire Vine. It's all hormones. An emotional roller-coaster. And having Cameron around so much doesn't help." She rolled her eyes.

"I talked to Herr Georg. You know, that

thing we talked about."

"You mean the judging?"

Candy nodded.

"Ooh, tell me. What did he say? Someone screwed up royally, right? Or maybe Sapphire just got her hooks into one of the judges — you know, bribery?"

Candy frowned and shook her head. "He wouldn't admit to anything. But I know it has to be something like that. There's no *way* she could have won that pageant without help from someone."

"Right. It goes against the laws of the universe."

"Something's definitely rotten in Denmark."

"Who gives a crap about Denmark? Something's rotten right here in good ol' Cape Willington."

They talked on for some time as they finished their food and were still gabbing away when they heard another voice nearby. "Hello, excuse me."

Candy and Maggie looked up. A curly-haired woman with a dark complexion, dark brown eyes, and a bright smile stood beside them.

"My name is Melody . . . Melody Barnes," the woman said, introducing herself. "I'm the proprietor of this little establishment. I just wanted to come by and introduce myself. You're Candy Holliday, right?"

"That's right." Candy held out her hand as she nodded toward Maggie. "And this is my friend Maggie Tremont. It's nice to meet you, Melody."

There were smiles and handshakes all around, after which Melody continued. "So how's the food? Are you enjoying it?"

"Excellent," said Maggie.

"The lobster roll is wonderful," added Candy. "These chunks of lobster are huge."

Melody seemed pleased. "I'm glad you're enjoying it. That's a specialty of the house. My grandmother's recipe. It's all in the spices, you know. Listen, I must tell you, there's a reason I wanted to meet you. I bought one of your blueberry pies on Saturday."

"Oh yes, I remember," Candy said pleasantly. "Did you like it?"

"It was one of the best I've ever tasted. I ate one piece myself and served the rest of the slices to some of my customers today. It's been a huge hit, especially with the tourists, and I was wondering, well, if you would consider baking pies for me on a regular basis, to serve here in the café?" Leaning a little closer, she whispered, "I've been told I need to upgrade my desserts!" She leaned back again as she continued. "But I just don't have the time to bake, since I'm so busy with the rest of the cooking. Anyway, your pies are so much better than anything I could make. I don't think I could improve on them. And if you could help me out, it would mean the world to me."

Candy's eyes lit up. "Really? Of course! I'd love to do that. How many would you need?"

They set to talking then, and by the time Candy and Maggie left the café fifteen minutes later, Candy had an order for eight pies a week, half to be delivered on Monday morning and the other half Thursday morning. For this first week, though, she had agreed to deliver five pies the following afternoon.

"Wasn't that nice?" Maggie said as they drove back to the insurance agency. "I guess things really are looking up for you, what with the festival, and now this."

Candy nodded, feeling all aglow. "It's great, isn't it? With the way things are going, I just might be able to pay my bills this month."

"Honey, with the way things are going, you'll be able to buy Pruitt Manor!"

ELEVEN

Candy awoke suddenly in the middle of the night. For a few moments she lay in the darkness as a warm breeze blew over her, trying to figure out what had pulled her so quickly out of deep sleep.

And then she heard it — the chickens were in a frenzy, squawking madly out in their coop about something.

She jumped out of bed, pulled on a bathrobe, and carefully made her way down the dark staircase. Doc kept a flashlight on the windowsill by the back door, for emergencies. Candy grabbed it, slipped into a pair of sandals, and headed out into the night, flicking on the flashlight as she went.

A three-quarter moon cast a faint glow on the landscape, giving it a ghostly appearance. Trying to ignore the creepy feeling that edged up her back, she hurried toward the barn and skirted around the side of it. As she approached the coop behind the barn, she could hear the chickens squawking in terror.

She stopped about ten feet away and shined the flashlight back and forth. Most of the girls were in a frenzy, their under-feathers flying everywhere, but a few still sat up in their roosts, their necks pulled way down into the feathers, clearly frightened out of their wits. Something had spooked them — but what?

Flicking the flashlight about, Candy searched the shadows around the coop while at the same time looking around for a weapon. This was a rural area, and there could be any number of critters about. If she had to tangle with anything too dangerous, she didn't want to do it bare-handed. She wished she had remembered to pull Doc's shotgun from the broom closet in the kitchen.

And then she saw it — an animal about the size of a small dog pawing at the chicken wire on the back side, trying to break into the coop.

"Hey! Get out of there!" Candy shouted suddenly, her voice breaking sharp in the night. She moved to her left, bent and scooped up a handful of stones, and flung them at the critter. It shied away when it saw her, its eyes luminescent in the flashlight's beam, watching her intently to see what she was going to do next.

She picked up a good-sized rock and threw it at the animal — a fairly large fox, she saw now. "Leave them alone! Git!"

She picked up a large stick and started toward the creature, but before she had taken even a few steps it turned suddenly and slunk away, seeming to simply disappear into the high grass and shadows that edged the blueberry field behind the barn.

"What's wrong?" came a voice behind her.

Candy jumped at the voice and twisted about. Doc was coming toward her wearing only a T-shirt and boxer shorts. His shotgun was tucked under one arm.

She held a hand to her rapidly beating heart. "A fox, trying to get at the girls."

Doc squinted into the darkness. "Did you chase it away?"

"Yeah, it's gone, I think."

"Damn critters. Are the girls okay?"

Candy walked toward the coop, shining the flashlight inside. The chickens were still clucking loudly, still frightened, though they were starting to calm down.

"They seem all right. Just scared as hell." She walked around the coop to where the fox had been pawing at it and bent to inspect the chicken wire. "Damn thing almost got in, though. I'm gonna have to fix this in the morning. We got any chicken wire left?"

Doc shook his head as he leaned the shotgun against the barn. "I don't think so. I'll tie a piece of plywood up against it for tonight. That'll help temporarily, but we'll have to stop by the hardware store in the morning."

Doc helped her patch up the coop as best they could, then they both went back to bed. But Candy found she couldn't fall asleep again, no matter how hard she tried. She turned and tossed for an hour or so and finally gave up. At first light she climbed out of bed, feeling tired and cranky. She put on the coffee, checked the girls again, and decided she might as well start baking pies to take into town later in the day.

She knew her arrangement with Melody wouldn't make her a lot of money, but every penny would help. It seemed that scraping around for money had become a way of life for her and Doc. She had made good money down in Boston, true, and had lived quite comfortably until Clark, her ex-husband, lost his job. As their marriage unraveled, they had to live on her paycheck, which made their finances tight, but they still had their savings — until Clark squandered most of that on his start-up tech company. When they divorced, they sold the house, but after paying off an equity loan, they weren't left with much. They split it up, and Candy used some of the money to make a few repairs around Blueberry Acres when she moved in with Doc. The place had needed a new roof, and they'd done some remodeling work inside, tearing out old carpet and putting in new wood floors. She'd also had to buy a new fridge and dishwasher when the old ones went out. The rest of the money she still had in a savings account at a bank in Bangor, but she was hesitant to touch it, thinking some day she might buy a place of her own.

For now they lived off Doc's Social Security and his retirement money from the university, from the twenty or thirty thousand they made every year selling blueberries, and from the odd jobs Candy did around town. For the most part they lived comfortably enough, until unexpected bills started to pile up or when something special was needed. There were days, when the checking account was near empty, that she considered heading up to Bangor or down to Portland to try to get back into a marketing firm. But every time she considered that option she quickly put it aside. Such a job, she knew, would bring back too many memories of her earlier life, and she resolved again to try to make her current situation work.

So she was grateful for any extra income — even if it meant making a few extra dollars a week by baking pies for Melody's Café.

Several hours later she pulled the last two pies out of the oven, set them on the counter to cool, walked out onto the porch to rest for a moment, and promptly fell asleep in a chaise lounge. The ringing phone woke her.

Maggie was on the other end of the line. She sounded frantic. "Are you watching TV?"

"No, I'm . . . I'm baking," Candy answered, still feeling groggy. "Why?"

"Turn it on. Now. Channel seven. I'll call you right back." She hung up.

Candy glanced up at the clock. It was just after noon. Had she slept that long?

She yawned, poured herself a cup of lukewarm coffee, and flicked on the small TV set in the corner of the kitchen counter. As the sound and picture came on, she heard the news announcer speaking, starting in midsentence.

". . . just after ten thirty this morning. The body was apparently discovered by a neighbor, who called the police. The victim has been identified as thirty-seven-year-old Sapphire Vine, who . . ."

Candy gasped. Her hand flew to her mouth as she watched the image of a stretcher being wheeled out of the front door of a Victorian house. The body lying on the stretcher was draped in a white sheet.

". . . was crowned as Cape Willington's Blueberry Queen just this past Saturday night. According to observers, Ms. Vine's appearance in the annual pageant was somewhat controversial, since contestants are usually limited to girls of high school age."

A homemade video of Sapphire dressed as a blueberry and reciting her poem appeared on screen. It was soon replaced by more shots of the ambulance and police cars.

The announcer continued. "Sources tell us that Ms. Vine was a columnist for the local newspaper and was a respected resident of the town. According to Cape Willington Chief of Police Daryl Durr, the death is being treated as a homicide, and police say they have arrested a suspect. He is identified as Ray Hutchins, a local handyman. An investigation is underway. We'll keep you posted on further developments. Now for a check on the local weather, we'll turn to our own Kimberly Frank, who tells us that it's going to turn stormy . . ."

TWELVE

Candy felt her legs go numb. Before they had a chance to collapse beneath her, she crossed to a chair and sat down heavily. Her fingertips were tingling, and there seemed to be a buzzing sound in her ears.

Sapphire murdered? Ray arrested?

How could that be?

She didn't have much time to consider an answer, because the phone rang again. Candy rose shakily to answer it and then sat back down.

"Did you see it?" Maggie asked breathlessly.

"I saw it. I don't believe it, but I saw it."

"Wasn't that utterly, totally bizarre? The way they brought her body out on a stretcher like that? It was so undignified, but at least she got her final moment in the spotlight. I half expected her to jump up in her cowgirl outfit and start reciting poetry."

"It doesn't seem real," Candy replied,

leaning forward and putting a hand to her forehead. She felt hot.

"Oh, it's real all right. Someone really, truly did it. Someone murdered our Blueberry Queen."

Candy took in a sharp breath. "That's right! I hadn't thought about it like that. Her Majesty is dead, isn't she?" She paused, thinking. "But if Sapphire's gone, that means . . ."

Maggie picked up the thread, finishing her thought. "It means, by decree, that the Blueberry Queen sash and crown must be handed over to the first runner-up."

"Haley Pruitt!"

"That would be her, the granddaughter of our dear old rich friend, Mrs. Pruitt."

"So justice is served — Haley will get what probably was rightfully hers in the first place."

"True, but doesn't it sound suspicious to you? If I didn't know better, I'd say Old Lady Pruitt had something to do with this."

Candy felt a jolt of realization shoot through her. "You think so? You really think she had Sapphire rubbed out?"

"Who knows? It's possible, isn't it? It sure would make a lot of sense."

"I suppose so, but . . . they said they've arrested Ray. They must think he had something to do with this."

Maggie snorted, a distorted blast of noise coming over the phone. "Ray Hutchins? Oh, come on! Do you really think he could do something like that?"

"I . . . I don't know," Candy said thoughtfully. "I guess not, since you put it that way. It doesn't seem possible, does it?"

"Are you kidding? It's ludicrous! Our little ol' Ray wouldn't hurt a fly. He tears up when he steps on a cockroach."

It's true, Candy thought, remembering the look on Ray's face a few days ago when he had put the sides of the booth on the wrong way. "But what's the connection? How'd he get himself arrested for killing Sapphire Vine?"

"Who knows? But I can tell you right now they're barking up the wrong tree with that guy."

"But if he didn't do it," Candy said, her mind working feverishly, "then who?" She paused as she collected her thoughts. It took her a few moments before she could put everything in order. "Even though she had motivation, I can't really imagine Mrs. Pruitt doing something like this — no matter how much she hated Sapphire and wanted Haley to win. And it couldn't have been one of the other contestants, could it?

Or the *parents* of one of the contestants?" She paused, then said jokingly, "*You* didn't kill Sapphire, did you?"

That got a chuckle out of Maggie. "Me? Hah! Listen, honey, don't think I didn't think about it more than once. In fact, I wish I *had* killed her. I sure could use the notoriety. And to tell you the truth, it *was* on my to-do list. But somebody beat me to it."

Candy smiled as Maggie continued, obviously on a roll. "Besides, if I'd done her in, I wouldn't make a secret of it. I'd be shouting it from the rooftops until they dragged me down and hauled me off to the looney bin. They'd probably even make a TV movie about me. *Maggie Tremont, Blueberry Queen Murderer.* I'd finally get my name in lights, just like I always wanted." She let out a final laugh. "So what about you? Are you the killer?"

"Me?" Candy sighed. "Not me. I didn't have any motive to kill her. I've got nothing to gain. Besides, I get woozy at the sight of blood — I have to lie down when I get a paper cut. I could never do anything like that."

"Well, if *I* didn't kill her, and *you* didn't kill her, and *Ray* didn't kill her, you know what that means, don't you?" Maggie asked ominously.

"No, what?"

"It means they've arrested the wrong person. And that means the *real* murderer is still running loose around Cape Willington."

That sent a chill skittering up Candy's spine. "You're right." Instinctively she looked up to see if the kitchen door was locked, and through the window saw Doc's pickup truck coming up the dirt lane. He had gone into town as usual that morning, telling her he had best get out of her way and let her bake.

Now she let out a breath of relief. "Doc's here. I've got to go."

"Okay. Call me tonight!" Maggie said as they hung up.

Candy walked out the door and stood on the back porch, her hands slipped into the back pockets of her jeans, as Doc pulled up and called out to her with the engine idling. "Have you heard?"

She nodded. "I've heard."

He motioned her toward the truck. "Get your things and come on."

"Where are we going?"

"To the police station. We're gonna look in on Ray and see if he's all right."

Candy nodded, ran back into the house to

get her purse and keys, closed the door behind her, and climbed into the cab beside Doc. He pulled the gearshift into reverse and wheeled the truck around.

"Whoever heard of such a thing?" he muttered as he drove back down the lane. "Arresting Ray Hutchins! A kinder, gentler soul doesn't exist on this planet. He must be frantic right about now. We've got to give him some moral support."

It took less than ten minutes to drive to the Cape Willington Police Department, which was located about half a mile outside of town in a relatively new one-story brick building on Route 196, also known locally as Loop Road. The village's police station had relocated there about ten years ago, after abandoning a cramped old wooden building at the far end of Main Street, which it had operated out of for the better part of a century.

Doc parked in the front lot, and he and Candy pushed silently through the wood-and-glass door and presented themselves at the information desk.

"We'd like to see Ray Hutchins," Doc announced to the stout woman behind the desk. She was nicely dressed, in a blouse, skirt, and silk scarf. "I believe you have him in custody in connection with the Sapphire

Vine murder."

"Oh, hi, Doc," the woman said, looking up and pushing her glasses up on her nose. "I thought that was you. Haven't seen you for a while."

"Hi, Carol. How're things going?"

"Oh, you know — Phil's lumbago is kicking up again and the wagon needs new tires. But other than that, as good as can be expected, what with all that's happened today. So, you're here to see Ray, huh? You're not family, are you?"

Doc shook his head. "Don't think he has much of a family. We're just here to lend moral support."

"Moral support. Okay, I see." Carol picked up a pen and nodded as she looked down at a sheet in front of her. She tapped at the sheet for a few moments with the pen, then looked back up. "Well, Doc, that's a real nice gesture, and I'd sure like to let you in to see him, and he'd probably be real glad to see you. But I don't think it's gonna happen today. He's still in booking, and after that they're gonna take him up to the county jail in Machias. We don't retain prisoners here, you know."

"What do you mean?"

"We don't have jail cells, Doc. We've got a secure area in back where we bring prisoners in to book them, but then they're taken to Machias or Bangor for incarceration."

"Oh." Doc's jaw tightened. He hadn't been aware of that. "No chance of seeing him before you ship him out?"

Carol glanced up at the clock, then back down at the sheet in front of her, shaking her head. "I don't think so. We just don't have the facility for such a thing, especially with a prisoner like Ray. There's the issue of personal safety, you know."

"Who's personal safety? Ours?"

"Sure. Look, Doc, it's crazy around here right now. Why don't you wait until all the booking and paperwork are done and then check on Ray tomorrow up in Machias. You should be able to get in to see him then."

Doc didn't seem to like that answer. He looked as though he were about to burst wide open, so Candy put a restraining hand on his shoulder. To Carol, she said pleadingly, "Isn't there any way we could see him today? We could wait around for a while, see what happens."

Carol pursed her lips. "I'd sure like to help you out, Candy, Doc, sure would, but it's just not in my power, you know. We got ourselves a murder investigation going on here. Everyone's real serious about it, being the rare event it is. Even got some detectives coming over from Augusta. Yup, it's real serious all right. We've got to do things by the book. You can understand that, can't you?" She gave them a tight smile that seemed to plead for their cooperation. "Try it tomorrow, okay? Up in Machias?"

Doc let out a long, painful sigh of resignation. "Okay, Carol. Listen, do me a favor then, will ya? If you see Ray, tell him we were here, and tell him we'll see him in the morning."

"I'll do that, Doc, Candy. Good to see you both."

Back outside, Doc was still steaming as he climbed into the truck. "I can't believe they won't let us in to see him."

"Poor Ray," Candy said as she slid in beside him. "He must be terrified in there."

"I still can't believe they arrested him. Anyone who knows Ray knows he could never have done anything like that. Someone's just making a huge mistake."

"Do you have any idea why they arrested him?" Candy asked as Doc started up the truck.

"Not yet, but I know where we can find out."

"The diner?"

Doc nodded emphatically. "The diner."

They drove back into town and parked on

Main Street. As Candy climbed out of the truck, she felt a strange sensation go through her. She stopped on the sidewalk and twisted around, her gaze roaming up and down the street. She wasn't sure what she expected to see in this town she had grown so accustomed to, but she was surprised to find that everything was essentially business as usual. Folks strolled about, gazing into shop windows, hurrying to or from work, snacking on ice cream, or chatting on cell phones. People were laughing. It all seemed so odd after what had happened over the past few days — that two people who had lived here, in this town, two people they all had known, had talked to (and in the case of Sapphire, frequently made fun of), people who had been alive and probably walked down this very street just a few days ago, were now gone, dead, one murdered not far from this very spot, the other dead after a suspicious plunge from a seaside cliff. And Sapphire's murderer still might be running loose around town! But despite that, everything seemed to be normal. And somehow that just didn't seem right to her.

Once they entered Duffy's Main Street Diner, however, Candy realized that things in town were not quite business as usual. The place was abuzz, and all the talk was about Sapphire Vine. Had she still been alive, she would have been mighty proud to have been the main topic of conversation.

"Hey, Doc!" someone yelled from a corner booth and waved at them.

"There they are." Doc pointed the way. "Hi, Juanita," he called out to the waitress behind the counter.

"Hey, Doc. Hey, Candy. You both having the usual?"

Doc nodded. "We'll be with the boys."

"Got it."

Finn, Artie, and Bumpy had staked out their usual place in the horseshoe-shaped corner booth, from which they could watch the comings and goings in the diner as well as the activity on the street outside. Finn scratched at his salt-and-pepper beard as he chewed on a toothpick, while Artie made notes on the ever-present clipboard and Bumpy eyed a handful of leftover fries on Artie's pushed-back plate. Doc greeted them as he slid into the booth on one side. Candy slid in on the other side, next to Bumpy.

Finn gave them a wink, Artie looked up and nodded, and Bumpy raised a couple of fingers in greeting. "Hey, Doc. Hey, Candy. Where've you two been? We were expecting you half an hour ago."

"We stopped over at the police station to talk to Ray," Doc explained, "but they wouldn't let us see him."

"I'm not surprised," Finn said knowingly. "Booking and all. Plus he's a murder suspect. They have to be careful how they handle these things."

Doc shifted restlessly. "So they said, though I can't imagine why they'd arrest him in the first place. Damn foolish, if you ask me."

"They must've had a reason," Bumpy said, giving into temptation and filching a French fry from Artie's plate. He dipped it generously in ketchup before he ate it. "They just don't arrest a person like that for nothing."

"What kinda reason could there possibly be for arresting Ray Hutchins?" Doc shot back. "That boy is as innocent as a newborn baby."

Finn cleared his throat. "Um, well, not necessarily."

They all looked over at him. For a moment everyone was silent.

"Well," Doc said finally, breaking the silence, "it's obvious you've heard something through your usual sources. You gonna tell us what you know or do we have to beat it out of you?"

"I think we should give him a sound rapping about the head and shoulders," Bumpy suggested.

"Naw, he'd probably enjoy it," Artie added with a grin.

Finn leaned forward over the table. "Okay, I'll tell you," he said, his voice conspiratorially low, "but you can't say nothing."

Everyone groaned. "Enough with the horseshit," Artie said.

"Yeah, cough it up," Doc added. "You know something, so spill it."

Finn's dark eyes shifted around the diner, as if to make sure no one was eavesdropping. Convinced he wasn't being overheard, he folded his arms on the table and lowered his voice even more, to a coarse whisper. "Well, like I said, you haven't heard this from me, but they arrested Ray because they have stone-cold evidence that he murdered that Vine woman."

"Evidence?" Candy said testily. "What kind of evidence could they possibly have?"

Even as she asked the question, she wasn't sure she wanted to know the answer. Finn told her anyway.

"From what I've heard from the boys inside, they found the murder weapon, right there at the scene of the crime, and they traced it right back to Ray."

Artie snorted. "Who would be stupid enough to leave the murder weapon at the scene of the crime?"

"Well, that's the point, isn't it?" Finn said. "Who *would* be stupid enough to do that?"

They all sat in silence for a moment as the question answered itself.

"So what was this murder weapon that incriminated Ray?" Candy finally asked, still refusing to believe.

Finn glanced over at her, then said to them all, with as much drama as he could muster, "A hammer. A brand-new red-handled hammer."

Candy closed her eyes as the air seemed to go out of her. "Oh no."

Finn nodded. "From what I've heard, someone — Ray, allegedly — took that hammer and bashed in Sapphire's skull from behind. Blunt trauma. Pretty gruesome, they say. She must have died instantly. Never knew what hit her."

"That's awful," Bumpy said.

"Terrible. Just terrible," Artie agreed, pushing his glasses up the bridge of his nose with his middle finger.

"But what makes them think Ray did it?" Doc asked angrily. "Did they find him there? Did anyone see him do it?"

Finn shook his head. "Not that I know of,

but there are witnesses who saw Ray's truck parked in front of Sapphire's house last night. And someone said they heard shouting coming from the house at around nine last night."

Candy opened her eyes but kept them focused on the table in front of her, unable to look at the others in the booth. It all seemed so unreal. She looked at her hands, but even those seemed foreign to her as she anxiously rubbed them together.

She had seen that hammer before — had held it in these very hands. And now it was a suspected murder weapon, wielded — apparently — by someone she knew.

At someone she knew.

Suddenly she felt very sick.

THIRTEEN

Their food was delivered, but Candy found she had lost her appetite. She sat for a while with Doc and the boys, listening to their back-and-forth banter, which turned quite salty, as it often did. She stayed as long as she could, her stomach churning, until finally she pushed the plate back and excused herself from the table. "I'm going to run over to Gumm's and pick up that chicken wire," she told Doc. "I'll meet you back at the truck in fifteen minutes."

He looked up, his gaze narrowing. "You all right? You're looking kinda pale."

She smiled weakly. "I just need some air."

"You gonna finish that?" Bumpy asked, pointing to her uneaten lunch.

"It's all yours." She left without another word, giving them a halfhearted wave before walking out of the dark coolness of the diner. Once in the bright sunlight of the midsummer afternoon and away from the talk of murder, she felt a bit better. The day was hot and the humidity was building again. Dark, ominous clouds were piling up above the western horizon. *It's going to turn stormy,* the news announcer had said on the noonday forecast.

She had been right in more ways than one.

Clutching her purse, Candy crossed Main Street, dodging cars and pedestrians, and headed down the block toward Gumm's Hardware Store at the far end. A few of the townsfolk said hello to her as she passed them on the way, but she replied absently, still feeling shaky.

Ray's hammer, she thought as she walked inattentively, head down. *The same hammer I used the other day when Ray came over to the farm to help with the booth. I held the murder weapon in my hand. I held the weapon that killed Sapphire Vine.*

She felt her stomach churning even more. For a moment she thought she was going to be physically sick, but she forced it back as another thought struck her: *My fingerprints are probably on the murder weapon. What if they think I had something to do with Sapphire's death?*

Now she really thought she was going to be sick.

Trying to shake off her queasiness, she

pushed through the front door of Gumm's and into the coolness again. Cameron, Amanda's boyfriend, stood behind the counter, looking incredibly bored.

"Hi, Cam," she said, giving him a wave.

"Oh, hi, Candy. How's it going?"

"Not so great right now. Where do you keep the chicken wire?"

He pointed, looking concerned. "Back corner, next to the rakes and shovels. Everything okay?"

"Yeah, it's just . . . things are a little crazy. So how's Amanda doing?" she asked as she started off down the aisle.

"She's okay. Glad the pageant's over."

"All of us are," Candy said as an image of a postpageant Sapphire Vine flashed unbidden through her mind. She saw Sapphire standing in the living room of her little yellow house, being struck in the head from behind by a shadowy figure that held a red-handled hammer . . .

Candy shook away the frightening image.

She'd been positive there was no way Ray could have done such a thing, but now she wasn't so sure. *Could he really have killed her?* she thought as she wandered back through the aisles of the hardware store, still feeling as if she were in a daze. *Of course he could have,* she realized after a moment. *Just about anyone can be pushed over the edge, given the right circumstances. Maybe she pressed him too hard about something, or maybe she was blackmailing him . . .*

Blackmail. Now *that* was an interesting thought.

There were rumors around town about that, Candy recalled. Some said, in whispers, that Sapphire found great joy in digging around for dirt on various townsfolk. It was said she even kept secret files on some people. Maybe Sapphire had turned up something about Ray's past that he didn't want known. It was a possibility, Candy realized. *What do you really know about him, anyway? Everyone has secrets. Maybe Sapphire found out what Ray's were. Could she have confronted him, put a good scare into him, backed him into a corner so he felt he had no choice but to hit her over the head with his shiny new hammer?*

But what could it have been? What could have provoked him into doing such a thing?

That was the question that gnawed at her as she blinked rapidly a few times and found herself standing in the back corner of the store. Forcing herself to focus, she ran her eyes up and down the shelves, back and forth. She finally spotted a few bundles of rolled-up chicken wire piled in the back of the bottom shelf, covered in dust.

As she knelt down and reached for a couple of bundles, she heard garbled voices from the front of the store. Cameron was talking to someone, but Candy couldn't quite make out what they were saying. She rose and absently wandered down the aisle, her eyes raking over the shelves and displays, trying to remember if she needed anything else while she was here.

She turned into the next aisle and stopped suddenly. Then just as suddenly she backed up around the corner. She froze as her heart raced.

A uniformed police officer stood in the center of the aisle she had been about to enter. He hadn't seen her; he was standing in front of bins of tools, his back to her, talking to Cameron.

"They're right here," Candy heard Cameron say to the officer. "We just got them in about a week ago."

"How many were in the initial shipment?" the policeman asked in an official-sounding tone.

"I think we ordered eight."

"There are five left. Who'd you sell the other three to?"

Cameron went silent a moment. Evidently he was thinking about his answer. "Well,

Ray bought the first one, the same day they came in. He loves buying new tools. He's in here all the time."

"Ray Hutchins?" the officer clarified.

"Yes, sir."

Candy thought she heard the scratch of a pen on a notepad. "What about the other two?"

"I think I sold one on Saturday morning to someone who came over from Town Hall. He said he needed it to work on the pageant set."

"Do you remember the name of the person who bought it?"

As they spoke, Candy edged along the aisle, trying to be as inconspicuous as possible. She pretended to look at chain saws as she eavesdropped on their conversation, just in case someone should come around the end of the aisle and spot her.

"I don't know his name," Cameron said. In her mind's eye she could see the teenager shrug, his bony shoulders rising and falling, his hands stuffed in the pockets of his worn jeans. "He was just one of the construction guys."

"A male then?"

"Yeah — um, yes, sir. A male."

"How old was he, would you say?"

"In his forties, I guess."

"I'll need you to give me a description of him. So who bought the third hammer?"

"I don't remember. I don't think I sold it." At that, Cameron shifted and called out toward the small office at the back of the store. "Hey, Mr. Gumm, did you sell one of these new Apex hammers to someone in the past few days?"

Candy heard someone grumbling and then a shuffling of feet. "Er, what was that?" came a thin, elderly voice from the office doorway.

"These hammers," Cameron repeated. "Officer Martin wants to know who we sold them to."

"What hammers?"

The shuffling feet came down the main aisle, which ran perpendicular to the one where Candy now stood, and then old Mr. Gumm appeared. Candy lowered her head and held still, hoping he would pass by the end of the aisle without see her. Fortunately, he was looking down at the floor as he walked past. He shuffled on by and turned into the next aisle.

"These Apex hammers," Cameron said again.

"What, the ones with the red fiberglass handles?"

"Yes, that's right, sir," said the police officer as Mr. Gumm approached them. "Allegedly three of these hammers have been sold. I need to know who you sold them to."

"Well, let me see now." The shuffling stopped as Mr. Gumm thought about this. "I sold one to that butler fellow who works up at Pruitt Manor. Unpleasant one, he is," Mr. Gumm grumbled. "Looks a lot like a bulldog, doesn't he?"

Candy's eyes grew wide as the policeman asked, "When was that, sir?"

"Well, now, let me see. Must've been Thursday or Friday last week, I guess. Yup, yup, that's right. Cam's off on Thursdays, so I was here by myself. That's when it was."

"I see. I'm afraid I'll need to confiscate the rest of these hammers," Officer Martin said. "They might be evidence."

"Evidence of what?"

"It's part of a murder investigation, sir."

"Murder? In Cape Willington? Who got murdered?"

"A woman named Sapphire Vine. A hammer just like one of these was used as the murder weapon."

"What?!" Cameron's voice came out as a disbelieving shout that made Candy jump, even though she was an aisle away. "What did you say?"

Calmly, Office Martin repeated his statement. "Someone murdered Sapphire Vine, using a hammer for a weapon."

"But that's impossible!" Cameron shouted, his voice so high it was almost a shriek.

"I'm sorry but it's true." Officer Martin's voice was strangely calm, almost cold.

"But she can't be dead! She can't be!" Cameron sounded as if he were about to cry.

"I know how shocking it can be," Officer Martin said, forcing sympathy into his voice.

"Shocking? Damn right it's shocking," Mr. Gumm said. "And with a hammer? Well, that's downright brutal."

"It was, sir. The hammer we found at the scene of the crime was brand new, just like these. Didn't have a scratch on it. Just to tie up any loose ends, we're running down all the other hammers like it in town. That's why I need to take custody of these. If more are sold it might foul up the investigation."

"Well, I'll have to charge you for them then," said Mr. Gumm. "Those are quality hammers — our top-of-the-line. Cost eighteen dollars each."

"Send a bill over to Town Hall. You can tag it with my name if you want."

Mr. Gumm grumbled at that. "Durn right

I'll put your name on it. And you ain't leaving here until you at least fix your signature to a sales receipt. I ain't made of money, you know. Got a business to run here."

"Yes, sir."

"Cameron, help him bag up those hammers. I guess we got to give them to him. Just got them in — durn shame."

"I'll need to bag them myself," Officer Martin said. "Special handling."

"Well, do what you have to do," Mr. Gumm said, and he began to shuffle away.

"I . . . I have to leave," Cameron said suddenly. Candy could hear his footsteps head away back down the aisle and toward the door.

"Hey, boy! Where're ya going?" Mr. Gumm called out, but there was no reply.

What was that all about? Candy wondered as she suddenly remembered that she had to meet Doc. She checked her watch. It was nearly one thirty. As quietly and carefully as she could, she walked to the end of the aisle and strolled nonchalantly up to the cash register, where Mr. Gumm was scribbling something down on a nearly used-up pad of sales receipts. He looked up at her as she placed the bundles of chicken wire down on the counter.

"Oh, Candy, it's you. Didn't know you

179

were here."

"I was way in the back, looking at chicken wire. I need to do a few repairs on the coop. Got a fox trying to get at the girls."

Mr. Gumm shook his head and had a chuckle at that. "Those foxes do love their chickens. Sneaky little critters. They got dark murdering hearts, they do."

Candy nodded grimly. "They're not the only ones."

"You got that right. Been strange goings-on in this town lately. Strange goings-on." The old man shook his gray head again and jabbed a crooked finger at the keys of an ancient cash register. "That'll be five twenty-five."

FOURTEEN

Doc was waiting for her in the truck. He gave her his best bored look, which he had perfected over the years, as she threw the chicken wire into the back and climbed into the cab.

"Took you long enough," he said evenly as he started the truck. "You said fifteen minutes."

"I got held up talking to Mr. Gumm."

"Ah, well, that'll happen. Get everything you needed?"

"Yup."

She wanted to tell him more — about eavesdropping on the conversation between Cameron and Officer Martin, and about Cameron's strange reaction upon hearing of Sapphire Vine's death — but she held back. She wasn't ready to talk about it just yet. Instead, she fell silently into her own thoughts as Doc backed up the truck, started off along Main Street, made a right

181

turn onto the Coastal Loop, and headed out of town. But as they came to the intersection of River Road, Candy impulsively signaled to the right.

"Dad, do me a favor and turn here," she said suddenly.

"What?"

"Make a right turn up here."

He looked puzzled. "I thought you needed to get home so you can deliver those pies to Melody's Place."

"It's called Melody's Café, and I need to stop at the Tremonts' first."

"The Tremonts'? Why would you wanna go there? Ed's away and Maggie's probably still at work."

Candy rubbed her forehead in thought. "I'm not sure. I just want to check on something. Indulge me. Please?"

He arched an eyebrow. "Well, I guess I've done that enough times," he said as his mouth worked itself into a grin, and made a right turn at the intersection.

The Tremonts lived on the north side of the English River, in an area locally known as Fowler's Corner. A hundred years ago, all this land had belonged to one of the town's most illustrious former citizens, a long-whiskered gentleman known as Edwin P. Fowler who had come to Cape Willington in the 1860s when he was still in his twenties, and in the decades that followed had made his fortune in logging, banking, and land speculation.

But most of Fowler's land had long since been sold off, and starting in the 1950s a number of side streets and cul-de-sacs had been built in the area. The majority of homes were little white capes with a few split-levels mingled in here and there. The Tremonts lived on a street of newer homes at the edge of town, in a three-bedroom green gabled house barely five years old.

Doc pulled into the driveway and Candy jumped out. "I'll be right back."

"Take your time," he said, turning off the engine but leaving the radio on. He leaned his head back. "Guess I'm not in a hurry."

Candy rang the doorbell and waited. After what seemed like an interminable period of time, the door cracked open and a curious eye peeked out. "Who's there?"

"Amanda? It's me, Candy."

"Oh, hi." The door opened a bit further. Amanda stood in the doorway, wearing white shorts and a pale pink sleeveless blouse, and eating a muffin. Candy noticed with a bit of dismay that the muffin wasn't one of hers. "Mom's at work."

"I'm not here to see your mom. I'm here

to see you."

"Oh. Okay." Amanda opened the door a little further. "You wanna come in?"

"Actually" — Candy looked past her into the house — "I was wondering . . . is Cameron here?"

"Cam?" Amanda turned and looked behind her as if she wasn't really sure. "Um, I don't think so. Why?"

"I need to talk to him."

Amanda's forehead crinkled. "About what?" she asked as she took another bite of the muffin.

"Oh, nothing really important. Listen, if he comes in, would you . . . ?"

At that moment she was interrupted by the sound of a door opening somewhere in the back of the house and a male voice calling out, "Amanda? You here?"

"Oh, there he is now," Amanda said, chewing loudly. "So you wanna come in?"

Candy nodded. "If it's okay."

"Sure."

They found Cameron in the kitchen, his nose stuck deep into the fridge. "Hey, 'Manda," he called as he heard them approaching, "where's the rest of that watermelon your mom —"

He stopped abruptly as he backed out of the fridge and saw Candy. "Oh. It's you," he said in a surprisingly cold tone. He slammed shut the refrigerator door and walked away toward the family room that adjoined the kitchen.

"Cameron, wait. I want to talk to you." Candy followed him, with Amanda trailing behind.

"What about?" he growled, stuffing his hands deep into the pockets of his jeans.

"I overheard you talking to Officer Martin at Gumm's."

"Oh, that. Yeah, I guess you were there, weren't you? I forgot about that." He plopped down on a relatively new brown sofa and searched around for the TV remote.

Candy stood in front of him with her arms crossed. She got right to the point. "You took the news about Sapphire pretty hard."

"Yeah, well, it just surprised me, that's all."

"I wasn't aware you knew Sapphire that well. Were you two friends?"

Cameron looked up at her crossly and then flicked his eyes to Amanda before he continued his search for the remote. "No."

"Then why the big scene at Gumm's?"

He gave her a dirty look. "What is this, the third degree?"

"Not at all. I was just worried about you.

You seemed pretty upset. I wanted to make sure you were okay."

"I'm fine. Just hungry, that's all." He finally found the remote, stuck down between the seat cushions. He fished it out, leaned back, and flicked on the TV.

"Cameron." Candy sat down beside him as he channel surfed. He wouldn't look at her. "Cameron, I want to talk to you about the hammers."

"What?"

"The hammers. The new red-handled hammers you got in at the store."

He breathed out through gritted teeth. "What about them?"

Candy took a deep breath and hesitated only a moment before plunging on. "You said you sold one of the hammers to someone from Town Hall. I was just wondering what he looked like. The person you sold it to, I mean."

Cameron glanced over at her with suspicion in his eyes. "Why?"

Candy paused again. It was a good question. What should she say? She didn't really know the answer herself, except that some sort of instinct seemed to be driving her on. "Something just doesn't quite make sense, that's all," she answered finally. "I guess I'm trying to figure a few things out."

He considered that as he stopped channel surfing at a sports news program on ESPN. Finally he shrugged. "It was just some guy. I've seen him in the store a bunch of times, but he never talks to me much. He mostly deals with Mr. Gumm."

"What does this guy look like?" Candy prodded.

Cameron's brow wrinkled in thought. "Kinda overweight, I guess, with this big beer belly. Glasses, black hair, black moustache." After a moment, Cameron added, "And he has kinda this red face."

Candy thought a moment. "Ned? Is that who it was? Ned Winetrop?"

Cameron shrugged. "Yeah, that sounds about right."

"And he bought the hammer from you on Saturday morning?"

Cameron nodded.

There was silence for a few moments. Candy could feel the tension coming off him. Finally she smiled and slapped her hands on her knees. "Well, okay. I guess that's about all I wanted to ask you." She looked at him closely. "You sure you're all right?"

"I'm fine." He got up and walked back into the kitchen, with Candy and Amanda following. He crossed to the fridge and opened it again. "I'm starving," he said, bending over so he could scrutinize the items inside.

Amanda edged past him and reached for the peanut butter and jelly. "I'll make you a sandwich."

He smiled up at her, and for the first time since he had walked in the door he looked like the teenage boy Candy knew so well. "Thanks, babe," he said to Amanda. "You're too good to me."

"Aww, you're worth it," she said, snuggling up against him.

Candy watched them wistfully for a moment, then smiled. "Well, I guess I'll be on my way. Like I said, I just wanted to make sure you were okay."

They seemed to barely hear her. In fact, she felt practically invisible.

She turned toward the door. "I'll just . . . let myself out. No, no, that's okay. No reason to see me to the door or anything silly like that. I'm a big girl. I'll be just fine."

They never noticed her leaving.

Back out in the truck, Doc was listening to a country song and tapping away noisily on the steering wheel. He started up the truck as Candy climbed in beside him.

"So, we good to go?" he asked.

"Yeah."

"I saw Cameron's car pull up a few minutes ago."

"Yup," Candy said.

"Something's going on, huh?" Doc glanced over at his daughter. "You up to no good?"

Candy gave him a sly smile. "Yup."

He laughed and patted her on the knee as he turned the truck back toward home. "That's my girl."

FIFTEEN

It was nearly three thirty by the time Candy dropped off the pies at Melody's Café. They had agreed to a price of nine dollars apiece, which was adequate for Candy and would still turn a nice profit for Melody, who planned to sell slices at three dollars apiece.

"That should hold me for this week," Melody told her. "They look lovely."

"Thanks. I'll have more for you on Monday."

Melody paid her in cash, which she pulled from the register, and with forty-five dollars in her pocket, Candy walked back out to the Jeep as a fierce gust of wind, full of the scent of earth and sea, swept down from the sky and assaulted her, whipping her hair about her face.

Though the morning had been fairly warm and pleasant, the day had steadily worsened as ominous clouds gathered on the western horizon. Those clouds had reached them now, the dark churning sky swallowing up the sun. Candy climbed into the driver's seat as the first few heavy raindrops pelted the sidewalk and street around her.

She sat for a moment as the sky broke open and the deluge began. Lightning crackled in the distance, and a roll of thunder shook like a fist of fury down from the skies.

Candy wasn't thinking about the storm, though. She was thinking about Sapphire Vine and Ray and that red-handled hammer. Something Maggie had said to her on the phone that morning kept nagging at her, tickling away at her brain: *Ray wouldn't hurt a fly,* Maggie had said. *He tears up when he steps on a cockroach.*

Maybe so. But they had found his hammer at the scene of the crime. And according to Finn Woodbury, someone had seen Ray's truck in front of Sapphire's house last night, when Sapphire had been murdered. What had he been doing there? And could he really have hit her with his hammer?

Candy recalled the way Ray had cradled the hammer when she had handed it back to him that day in the barn. Suddenly she knew what had been bothering her all day.

Ray loves that hammer, she thought. *The*

*other day, he treated it like some sort of pre-
cious thing, almost as though he were in love
with it. He didn't even want me to touch it. He
didn't want it to get damaged at all. So if he
loves that hammer so much, why would he
muck it all up by hitting Sapphire in the skull
with it? And why would he leave it there after
he hit her?*

None of it made any sense.

Candy started up the Jeep. She decided
she had to talk to Maggie again, to try to
sort it all out. She drove to the intersection
of River Road and the Loop, made a left
turn, then another left onto Main Street and
a right onto Ocean Avenue. It could be difficult to find a parking space along here in
the afternoons, but she lucked out and
found a spot practically right in front of
Stone & Milbury's. Ignoring the pelting
rain, she jumped out of the Jeep and dashed
toward the insurance agency's front door.

It was only a dozen steps or so, but she
was soaking wet by the time she made it
inside. "Whoa, is it raining hard out there!"
she exclaimed as she walked through the
reception area and turned the corner into
Maggie's office.

She stopped dead. Three curious faces
looked up at her.

Maggie sat behind her desk, with two

stacks of papers in front of her. A middle-aged couple sat in front of the desk, facing Maggie.

"Oh, I'm sorry!" Candy said in surprise. "I didn't realize you had customers."

With the height of professionalism, Maggie rose and gave the couple a pleasant smile. "Excuse me for a moment," she said to them. "A friend of mine. I'll be right back."

Taking Candy by the arm, Maggie steered her out of the office.

"I'm so sorry," Candy said in embarrassment as they walked back into the reception area.

"Don't worry about it." Maggie dismissed the interruption with a wave of her hand. "We're just finishing up some things. Where've you been? You look like a drowned rat."

"It's raining."

Maggie scowled. "You know, they have these neat little things called umbrellas. Fabulous invention. They do a great job of keeping you dry when it rains. You might want to check one out sometime."

"Ha, ha, very funny. Listen, I have to talk to you about something."

"Can't right now, honey. I'm in the middle of a meeting." She leaned a little toward her office and called to her clients in the friendliest possible tone, "I'll be right there!"

"When are you free?" Candy asked.

"I'm here 'til five thirty."

"Meet for drinks after work?"

Maggie considered that for a moment. "Don't know if I can, but I'll try. Call me around five, okay?"

"Got it. Good luck with your customers."

"And you get yourself an umbrella, girl. Better yet, take this one." Maggie reached toward a twenty-year-old metal coatrack that stood near the door. A battered old black umbrella was leaning against one of the posts. "Someone left it and never came back for it, so it's yours."

"Thanks, you're a doll."

"That's what all my boyfriends tell me," Maggie said with a grin as she sashayed back into her office.

Outside, the wind was whipping so hard that it threatened to rip the umbrella right out of Candy's hand. Before she knew what was happening, she was blown sideways down the street. She ducked into an alcove and stood there for a moment in the shelter of an overhang, fiddling with the umbrella, which had flipped outward, and trying to gather up the courage to make a run for her Jeep. Then a door pushed opened behind her and a tall, thirty-something man emerged from the building, nearly running her over in his haste.

"Oh, I'm sorry!" the man said, looking up.

"No, it was my fault. I just had to take refuge from the rain for a few minutes."

The man stopped beside her and squinted up into the sky. "It is coming down heavy, isn't it?" He looked over at her. "I love summer storms like this, don't you?"

"Well, yes," said Candy a bit bashfully, "but it doesn't do much for one's appearance." She pushed some of the wet locks off her forehead.

He laughed pleasantly. "You look just fine to me." He studied her a little closer. "You're Candy Holliday, aren't you? You live with Doc out at Blueberry Acres?"

"That's right. Have we met before?"

He held out his hand. "Name's Ben Clayton."

"Oh! We *have* met, I think," Candy said, shaking hands with him, "though for the life of me I can't remember where. You work for the *Cape Crier*, right?" The *Cape Crier* was the local weekly newspaper — *The Voice of Downeast Maine,* as its tagline claimed. It went out to readers in parts of two counties — Hancock and Washington.

195

"Actually, I'm the editor," Ben said.

"Oh, that's right. I've seen your name in the paper. What a fun job." But as the words left her mouth, the smile fell from her face as she realized what that meant. "Oh! You must have worked with Sapphire."

His expression, too, took on a measure of seriousness. "I was her boss."

"I didn't realize," Candy said. "I'm so sorry."

Ben nodded. He was taller than she was, just shy of six feet, she guessed, and lean, with a rugged face and light brown hair that he had let grow a bit long in the back. He wore jeans and an open-collar blue shirt, and carried a scuffed, dark brown leather satchel. Candy wondered why she hadn't noticed him much around town before.

"Sapphire's death was a shock to us all," he said heavily. "It's tragic how something like that can happen so quickly, and someone you knew and liked and worked with is just . . . gone, just like that."

"It's terrible, just terrible," Candy agreed, eyes downcast.

They both were silent for a moment. Then Ben asked, "Were you a friend of hers?"

"An acquaintance," Candy hedged. "We knew each other, but we didn't hang around socially or anything like that."

"Hmm," Ben said, watching her.

What does that mean? Candy wondered.

"You know, this may sound strange," he continued after a moment, "but it seems to me that Sapphire didn't have many friends. Oh, she knew a lot of people — I was always astounded by how many people she knew — but she didn't seem to be close to many of them."

Candy wasn't sure how to reply to that. "Well," she responded tactfully, "maybe it's because she was such a . . . unique personality."

"You can say that again."

They stood awkwardly in silence for a moment. Finally Candy looked out at the sky. "Well, I guess I should make a run for it. . . ."

She straightened out the umbrella and turned up her collar, preparing to brave the rain, but then Ben touched her by the elbow. "Candy, before you go, can I ask you something?"

Candy looked at him curiously. *Oh my God,* she thought as a small smile flickered across her face, *is he gonna ask me on a date?* Swallowing, she said, "Sure."

"This may sound odd," he began, then hesitated. He seemed to reconsider what he was about to do. "Maybe . . . maybe I

197

should wait until another time."

Candy forced her smile just a bit as she turned to face him. "No, go ahead. I'd like to hear your question."

"Well, all right, then. I have to confess that I've done some checking up on you."

That took Candy by surprise. "You have?"

He laughed and looked a bit embarrassed. "I hope that didn't come out the way it sounded. You see, Sapphire keeps these files on people in town, including you." As the smile fell from Candy's face, he added quickly, "For her column, you know. She does extensive research. I've never seen anyone work as hard as she does — um, *did* — in, um, ensuring the accuracy of her columns. She collected everything — clippings, biographical histories, business cards and announcements, magazine articles, press releases, anything she could get her hands on. And all that information went into her files, for research."

"And she has a file on me?" Candy asked incredulously.

Ben nodded. "The police left just about an hour ago. They wanted to go through Sapphire's office and files. Just routine, they said. They didn't find much, but they sure made a mess of the place. Anyway, as I was straightening up, I came across your file

198

stuck in the back of one of the drawers, so I flipped through it. I guess curiosity got the better of me. Anyway, I noticed that you've done some writing in your career."

"Oh. That." Candy made a face. "That was years ago. I worked for a marketing firm in Boston for ten years, and I wrote a few magazine articles on the side — personality profiles, mostly, interesting business people around town, that sort of thing."

"Published in some of the local newspapers," Ben prompted.

"They were small papers. I'm not sure anyone even read them. And they paid practically nothing."

"But you *have* written and been published?"

"Well, yes, but —" Candy paused and tilted her head, unable to keep a confused look off her face.

"I guess I should get to the point," Ben said, sounding professional again. "As you know, Sapphire's weekly gossip column was one of the mainstays of the newspaper. In fact, I probably would not be exaggerating if I said it was one of the best-read features in the paper. That and the school lunch menu. And the police blotter, of course." He sighed and went on. "I'd probably also be accurate if I said that we sold a lot of papers strictly *because* of Sapphire's column. And now that she's gone . . ."

"Yes?"

"Well, I'm in a bind, and I was wondering if, well, if you'd like to take over the writing of her column."

Candy eyes widened. "You're kidding."

"No, I'm completely serious," Ben continued quickly. "Here's the thing. I have to get someone on that column right away, or else I'm going to have a big hole in next week's paper. I'd do it myself, but I've got my hands full with Sapphire's murder investigation and Jock's death and the festival and everything else that's been going on around town. Wow, what a week." He made a face and shook his head. "Plus, I'm a bit thin on staff because of summer vacations. And a lot of my volunteers have been bailing on me. I just need someone to write up some info about the pageant and contestants, plus some local gossip stuff. You know, the sort of thing Sapphire used to do. Jane Doe got married, Bobby Jones scraped his knee, Eddie and Edith's kid joined the Navy, that sort of thing. Community news."

Candy wasn't sure what to say. "Well, I don't know."

"I'm sure you wouldn't have much trouble doing it, not with your writing experience. I can show you, if it would help to convince you." He pointed up the stairs behind them. "You got a minute?"

Candy looked out at the rain, which if anything was coming down harder than before, and then looked over at Ben Clayton.

Tall Ben. Handsome, lean, rugged Ben. Smart Ben. Very smart Ben.

A newspaper editor. *Employed* Ben.

Without seeming too conspicuous about it, she glanced down at his left hand.

No ring.

Tall, handsome, rugged, smart, employed, *single* Ben.

"Well, sure, okay, I guess I have a few minutes," Candy finally said with a sweet smile.

He flashed a broad grin, showing off beautiful teeth. "Great! Come on, I'll take you up to our offices."

The *Cape Crier* was run out of cramped quarters above a real estate office. An ancient dark staircase led up to the rabbit warren of rooms that wound their way back into the nether regions of the building. "It's a bit of a mess up here," Ben apologized as he led Candy to a small, windowless office not much bigger than a closet. He pulled a string attached to a porcelain light fixture screwed into the ceiling. The room was cast in the harsh light of a single naked bulb.

"This is — sorry, *was* — this *was* Sapphire's office."

Candy wasn't impressed. In fact, she found it hard to hide her disappointment. The newspaper business always sounded so glamorous to her, but this was far from what she expected.

A small metal desk was shoved into one corner. A computer that must have been five years old — at least — sat to one side of the desktop. On the other side were metal trays overflowing with files, notes, and papers in disarray. A gray metal file cabinet and a rickety old chair were lined up against the opposite wall.

Sapphire had done her best to add some spice to the place. Posters of kitties and horses covered cracks in the walls, and a Tiffany-style lamp sat on one corner of the desk. A colorful, cozy-looking knitted cushion covered the seat of the desk chair. Knickknacks and paperback novels lined a sad-looking shelf. Dated press passes were thumbtacked to a small bulletin board on the wall in front of the desk, along with neatly printed three-by-five cards that said things like, "You look mahhhvelous today" and "You go, girl!"

It all made Candy feel incredibly depressed.

Barely noticing the clutter, Ben crossed to the desk and plucked a green file folder from the top tray. "Like I said, the police have been through here, so it's a bit of a mess."

How could you tell? Candy nearly blurted out.

"Anyway," Ben said as he flipped open the folder and ruffled through the papers inside, "here are some clippings of Sapphire's previous columns, so you can see the kinds of things we're looking for. I've also included some notes that she made at . . . um . . . at the end of last week, as well as a few notes of my own. Unfortunately, she never really had a chance to get started on this week's column. It was supposed to be a firsthand account of the pageant, of course. I thought she had done some preliminary research work on it, but I haven't been able to locate any of that information yet. Once I dig around a little it'll probably turn up."

He closed the file and held it out to Candy, who took it tentatively. She looked around. "You mentioned something about other files?"

Ben held up a finger. "Right." He turned to the file cabinet and pulled open one of the drawers. "She kept all her research in here." He ran a finger along a long line of files, arranged alphabetically by name, Candy saw. Many of the names she recognized.

Ben continued. "A few of them are gone, of course. The police took Ray's and a few others. But they didn't find much. I've been through a lot of these. There's nothing you'd call injurious or scandalous in them. It's all pretty harmless."

He drew out a few of them and flipped through the papers inside to show her.

"Can I see the file she kept on me?"

"Huh? Oh, sure." Ben turned, dug back into the filing cabinet, and pulled out a blue file. "This is yours." He handed it over, a bit sheepishly, she thought.

With some trepidation Candy flipped open the cover and glanced at the contents, but Ben had been right. A few clippings about Blueberry Acres, a photocopy of a newspaper article Candy had written a half dozen years ago (though she had no idea where Sapphire had found *that*), and a loose-leaf page with a few notes jotted on it. One scribbled line in particular caught Candy's attention. It read, "lonely divorcee." Candy noticed that there was a little heart over the *i* in *divorcee*.

Lonely? Was that how she seemed to Sapphire?

Funny, but of all the words Candy would have used to describe herself, and after all she had been through, she never would have considered herself lonely. In fact, she felt quite the opposite most of the time.

"So, are you interested?"

Candy looked up. Ben was watching her with a hopeful look in his deep brown eyes. "What?"

"In taking over Sapphire's column."

"Oh. That." Candy let out a sigh as she closed the folder. "I just don't know, Ben. I'll have to think about it."

"Well, like I said, I sure could use your help. Of course, I'd pay you for your work."

That perked up her ears. "Pay? As in money? Cash?"

He chuckled. "We're on a tight budget, unfortunately, so I can't afford much. Maybe seventy-five dollars a week?"

It wasn't much. Not enough to make her jump at a job she wasn't sure she wanted.

"Let me think about it," she said again.

Ben nodded. "Okay, but — not to put too much pressure on you — I need an answer fairly quickly. By, say, sometime tomorrow?"

Candy nodded. "I can do that. I'll call you in the morning, okay?"

"Fine, fine." He dug into a shirt pocket and pulled out a card. "Here's my number."

Candy glanced down at the business card. BEN CLAYTON, EDITOR, it read in the center of the card in raised black letters. The name of the paper was in the upper left corner, followed by the address. The e-mail address and phone and fax numbers were at the bottom.

Candy shoved the card into a back pocket as Ben reached up and flicked off the light. He led her back through the offices and down the stairs. Outside, the rain had let up a little.

"I hope you'll consider the offer," he said as they stood in the alcove again. "I sure could use the help."

"It might be fun," Candy said, trying to sound positive, though something about the whole thing bothered her. Maybe it was the fact that she would be taking Sapphire's old job.

She raced back to the Jeep and jumped into the front seat, but sat for a few minutes before she started it up, considering Ben's offer. She believed in going with her gut instinct, and that instinct told her to take a pass on the job. Still, she had promised him she would think about it, and she decided that that was what she would do.

But first, she had a friend to save, and a stop to make.

Sixteen

Even as she walked up to the front door, she wasn't sure why she had come.

Ned Winetrop lived in what was commonly called a New Englander — a catchall term for a two-story, high-peaked-roof affair that couldn't quite be classified as a Victorian, cape, ranch, or anything else. This one had obviously once been known euphemistically as a "fixer-upper," but Ned, being a carpenter, had done quite a bit of work on it over the years. It was now fairly presentable, though still rather plain looking, with its simple lines and white clapboard exterior.

Candy was somewhat surprised to find Ned's old, dark blue Reading-bodied work truck in the driveway. Some part of her had been hoping he wouldn't be home, but he was, so she had no excuse for driving away without talking to him.

She had been uncertain at first of what

she was going to say to him, but on the ride over she had worked it out in her head. She rehearsed it mentally one last time as she climbed the cement steps, pulled open the screen door, and rapped loudly on the front door, which looked as though it had just been given a fresh coat of burgundy-colored paint.

She heard movement inside. A moment later the door opened and Ned peered out, holding a half-eaten sandwich in one hand. "Yeah?"

"Hi, Ned. It's Candy Holliday."

He looked surprised to see her. "Oh, hi, Candy." He leaned out and glanced back and forth. "Doc with you?"

"No, I'm here alone. I wondered if I could have a few minutes of your time."

Ned took a bite out of the sandwich. He had a pudgy face with high cheeks, and the combination partially obscured his dark eyes, as though burying them amongst a jumble of deep red pillows. "Sure, guess so. What about?"

"The Blueberry Queen Pageant." Candy flashed the business card Ben Clayton had given her, though she was careful to hold her thumb over Ben's name, so that just the newspaper's name and address at the top showed. "I'm working for the *Cape Crier* now. Ben, the editor, asked me to write an article about the pageant. I thought I'd include something about your efforts."

"Really?" Ned's eyes widened, he grinned oddly, and with his ample hip he pushed the front door open all the way. "Come on in."

The living room was neat and welcoming, though it was clear Mrs. Ned subscribed to the Wal-Mart School of Decorating. "Wanna sit down?" Ned indicated the olive green sofa, which obviously was not from the Ethan Allen collection.

"Okay, sure."

"Can I get you something to eat or drink?"

Candy shook her head as she settled into the sofa. "I don't want to take too much of your time."

Ned finished his sandwich in three bites and dusted his fingers on the front of his shirt. "So what can I help you with?" he asked around a mouthful of ham, cheese, and French's mustard.

"Well, I know you did a lot of work on the set for the pageant."

He nodded as he settled into a well-worn armchair. "Yup, yup."

"I was just curious about some of the stuff you did, how long it took, that sort of thing."

Ned scratched his head. "Well, you know,

it wasn't that tough of a job. I helped build the backdrop and did some of the decorating . . . ," and he went on to describe his contributions to the pageant.

"So you were in Town Hall most of the afternoon, then?" Candy asked. "On Saturday, I mean."

"Yup, on Saturday. I wasn't there that long. Just a couple of hours."

"I heard you needed some new tools to do some of the work."

Ned's thick dark brows fell into a questioning look. "Tools?"

"Yeah, you know, I heard you had to buy a new hammer."

"Oh, that." He relaxed a bit. "You know, there's a funny story about that. I loaned my best hammer to a friend, and would you believe he busted it trying to get a tire off his van?" Ned laughed. "He had a flat, and the tire was stuck — they'll do that sometimes, you know. Most times you just have to give it a good kick with the heel of your boot, but he didn't know that, so he banged on the metal wheel one too many times with my hammer. Shattered the handle. 'Course, he gave me some money to pay for a new one, and I had to make a trip to Gumm's that morning. Bought this nice new red-handled job. And would you believe I lost it that same day?"

"You lost it?" Trying to remain nonchalant, Candy laughed with him — a good acting job, she thought.

"It sounds funny now, but I'll tell you I was pretty burned up about it at the time. I set that thing down on the stage — at least, that's where I thought I put it — and when I went back to get it, it was gone. Either someone stole it or . . ."

It must have dawned on him then what he was saying, because he stopped suddenly and looked at her with a strange expression on his red face. "Why are you asking me about the hammer?" he asked, suspicion creeping into his voice.

Candy waved a hand at him and laughed nervously. "Oh, I don't know," she said, trying to sound light and airy, though it came out incredibly forced. "It just sounded like an interesting story."

Ned stared at her for the longest time, his face an unreadable mask as his mind worked back over the conversation. Finally he asked, "How did you know I bought a new hammer?"

"Oh." Candy bit her lip, trying to think fast, but nothing much came to her. She shrugged, attempting to remain calm. "I guess I just heard it somewhere. It's not that important. I wanted to ask you about Ray . . ."

"Ray?"

"Yeah, I know he helped you out on Saturday and —"

"Candy, does this have anything to do with that murder?"

"Murder?" Candy repeated parrotlike, putting on her best surprised look. "You mean Sapphire Vine? Why, no, of course not, I, I . . ."

Ned rose abruptly. "I don't think I should answer any more questions," he said stiffly.

Candy felt her heart thump in her chest as she rose too. "Why not?"

He let out a long breath through his nose. "I don't think I should say anything about it right now."

"Have the police talked to you?"

"Candy . . ." Ned's voice trailed off as he crossed his arms and admonished her with his eyes.

"Okay, okay," she said quickly. "I'm sorry if I've said anything to offend you. I was just trying to get some info for my story."

"Well . . ." He rolled his eyes. "No harm done, I guess, but I just can't say anything else about what happened that day."

"Oh no, of course not, I completely understand," Candy said awkwardly, and made her way to the door.

I guess that was a stupid thing to do, she thought as she climbed back into the Jeep and drove home.

On the other hand, it had worked. She had found out an important piece of information about that day — Ned had lost his hammer. She sensed she was on to something.

In a moment of clarity, she knew what she had to do next.

When she got home, she walked around to the back of the barn. Doc was working on the coop, attaching the new chicken wire with a staple gun. "I'll be right there to help, Dad," she called to him, then turned, walked into the kitchen, and picked up the phone.

She called Maggie first. "Can't meet you today," Maggie said hurriedly. "Just got too much to do. Tomorrow, lunch?"

"Sure. I'll meet you at Duffy's at twelve thirty. I have a lot to tell you."

"I can't wait. See you then."

After she hung up, Candy took Ben's card from her pocket and dialed his number. "Hi, it's Candy Holliday," she said when he answered the phone at the other end.

"Oh, hi, Candy. What's up?"

"About that job you offered me? I've decided to accept it."

SEVENTEEN

The next morning, Candy and Doc climbed into the Jeep Cherokee and headed up to Route 1, where they turned east toward the town of Machias, the county seat. The day was overcast, the remnants of the previous day's storm still clinging stubbornly to the coast, which only added to their somber moods.

They were silent for most of the forty-minute drive, which took them through small settlements and past boulder-strewn blueberry fields ripe for the harvest. Candy kept the radio tuned to an AM news station, though they heard more static than news as the signal faded in and out. They were eager for the latest information about the investigation into Sapphire Vine's murder, but there was nothing to be heard, which only made Candy more morose and Doc more restless.

The Washington County Sheriff's Office

was located on Court Street just off Machias's main street, in a red brick building next to the Superior Court. They parked in the side visitor's lot, checked in at the front desk, and at just after ten o'clock were shown into an empty room by a young, straight-backed, mustachioed officer named Wayne Safford. "You can wait for Ray in here," he told them. "He'll be right in."

It was a small, windowless, cheerless room with a freshly waxed brown and white tile floor and walls painted a dull institutional beige. At its center was a narrow folding table surrounded by four metal folding chairs. A U.S. flag stood in one corner, next to a flag of the great State of Maine, with its moose and pine tree, farmer and seaman, set on a blue field under the North Star. There was no other furniture in the room — no pictures or photos on the walls, no one-way mirrors. The place smelled old yet efficient.

"Well," Doc said as he dropped into one of the chairs with a grunt, "at least they let us in to see him. I thought they'd give us a hard time."

Candy nodded her agreement and stood with her arms folded across her chest, hugging her shoulders. The air conditioning in the building must have been set on high, or perhaps it was all funneled into this small room. Feeling chilled, she wished she had brought a sweater with her. But who travels with a sweater when it's eighty degrees outside?

She thought of sitting down beside Doc but realized she was too nervous for that, so she paced the perimeter of the room, looking for anything the least bit interesting to occupy her time, and failing miserably.

Fortunately, they didn't have to wait too long. Sooner than she expected, the door swung open and Ray shuffled in, his head bowed low. He looked terrible. Even when he saw Candy and Doc, the most he could manage was the most pitiful smile she had ever seen. He sank heavily into a chair opposite Doc. His gaze dropped to the table and stayed there.

"I'll be back in fifteen minutes," Officer Safford said. He left, closing the door firmly behind him.

A loud click told them the door locked itself as it shut.

Doc tried to ignore that disconcerting fact. "Well, how ya doing, Ray?" he said in a lively tone that sounded much too forced. He managed a smile as he leaned closer to the handyman. "Are they treating you all right?"

Ray shrugged, a quick movement that showed defeat. He let out a long shuddering breath. "Oh, they been okay to me." His bottom lip puffed out a little. He seemed to be fighting back tears.

Candy felt the despair, embarrassment, and confusion radiating off him in waves. "Are they feeding you, Ray?" she asked, looking worried. "Are you eating?"

Ray nodded, though he still stared at the tabletop. "I had donuts and flapjacks for breakfast. They even gave me some blueberry syrup. I been eatin'."

Candy went to stand beside him, and she couldn't help reaching out and placing a comforting hand on his shoulder. "Ray," she said softly, "do you want to tell us what happened?"

That did it. The tear ducts opened, the emotions bubbled up, and he shook like a house in a hurricane. "I . . . I didn't do it," he stuttered between sobs. "I didn't do that terrible thing they said I did." He glanced up at Candy, a horrified look in his eyes. "How could they say I did it? They don't know me. I could never do somethin' terrible like that."

"I know, Ray, I know," Candy said sympathetically.

"We know you didn't do it," Doc added,

"but what happened? How'd you get mixed up in this mess?"

"I don't know, Doc, I just don't know," Ray wailed, shaking his head frenetically and dropping it into his open hands.

"Try to stay calm," Candy told him, sinking into the chair beside him and looking at him intently. "Take a few deep breaths."

He listened to her. He straightened and took a breath, then another, shaking with grief the whole time. That calmed him a bit, though the distress he felt was still evident on his face. "Why do they think I did it?" he asked finally, looking over at her, his eyes reddened.

Doc leaned forward in his chair, his hands clasped together on the tabletop. "Well, for one thing, Ray, they have witnesses who say they saw your truck at Sapphire's house Monday night, right before she was murdered," he explained as gently as possible.

Ray nodded as his lips trembled. "Yeah, that's right. I was there all right. She left me a note. Said she wanted me to come over at nine thirty and help her fix something. It was late, but I went over there anyway, just like she said. But when I got there she got mad at me for some reason. She yelled at me and told me to go home. I didn't know what to do. So I left. But I didn't kill her."

Candy exchanged a questioning glance with Doc. "Did you tell the police what you just told us?"

Ray nodded emphatically. "I told them — over and over I told them. But they won't listen. They said I did it. They said they have *evidence*."

"They do," Doc said quietly. "They found your hammer at her house, next to her body."

Candy watched Ray to see his reaction to this piece of information, and what she saw surprised her. His expression changed in an instant. He looked as though he had just been accused of the worst crime in the world — something far worse than murder, if that were possible. He started to wail in a high voice, a strange sound that reminded Candy of a wet kitten mewling pitifully.

"My . . . my hammer," he said softly. "But how'd it get there?" He lost his composure then and broke down again, crying uncontrollably now.

Candy and Doc sat silently for a moment, feeling helpless. Neither of them knew what to say. They tried to comfort him, but this time it didn't help. He just shook his head over and over and wouldn't say anything else.

"Ray," Doc said finally, trying to get the

handyman to look at him. "Ray, do you have a lawyer yet? Have they appointed someone to help you?"

But Ray wouldn't answer. The sobs finally lessened, but he sat crouched over, his hands around his knees, his shoulders hunched and arms tucked in at his sides, rocking back and forth. And then he started humming something.

Candy put her arm around his shoulders. "Listen, Ray," she said, leaning close to him, "we're going to help you any way we can. You hear that? Don't you worry. We know you didn't have anything to do with this. And we're going to do everything we can to prove it. We're going to get you out of here. That's a promise."

She didn't realize until that moment that there were tears in her eyes. She wiped them away quickly with her fingertips. Doc reached across the table and handed her his handkerchief.

When Officer Safford finally unlocked the door and peered into the room, Ray was still sitting in that same position, rocking back and forth. Doc and Candy were standing quietly beside him. There was nothing more to say.

"Does he have an attorney?" Doc asked as Ray was coaxed to his feet.

Officer Safford nodded. "He's got someone. And a county social worker has been assigned to him also. He's in good hands."

"What's the lawyer's name?" Candy asked.

"Big-time guy by the name of Cromwell. Down from Bangor."

With that, Ray was led away, and Candy and Doc were left alone in an empty room.

EIGHTEEN

As Candy and Doc drove into Cape Willington, the sun finally broke through the coastal clouds, brightening the day, but it did little to lift their spirits. They had talked themselves out on the drive home and had ridden the last twenty minutes or so in silence. But as they approached the Coastal Loop, Doc straightened, rubbed at his eyes, stretched, and then looked over at her. "You want to stop at the diner for a while? Get a cup of coffee maybe, see if Finn's got any news about the investigation?"

Candy glanced at her watch. It was eleven fifteen. She was supposed to meet Maggie at the diner at twelve thirty for lunch, but she knew she'd have a hard time sitting still until then. She shook her head. "How 'bout I drop you off and meet you back there in a bit?"

"You got something planned?"

Candy shrugged, trying to dispel the

disheartening feeling that had settled over her. "Ben asked me to stop by the *Crier* offices to pick up some files and sign a few forms, so I guess I'll run over there and see what's up."

Doc nodded approvingly. "Good idea. While you're there, see what you can find out about Ray's case. Maybe Ben's heard something. And I'll talk to Finn and the boys. Then we can compare notes and see what our next move is."

Candy felt only the faintest ray of hope, but at least they were doing something. "Sounds like a plan."

She drove into town, turned onto Main Street, and pulled up to the curb in front of Duffy's. Doc opened the passenger door and climbed out while the Jeep idled noisily.

"I'll be back around in an hour or so," Candy called to her father. "Will you be okay 'til then?"

"Don't worry about me. Just don't forget to pick me up on your way back through."

She gave him an indulgent look. "I won't forget, Dad."

Doc closed the door and, leaning in the window, smiled at her. "I know you won't, pumpkin."

"Dad . . ." she began, then allowed herself

the briefest smile when she saw the mischievous twinkle in his eyes.

"You know, you're mighty pretty when you smile like that," he said with a wink. Then, slapping the side of the Jeep in farewell, he ambled off toward Duffy's Diner.

Candy pulled back out onto Main Street and made an almost immediate left onto Ocean Avenue, her eyes scanning both sides of the street for a parking spot. But not surprisingly, there was none to be found.

She swore under her breath and considered making a U-turn right there in the center of town but thought better of it when she saw a police car in her rearview mirror. So, with no other options, she decided she'd just have to circle back around on the Loop and make another pass along Main Street. Maybe, with luck, she'd find an open spot.

At the bottom of Ocean Avenue she dutifully put on her turn signal and, after pausing an appropriate amount of time at the stop sign, made a right turn onto the Loop, which took her southward along the coastline. A moist warm breeze blew in the window, bringing with it the heady, comforting smells of the sea.

She couldn't help glancing off to her left, out over at the ocean, as she drove. It was a magnificent shade of deep blue today, rich and lively, a color that reminded her of nothing less than cool, ripe blueberries. The sea tossed restlessly. A sail or two could be seen on the hazy horizon. Flocks of gulls, cawing raucously, swarmed after whatever tidbits their dark questing eyes could find.

Candy loved being by the ocean. Despite the fact that she drove past it several times a week, she still marveled at it every time she saw it. There was something magical about the sea — perhaps, she thought, because it was constantly moving, always changing yet always the same, unending, unstoppable. It could be graceful and generous, yet dangerous and sometimes deadly, demanding respect.

But there was more to it than that. The sea had become almost spiritual to her. It had a way of flowing into her, *inhabiting* her, *fulfilling* her. For those few moments, as she gazed out over the ocean, the cares of the everyday world seemed trivial, so small in comparison to the vastness and majesty of the sea.

Whenever she was feeling down, or stressed, or overwhelmed by the constant jabs and distractions of the world, or when she felt she had lost her way, she had only to stand here upon these jutting black rocks that lined the coast and look out to the sea, and she would feel at peace again.

But she had no time to gaze too long at the sea today. The troubles of the world were pressing in, poking at her, like thorns on a rosebush.

Speaking of thorns . . .

As she angled southwestward along the Loop, the pointed rooftops of Pruitt Manor came into view above the tops of a few thick-trunked pines that had made a bold stand on Kimball Point. The place seemed to beckon to her, and she felt compelled to respond.

Before she knew what she was doing, Candy had flicked on her left-turn blinker and steered the Jeep sharply onto a private driveway that led between two five-foot-tall stone pillars. The iron gate stood open, so she drove on through, still not quite sure what she was doing. A small, tasteful sign alongside the road announced PRUITT MANOR — PRIVATE PROPERTY.

She had been here only once before that she could recall, when Mrs. Pruitt had opened the place to the Cape Willington Garden Society. Candy and Maggie were only occasional Society members, but they had made sure they were there that day, dressed in cool summer frocks like the other ladies, wearing broad-brimmed straw hats as they strolled the grounds under the watchful eyes of Mrs. Pruitt and her staff. They had even been invited into certain sections of the house — the foyer, the formal sitting room, the music room, and a few other rooms on the main level, plus the conservatory, a magnificent gabled glass-and-mahogany structure at the back of the house, from which double doors and a blue-stone staircase led down to a wide lawn that stopped at a jumble of rocks perched above the roiling sea.

The place had taken Candy's breath away. Mrs. Pruitt had even been reasonably hospitable that day, offering the ladies of the Society tea and trays full of finger foods as she pointed out her herb, rose, and perennial gardens abloom with pulmonarias, primulas, nepetas, and verbascums. That had been the first time Candy had noticed Hopkins (or whatever his name was), the pug-faced butler/chauffeur who never seemed to be too far from Mrs. Pruitt's side.

Even now, as she followed the winding gravel driveway toward Pruitt Manor and pulled into the wide paved courtyard that fronted the house, Candy half expected the butler to dash suddenly from the mansion's front door, arms flailing wildly in protest of her appearance here.

And, in truth, she did feel like a pauper in a princess's court as she shut off the Jeep's engine and leaned forward to gaze through the windshield, up at the imposing English Tudor façade of Pruitt Manor.

"Oh man," she said softly to herself.

It took all the will she could muster to open the door and step out of the vehicle. She wished then that she had worn something more presentable, instead of her regular faded jeans and sleeveless cotton blouse. But no matter — she was here now. She might as well do what she had come here to do.

And what exactly is that? she wondered to herself.

"Girl, you've been doing some mighty strange things lately," she muttered to herself with a shake of her head as she followed a flagstone walkway past impeccably manicured lawns and neatly clipped bushes to the manor's recessed entryway. Taking a breath, she rang the doorbell. "If I didn't know better, I'd say you were in way over your head."

She waited, trying to quickly sort out what she was going to say. Then, as she heard footsteps approaching inside, saw the door handle twist and the door inch open, she pasted her most pleasant smile on her face.

The door opened fully, and there, naturally, stood Hopkins (or whatever his name was).

He gazed at her without expression. "Yes?"

"Oh, hello, I'm, ah, I'm Candy Holliday. I was wondering if Mrs. Pruitt or Haley is here today?"

The butler was silent a moment, eyeing her up and down. "Yes?"

"Well, I was wondering if I might see them. I'm, um, I'm writing a story for the *Cape Crier* — the local newspaper, you know. And I, um, I wanted to ask Mrs. Pruitt a few questions about the pageant."

"Do you have an appointment?"

"No." Candy swallowed. "No, I don't."

The butler bowed his head slightly. "I shall inquire as to whether Mrs. Pruitt is available." He held the door open a little further. "Won't you come in?"

"Yes, thank you."

She followed the butler into the Italian-tiled foyer, where he turned to face her. "If you would wait here, please, I'll be back momentarily."

"Of course. Thank you," Candy said again.

He nodded obliquely at her and disappeared through a side archway, into the room beyond.

"Well," Candy said to herself as her gaze wandered up the grand staircase and to the ceiling high above, "at least you made it this far."

The place was elegantly decorated in the English Tudor style, reflecting the exterior of the manor. Queen Anne–style chairs, ornate wood paneling, heraldic designs, and stylish floor tile featuring an oak leaf and acorn design gave the foyer a warm yet aristocratic feel. A chandelier suspended over her head — a hefty wood-beam and brass affair with lights that resembled thick candles — looked like something from a medieval hunting lodge. Portraits of austere, rich-looking folk, probably long dead, adorned the walls. They peered down their long noses at Candy, as if to inquire, quite snobbishly, about her presence here. She sneered back at them, hoping belatedly that some hidden security camera hadn't captured the face she had just made.

She was debating whether to sit in one of the Queen Anne chairs when she heard approaching steps. It was the butler again, looking as stiff and disapproving as the people in the portraits.

"Madame will see you now," he announced formally with a slight nod of his head. His elbows were held back against his sides as if he were pinioned. "If you will follow me, she will see you in the tea room."

Ohh, the tea room! Candy thought excitedly, though to the butler she said, trying to match his formality, "That will be fine. Thank you."

He turned abruptly and led her back through a hallway and past a series of rooms, each more ornate and stylish than the one before — a formal sitting room, a music room with a grand piano, an elegant dining room with a mahogany table large enough for a dozen or more dinner guests. Toward the rear of the house the roar of the ocean became louder, and as she entered the tea room she saw why.

It was a small sitting area that opened onto the conservatory and the gardens and ocean beyond. Mrs. Pruitt, perched nonchalantly in a wicker armchair, perusing a home and garden magazine, looked up as Candy and the butler approached.

"Ms. Candy Holliday to see you, madame," the butler announced formally as he presented Candy to his mistress.

"Thank you, Hobbins. Would you tell Cook that she may serve us now?"

Hobbins! That's the butler's name! Candy made a mental effort to lock it into her brain.

"Of course, madame," Hobbins the butler said, using a tone that was more polite and respectful than the one he'd used with Candy. He pivoted perfectly on his heel and left the room.

Mrs. Pruitt set aside her magazine and held out a hand without rising. "Candy dear, how nice to see you again," she said, a practiced smile on her aging face.

She was a handsome enough woman, Candy now saw close up, though thin as a stork. Her gray hair was cleverly arranged and amazingly well maintained, even in the summer heat. Her eyes were intelligent and watchful, her complexion clear and creamy. Even her wrinkles looked artful, giving her a sophisticated appearance in keeping with her carefully honed image.

"Won't you please sit down?" Mrs. Pruitt motioned to a chair opposite her.

"Thank you for seeing me," Candy said as she settled into the wicker chair. "Your house is beautiful."

"Well, thank you for saying so." Mrs. Pruitt nodded graciously. "But you've been here before, haven't you?"

Candy's head bobbed up and down. "Three years ago, with the Garden Society."

"Yes, I thought so. With your friend — her name was . . ."

"Maggie," Candy finished for her. "Maggie Tremont."

"That's right. Maggie. A delightful woman. Wonderful sense of humor. She's doing well, I hope?"

And so it continued as Mrs. Pruitt's cook appeared bearing a sterling silver tray. Upon the tray sat a flowered china teapot in shades of pink and apricot, matching Royal Doulton teacups and saucers, and a silver serving plate piled high with cookies, cakes, and other assorted goodies.

Mrs. Pruitt poured, and gazing out over the sea, they sipped and chatted pleasantly about various community-related subjects and people until Mrs. Pruitt finally said quite pointedly, "I suppose you're here to ask me about that Vine woman and the pageant."

"Oh." Candy had to set her teacup down so she could focus. "Well, yes, actually. That *is* why I wanted to talk to you. I'm working on a column for the *Cape Crier* about the event, and I wanted to ask you a few questions about that night."

Mrs. Pruitt swiveled toward her, giving Candy her full attention. "What would you like to know?"

Candy paused a moment, organizing her thoughts. She wished she had brought a pen and notepad so she appeared more official. "Well, I was wondering" — she cleared her throat — "I was wondering if you could tell me your reaction to what happened that night."

"My reaction?" Mrs. Pruitt frowned. "My reaction," she repeated. "Hmm." She considered this a moment. "Well, as you probably are aware, I was quite upset by the whole affair. It was simply horrendous of them to crown that Vine woman as the Blueberry Queen. Totally irresponsible, and a total travesty. To think that anyone on that stage was better than my Haley is simply ludicrous," Mrs. Pruitt said with a flare of righteous anger. It was as if she had been waiting for days for someone to ask her opinion of what had happened that night, and it all came pouring out of her, but she quickly caught herself and, straightening her shoulders, adjusted her tone. "Of course, with what has happened in the past day or so, the events of that night have been completely overshadowed. Naturally, Ms. Vine's untimely death is a terrible occurrence. Nonetheless, she did not deserve to win that crown."

Mrs. Pruitt nodded her head sharply, as if to put a fine point on her statement.

Candy picked up the teacup again and

took a sip of tea before proceeding, holding the cup with both hands, giving herself a moment to form her next question. "So is it your opinion that you — or, er, Haley was unfairly treated?"

"Of course! It's obvious the judges were in error," Mrs. Pruitt stated adamantly. "As I have said, Haley clearly was the best contestant in the pageant. Anyone who was there could see that. Talentwise, she was far superior to the other girls." Mrs. Pruitt sharpened her gaze on Candy. "Do you believe otherwise?"

Candy had to admit that she didn't. "Haley's performance was clearly the best."

Mrs. Pruitt nodded approvingly.

"But if that's true — and we both agree that it is," Candy went on, thinking out loud, "and if it was as obvious to others in the audience, including the judges, as it is to you and me, then how did Sapphire win? Why wasn't Haley crowned the Blueberry Queen?"

"An excellent question," said Mrs. Pruitt. "You said you work for the newspaper. Perhaps you should investigate."

"Perhaps I should," Candy said thoughtfully. She leaned forward in her chair. "You don't suppose . . ." she trailed off, thinking.

After a moment, Mrs. Pruitt prompted,

237

"What, dear?"

Candy let out a breath. She decided that she might as well say what was on her mind. "Well, you don't suppose there was something . . . strange going on?"

"Bribery, you mean?"

"Bribery?" That wasn't what Candy had been thinking, and it surprised her, though she seemed to recall Maggie saying something about bribery also. "Do you really think so?"

"Yes."

"One of the judges?"

Mrs. Pruitt nodded.

Candy mulled that over. "I would have thought it would have been something a little less . . . conspiratorial. An error in scoring, perhaps."

Mrs. Pruitt made a somewhat surprising noise through her nose. "If you believe that, you really are as naive as you look."

I look naive? Candy thought sadly. *And Sapphire thought I was lonely. I really must do something about my image . . .*

"But if what you say is true," Candy went on, "that someone was being bribed by Sapphire, then which of the judges was it?"

Mrs. Pruitt shrugged. "Probably all of them."

Candy's mouth nearly dropped open. "All

of them?"

Mrs. Pruitt seemed annoyed by the question. "I wouldn't put it past that Sapphire Vine woman. You saw her up there. You know what she's like. She would have stopped at nothing to win that pageant." Mrs. Pruitt leaned forward in her chair, and said emphatically, *"Nothing."*

"But how?" Candy asked, clearly taken aback.

"I'm sure you'll figure it out, dear. I'm sure you can follow the clues."

That sparked another thought. "You don't suppose there's a link between her death and the fact that she won the Blueberry Queen Pageant, do you?"

"Well," said Mrs. Pruitt evenly as she refreshed Candy's cup of tea, "that's the big question, isn't it? So, tell me, how is your blueberry farm doing?"

Caught off guard by the sudden shift in the conversation, Candy answered quickly. "Oh, well, fine, just fine, thank you."

"You know, my grandfather once owned that property . . ."

Some time later, with the interview complete, Candy thanked Mrs. Pruitt, who rose and showed her to the door. Hobbins, it appeared, was preoccupied.

As Candy was in the foyer about to leave,

Haley Pruitt came dashing down the grand staircase, though she came to an abrupt stop when she saw her grandmother.

"Ah, here's Haley now," said Mrs. Pruitt, giving her granddaughter a disapproving look. To Haley, she said, "Candy Holliday stopped by to talk about the pageant, dear."

"Isn't it exciting?" Haley asked, crossing to her grandmother's side. She practically bubbled. "I'm going to be the Blueberry Queen!"

"They've contacted you then?" Candy asked.

"We heard from the pageant committee this morning," Mrs. Pruitt replied smugly. "There will be a short ceremony at Town Hall on Sunday morning."

"Well, I'm sure you'll make a wonderful Blueberry Queen," Candy said diplomatically. In a fleeting moment, she thought of asking Haley her thoughts about Sapphire's death but decided that it might seem inappropriate at the moment. Instead, she thanked Mrs. Pruitt for seeing her and asked for permission to contact her should she have any further questions.

A few moments later she was ushered politely outside, and the heavy front door closed firmly behind her.

As she walked toward the Jeep, digging in

her pocket for her keys, she turned and took one last look back at the manor. Its stucco-and-timber exterior was well maintained, and the multiple gables, overhanging upper stories, and tall brick chimneys gave the place an unmistakable medieval appearance.

She turned, her gaze wandering. A walkway that branched off led to a flowing fountain, and farther off to the right was a four-bay garage. Several of the garage doors were open. Candy could see the tail-end of the Bentley sitting in the cool shade of the garage, and also what looked like a Mercedes SUV.

Along the wall in the far-right bay was a long workbench, with a variety of toolboxes, an air pump, and other mechanical devices scattered across its surface.

I wonder, Candy thought.

She checked over her right shoulder, then her left. She made a complete about-face.

No one around. She was completely alone.

Trying to appear as inconspicuous as possible, she meandered along the walkway toward the garage, stopping and turning frequently, pretending to admire the estate and the grounds. As she got closer to the garage, she angled sharply toward the Bentley, deciding to use that as an excuse if anyone spotted her, but veered at the last moment into the far-right bay. Nervously she scanned the workbench, then flipped open the lids of a few toolboxes, searching inside.

No red-handled hammer.

Cameron had told Officer Martin that one of the hammers had been sold to the butler at Pruitt Manor — Hobbins.

If that was true, it had to be here somewhere. She had to check on it, just to satisfy her curiosity.

She opened a few drawers and scanned the shelves above the workbench but found nothing. She was just about to turn and leave when a voice behind her asked, "Can I help you?"

Candy spun, her heart nearly leaping out of her chest.

Standing at the entrance to the bay, and blocking her exit, was Hobbins.

He had removed his suit jacket and now wore a dark-green work apron. His starched shirtsleeves were rolled up to mid-forearm.

In his hand was a hammer. A red-handled hammer.

Candy was so surprised she stuttered and stammered, unable to get out any actual words. "I . . . I . . . um . . . uh . . ."

"Are you looking for something?" the butler asked suspiciously.

"No, I . . . uh, uh . . . I was, uh . . . I just wanted to look at your Bentley," she finally managed to say in a rush.

"Oh." Letting out a breath, Hobbins carelessly tossed the hammer onto the workbench and waved. "Well come on then. You can have a look at it."

"Oh, um, good. Thank you very much." Candy forced a smile.

"It's a ninety-three Brooklands Saloon style, as you can see," said Hobbins as he walked to the car. "All the standard amenities — alloy wheels, heated seats, wood trim, traction assist, dual horns. Six-point-seven-five-liter engine capacity. Black with gray interior. Handles like a dream . . ."

Five minutes later, still shaking a little after the unexpected encounter with the butler, Candy climbed gratefully into the Jeep, started the engine, and drove back down the gravel driveway.

"You have to stop doing this to yourself," she muttered as she turned toward town.

But at the same time she sensed she was making some progress.

Possible bribery. Missing hammers — and a hammer that wasn't missing. And was there a link between the pageant itself and Sapphire's death?

It all would make for interesting conversa-

tion when she met with Maggie for lunch at
Duffy's.

NINETEEN

Doc and his buddies were gone. The corner booth at Duffy's where they usually held court was occupied by a suburbanite family, obviously tourists, with three bouncing children, one of whom had climbed on top of the leatherette booth seatback and was riding it like a horsey. Dolores the waitress, looking exasperated, was trying to coax the young boy back down into a normal sitting position. The parents seemed more annoyed at Dolores than at their own child.

"Hey, Dolores," Candy called as the waitress approached her after having had little success with the family in the corner booth. "Have you seen Doc?"

"He left awhile ago with his posse."

"Do you know where they went?"

Dolores shrugged. "Don't know, honey. Sorry."

As the harried waitress rushed away to deal with her demanding customers, another voice nearby spoke up. "Excuse me, but they said they were headed over to the Rusty Moose to play some pool."

Candy turned. "Sorry?"

Sebastian J. Quinn sat in a nearby booth, alone. He had almost finished what looked like a hot turkey sandwich and mashed potatoes swamped in a river of brown gravy.

"I heard them talking," Sebastian went on, pointing with a thumb to the corner booth behind him, "before they left."

Candy nodded gratefully. "Oh, okay. Thanks, um, Mr. Quinn."

"Please, call me Sebastian." He motioned to the seat opposite him. "I believe they said they'd be back fairly quickly. You're welcome to sit and wait for them, if you'd like."

"Oh! Well . . ." Candy glanced around at the clock on the wall behind the counter. Twenty after twelve. She was to meet Maggie for lunch at twelve thirty. "I'm supposed to be meeting someone . . ."

"Wait with me then," Sebastian said without a hint of desperation. "We can keep each other company. I'll buy you a cup of coffee."

Candy allowed herself a smile. "To tell you the truth, that does sound pretty good." And despite her reservations, she slid into the booth across the table from Sebastian as he summoned Dolores.

After Candy had ordered, Sebastian said, "So, who are you meeting, if you don't mind my asking?"

"Oh, just a friend of mine. Maggie Tremont."

"Tremont?" Sebastian's fork perched above his plate. "Any relation to Amanda?"

"Her mother."

"Ahh." He scooped up a forkful of mashed potatoes, dripping gravy, which he shoveled into his mouth. "Amanda did a good job Saturday night. She seems like a delightful young lady."

"She's a good kid. She worked really hard to prepare for the pageant. All the girls did. It was a wonderful show, though it ended strangely."

"Yes it did."

"It's too bad," Candy went on, giving Dolores a nod of thanks as her coffee arrived, "because everything that's happened since then has overshadowed the efforts of those girls up on the stage that night."

"I suppose everyone's in shock over the news of Sapphire's death."

"That's putting it mildly." Candy ripped open a packet of Equal and stirred it into her coffee. "Nothing like that has ever happened in this little town before, at least as far as I know. It just doesn't seem, well, it doesn't seem real."

"Are you familiar with this Ray fellow — the one they've arrested?"

"Oh sure." Candy took a sip of her coffee. It was good and hot though a bit bitter even with the sugar — typical diner coffee. "Ray's a good friend and a really sweet person. I just can't believe he had anything to do with this."

"The murder, you mean? Why is that?"

Candy sighed. "Well, you'd have to know Ray. He's a gentle sort. He wouldn't hurt a fly."

"So you think he's innocent?"

"I *know* he's innocent," Candy said adamantly, "and I'm going to prove it."

The ends of Sebastian's wide mouth arced up in a smirk. "Really? That sounds quite noble of you. And how do you plan to do that?" He watched her in amusement as he scooped up the last of the mashed potatoes and gravy on his plate.

Candy wasn't put off by his condescending tone. "By finding out who really murdered Sapphire, of course," she said simply.

"So you're a private investigator?"

Candy snorted. "Far from it. I'm not nearly anything as important sounding as that. I'm just a private citizen trying to do her civic duty."

"Well, that's commendable." Sebastian placed his knife and fork on the empty plate and pushed it toward the end of the table, then picked up the napkin, which he dabbed at mouth and beard. "And how is the investigation progressing?"

Candy arched an eyebrow. "Just between you and me, I've turned up a few curious clues that so far haven't added up to much."

Sebastian grinned conspiratorially as he put his arms on the table and leaned forward. "I love a good mystery. Care to share what you've learned so far?"

"Not yet," Candy said enigmatically, "but if I uncover anything particularly troublesome, I'll let you know."

"I'd be glad to lend a hand any way I can, of course. I'm quite adept at unraveling mysteries. I've been known to regularly figure out those mysteries on TV long before the third commercial break."

"Oh my. A real pro." Candy feigned an impressed tone, then looked at him catlike as she saw an opportunity. She leaned closer too. "Well, if you really want to help, there *is* one thing I'm curious about — something you might know."

"What would that be?"

"Well, there's a rumor going around town

that one of the judges was bribed by Sapphire — so she could win the crown. I don't suppose you'd know anything about that?"

As she asked the question, she saw, just for an instant, a look of surprise flash through his eyes. "Bribery?"

"That's the scuttlebutt."

"Scuttlebutt?" He laughed, at ease again, though it seemed a bit forced. "That's a strange word. You learn that in the military?"

"Actually, from Doc. He was in the Navy back in the sixties. Went through college on the G.I. Bill. So?"

But before Sebastian could answer, Maggie huffed up to the table and in a flurry of movement slid into the booth beside Candy. "Hi, honey, made it! Sorry I'm late! It's just been a hectic week."

"Oh, hi, Mags."

As Maggie settled herself, she cast an appraising eye at Sebastian. "So . . . I'm not barging in on anything, am I? I'd hate to break up a romantic rendezvous."

"Maggie!" Candy yelped, offended.

"Candy and I were just having a pleasant conversation," Sebastian said diplomatically.

"Is that what they call it these days?" Maggie gave him a wink.

"If you must know," Candy said archly, "I was just asking Sebastian about the rumors that Sapphire had bribed one of the pageant judges."

"Ooh." Maggie rubbed her hands together excitedly. "Sounds like I made it here just in time." She looked pointedly at Sebastian, as did Candy. "So?"

For a few long moments Sebastian J. Quinn stared back at them with something approaching disbelief in his eyes. Then he laughed as he signaled for the check. "Ladies, ladies, you know I can't talk about anything like that. I'm sworn to secrecy. Besides, I think you're barking up the wrong tree. Perhaps the rumors are wrong. Perhaps Ms. Vine won the pageant fair and square."

Candy tilted her head thoughtfully, sharpening her gaze on him. "That's what Herr Georg said. Sounds like we have a conspiracy on our hands."

"Then you also have quite an investigation on your hands," Sebastian said as he slid from the booth and reached into a pocket, pulling out a wad of bills. He dropped a ten onto the table. "I wish I could continue this delightful conversation, ladies, but I have a few poems to write. If you'll excuse me . . ."

After he left, Maggie slipped around to the other side of the booth. "I guess we chased him off."

"Think he's hiding something?"

"No doubt about it. He knows something, that's for sure."

"Maybe he knows how Sapphire won that pageant."

"He's probably covering up for someone," Maggie said as she pulled a menu out from its place between the plastic bottles of ketchup and mustard at the end of the table. "I'm telling you, that whole thing was rigged."

"That's what Mrs. Pruitt thinks too."

"Mrs. Pruitt?" Maggie looked surprised. "You talked to her?"

Candy nodded. "About an hour ago."

"What! And you didn't tell me?"

"You just got here."

"Well, what are you waiting for? Get talking, girl. And don't you dare leave out a single tidbit. I want to know *everything*."

So as they ordered — a grilled chicken salad with extra alfalfa sprouts and tomatoes for Maggie, a veggie burger with mushrooms and onions, and coleslaw on the side for Candy — the topic of conversation focused on Candy's visit with Mrs. Pruitt. That led to a discussion of Candy's red-handled hammer theory, which was still under development — that somehow Ray's hammer had become mixed up with another one, which had been the actual murder weapon.

"It's the only explanation," Candy said as she took a bite of her veggie burger. "Ned even told me that his hammer is missing, which I find incredibly suspicious. I know the answer to this whole mess has something to do with those damned hammers."

"Have you asked Ray about it?"

"Yeah, Doc and I talked to him this morning, but we got nowhere. He was too much of an emotional mess to tell us much of anything. I doubt he's told the police much either."

"Have they charged him with anything yet?"

Candy shook her head. "I didn't think to ask." After a moment, she added, "How do things like this work? With the police, I mean?"

"Well," Maggie said thoughtfully as she munched on her salad greens, "after the perp has been arrested, he's booked and there's an arraignment, I think, and a bail hearing. And then I think he's formally charged, probably at the county courthouse in Machias. Or something like that."

"How long does all that take?"

Maggie scrunched up her nose. "A couple of days, I think?"

"Hmm." Candy's mouth twisted as she thought. "There's not much time left then. I've got to figure this thing out pretty quickly, or Ray's going to be in a heap of trouble."

"News flash, sweetie. He's already in a heap of trouble!"

"That's true, isn't it? Guess I've got to do some more digging to see if I can get to the bottom of this whole mess. Speaking of digging, did I tell you that I was in Sapphire's office yesterday? And that I got a job offer? From Ben Clayton?"

"What?" squeaked Maggie. "No, you didn't! You little weasel! You know you're supposed to tell me these things the moment they happen! Why didn't you call me? When did all this take place?"

"Yesterday afternoon, right after I left your office."

"Did he rescue you from that rainstorm?"

"Something like that, yeah."

"And he wants you to work for him? Doing what?"

"Writing a column. Actually, taking over Sapphire's column."

Maggie was almost beside herself with excitement. "And you accepted his offer, right?"

"After thinking it over for a while, yes, I did."

"You had to think it over?" Maggie looked stunned.

"I wasn't sure I wanted to do it."

"Are you daft, girl?"

"It's a big commitment. A column a week."

"So what's the problem? You're smart. You can do that standing on your head with one hand tied behind your back. Is he paying you?"

"We agreed to seventy-five dollars a week."

"Honey, you'll be loaded!" Maggie beamed for a moment, but the smile slipped from her face, and she suddenly looked depressed. "How did I miss all this? I guess I really am out of the loop, aren't I?"

"You're definitely missing out on the good stuff."

"I've got to get out more. See more people."

"Tell you what," Candy said with mock sympathy. "I'm headed over to Ben's office after lunch. He wants me to pick up some files and fill out a few forms. Why don't you come with me? You can see Sapphire's office — you know, check out the place where she worked."

Maggie's jaw dropped. She looked as if

she had just won the lottery. "Honey, just try to keep me away!"

TWENTY

Maggie walked over to the *Cape Crier*'s office on Ocean Avenue, since it was just a block away, but Candy drove the Jeep, thinking she might need it. She found a parking spot down toward the end of the block, across from the town park. Upstairs, Ben was pleased to see her. "Hi, Candy."

"Hi, Ben. I've brought a friend of mine along. You know Maggie Tremont, right?"

"Sure. Maggie and I practically work next door to each other. Hi, Maggie."

"Hi, Ben. This is really exciting — for Candy, I mean."

He smiled, though he looked a bit frazzled. The sleeves of his blue oxford shirt were rolled up, his tie discarded, and his long brown hair was charmingly askew. He looked like a preppy school kid studying for exams.

"I'm really glad you decided to take this job, Candy," he said honestly. "I've got everything ready for you."

He handed her a manila folder. "Here are some forms for you to sign — a W-2, workman's comp, that sort of thing," he said, talking fast. "If you could get them back to me in a day or so, that'd be great. I'll need your Social Security number so I can get you set up with payroll. You'll also find a list of publishing dates for the rest of this year, and the deadlines for your column. Generally, it's due every Monday at noon. Keep in mind that we suspend publication for two weeks at the end of August, which should work out pretty well for you — you'll have only two columns due before the break, so you'll have a little extra time to get your sea legs before we hit the fall issues, which can get hectic. Let's see, what else? Don't worry too much about a headline and deck — I'll write those or the copy editor will. She's a volunteer — great person — you'll really like her. Anyway, about seven hundred words should do it each week — three pages typewritten. Nothing fancy with formatting. We use Microsoft Word. You can just e-mail the column to me — send it as an attachment." He snapped his finger, as if he had just remembered something. "That's right — I've got to set you up with a new e-mail address. You've got a computer at home, right?"

Candy nodded. It had been awhile since she worked a regular job, and she had gotten out of the habit of the daily grind, but she was keeping up with him okay. She wished again that she had brought a pen along to take notes. That's something she would have to remember in the future, now that she was a columnist.

"Of course, you can use Sapphire's office if you want to," Ben continued. "There's an old computer in there if you need it. It's loaded with all the software we use. We can probably find some of her past columns on it so you can follow her formatting."

Candy gulped, her enthusiasm suddenly zapped. "Sapphire's office?"

Something in her tone made him pause. "Is that a problem?"

"Well . . ."

"The police have everything they need out of there, so don't worry about that."

"It's just that . . ."

Ben's brow fell, and he looked confused for a few moments, until Maggie piped in to help translate. "She's worried about working in a dead woman's office," Maggie said matter-of-factly.

"Oh, I see." But it was clear from the tone

of his voice that he still didn't totally understand.

"Maybe if we changed things around in there a little," Maggie said helpfully to Candy. "You know, make the place your own."

Candy shook her head doubtfully. She was wondering again if this was such a good idea after all. "I . . . I don't know."

"Tell you what," Ben said. "Why don't you two have a look around in there? You remember how to find it, right? See what you think. If it doesn't work out, I can try to move you somewhere else, or maybe you can just work out of your home until we get it figured out, okay?"

Candy nodded, feeling slightly better. "That sounds acceptable."

"Just give me a holler if you need anything. I'll be around. Oh, and I'm having new business cards made up for you. They should be ready in a few days. In the meantime, you can use some of the generic cards we have floating around here. There might be some in Sapphire's desk. If not, let me know and I'll scrounge some up for you."

Even with directions from Ben, it took Candy and Maggie more than five minutes to find Sapphire's office in the rabbit warren of hallways and offices, which the *Crier* shared with a web-hosting company and a local quarterly real-estate publication. They made two wrong turns, winding up in a broom closet the first time and at a brick wall the next. But finally they opened a door and entered what had, until recently, been Sapphire Vine's exclusive domain.

Maggie was thrilled with what she saw. "It's just as I always dreamed it would be," she said breathlessly. "This proves that she was a really, really twisted person."

"Remember, you're speaking of the dead," Candy cautioned as she stood uneasily by the doorway.

Maggie ignored her. "Look, she has kitties on the walls! And look at all these cute little notes she wrote to herself! It's all so wonderful!"

But while Maggie was thrilled with the unexpected treasures she found, Candy felt just the opposite. She swore she could feel Sapphire's ghost inhabiting the place — and it wasn't a happy ghost.

"I can't work in here," she said suddenly.

"Well, I agree, it is a bit dreary," Maggie said, looking around. "It could use some sprucing up, maybe better artwork, and it needs a fresh coat of paint. That would help a lot. A nice eggshell, maybe? Or a soft mauve?"

"That won't work."

"Some new furniture?"

"Nope."

"Flowers? Doilies? I could stencil a nice design around the walls for you."

Candy shook her head.

"Well, what do you want to do then?"

Candy motioned to the computer. "Ben said there were some past columns on there. I'll pull them off and put them on a disk. And I'll dig around and grab some files, haul everything back home, and work from there. Maybe Ben can find another office for me in the next week or so."

Maggie sighed. "Okay, if that's *really* what you want to do, I'll help you, but it sure seems like a wasted opportunity to me."

They set to work, but Maggie couldn't stay long — she had to head back to work at one thirty. Forty-five minutes later, Candy had assembled everything she thought she'd need, including many of the files from the cabinet, notebooks with scribbled messages, stacks of newspapers with Sapphire's past printed columns in them, a handful of generic business cards, assorted business cards of individuals and companies around town that might serve as story leads, a well-thumbed address book, and copies of some of Sapphire's e-mails she had printed out for later viewing.

She shut down the computer, loaded everything into two battered old banker's storage boxes she had pulled out of the back of a closet, carried them down to the Jeep, then stopped back in to see Ben.

"We'll work it out," Ben said optimistically after she had explained everything to him. "Don't worry about it for now. Just work on your column, and keep in touch. I'm here if you need anything. And I'll find you another place to work. At the very least, I'll move you in with someone else temporarily."

She flashed him a smile. "Thanks for understanding. Sorry to be so childish about this whole thing."

He waved a hand at her. "Don't even think about it. I understand completely. Besides, like I said, you're doing me a favor, right?"

"Right. Thanks, Ben," she said as she headed out the door. "You're a doll."

And she meant it.

TWENTY-ONE

Candy stopped back at Duffy's to pick up Doc, who had finished his game of pool and was back in the corner booth with the boys, and together they drove home. Before she unloaded the Jeep, she checked on the girls, who seemed as happy as ever. She gave them a few cupfuls of cracked corn and egg-laying pellets, freshened their water, gathered their eggs, and laid some clean straw in their roosts.

Then she carried one of the boxes filled with Sapphire's papers and files into the house.

"What's that?" Doc asked as he opened a bottle of beer, a good local brand called Thunder Hole Ale, brewed in Bar Harbor.

"Homework," Candy said as she dropped the box onto the kitchen table.

"Got more in the Jeep? Want me to grab them?"

"One more. That would be great."

"Coming right up," Doc said, setting his beer aside as he walked out to the Jeep and retrieved the other box.

"What's in here anyway?" he asked as he set the second box down on the table, beside the first.

"Sapphire Vine's old papers, notes, and files. Ben thought it might help if I went through them, so I could see what kind of research she'd done — formatting, contacts, that sort of thing."

"Well, you've got pretty big shoes to fill. Her columns were mighty popular, you know." Doc at least had the good sense to add after a few moments, "But I'm sure yours will be just as good."

She gave him a sideways smirk. "Yeah, right, thanks for the vote of confidence."

"Hey, let me know if you need any help. I've got some experience as a wordsmith. And not just that ancient history stuff I've been working on. I've written about modern topics, for newspapers and magazines. They don't give full professorships to monkeys, you know. You have to be published."

"I'll keep that in mind, Bonzo."

"Hey, I heard that!" Doc called as he walked into the living room, flicked on the TV, and settled himself in to watch *Ellen.*

Candy sat at the kitchen table, unloaded

both boxes, and started sifting through the files. Most contained worthless stuff — nothing much she could use. She tossed those files onto a discard pile on one side of the table.

A few files contained some notes and interesting stories that might be helpful in the future. Candy set those aside, intending to start her own filing system.

Then there were a few that confused her. Most of the files were labeled on their front tabs with names or subjects — not much guessing was required to figure out what was in them. But she found a handful of files — fewer than a dozen — that had no labels or names on them, and no indication of what was inside.

One, for instance, had the mysterious nomenclature BAK1946 printed in Sapphire's childish letters on the inside front cover. It contained only a few e-mails, which Sapphire had printed out.

"We must come to an agreement about this, or else," read one of the e-mails, one that had been sent by Sapphire. *A rather threatening comment,* Candy thought. Underneath that line, and indented a few spaces, was the message Sapphire had replied to. It read, "I've asked you not to contact me about this again. I cannot help you."

Candy's brow furrowed in thought. Whatever message from Sapphire this mysterious person had replied to had been deleted.

She flipped back through the other pages in the file. There were a few copies of printed e-mails with messages similar to the first one. Sapphire's notes and tone grew increasingly threatening, and the unnamed person who replied grew increasingly reticent to do whatever it was she was asking. But there was no indication of the name of the person Sapphire had been exchanging e-mails with, or even the person's gender.

There wasn't much more in the file. A photocopy of an aged black-and-white photograph, showing a mother with a young child sitting on her lap. A yellowed newspaper clipping in German, which Candy couldn't read. A few notes that made no sense.

German?

Candy looked back at the inside front cover.

BAK1946.

BAK? Could that stand for Baker? Herr Georg? *What year had he been born?* she wondered. He was in his early to mid sixties, she guessed. Counting back, she realized it was entirely possible he could have been born in 1946. But it didn't make any sense. Why was Sapphire e-mailing Herr Georg? And what was it that she wanted him to do?

The thought crossed Candy's mind that it might have something to do with the pageant. Maybe she *was* trying to bribe him.

Or maybe she was *blackmailing* him.

That could open up a whole new bucket of worms.

Candy set that file aside and picked up another. This one was just as intriguing as the first. It had information in it about all five judges of the Blueberry Queen Pageant, including phone numbers and e-mail addresses. Sapphire had placed checks beside the names of all five judges and circled two of the checks — those beside the names of Herr Georg and Sebastian J. Quinn.

That might fit, she thought, *if she was blackmailing both of them.* But if Herr Georg's file was here, where was Sebastian's? She double-checked. There was no file with his name on it, nor any that looked as if it contained any information about him.

Curious.

She opened a third mysterious file. This one intrigued her the most. On the inside front cover were the initials *C. Z.* It didn't take Candy long to figure out who that might be — Cameron Zimmerman.

Amanda's boyfriend.

Unlike the others, this was a thick file, with clippings, photographs, and photocopies of old papers going back nearly twenty years. Sapphire had obviously done a lot of research on Cameron. There were numerous newspaper clippings of his educational and athletic achievements — making the honor roll in seventh grade, scoring a goal in junior varsity soccer, that sort of thing. A number of fuzzy candid snapshots of him that looked like spy photos, taken from behind bushes or at great distances, apparently without his knowledge. Candy even found a few pages that had been ripped from high school yearbooks, on which his images appeared.

Candy was surprised by the detail of the information she found. *Sapphire's been stalking him for years,* she realized. *But why?*

There were also pages and pages of notes that traced Cameron's history over a period of nearly fifteen years. Addresses and phone numbers. Detailed information about his parents, Moe and Debbie Zimmerman. Moe was a trucker; Debbie worked at a hair salon. Cam was their only child.

Candy read through the papers with growing interest. But it was a notation scribbled at the bottom of one of the last pages that caught her attention and made her sit up straight in her chair.

He's the one, it read.

"The one?" Candy said out loud. "The one what?"

"What?" Doc called from the living room.

"Nothing!" Candy called back.

"Hey, you should see this," Doc said. "Ellen's giving away iPods to her studio audience again. And you should see what else they're getting."

"Just a minute, Dad."

Candy started going back through the files again, searching for other notations, but there was nothing unusual that jumped out at her.

Except, she realized with a start, for the fact that despite all she had found in Sapphire's office, there was a lot of information that seemed to be missing — information that Sapphire, as thorough as she seemed to have been, should have collected.

In other words, there were huge gaps in Sapphire's research.

For instance, there was a file on Cameron but practically nothing about any other student, or any teachers or school administrators. Practically nothing on the local police force or town council or county commissioners. Nothing about local businesspeople. Nothing on Mrs. Pruitt. Nothing on Maggie or Amanda.

And nothing on any of the other beauty pageant judges. Or any of the other beauty pageant *contestants,* for that matter.

In fact, nothing at all about the pageant.

Now that's odd, Candy thought, scratching her head. Ben had told her Sapphire was going to write her next column on the pageant, and that she had done some research on it. But there was nothing here about the pageant. Nada.

That doesn't make any sense, Candy thought, *especially when she was a contestant herself. There should be reams of information.*

But there was nothing.

Maybe the police took those files, she thought, *or maybe Ben has them.*

Or maybe Sapphire kept those files somewhere else — someplace private, where no one else could get a look at them . . .

Candy was still sifting through the files, mulling them over, when Doc walked back out into the kitchen. Candy barely noticed him.

"That was a pretty good show," he said in

a conversational tone. "Too bad you missed it."

"Huh?" Candy looked up.

"Ellen."

"Oh. That's great, Dad."

"Hey, I'm gonna take a walk up through the fields before dinner. Want to join me?"

"No thanks. I'm going to work here awhile longer, then I'll start dinner."

"Okay."

He was almost out the door when he stopped and turned back. "Oh, by the way, I almost forgot to tell you. I got some new information from Finn today. He talked to his source at the police department this morning. That guy we met, Officer Safford, was right about Ray's lawyer. Seems he's some superexpensive guy who works for a big firm up in Bangor. And guess who's picking up the tab for his services?"

That caught Candy's attention. She looked up. "Who?"

"You won't believe it if I told you."

"Daaad . . ."

"Okay, okay. It's Mrs. Pruitt."

Candy scrunched up her face. "Mrs. Pruitt is paying for Ray's lawyer?"

"That's what I said. In fact, this guy she's hired is associated with the firm that handles all her estate and business affairs. Strange, huh?"

"Very."

"Something else. They've been interrogating Ray —"

"Interrogating him?"

Doc nodded. "— and apparently he just keeps repeating the same thing over and over. Says he didn't do it and says it's up at the fort. The police have no idea what he's talking about, and he's not telling them. You know what he might mean by that?"

Candy had to think about that one. Finally she shook her head. "I don't think so. The only fort I can think of is Fort O'Brien, that old Revolution-era fort up by Machias. But it's just a ruin now, isn't it? Just the foundations or something like that? I don't know what that would have to do with anything."

"Yeah, I thought the same thing. Well, I guess we'll let the police figure it out. Just thought I'd ask."

He gave her a wave and disappeared out the door, leaving Candy sitting at the kitchen table, gazing over the remnants of Sapphire Vine's life.

But only partial remnants, Candy realized.

There had to be more.

She crossed to the phone, picked it up, and dialed Maggie at the insurance office.

"I've only got a second," Maggie said. "What's up?"

"You got any plans for tonight?"

"What do you have in mind?"

"You're going to say I'm crazy, but I'm thinking about breaking and entering."

"The old B-and-E? You *are* crazy. You can get yourself arrested for that, you know."

"So I've heard. But I've got to do it. It just might save Ray. You with me?"

"Of course! How could I pass up an offer like that? So whose house are we breaking into?"

"Sapphire Vine's."

Twenty-Two

"Tell me again what we're doing and why we're doing it, just so I know what to say to the nice police officer when he's slapping the handcuffs on me and reading me my Miranda rights."

Maggie had moments ago settled into the passenger seat of Candy's Jeep, and the two were now headed at a steady though law-abiding clip toward Sapphire Vine's house, with Candy at the wheel.

"It's simple," Candy replied, keeping her eyes trained on the dark road in front of her. "I went through Sapphire's files, but there's a lot of critical information missing. I figure she must have kept another set of files at her house. So we're going to break in and see if we can find them."

"But wouldn't the police have confiscated them already? I'm sure they must've searched her house. Hey, did you see that? It looked like a skunk."

Candy swerved out a little to avoid a furry critter that was scurrying back off the road. "I saw it. It was a fisher cat."

"They eat horses, don't they?"

"It's 'They *shoot* horses, don't they?' And no, they don't. But they do eat small rodents, rabbits, that sort of thing. I've heard they have a particular affinity for cats."

"Who? Horses?"

"No. Fisher cats."

"Eww, that's so cruel."

"Simple way to solve it: don't let your cats out at night."

"But Mr. Biggles loves to go out catting around at night. Just like me." Maggie stared out at the darkness beyond the headlights. "So you haven't said anything about my black outfit. Do you like it?"

"It's very chic."

"Thanks. I thought I'd dress for the occasion. You know, black can be very slimming. Hey, this is fun. Doesn't it remind you of something Lucy and Ethel would do?"

"I hadn't thought about it that way, but now that you mention it, yes."

"Good thing Ricky's not around. What do you suppose he'd say if he caught Lucy doing this? Probably something like, 'Luuucy, you got some 'splaining to do!' " She laughed at her own joke. "You know, it's great having a friend like you. We should get out more often. Burgle a few houses, steal a car or two — you know, girl stuff." She paused, then asked, "So what are we doing out here again?"

Candy sighed and drove on.

Sapphire Vine had lived in a well-kept Queen Anne Victorian on Gleason Street in an older neighborhood near the center of town. Candy had no idea how Sapphire could afford such a place, since the only job she seemed to have had was her part-time position as columnist for the *Cape Crier*. After talking with Ben, Candy knew she hadn't been paid much. So where had the money come from?

It was just another question to fuel the ever-growing mystery surrounding Sapphire Vine.

Candy had driven past Sapphire's house numerous times, but she had never been inside, though it looked nice enough. Its vintage scalloped siding was painted an old, thick buttery yellow, and the trim was cocoa brown, which made for a nice contrast. The front porch was wide and inviting, dotted with rockers and potted plants. Lace curtains hung in the windows, and flower beds and old shade trees added some stateliness to the front yard.

It was near midnight when Candy pulled over to the side of the road, switched off the headlights, and killed the engine.

"Why are we parking here?" Maggie asked, looking around. "We're still a block away."

"Just a precaution. I thought it would be too obvious if we parked right in front of her house. We *are* breaking into the place, after all."

"Right. Good idea."

"I figured we'd circle back through the woods on the empty lot behind her house and come around from the rear. We probably don't want to just walk right up to the front door and barge our way in."

As Candy spoke, she reached into the backseat. She pulled a black canvas tote bag into her lap and dug around inside until she found two flashlights. She handed one to Maggie, then climbed out of the Jeep, slipping the bag's strap over her shoulder.

"Boy, you thought of everything," Maggie observed as she flicked on her flashlight and joined Candy. "How many homes have you broken into?"

"This is the first one."

"I'm impressed by your preparation."

Candy shrugged. "Seems pretty obvious. It's just common sense, you know."

"That's what Jesse James used to say —

or so I've heard."

"Close friend of his, were you?"

"Honey, you don't know the half of it."

Keeping their flashlights aimed low, they left the street and angled back through the woods toward the house in which Sapphire Vine had once lived. Now that they were out of the Jeep and into the night air, they walked in silence. When they did talk, they did so in low whispers.

The woods were overgrown and tricky to traverse. Maggie jumped noisily more than once as she was spooked by night creatures, and almost tripped a couple of times, cursing angrily under her breath. But they picked their way through without too much trouble and soon emerged from the woods, pausing at the edge of Sapphire's backyard.

Candy reached back inside the bag she carried and handed something to Maggie. "Here, you'll need these."

Maggie shined her flashlight on the objects she had been handed. "Isotoner gloves?"

"It's all I had. We can't leave fingerprints."

"But aren't we supposed to wear those little latex gloves like they have in hospitals or at the deli counter? You know, like when they slice your cheese for you?" She held out an imaginary slice, as if for a customer. " 'How's this?' " she mimicked. "And what about those people who say, 'Oh, can I have that a hundredth of an inch thinner'? I mean, come *on* — it's a piece of *cheese!* Get a life!"

"Shh! Get your Isotoners on," Candy said, pulling her friend along by the arm. "We're going in."

As they walked across the yard toward the back of the house, Candy slipped on a pair of lavender Polartec winter gloves — the only other ones she had except for a few pairs of grimy old gardening gloves, which were totally inappropriate for this kind of delicate operation. Candy was just snugging her fingers into them when she looked up — and stopped dead in her tracks. Maggie, who was following behind, plowed into her.

"Hey, what's going on?" Maggie whispered harshly.

Candy pointed up at the house. "Look there."

Maggie raised her eyes, following Candy's finger.

A dim light showed through a small window nestled into the very highest peak of the house's gabled roof.

"You think someone's home?" Maggie whispered, sounding worried.

Candy shook her head. "No one lives here anymore — Sapphire probably just left a night light on or something like that. Come on."

"But what if someone's moved in and . . ."

"Shh! Wait here."

"Where are you going?" Maggie whispered, but Candy had already moved away. She disappeared into the shadows at the back of the house. Maggie heard her jiggle the knob on the back door.

"It's locked. And it's got yellow police tape across it," came Candy's faint whisper. "I'm checking around the side. Be right back."

As Candy disappeared into the night, Maggie waited nervously. Time seemed to drag on. She tapped her feet, looked up at the stars, and bit her lip. "Candy, you there?" she finally whispered into the shadows.

No answer. "Candy?"

She was just about to investigate when a dark shape loomed from around the other side of the house and approached her at a fast pace.

"Halt! Who goes there!" Maggie squeaked.

"Shh! It's just me."

"What are you doing?"

"Looking for a way in, silly. All the windows are locked."

"Well there's a surprise. What are we going to do now?"

"I'll guess I'll have to put the *break* into breaking and entering. I need a big rock or a brick."

"Why? What are you gonna do?"

"Break a window. Got any other bright ideas?"

"How about looking for a spare key? Everyone leaves a spare key around somewhere outside, right?"

"Good idea. I'm glad I brought you along. Let's see what we can find."

It took some searching, but Maggie finally located a key hidden on top of one of the back window frames. "Here it is!"

"You're a genius! We're in business."

Candy slipped the key in the lock, turned the knob, and pushed open the door. "Here, put this back where you found it," she said, handing the key to Maggie. Then she ducked under the police tape.

Maggie hid the key in its secret place, then rejoined Candy.

They were in.

The door opened onto a long dark hall. Maggie closed the door behind them as they shone their lights around. A door to the left led to the kitchen. On the right was a small bathroom and a storage space under the staircase. Straight ahead was what looked like the living room.

Everything seemed to be in disarray — probably from the police search of the house, Candy guessed.

"Where do you think she bought it?" Maggie asked quietly, coming up behind Candy.

"What?"

"Where do you think Sapphire was when she was — you know — killed?"

"Oh." Candy took a few tentative steps forward and peered into the living room. She pointed to a spot on the living room floor marked in an X with masking tape, which seemed to glow in the beam of her flashlight. "There."

Maggie made a face. "Yuck. Let's go this way." She angled off to her left, into the kitchen, but Candy hesitated in the back hall. "Do you suppose we should wipe our shoes or something?" she asked.

"Why would we want to do that?" came Maggie's harshly whispered response.

"Well, mine are kinda muddy from the woods. The police can't match shoe prints, can they?"

Maggie's face appeared back around the door frame. "I never thought of that."

"Can they?"

"Yeah, I think so."

Candy thought a moment. "Guess we'd

better take off our shoes then. We can leave them here by the back door."

"Good idea."

Their shoes off and carefully set on the back-door mat, the two of them began to explore the house in their stocking feet. They started in the kitchen. As carefully and quietly as possible, Candy checked all the cupboards and opened all the drawers. While Maggie cooed with pleasure over the Betty Boop cookie jar and Sapphire's collection of whimsical salt and pepper shakers, Candy searched through a small stack of unpaid bills on the breakfast table. She even poked into the trash can but found nothing.

Moving quietly and methodically, they next checked a small laundry room attached to the kitchen, the downstairs bathroom, and the dining room. Then, respectfully, they walked into the living room, careful to stay to the outer edges, avoiding the center of the room, where Sapphire Vine had died a violent death after stopping the business end of a hammer with her head.

Maggie looked around with a mixture of fascination and repugnance. "I love the fact that we're here," she whispered, unable to take her eyes off the masking-tape X on the floor, "but you have to admit this is kind of creepy. I didn't think it would be so tomb-like. It's like a dead person lives here."

"A dead person *did* live here, but she's gone now, so she won't mind if we nose around a little."

"You sure about that?"

"Well, no, not really."

Maggie tilted her head pleasantly. "Okay, that's good enough for me. Let's get back to business."

Tiptoeing about cautiously, they shined their flashlights into various nooks and crannies, checking the room. It was actually tastefully decorated, they were surprised to discover, with a fairly new rust-colored furniture set, Mission-style coffee and end tables, a well-stuffed bookshelf, a comfortable-looking rocking chair, a large TV, and an upright piano. There were only small touches that indicated Sapphire Vine had once lived here — a collection of cat and angel porcelain figurines arranged lovingly on a bookshelf, an embroidered pillow on the sofa that read, "The World's Gutsiest Gal."

Candy and Maggie examined these items curiously, then moved on to the piano. A dozen or so old family photos in antique silver frames were lined up along its top. "I wonder why Sapphire never told us anything about her family," Maggie said softly.

"Maybe because we never asked."

"Good point. Look, here's a photo of her when she was younger — about twenty years old or so, I'd say. Handsome guy with her."

Candy studied it, focusing in on the innocent young couple, who in the photo appeared to be extremely happy. Sapphire's hair was longer, her face more cherubic, and she looked heavier than she had in more recent days. The young man she stood next to was tall and lean with dark curly hair. He had an easy smile and wore an old gray sweatshirt with the letters *USM* on it in faded blue. "I wonder what happened to him."

Maggie shook her head. "She probably chased him away with her sharp wit."

"Yeah, sure."

When they found nothing else of interest on the first floor, they moved to the second. There they found another bathroom and three bedrooms, two of which were furnished and one empty except for some boxes, an ancient weight-lifting set, some old pieces of furniture, and as sorted piles of clothes and books stacked in haphazard piles.

Candy pointed to the furnished bedrooms.

"You take the one on the right, I'll take the other. Check everything."

Maggie did as instructed. She searched through dresser drawers, the nightstand drawer, an oak hope chest, even the storage boxes under the bed.

"Nothing!" she called out.

Candy walked back out of the other bedroom. "Nothing in there either. She must keep her papers around here somewhere. There's got to be a workspace or something — someplace where she writes and keeps her files."

"Maybe in the basement," Maggie suggested.

"Maybe." Candy shined her light around. She turned a complete circle, then walked back in and checked all the bedrooms. She seemed to be searching for something.

"What's wrong?" Maggie hissed.

Candy shook her head. "Where are the stairs to the top floor?"

"The what?"

"The top floor. Remember that light we saw in the window? Well, there's no light on here. There must be another floor above this one. Look around for a set of stairs."

"It's probably right here," Maggie said, motioning to a door that led to the space over the lower staircase. But when she opened the door, she found that it was only a closet, stuffed with blankets, a vacuum cleaner, old shoes, and more boxes. "Nope, that's not it."

"Hmm. There must be a way to get to the top level — maybe in a closet or behind a closed door. Let's look."

So they drifted off, walking the floor, exploring the bedrooms again, searching everywhere. But they found nothing.

"That's so weird," Candy said as they met back in the hallway. "I know I saw a light in that top window, but how do we get up there?"

"Maybe there's a secret door," Maggie guessed.

"Hmm. Could be. This place must be a hundred years old, at least. It's possible they could have put a secret door or panel someplace. Let's look again, more carefully this time."

"Okay. You take that side of the hallway, and I'll look over here."

The minutes passed as they each searched a room, which wasn't easy, since they had only their flashlights to see by. Candy desperately wanted to flick on an overhead light but knew that was taboo. She rapped on the walls with her knuckles, listening for any hollow sound. But then she realized that it all sounded the same to her. Even if she found a secret door, she didn't know what it would sound like.

She decided to check the closet more carefully. She guessed that she was in the spare bedroom, since it was sparsely decorated, and Sapphire's winter clothes were hanging from the bar in the closet. The shelf above was filled with boxes.

Then she looked again, shining the light around. The shelf was only half-full, she saw now. And the far end of the shelf was missing.

Curious, Candy walked to that end of the closet and shined her light up along the wall. That's when she noticed a narrow wooden ladder leaned up against the back wall of the closet. Her eyes followed the ladder up to the ceiling.

Then she saw it — a trap door.

"Found it!" she called out as loudly as she dared.

She heard footsteps approaching at a run. "What? Let me see!"

"Right there. Look."

Maggie shone her light up with Candy's. "Ooh, yes, that's it! A trap door. How clever! I bet the police didn't see that! Who's going up first?"

"I don't suppose you want to volunteer?"

Maggie gave her a look. "Just be careful. I'll watch your back."

"Thanks. That makes me feel *so* much better. Here, hold this."

Candy passed her flashlight and the tote bag to Maggie, then grabbed on to one of the ladder's rungs. She put a foot on a lower rug, testing it carefully to make sure it would hold her weight, then hoisted herself up slowly, a rung at a time, until she was high enough to reach the trap door in the ceiling. Holding onto the ladder with one hand, she pushed up on the trap door with the other. It gave way easily, opening a few inches with a low creak.

"I'm going up," she called back down in a loud whisper. "Pass the flashlight to me when I get up there."

"Roger that," Maggie called efficiently.

Candy pushed the trap door all the way open and saw a faint glow of light filtering down into the closet. Grabbing the wood frame of the opening, she pulled herself up and into the room above.

Twenty-Three

She sat for a moment on the edge with her legs dangling down and looked around warily. But it was just as she expected — a cozy attic hideaway that had been Sapphire's secret retreat.

Because of the size of the trap door, it must have been difficult to get big pieces of furniture up here, so what Candy saw was a makeshift arrangement. A narrow folding table, pushed into one corner, made for a desk. The room also contained a trio of fold-up-style director's chairs, a small wicker chair, several cinder-block-and-board shelves lined with books, a portable TV set on top of a green plastic crate, a CD player/radio on the floor beside it, a few tall boxes that had been turned upside down to serve as end tables, and — strangely enough — a thin twin-sized mattress laid on the floor along one wall, with a pillow and blankets scattered across it.

"Let me see, let me see!" Maggie exclaimed excitedly as she came up the ladder behind Candy, handing up the tote bag and flashlight. "What have you found?"

"It's Sapphire's secret lair."

"The center of the spider's nest. This just keeps getting better and better."

Candy swung her legs up underneath her, rose — and immediately bumped her head on the sloped ceiling. They were at the very top of the house, and though the ceiling was high enough in the center of the room that she could stand, it sloped down sharply at the sides.

There was a small window that looked out over the backyard, dark now except for a small patch faintly illuminated far below. An antique floor lamp with a low-wattage bulb had been left on; that had been the light they had seen from the yard.

Candy crossed to the folding table that served as a desk. It was a primitive setup, but everything Sapphire had needed appeared to be here. On the table was a fairly new notebook computer. Candy spotted a phone line that ran down through a crude hole cut in a corner of the floor, probably used for an Internet connection, though she saw it was now unplugged; Sapphire had apparently upgraded to wireless. The desktop had been kept nice and neat, as expected of Sapphire. Papers, files, and magazines were carefully organized in a variety of plastic desktop trays and sorters. Sharpened pencils and pastel-colored pens were stored in old coffee cups that served as pencil holders. Another address book — this one with a glossy pink cover decorated with stickers of ice cream cones and flowers — sat to one side of the computer. A Rolodex nearby looked as though it had been frequently used and regularly updated. The handset of a wireless phone sat beside the address book.

No one could ever say Sapphire had been a slouch when it came to organization.

A two-drawer cardboard file cabinet — one of those cheapie jobs you could buy at an office supply store — sat to one side of the desk. Slipping off her Polartec gloves and setting them down on the floor with the tote bag and flashlight, Candy dropped into the chair behind Sapphire's desk and gingerly pulled open the file cabinet's top drawer. It was heavy and stuffed full, just as she suspected. She started fingering her way back through the files.

"Would you look at this?" Maggie asked from the other side of the room. She had wasted no time in exploring the surroundings.

Candy turned and looked up. Maggie held a photo album open in her hands. She was paging through it. "There are pictures of her in here going back to when she was a baby. And look at this." She closed the album and held it out so Candy could see it.

Along the bottom right corner of the album cover, in gold block letters, was the inscription *Susan Jane Vincent.*

Candy's brows knit together. "Who's Susan Jane Vincent?"

"Don't you get it?" Maggie's eyes were huge. "It's Sapphire! That must be her real name! She must have changed it somewhere along the line."

"Well I'll be damned."

"You didn't think Sapphire Vine was her real name, did you? I always suspected she must have changed it at some point, maybe to hide a sordid past. And here's the proof."

"Susan Jane Vincent, huh? So she's just an ordinary plain Jane after all."

"I wonder if the police know about this," Maggie said absently to herself as she paged through the album.

Candy looked around the room with fresh eyes. "They might have discovered her real name by now, but my guess is they haven't found this place yet. They must have missed it when they searched the house."

Maggie set the album aside and looked over at Candy. "Are we going to tell them?"

Candy shrugged. "I don't know yet. Keep looking. See what else you can find."

"Right, Chief!" Almost immediately Maggie chimed up again. "Here's something." She reached toward a book on a narrow shelf, pulling it out and holding it up, just as she had with the album.

"I can't see it from here," Candy said, squinting from her spot across the room, so Maggie walked over and placed it in her hands.

Candy realized after a moment that she had seen the book before — or one just like it. She turned it sideways and read the gold-lettered title on the spine. "*The Bell of Chaos.*"

"By none other than that great peacock himself, Sebastian J. Quinn."

Candy tilted her head thoughtfully as she flipped through the pages. "Why would Sapphire have this?"

"Maybe she's a lover of bad poetry."

"Or maybe she was doing research on the judges." As Candy flipped through it, the book's pages fell open to a section in back, revealing a yellowed newspaper clipping tucked inside. "What's this?" Curiously she pulled it out and unfolded it.

Maggie crowded in next to her, reading over her shoulder. After a moment she said, "It looks like an obituary."

"It is." Candy scanned down through the clipping. "Somebody named David Squires. Looks like he died in a car accident. Almost twenty years ago, according to the date."

"A friend of Sapphire's?"

Candy shrugged, and started folding the clipping back up, then stopped. Suddenly curious, she unfolded it again, this time studying it more closely. She pointed with her pinky at the faded photo of David Squires that accompanied the article. "Does he look familiar to you?" He was a handsome, curly haired young man wearing a coat and tie; the photo had obviously been taken for his high school yearbook, when he had been a senior.

Maggie leaned in closer, scrutinizing the photo. After a few moments her face lit up. "He's the same kid we saw in the photo downstairs with Sapphire!"

Candy nodded. "I think you're right."

"So now we know what happened to him," Maggie said softly.

"That we do." Candy finally folded up the

newspaper clipping, placed it inside the book, and laid it on the desktop. "So that's one mystery solved — sort of. But there are plenty more that need figuring out. Let's keep looking."

"Righto!" As Maggie bounced away to continue her snooping, Candy turned back to the cardboard filing cabinet. She took a moment to orient herself, glancing at the labels on the manila folders. Yes, she realized almost immediately, these were all the files she had been seeking.

Toward the front she found a file devoted to each of the Blueberry Queen Pageant contestants, including Amanda. Maggie would want to see that one. Candy pulled it out and set it on top of the makeshift desk, beside the copy of Sebastian J. Quinn's book of poetry.

Behind the contestants' files were a thick file on Mrs. Pruitt, and a separate, much thinner one for Hobbins the butler. *Those two files will bear checking out later,* Candy thought. *Probably some real interesting stuff in there.* She pulled them out as well.

Paging on back, she came to a file on Jock Larson. That caught her attention. What had Sapphire known about Jock? Probably a lot, Candy guessed. She pulled it out and flipped open the cover. Inside she found a stack of lined yellow pages filled with Sapphire's neat handwriting, and long lists of names, dates, times, addresses, phone numbers, license plate numbers, family histories, even notes on what Jock and his various female companions had been wearing when they had been spied upon by Sapphire. Candy thumbed randomly back through the pages, spotting a vaguely familiar name here and there, though most of the notes seemed to predate her arrival in Cape Willington. The most recent entry was dated about six months earlier.

Failing to find anything particularly revealing, she was about to flip the folder closed when she noticed a small plastic ziplock bag tucked in the back. It looked empty, but when Candy lifted it out and gingerly held it up to the light, she saw that it contained a few strands of long white hair.

She puzzled over that for a moment, then placed the bag back in the folder, closed it, and set it aside with the others, planning to examine it more closely later. For now, she turned her attention back to the file cabinet. She continued on toward the back, her fingers tugging at the well-worn manila folders, glancing at the names on the neatly hand-printed labels. There were no other files on her or Doc, or on Maggie, thank goodness, but she found another one on Cameron, which she pulled out. A bit further on, she found one on Ben Clayton, which she also removed, thinking it could make interesting reading. No doubt Sapphire had collected a few tasty secrets about tall, handsome Ben.

At the very back she found a folder devoted to each of the Blueberry Queen Pageant judges, including Oliver LaForce, the owner of the Lightkeeper's Inn, and even one on Sebastian J. Quinn. And at the very back, a thick file on Herr Georg.

Hesitating just a moment, Candy pulled the file out and flipped open the cover. More e-mails to and from Sapphire and BAK1946 — obviously Herr Georg. These were more direct and threatening than the others Candy had seen. She shuffled back through the folder. Obscure newspaper clippings, apparently decades old. Fuzzy photocopies of what looked like birth records in German. And then something that surprised her: documents that looked like genealogical and military records, some with the swastika stamped ominously at the top of the page.

As she worked her way back through the documents, Candy's dread grew. She wondered how Sapphire had gotten her hands on all this material — and if, finally, here was a real motive for murder. It all began to make sense. If Sapphire, with her relentless digging, had turned up some dark secret from Herr Georg's past, had she used that knowledge to blackmail him? And had that driven him to the unthinkable?

Candy shuddered, knowing what her next step would have to be.

She was still scanning the documents when Maggie spoke out in shock. "Oh my God!"

Candy started, her gaze shooting to Maggie. "What? What's wrong?"

Maggie was standing beside the twin mattress, bending over it. She held up a discarded Phish T-shirt and a well-worn Red Sox baseball cap. "Cameron was here!"

"What?"

She shook the items she held, the distress evident on her face. "These belong to Cameron!"

"Cameron who?"

"Our Cameron! *My* Cameron. Cameron Zimmerman!"

Candy shook her head. "That's crazy. You're jumping to conclusions. Those clothes could belong to anyone."

"They belong to *Cameron*. I've seen him *wearing* them. Plus, his *initials* are on the headband inside the cap."

Candy shook her head in confusion. "That doesn't make any sense. What would they be doing up here? You think Sapphire stole them from him?"

"No! Don't you see? Cameron was *here!*" Maggie pointed emphatically to the bed. "He's *slept* here!"

"Here?" Candy's gaze was drawn inexorably to the bed. "But why would he . . . ?"

Maggie rolled her eyes. "Don't you get it?"

"Get what?"

"It's simple! Cameron and Sapphire were having an affair!"

TWENTY-FOUR

A sudden gust of wind rattled the old house. Candy glanced uneasily up at the ceiling, then back at Maggie, making a face that communicated her disbelief. "You can't be serious."

"I'm totally serious! The evidence is right here. This must have been their secret love shack!"

Candy's response was a muted half laugh. "Do you know how crazy that sounds? I mean, come on! Cameron's barely eighteen. What would he ever see in Sapphire? He's much too young for her."

"She's a cradle robber! I always knew she was creepy!"

Candy shook her head. "I don't believe a word of it. There must be some other explanation. Maybe . . ."

But she gulped down her words as they heard a door open and then close somewhere downstairs.

For a moment Candy and Maggie stared at each other in shocked silence. Then Maggie hissed, "Someone's here!"

"Douse the lights!"

"We're trapped!"

"Shh. No one knows we're up here. Just keep cool and we'll be fine."

They switched off their flashlights, drifted back into the low corners of the room, and waited.

They could hear footsteps walking through the house two floors below.

"Should we turn out that other light?" Maggie whispered from her hiding place, motioning to the floor lamp.

"No, just leave it on."

"The trap door's still open!" Maggie started toward it, but Candy urged her back.

"Just leave it alone! Don't make a sound."

Maggie edged back into her corner, crouched, and waited.

Heavy footsteps were coming up the stairs, two at a time.

"They're coming up!"

"Shh!"

Maggie shushed, though Candy could hear her whimpering quietly. They both waited nervously. The footsteps were closer now, turning into the bedroom below. Candy's heart thumped in her chest and blood rushed through her ears. What if it was someone dangerous? What if the person who had killed Sapphire — not Ray, but the *real* killer — had come to kill *them?*

Candy looked around for a weapon as she heard the footsteps enter the closet and pause just below the trap door.

She spotted a camera tripod near her, tucked into the corner. Carefully she picked it up and held it in her right hand, ready to swing if necessary. It wasn't the best weapon in the world, but it was metal and it was hard and it would do in a pinch.

And they were definitely in a pinch.

She heard someone climbing the ladder, slowly, cautiously. Candy shrank back into the shadows as far as she could go, her gaze riveted on the opening in the floor not six feet from her.

A shaggy head popped up. "Is someone up here?" a nervous male voice asked.

For a moment there was no answer. Then Maggie said in disbelief, from the other side of the room, "Cameron? Is that you?"

"Mrs. Tremont?" He was halfway up the ladder. Only his head and shoulders emerged through the opening, but it was enough.

Maggie stepped from her hiding place and gasped. "It *is* you! I can't believe it! What are you doing here?"

"What are *you* doing here?" Instead of sounding surprised, his tone was accusatory.

"What do you think we're doing? We're snooping around."

"We? Who else . . . ?" His head swiveled around and he saw Candy. A dark look came to his eyes. "Who said you could do that?"

"We're trying to find out who murdered Sapphire," Candy said, sounding apologetic.

"I didn't do it!"

"No one said you did."

"Then why are you . . . ?"

But before he could finish, Maggie cut in. "Are you sleeping here?" she demanded to know, pointing to the bed.

At first he seemed surprised by the question, but then his face grew hard. "What if I am?"

"Cameron . . ." Candy set the tripod down and took a step toward him. "We're just trying to find out what's going on here."

"Well I don't know," he said stubbornly.

"But your things are here. Your clothes."

"Were you and Sapphire Vine having an affair?" Maggie asked hotly.

"What?"

"You heard me, mister! Answer my question. Were you and Sapphire fooling around?"

His head shook furiously and he glared at her. "You're crazy!"

"Don't you talk to me in that kind of voice, young man."

"I can talk to you any way I want! You're not my mother."

"Cameron, I want some answers and I want them now!"

"I'm leaving!"

"Don't you dare . . ."

But it was too late. Cameron had dropped back down the ladder. Candy could hear his footsteps retreating back across the bedroom, out into the hall, and down the stairs.

"Cameron! Wait!" Maggie dashed to the opening and started down after him. "Don't you run away from me!"

Candy heard him shout something back at her, but the words were muffled. A few moments later the back door opened again. Maggie's shouts could be heard as she ran out into the backyard after him.

"Oh boy. What a mess." Candy shook her head in disbelief, knowing the neighbors might have heard all the commotion. "Time to get out of here."

She started toward the trap door but

turned back, her mind working furiously. She didn't want to leave anything here that might incriminate them. She spotted her tote bag sitting on the floor near the desk, right where she had left it. She crossed to it, picked it up along with her flashlight and gloves, and started to leave.

But she turned back again. She looked at the files on the desk. She should put them back into the filing cabinet, she thought, just in case someone else found this place. She could try to get a look at them later.

But immediately she reconsidered that. Who knew when she would have a chance to sneak in here again? And who knew if the files would be here if she made it back?

Better, she thought, just to take them with her. No one knew they were here anyway, she rationalized. No one would ever know they were missing.

She tried not to think about the consequences of removing evidence from the scene of a crime. Before she changed her mind again, she stepped back to the desk, picked up Jock's and Herr Georg's files, and stuffed them into the tote bag. Then she added others — files for Amanda and Cameron, Mrs. Pruitt and Hobbins, and tall, handsome Ben. They fit snugly, but she got them all in.

Her gaze darted across the desk. She grabbed the address book too and tucked the Rolodex under her arm.

Before she left, she spotted one more thing she decided she wanted to take with her — the photo album with Susan Jane Vincent's name on it.

That was all she could carry. After a last look around, she quickly dropped down the ladder, pulling the trap door closed after her, and dashed down the stairs. She pulled on her shoes by the back door and ducked out under the police tape. Then, pushing the lock button on the door knob and shutting the back door tightly behind her, she raced out into the dark backyard.

TWENTY-FIVE

The phone rang at just after eight in the morning. Jolted out of a deep sleep, Candy groaned as she reached over and blindly grabbed for the receiver. "Hello?"

"Good morning, *liebchen!*"

"Herr Georg?"

"Yes, Candy, it's me. How are you today? I hope I didn't wake you. Were you asleep?"

"Um, no, well, actually I was just getting up."

"Oh dear. Should I call back?"

"No, no, that's okay." Rubbing her eyes, she sat up, threw her legs over the side of the bed, and pushed her hair back from her forehead. "What's going on?"

"I have a favor to ask. Rosemary, my regular girl, can't make it in today. She's out sick, or so she says, though I doubt that. It's a suspiciously nice day. Still, she won't be in, and I need counter help for a few hours while I'm in the kitchen. I don't suppose you'd be willing to come in and help out?"

Candy squinted at the clock. "What time do you need me?"

"Around nine?"

"I'll be there."

"My *liebchen,* you are an angel!"

"I'm glad to help out." She didn't mention she was secretly relieved he had called. She had been trying to figure out how to approach him about what she had seen in his file the night before.

"Fine, fine. See you in an hour. Thank you so much!"

She started to say more but held back. She decided it would be best to wait until she could talk to him face-to-face to ask him the questions she really didn't want to ask.

But as difficult as she knew it was going to be, she had to confront him about the documents she found the night before — or, to be accurate, the ones Sapphire had found. Though many of the faded, yellowed documents were in German, which she couldn't read, she had a good idea of what they said, and they greatly disturbed her. They raised more questions than they answered — and led her to conclusions she refused to accept.

Ever since she first heard about the violent death of Sapphire Vine, Candy had been trying to fit the pieces together, to unravel the mystery of not only *who* murdered Sapphire (for Candy was now more convinced than ever that Ray had *not* done it) but also *why* she was murdered.

Now she had at least one possible answer — but she didn't like it at all.

As much as she hated to admit it, Herr Georg seemed to be the one with the most to gain by Sapphire's death. That troubled Candy more than she could say. It actually made her heart ache, for she couldn't imagine Herr Georg doing anything so destructive.

But she had seen the e-mails, documents, and newspaper clippings herself. They were all there in the file, which still sat on her kitchen table, evidence of a hidden past that just possibly was a motive for murder.

Following her adventure with Maggie at Sapphire's house the night before, she had arrived back home at some time after one in the morning. She had been dead-flat exhausted and upset with herself over how the whole thing ended.

By the time she had dashed out the back door of Sapphire's house and into the yard, Cameron was long gone. She finally found

311

Maggie wandering around blindly in the dark woods, desperately searching for the teenager. But it soon became evident he wouldn't be found that night, so reluctantly they gave up the search. They had found what they came for and decided it was time to disappear into the night before anyone else stumbled upon their questionable activities.

So, emotionally and physically drained, they had trudged back to the Jeep, Candy lugging the bulging tote bag heavy with files and papers.

"That was . . . fun," Maggie said on the way home, sounding not at all convincing. "We really should do that again sometime — like maybe in a decade or two."

Candy had been too tired to smile. "I think our burgling career started and ended tonight."

"You are *so* right about that."

Once back at Blueberry Acres, Candy had emptied the tote bag of files onto the kitchen table, sat wearily, and spent the next half hour or so paging through Herr Georg's file, trying to decipher some of the ancient, faded German documents within. But when she nearly fell asleep at the table, she finally gave up and crawled into bed.

Now it seemed that, much sooner than

she expected, she would have a chance to talk to Herr Georg about what she had found.

As she rose, showered, dressed, and headed down to the kitchen, her mind was already churning, trying to figure out how she was going to broach the subject with him.

Downstairs, Doc was drinking a cup of coffee at the kitchen table. Sapphire's files were piled neatly on the table in front of him. Candy couldn't remember leaving them like that. Her brow furrowed as she realized Doc must have been looking through them. By the look on his face she knew instantly that he disapproved.

In silence, Candy walked to the counter, dropped a slice of bread into the toaster, and poured a cup of coffee. She moved about silverware and saucers and glasses, trying to fill the uncomfortable quietness. All the while she kept her back to Doc, but she could feel his eyes on her. She had seen him in these moods before — though rarely — and she wasn't quite sure what to expect.

But there was no way around it. She had to face him. She turned, holding the cup of coffee up toward her face with two hands. He was looking right at her.

He pointed with the subtlest of gestures

toward the files on the table. "What have you been up to?"

For a moment she was a child again, a little girl being admonished by her stern father. Old feelings she hadn't experienced in decades sprang into her heart and mind. But then she reminded herself that she was a woman in her thirties, responsible for her own decisions, and that she had made those decisions for a very good reason.

"Dad, I'm trying to save Ray."

"And these will help?" Doc tilted his head toward the files.

"They might. I think so, yes."

Doc didn't ask where the files came from; he seemed to know that answer — or if he didn't, he didn't seem to care. It was obvious that his concern was for Candy, and for her alone. With a foot he reached under the table and kicked back one of the chairs. "Have a seat."

Candy looked at him suspiciously. "Okaaay."

"I just want to talk for a few minutes," Doc said as she sat down.

Candy placed the coffee cup on the table before her. "About what?"

"About you."

"Me? What about me?"

"To be honest . . . I'm worried about you,"

Doc said.

The toast popped up then, and Candy jumped up to place it on a plate and butter it. "Why are you worried about me?" she asked over her shoulder as she worked.

Doc sighed and waited until she had settled herself again, then leaned forward and folded his hands on the table in front of him. "Are you happy?"

Candy had taken a bite of the toast but stopped chewing at the question. "Am I happy?" she repeated with her mouth full, looking just a bit unglamorous.

"This whole thing with Sapphire and Ray, and the way you've become so . . . involved in it. It's got me to thinking."

Candy started chewing again, and this time swallowed before she spoke. "Dad, what's on your mind?" She glanced at the clock on the wall. "I have to leave soon. Herr Georg needs me to work in the shop."

Doc nodded in acknowledgment, then got quickly to the point. "I've been watching you all week, and I realized that I haven't seen you this dedicated to anything in a long time, not since you've moved up here — except for those damned chickens of yours. And it's got me to thinking. Maybe you're so involved with this Ray thing because you, well, because you haven't had much direction in your life recently."

Candy rolled her eyes. "Dad . . ."

Doc held up a hand. "Now hear me out. This is something I've got to say." He took a deep breath, then continued. "When you were a little girl, you didn't seem to know what you wanted to do when you grew up. Other little girls wanted to be teachers or doctors or lawyers or movie stars, but you had a hard time figuring it all out. Your mother and I were worried a bit about you then, but we knew eventually you'd find your way. And you did in college. You discovered a career, and then you met Clark, and for a while your life seemed to be on a fast track."

"You're right about that," Candy said, finishing up the last few bites of toast and wiping her hands with a paper napkin as she glanced at the clock again.

Doc knew his time was running out, but he refused to be hurried. "And then life took some hard turns, for both you and me. I want you to know," he said, reaching across the table to rest his hand on one of hers, "that having you move in here with me was one of the best things to happen to me in a long time. I've loved having you around again. But I can't help wondering . . ." He paused, hesitant to go on, then said finally,

"Well, I can't help wondering if you're here more for me than for yourself."

Candy started to protest, but Doc went on, quickly now. "You need more in your life than just me, sweetie. But it's more than that," he said before she could get anything out. "I have to ask — or I think you have to ask — what do you want to do with your life?"

Candy almost laughed, though she held back because she knew her father was serious. She thought a moment, then rose, placed her coffee cup in the sink, and returned to the table. She kissed her father on the forehead and held up his chin as she looked into his eyes. "Dad, I think it's really sweet you're concerned about my life, but don't worry so much. I'm just fine."

Doc smiled up at her. "I just want you to be happy, pumpkin."

"I know. Me too." Candy kissed him again, then grabbed her purse and a manila envelope from the table by the back door. "I hate to run, but Herr Georg's waiting for me. We'll talk later, okay?"

"Okay." After a brief pause he added, "Just take care of yourself."

"I will." And with that she was out the door. She jumped into the Jeep, headed down the dirt road toward town, and a few minutes before nine, she walked into the Black Forest Bakery on Main Street.

Herr Georg was in the back kitchen, wearing a long white apron and a chef's hat, his hands covered with flour. When he saw her, a wide smile broke out on his face beneath the curling white moustache.

"Ahh, Candy, there you are, just in time," he greeted her as she dropped her purse and the manila envelope onto a cane chair in a corner.

She said hello, and as she grabbed an apron and tied it about her waist, she added hesitantly, "I have something I need to talk to you about when we have a break."

"Yes, yes, of course. We'll have some time later. Have you had breakfast?"

"Just a cup of coffee and a piece of toast."

He clucked at her with his tongue. "Candy, Candy, that is not enough for you! You are a grown woman! You dash about here and there! You need something to help you keep your energy level up. Here, try one of these. I just took them from the oven." He handed her a raspberry cheese croissant oozing warm filling and giving off that luscious, just-baked smell, so powerful and redolent it almost made her dizzy.

Light, flaky, and golden brown, it practically melted in her mouth. "Hmm, hmm,

hmm. It's a good thing I don't work here regularly," she told him as she licked her lips and savored each bite, "or I wouldn't be able to fit through your shop's front door, that's for sure. Besides, I'd probably eat through all your profits!"

He laughed heartily, his eyes twinkling, just as the bell over the front door tinkled. Candy quickly finished the croissant and wiped her hands on her apron. "The first customer of the day," she announced as she darted out to the front counter.

A flood of customers, as it turned out, came through the door, one after another, keeping her quite busy for the next few hours, and the morning passed in a rush. At times it reminded her of a feeding frenzy of great white sharks, and she was the chum. The smells coming out of the kitchen were heavenly, spurring on the near-rabid customers, who kept Candy hustling as she filled dozens and dozens of white bakery bags with Herr Georg's delicacies and rang up sales on the old register. While the customers browsed and sampled the pastries, they sipped tea and coffee and chatted about family, friends, and work. In amongst the talk about the weather, the summer traffic, vacation plans, and the score of the latest Red Sox game, there were worried glances and whispers about Sapphire Vine, Ray Hutchins, and Jock Larson. Murder was still a topic that occupied the minds of many Capers, but few seemed willing to discuss the terrible events of the past week out in the open, preferring to talk in the far corners of the room, in lowered tones, so as not to disturb the more sensitive among Herr Georg's patrons.

As noon approached, the steady onslaught of customers slowed, and by one o'clock thinned to a trickle. Herr Georg picked up the phone, called Duffy's, and ordered deli sandwiches and salads for lunch. Then, the morning's baking done, he wandered out into the front room to check on Candy and the day's sales.

"We've had a busy morning," she said, showing him the sales register receipts.

"Hmm, yes, that's very good. It's all the tourists, you know. They're always hungry."

Fifteen minutes later, a delivery boy dropped off their sandwiches and salads. Herr Georg suggested they eat at a small table in the back room.

As they sat, Candy decided that the time to confront him had finally come.

"Herr Georg," she began, "I have something to talk to you about — something that's been bothering me."

"Yes?" He looked at her inquisitively as he took a bite of his smoked turkey and Swiss cheese sandwich, piled high with lettuce and tomato.

Candy hesitated. "Well, it's about Sapphire Vine."

That seemed to suck the life right out of him. The energy and optimism he had exhibited all morning disappeared in a flash, and his expression became solemn. He set his sandwich down on its wrapper. He seemed to have suddenly lost his appetite. "What about her?"

Candy took a deep breath, then plunged on, explaining how she had been hired to write a column for the *Cape Crier,* and that she was given access to Sapphire's files. She left out the part about breaking into Sapphire's house the night before, but told him that, much to her regret, she had come across a file that contained damaging information about him. She reached for the manila envelope, opened the flap, and withdrew a handful of yellowed, crinkly documents, which she handed to him. "I found these."

His face went white. He seemed to know in an instant what they were. He took them from her as if they contained his death warrant, and read over them silently for some time, his lips tight, his eyes dark and hollow. "So," he said finally, letting out a long breath as he set the documents down on the table, "it is true then. I hoped it was all a bluff."

"What's true? What's going on?" She felt a chill go through her. "This doesn't have anything to do with Sapphire's death, does it?"

He looked up at her, horror-stricken. "Oh no, of course not! Nothing like that!"

"Then what?" Candy's tone was sympathetic. She reached out and put her hand on top of his. She couldn't help noticing that, despite the warmth of the day, his hand was cold. "I'm not sure what this is about, but if there's any way I can help . . ."

He held her gaze for the longest time, as if considering what to tell her. Finally he nodded once, as if he had made a decision. He rose. "Come, we must talk."

TWENTY-SIX

Leaving their half-eaten sandwiches and the yellowed German documents behind, Herr Georg took her by the hand and walked to the front door. He flipped the OPEN sign that hung in the door window around so it read CLOSED, walked outside with Candy, and locked the door behind them.

"You're closing in the middle of the day?" she asked him curiously.

"I must be outside, away from here, to talk about these things," Herr Georg told her with a hesitant shrug. "This is more important than a few extra dollars, and it's such a nice day. Let's walk."

Sensing the import of what he was about to tell her, she let him lead the way. "Okay, let's walk."

With an expressionless face, he started off. Saying barely a word to each other, they crossed Main Street and angled toward Ocean Avenue, which was busy with pedestrians window-shopping and scurrying about. It was a warm day with clouds building overhead. The humidity was on the rise, and the air was sharp with the unmistakable tang of salt and the sea. A flock of gulls arced above, cawing in their hunger and unending quest for sustenance.

As he walked, Herr Georg kept his head turned down, his hands clasped firmly behind his back. Candy tagged along as they turned down Ocean Avenue, passed the doorway that led up to the *Cape Crier*'s offices and, a little farther on, the glass front of Stone & Milbury's. They crossed the street in front of the Pruitt Opera House and walked the rest of the way down the avenue, to Town Park.

With the dull roar of the rolling sea in their ears, they strolled past well-kept flower beds and over freshly mown grass, until Herr Georg spotted a bench in the shade of a thick oak tree. He approached it purposefully, sat down, and beckoned Candy to sit beside him.

"Do you know why I came here? Here, to Cape Willington?" he asked after they had settled themselves. When Candy shook her head, he gave her a melancholy smile. "No one knows, of course, except me — and, for a time, Sapphire Vine. But she is gone now.

I had hoped that my secret would die with her, but it appears now that it will live on."

He let out a tired breath. "I have run from that secret all my life. It is time for me to tell the story, to let it out into the world, for good or bad."

Candy sensed the turmoil going through him. She felt deep regret at having brought the whole subject up in the first place. But, she reminded herself sadly, she had had no choice. She was on a quest to know the truth — and to save Ray. Still . . .

"Herr Georg, you don't have to tell me if . . ."

He held up a hand, silencing her. "You're right. I *don't* have to tell you. But I *want* to. I have kept it inside for too long. The time has come for the story to be told. And you are the one I must tell it to, Candy. I am *compelled* to tell it, you understand, with all that has happened this week. You have been a good friend to me. I know I can trust you."

"Of course you can trust me," she said, "no matter what it is."

He patted her hand. "I know, I know. But the story I have to tell is a painful one for me. It eats at my soul. You see," he said, and his gaze shifted, out to the sea, far off to the east, "I was born on the other side of that ocean, on the distant shore, in Germany, just after the war — in the town of Wittenberg, along the Elbe River, southeast of Hamburg. I don't remember much of my life there. Oh, small snips and bits here and there, a fleeting memory or two, but most of it is lost to me. My mother fled our home country a few years after the end of the war, taking me with her."

"World War II?" Candy asked in clarification.

"Yes, yes, of course. I was born in 1946. We left in forty-eight. Not because we had to, but because my mother wanted to take me away from the fatherland — and away from my father." Herr Georg's gaze shifted back to her, and he looked hard into Candy's eyes, unwilling to run anymore from his past. "My father was a war criminal — or so I was told by my mother, in her last breaths, before she passed from this earth. She told me he committed terrible atrocities — awful, terrible things — for which he was arrested and tried after the war. It was a dreadful time in our country's history. My mother, to shield me from what was happening, to protect me from the repercussions of what might occur because of my father's acts, took me first to England, then brought me here, to the United States, hoping to start a new life. And together we did just that."

Herr Georg's gaze shifted away again as he went on. "We took a steamer to New York City, where we lived for a few years. I remember the transatlantic passage well, and many of my earliest memories are of that city. We changed our name, tried to start a new life — but our history was soon discovered. The sins of my father followed us to our adopted country. So we moved again, northward — to Worcester, then to Lewiston, and finally to Calais, at the far eastern edge of Maine — as far as we could go and still remain in this country. My mother loved it there — she said she felt as close to the fatherland as she could be and still live in America. You see, even though she hated what her country had done, she never forgot her heritage, and she would not let me forget it. To make ends meet, she worked as a cook, then as a baker. She was quite accomplished and made a small name for herself, and so I learned from her. When she died I came here, because I loved this village when I visited once with my mother. I love the sea, and I loved the people here. And here I have been ever since — and my secret has remained buried . . . until Sapphire Vine started digging around in my past."

"How did she find out about it?" Candy asked in a hushed tone.

Herr Georg shrugged. "Who knows? She was a gossip, you know — she talked to so many people. Somehow, somewhere, she heard rumors about me, or read something about me that sparked her curiosity — I don't know for certain — but she soon found out about my past, and my father's atrocities. One day — five years ago or so — she confronted me, almost as you just did in the shop. She told me she had evidence — documents. I didn't believe her at first. I told her she was mistaken. Then she showed me one of them. She had many more, she said. I didn't know whether to believe her or not, but I could not take the chance."

Candy felt a flash of anger go through her. "What an awful woman!"

"Oh yes, she certainly was that," Herr Georg said, "and much worse than you even know. You see, she threatened to reveal what she had discovered about me — that my father was a Nazi war criminal. Of course, I couldn't let that information get out to the public — I have a reputation to protect, you know, one that I have spent many years building. If such a story were to leak out, I would be ruined."

"So what happened?"

Herr Georg sighed and shook his head. "What could I do? I offered to pay her to keep her silent."

"She blackmailed you?"

"Yes, blackmail."

"And she's been blackmailing you ever since?"

He nodded.

"How much have you paid her?"

Herr Georg shrugged. "Thousands, perhaps tens of thousands. I honestly don't know. Every few months, when she needed money, she would call me up or send an e-mail. And not just money. The woman was relentless."

It took a moment for the rest of Herr Georg's statement to register with her, and like a knife it struck her deep. Instantly she knew what he was talking about. She couldn't help gasping. "Not just money? You mean the pageant!"

Herr Georg's head fell again. Almost imperceptibly, he nodded.

Candy quickly put it together. "She threatened to reveal your past . . . unless you rigged the scoring so she would win!"

Herr Georg shook his head. "Oh no, no, nothing as conspiratorial as that! Yes, I gave her much higher scores than she deserved, and I scored the other contestants lower than they deserved. But that is all. I didn't change the scores for the other judges! You must believe me, Candy, when I tell you that I didn't think it would make any difference. I honestly didn't! I thought my scores would have no effect on the outcome of the pageant. There were four other judges. I was certain Haley would win by enough points that mine wouldn't alter the outcome."

He raised his eyebrows, let out a breath. "But, of course, it did. I have lived with this terrible thing I have done ever since."

"Herr Georg, I . . . I don't know what to say."

"Please, Candy, don't think ill of me. I had no choice. I had to do as she asked. You see that, don't you?"

"Well," Candy said after many long moments, "I can understand why you voted for Sapphire, yes, and why you gave her money. But it was a foolish thing to do in the first place. No one cares about your past. It wouldn't have mattered to anyone. And now — well, now you're in a tight spot. You realize that if the police find out about this, you will become the prime suspect in Sapphire's death. After all, you had motive. You're the only person so far who's had good reason to see Sapphire dead."

He turned to her then, a pleading look in his eyes. "But they must not find out about this, Candy. They must not! I despised Sapphire, yes — I hated what she was doing to me. But I didn't kill her! I could never do such a thing! You must believe me!"

For whatever reason, Candy knew he was telling the truth. "I believe you, Herr Georg — I really do — but the question is, will anyone else? And there's another question that's even more important."

"What's that?"

"Well, if you didn't kill Sapphire, and Ray didn't . . . who did?"

TWENTY-SEVEN

Who did?

Who really killed Susan Jane Vincent, alias Sapphire Vine, the Blueberry Queen of Cape Willington, Maine?

That was the question that plagued Candy as she and Herr Georg walked back up Ocean Avenue to the Black Forest. They spoke little now, both of them lost in their thoughts. When they reached the bakery, as Herr Georg nervously tidied up around the front counter and checked on his wares, Candy walked into the back room, gathered up the faded documents from the table where she had left them, walked back out into the front room, and handed the documents to the baker.

"You should have these," she told him.

He hesitated before reaching for them. "Candy, are you sure you want to do this?"

She nodded. "I'll give you all the other documents as well. I've got them back at the house. You can decide what to do with them. It's not up to me — and now that Sapphire's gone, your secret is safe. Let's talk about it no more."

And they didn't. Since Herr Georg had finished in the kitchen, and the crowds had lightened considerably since the morning rush, Candy gave Herr Georg a hug, and walked out into the summer day.

As she headed up the street to her car, she felt she had done the right thing in returning the documents to Herr Georg. Still, now that she had left his shop, she couldn't keep a lingering doubt from creeping in. His story made sense and the documents appeared to back it up. And if he was indeed telling the truth, as she honestly felt he was, then it followed logically that Sapphire found out about his past and blackmailed him. After all, she had all those documents in her possession, which made Herr Georg's story all the more likely.

But the fact remained that Sapphire Vine was dead. Someone had killed her. And though Candy found it not only absurd but also literally painful to think that Herr Georg could have plunged a hammer into the back of Sapphire's head (not to mention how painful it must have been for Sapphire herself), the fact remained that he had an excellent motive for doing just that.

As Candy reached the Jeep Cherokee, she was torn as to what to do next. She toyed briefly with the idea of walking to the *Cape Crier* office to drop in on Ben and find out if he had heard anything new about the investigation into Sapphire's murder, but she decided against it. She hadn't started working on her column yet, which was due to Ben on Monday. She hadn't given much thought to it at all. She knew he would ask about it, and it probably wasn't the best idea to tell Ben she had made no progress whatsoever. He had enough to worry about; she didn't want to add to his concerns.

So that was out.

She thought of walking over to Duffy's or stopping in to see Maggie, but decided against both of those also. She realized that conversation was not what she sought at the moment — what she needed was to be alone, to think, to sort out all the details of Sapphire's death, to mull over all she had learned during the past few days.

So she pulled her keys out of her purse, hopped in the Jeep, and drove down Ocean Avenue to Waterfront Walk, a public park area with a half mile gravel pathway that meandered along the salt-sprayed shoreline. The path was lined with teaberry bushes and thick stands of rosehips, fragrant with summer blossoms, and benches were located at strategic places all along the walk, affording magnificent views of the coastline and the sea beyond.

She parked in the lot and, climbing out of the Jeep, was immediately assaulted by a stiff sea breeze thick with the smell of fish and salt. She walked a short distance, hands pushed deep into the pockets of her jeans, finally settling onto a lonely bench that looked out over the churning waves.

Mentally she began to form a list of all she had learned so far. Her thoughts went something like this:

- Sapphire had been killed by someone using a red-handled hammer bought at Gumm's Hardware Store. In all, three of the suspect hammers had been sold — one to Ray, one to Ned Winetrop, and one to Hobbins the butler up at Pruitt Manor. Ray's hammer was allegedly found at the scene of the crime. Ned lost his hammer on Saturday while he was at Town Hall working on the pageant set. Hobbins still had his hammer and was using it around Pruitt Manor.
- Ray was at Sapphire's house the night

she was killed — he didn't deny that. Neighbors saw his truck there and heard Sapphire yelling at him.

- Ray had a big-time — and expensive — lawyer from Bangor who was being paid by Mrs. Pruitt. The lawyer was associated with the firm that handled Mrs. Pruitt's business affairs.

- Sapphire kept secret files on everyone in town, including Jock, Mrs. Pruitt, Amanda, Cameron, Herr Georg, Ben, Sebastian J. Quinn, all of the pageant contestants and judges, even on Candy herself. Sapphire hid the files in a secret attic room that was known only to her and, apparently, to Cameron.

- Sapphire used the information she had collected to blackmail Herr Georg into altering his scores so she could win the pageant, though Herr Georg seemed to think his scores alone could not have affected the eventual outcome.

- Cameron had been shocked to hear about Sapphire's death. And he had been staying in her attic, apparently sleeping there on occasion. He worked at Gumm's and had sold two of the red-handled hammers to customers. He had access to all of the new hammers.

- At the bottom of one of the papers in Cameron's file, Sapphire had written the words *He's the one.*
- Sapphire's real name was Susan Jane Vincent. She changed it at some point in her life, evidently before she had moved to Cape Willington. One reason she may have had for changing her name was to escape some past indiscretion, or perhaps even criminal activity.
- Mrs. Pruitt strongly believed that somehow, some way, Sapphire rigged the pageant — bribed or blackmailed one or more of the judges. She had been right about that, of course, though she knew nothing about Herr Georg and his past.

That was a pretty accurate list, Candy thought. But there was something else — something Doc had said to her. What was it?

She wracked her brain, trying to remember.

And then it struck her. A fort! What had Doc told her? That's right, she remembered now: *They've been interrogating Ray,* Doc had said, *and apparently he keeps repeating the same thing over and over. Says he didn't do it and says it's up at the fort.*

What had Ray meant by that? What exactly was up at the fort? And what fort was he talking about?

Doc hadn't known. The police hadn't known. Candy had suggested Fort O'Brien, located up the coast near Machias, the county seat. Fort O'Brien dated back to the Revolutionary War days and was now just old ruins, but it was a popular historic site, with picnic tables, a few trails, and magnificent views of Machias Bay.

But what could those old ruins possibly have to do with Ray?

As far as Candy knew, he rarely left town. Why would he have gone up to an old fort? And if he had, what would he have hidden up there?

Candy rubbed her cheeks absently as she thought and stared out to the sea. There had to be an explanation, had to be an answer to this puzzle. But she just couldn't figure it out.

Maybe, she thought, she should drive up to Fort O'Brien and have a look around, to see what she could find.

But she shook her head. She sensed that would be a worthless trip — a wild-goose chase. Her instincts told her that the answers she sought were right here, in Cape Willington. She just had to find them.

All of the questions that charged around her mind led back to one person — Ray Hutchins. *He* was the person at the center of this whole mess. *He* was the one who allegedly owned the hammer that killed Sapphire Vine. *He* had been at her house the night of her murder. *He* was the one sitting in the county jail, charged with her murder.

Ray, she decided, was the key. And she had to follow that key wherever it led.

Suddenly she knew what she had to do. Rising purposefully from the bench, she walked briskly to the Jeep, climbed in, started it up, and drove back out onto the Loop. She headed south. The road curved around southwestward, taking her past Pruitt Manor, and then angled northwestward, past the Lobster Shack, past a thin strip of sand that was the town beach, and back up the Cape. She drove out of town, and kept going.

Ten minutes later she turned off the main road onto a dusty lane that led back to an old two-bedroom shack, which sat on a deserted piece of land framed by stands of old pines and low bushes.

Ray's home.

He had lived here with his mother when she had been alive, and by himself for the past three or four years. It was a sad, lonely looking place, without much character. The little house did have a fresh coat of dull gray paint on it and a porch swing that looked like something Andy Griffith might have sat on in the evenings with Aunt Bee. A rusty old pickup, much older than Doc's, sat up on blocks, its tires missing. In front of the house and off to one side was a small, weathered barn with a roof so swaybacked that it seemed it would collapse at any moment.

Candy pulled up in front of the house and shut off the engine. She sat for a moment looking around, feeling strangely out of place. She had been here a few times before, but always with Doc, and always when Ray was around. Being here now, alone, with Ray in jail and the place empty and ghost-like made her feel like a trespasser.

But no, it was nothing like that, she reminded herself. She was here to *help* Ray, not to foreclose on his property or tear it down. She was here to *investigate.*

So investigate she would.

Cautiously she climbed out of the Jeep. Birds sang in the high trees. The barn door's rusted hinges creaked slightly in the breeze. Sounds of cars passing by on the Loop were faintly audible.

Candy slammed shut the car door and walked around to one side of Ray's old house, squinting up at it, studying it as if she were a prospective buyer considering its aesthetic value. It looked smaller than she remembered. There couldn't have been more than eight hundred or a thousand square feet inside. The front porch was a newer addition. In the back there was only a cement stoop with an old metal garden chair on it, its faded pink paint rusting in spots. A few dead flowers in pots had been set out back.

Candy tried to peek into a few of the windows, but they were locked tight with the shades pulled down, so she couldn't see much.

In fact, there wasn't much at all to see. She walked to the barn, peered in the door, but except for old shovels and rakes, a few bales of moldy hay, and some long-abandoned farm equipment, it was empty. The flooring looked rotted. She decided it was too dangerous to enter, and in fact, she decided, the whole thing should probably just have been torn down.

"I guess this was a bad idea," she said to herself, shaking her head. "There's nothing here."

She started toward the Jeep, pulled open

the door . . . but something held her back, kept her from climbing up into the seat. She turned and looked around. It was only an instinct, something gnawing at her, that made her close the door again and take a final walk around the house, with sharper eyes this time.

And that's when she noticed the well-worn path, angling off through the grassy field behind the house, toward a copse of trees in the distance.

Now *that* was curious.

I wonder where that leads?

Her gaze rose, following the path into the distance. From what she could see, there were no houses back in that direction — no noticeable destination to which the path might lead. Perhaps it led to a garden, or a fire pit where Ray burned his trash.

Yes, that was probably it.

Still, her curiosity was piqued.

Before she had even fully thought it through, she started along the path that cut a fine thin line through knee-high grasses, goldenrod, Queen Anne's lace, and other weeds and wildflowers. This part of the property had obviously been neglected for years. At one time it might have been a well-tended field, lush with peas or beans, carrots, radishes and beets, corn and rhubarb and squash. Strawberries or raspberries might have been grown here, asparagus or new potatoes. But now it had gone to seed and showed no signs that it would change anytime soon.

As she moved further on, the field gave way to a thick fringe of black chokeberry bushes, and then she was in amongst the trees . . .

. . . and there it was, partially hidden by the leaves and branches.

There was no missing it or mistaking it. Ten feet or so off the ground, utilizing the thick trunks of a half dozen trees set closely together, meticulously crafted with plywood walls, a shingled roof, and even real windows, was a tree house.

Or rather, Candy thought as a jolt of realization shot through her, a tree *fort*.

The reality of it all, of what she had just discovered, took her breath away.

"Wow," was all she could say.

She stood there looking at it, studying it, for what seemed like the longest time, until she finally edged forward, toward it, then underneath it. It was fully a tenth of the size of the small shack in which Ray lived, and looked to be much more richly appointed and much more carefully cared for. It was obvious that Ray had spent not days, even weeks or months, but years tending to his hideaway.

Not unlike Sapphire's little attic hideaway, Candy thought. *Strange how both of them felt a need to hide a part of themselves away from the public eye, and how both of them were irrevocably linked, in life and death.*

Shaking away these curious thoughts, Candy looked around for a way up. Finding a knotted rope that hung down from the underside of the tree fort, she gave it a tug, which revealed a spring-operated drop-down ladder that fell neatly into place, with its bottom step resting just a few inches above the ground.

"Wow," Candy said again.

With a sense of discovery and expectation, she climbed the ladder and emerged at the top into a magnificent room, with a polished wide pine floor, a table and chairs, a rocker in one corner, a built-in bed with a mattress, a wood stove, and just about every imaginable amenity with the exception of electricity, though Candy had no doubt that Ray could have rigged that too if he had a mind to.

And there, sitting at the center of the table, was a red-handled hammer.

Just as Ray had said.

She walked closer to get a better look at it

but didn't touch it. She didn't want to get her fingerprints on it.

She leaned forward, holding her breath.

Sure enough, on the handle just below the claw head, was a small, almost imperceptible nick — a nick she had put there herself, when she mistreated the hammer while building her booth last Friday, almost a week ago.

This was Ray's hammer — there was no mistake about it. He had brought it here, to keep it safe.

Which meant the hammer found in Sapphire's house — the hammer that was used to kill her — had not been Ray's.

That hammer must have been the one that belonged to Ned Winetrop.

It was evidence that just might prove Ray's innocence.

Candy knew she had to call the police — she couldn't keep information like this to herself. Once the police saw what she had found, they would have to release Ray.

She was turning to leave when something else caught her eye — a note card set on a side shelf. She couldn't say what attracted her to it, except for perhaps the way it was displayed, as if in an honored position. Candy crossed to it, took it off the shelf, and read the typed message on the inside:

Come to my house this evening at 9:30. Bring your toolbox. I need your help.

It was signed *Sapphire* in a flowery script, with a swooping *S* and a little heart over the *i.*

TWENTY-EIGHT

Candy knew instantly what it was. The note Sapphire left for Ray, asking him to come to her house that night — the night she was murdered.

So Ray had been telling the truth about the note too. More proof that he was probably innocent.

Which meant, as Maggie said a few days earlier, the real killer could still be lurking somewhere around Cape Willington.

That thought gave Candy a chill. Suddenly spooked, she put the note back on the shelf, right where she had found it, and climbed back down the ladder. She started off through the trees toward the house, all the while looking around her, expecting at any moment to be ambushed by the real killer. But if there really was such a person, he or she wasn't hiding in these woods.

Half walking, half running, she passed through the field, circled the house, and climbed into the Jeep. She panicked for a moment when she thought she had lost her keys but found them in her back pocket. "Candy, stop trying to scare yourself," she muttered as she started up the engine. But as a precaution she made sure all the doors were locked. Then, tires spinning and shooting up clouds of dust and gravel, she whipped the Jeep around and sped back to Blueberry Acres.

She was grateful to see Doc's truck parked in the driveway. He was out behind the house on the lawn tractor, mowing the yard. Candy waved to him and he waved back, thinking she was just saying hello. When she waved more frantically, he shut down the mower. "What's wrong?"

"I found Ray's fort!" she called to him. "And his hammer. I'm calling the police."

That brought Doc running. He followed her inside and paced impatiently around the kitchen as she called the police station. She talked directly to Daryl Durr, Cape Willington's chief of police, and told him what she had found. She agreed to meet him back at Ray's place in ten minutes.

"Come on," she said to Doc. Candy was too nervous to drive, so they climbed into Doc's truck and off they went, down to River Road and across to the Loop at the opposite end of the Cape, then out of town to Ray's place.

It took the better part of an hour for the police to search the tree house, since they had to conduct a thorough investigation. The hammer, Sapphire's note, and other items they deemed important went into paper evidence bags. After that, they searched the surrounding woods as well as the inside of Ray's house again and questioned Candy at length. Chief Durr frowned when he heard her story. "What were you doing out here in the first place?" he asked in a gruff tone. She had thought about how she was going to answer that, knowing she would be asked, and decided it was best just to tell the truth — that she heard that Ray had mentioned something about a fort, and she set out to find it.

"Well, it seems we have some loose lips around the station," the chief said angrily. "You're aware that this is an official police investigation, Miss Holliday? And that what you've done is completely out of line? Not to mention dangerous?"

"Yes, I realize that," Candy said contritely, "but I just wanted to help. Ray's our friend. I knew he couldn't have killed Sapphire Vine."

"Well, you did the right thing in calling us

right away. This does shed some new light on the situation." The chief looked over as one of his sergeants walked past with the evidence bags. Then his gaze shot back to Candy.

"We'll take a look at what we've got and reassess the case." He leveled a finger at her. "But I'll have no more interference from you, ya hear? Your investigating days are over, right?"

"Um, yes, Chief Durr."

He held her gaze for a few moments, trying to intimidate her with his stare, then turned away. "Well, all right then. I'll let you off the hook this time. Besides, I've got more important things to do than lecture you. Seems like all hell is breaking loose in this town." He shook his head and frowned. "We've got your statement, so you can head back home. We'll call you if I need anything else."

"What about Ray?" Doc asked. "He can go free now, right?"

Chief Durr shook his head. "That's up to a judge to decide. He'll hear the evidence in the morning, or maybe this afternoon if we can hook up with him. Can't make any promises, though."

"But you have the evidence right there that he didn't do it," Candy persisted. "It

350

was Ned Winetrop's hammer that killed Sapphire — not Ray's. He deserves to be let go."

"Well, now, we have to go by the book on this one. Got a lot of people watching how we handle this thing. We're not a bunch of hicks, you know. We've got procedures to follow."

"You gonna pick up Ned Winetrop?" Doc asked.

Chief Durr scratched the back of his head and scowled. "You know I can't comment on that officially, Doc . . . but unofficially, sure, we'll pick him up and bring him down to the station for questioning. That's all you'll get out of me today, though. You folks head back home now. There's nothing else to do, and I'm in no mood to be quizzed anymore on our procedures."

Candy hesitated. She wanted to say more, to know more. But Doc, sensing Chief Durr's building annoyance and his daughter's exasperating stubbornness, put his arm around her shoulder. "Come on, Sherlock," he said, steering her away from the police chief. "You've done all you can do here. Let's go home."

TWENTY-NINE

It was well past four-thirty by the time they arrived back at Blueberry Acres. The sun that had been so bright that morning had disappeared behind a shield of low clouds blowing in from the west, pushed across the sky by a strong wind. Doc pulled up in front of the barn but left the truck idling. Candy started to climb out, then hesitated. "You're not staying?" she asked in surprise.

Doc gave her that look he gave her so often these days, the one that told her he just couldn't sit still right now. "I think I'm going to run over to the police station, see what I can find out about Ray. Maybe I can speed up the process to spring him."

"But Dad, he's not even there. He's up in Machias, and so is the judge. These things take time."

Doc shrugged impatiently. "I got to do something. Can't just sit around here waiting." He pulled the gear shift into reverse and revved the engine. "Want to come along?"

Candy didn't have to think long before she gave him an answer. "No thanks. I've done enough of the Cagney and Lacey bit this week. It's time for a break. I'm going to check on the girls, grab a glass of wine, and sit for a while."

Doc nodded. "I shouldn't be too long. Tell you what. I'll swing back by to pick you up, and we can head to Duffy's for dinner. It's Thursday — you know what that means."

"Duffy's world-famous meatloaf special?"

Doc grinned. "Dripping in gravy with smashed potatoes and buttered peas. It's a hard deal to pass up. What do you say?"

"Mmm, mmm." Candy stepped back and swung shut the cab door. "My mouth is watering already."

He laughed. "I knew I could tempt you. See you in forty-five minutes or so."

Candy gave him a wave as she headed around the barn to the chicken coop. The girls were clucking away, happy and guileless as ever, scratching at the earth and poking around their coop. She fed and watered them, then checked to see if there were any other signs of forced entry — paw prints in the dirt around the exterior, dug-up earth, any place some predator might be trying to widen a gap in the cage with a sniffing nose or a clawing paw. But there was no evidence to be seen. The critter that had come around a few nights earlier hadn't made another appearance — but that didn't mean it wouldn't be back. With the blueberries ripe in the fields, animals came from all over to partake of a free meal. Birds were the worst culprits, of course — some days it looked like a feathered convention out there in the barrens — but deer also frequented the fields in the early mornings, and even a stray bear might wander out among the bushes at this time of year.

Candy made a mental note to keep Doc's shotgun close by the back door.

She took a cursory walking tour of the property, just to check on things, then angled toward the house. Her mind wandering off on a myriad of different things, she climbed the steps onto the back porch, reached in her pocket for the house key — and froze.

Shards of glass littered the back porch near the door.

Her eyes jerked up.

One of the window panes in the door was broken, and the door itself was ajar.

Candy took a step back, forcing herself to stay calm as her heart thumped in her chest.

She cast a look behind her, wishing Doc hadn't left so quickly. But he was gone. She was alone.

Whatever was going on here, she would have to handle it herself.

She knew the smartest move would probably be to jump right into the Jeep and get the hell out of here. But this was *her* house, and Doc's — she wasn't about to abandon it to some wayward thief.

She took a few steps forward, avoiding the glass on the porch, and looked in through the door window. From here, she could see no one in the kitchen, no movement, no shadows that shouldn't be there.

The place looked empty, but someone could still be here, in another part of the house.

She listened for a moment, holding her breath.

No stray footsteps, creaking floorboards, door hinges squeaking, heavy breathing — nothing to indicate that the person who had broken the window was still around.

Moving quickly and quietly, she pushed open the door, tiptoed to the kitchen closet, yanked it open, and pulled out Doc's shotgun. Her eyes constantly scanning, on the lookout for a hostile intruder, she crossed to the junk drawer, pulled it open, and reached way in the back, her fingers groping for a box of cartridges. She grabbed half a dozen and pushed two into the gun's magazine.

She pumped the action, thumbed off the safety, and tucked the butt into her shoulder, her finger resting lightly on the trigger guard.

She moved forward purposefully then, stepping first into the living room, turning a complete circle, searching everywhere at once, eyeing along the gun's sights. Next, she went into Doc's den at the back of the house. She searched quickly and thoroughly. Then on to the dining room, the downstairs bathroom, and the laundry room, working her way back to the kitchen.

Nothing.

She paused and listened again for any unfamiliar or revealing sound. But again, nothing.

Tucking the butt of the weapon deeper into her shoulder, lining up along the sights, she moved upstairs as carefully and quietly as possible. Naturally several of the steps creaked under her sneakers, but that couldn't be helped.

Still, if anyone was up there waiting for her, they would know she was coming.

Adrenaline rushed through her body, her

ears roared, her breathing sounded monstrously loud. But she ignored all those things. When she reached the top of the stairs, she moved efficiently, starting with the room to her left — a guest room. She checked the closet, under the bed, in the back corner behind the bureau.

Next was Doc's bedroom. Same procedure, same results.

The upstairs bathroom, and then her room.

Five minutes later she was back downstairs in the damp, dimly lit basement, holding down her nervousness as she checked every corner, every shadow. Again, the search turned up nothing.

She lowered the shotgun and climbed the stairs back to the kitchen, her gaze still wandering watchfully. But she was fairly certain now that whoever had broken the window must have taken what they wanted and left.

Or maybe, she thought, it was just an accident — someone had come by to visit, gotten careless, and left guiltily before she and Doc arrived. But that seemed farfetched.

More than likely, they had been robbed. Burglary was uncommon around these parts — some folks still left doors and windows unlocked — but not unheard of. Candy did a more thorough search of the house, still carrying the shotgun with her. Nothing seemed to have been taken — the TV, DVD player, checkbooks, and what little diamond jewelry she owned were all still in their places. Even the engagement ring Clark had given her way back when was still tucked into its place in a corner of her jewelry box.

She walked back into the kitchen. That's when she noticed what was missing.

Sapphire's files were gone — all of them.

Last she remembered, they had been sitting on the table in two piles, in front of Doc. Could he have taken them? It was possible, she thought, but that didn't make sense. Where would he have taken them, and why hadn't he told her if he had?

No, someone else must have taken them — someone who broke into their house for that purpose. But who? Who even knew she had them? She hadn't told anyone about the files, except Herr Georg that morning, and she told him only about his own file. He couldn't have known she had more. Ben knew she had some files, of course, and Maggie. But why would they steal the files from her? They could have had access to the files at any time — all they had to do was ask.

Candy was about to pick up the phone and call the police to report the break-in when it rang, making her nearly jump out of her skin.

"Damn, I hate phones," she muttered to herself as she set the shotgun aside and picked up the receiver. "Hello?"

"Candy! It's Maggie!"

"Oh, hi, I —"

"Amanda's gone!" Maggie cut in, sounding almost hysterical. "She's run away! With Cameron!"

"What?"

"Amanda and Cameron — they're gone! They took off!"

"Took off? Where? When?"

"I don't know. I just got home. Amanda left a note. They must have left sometime this morning, after I went to work. They took Cameron's car."

Inexorably, Candy's gaze was drawn to the place where Sapphire's files had been.

"Cameron!" she shouted in realization. "That's who took them! He's the only other person who knew about them!"

"Knew about what?"

"Never mind. I'll tell you later. Do you know where they went?"

Candy could sense Maggie's anxiety. "I . . . I'm not sure. What's going on? What's this all about?"

"I don't know yet," Candy said, "but we're going to find out. Stay where you are. I'm coming to you. I'll be there in ten minutes."

After she hung up, Candy made one more call, to the police station. She left word with Carol at the front desk, asking her to pass a message on to Doc: The house had been broken into. He needed to get back home as soon as possible.

Then she grabbed her purse and keys and headed out to the Jeep, sighing as she went. She had hoped to spend a quiet evening at home with a glass of wine and perhaps a good book. But it was not meant to be. She had more important things to do now.

Cameron. She shook her head in disbelief as she climbed into the front seat and started the engine. How had he got himself mixed up in all this? Why had he been so upset to hear about Sapphire's death? What had he been doing in her secret room? And why would he have stolen the files?

What was he trying to hide?

She didn't know, but she promised herself she would find out, one way or the other.

THIRTY

Maggie threw up her hands, deep frustration showing on her face. "I can't believe they're doing this to me. What are they up to? Where can they be? We've checked everywhere."

Candy nodded. *It's true,* she thought, both hands tightly gripping the steering wheel. She felt edgy, ragged, and thirsty; her brain hurt and her fingers felt numb. She knew she was rapidly wearing out — it had been a long day, and it showed no signs of ending soon.

They had been combing the town for the past two hours, starting at Cameron's home, which they found dark and lifeless, then on to all his favorite haunts, including McCoy's, the only burger joint in town, where the high school kids hung out in the summer evenings, and the teen center in the basement of the Episcopal church. They had come up empty everywhere they looked.

Maggie had tried to use her cell phone to call folks around town, to ask if anyone had seen Cameron and Amanda, but the reception was lousy, fading in and out. It was sporadic even on a good day, which was why Candy had gotten out of the habit of carrying her own cell phone. But when inclement weather set in, it was near impossible to get a signal — so they had been forced to stop back at Maggie's house to use a land line. They wasted another twenty minutes there, and even that effort turned up nothing positive.

That's when Candy had an idea, and that brought them here, to Sapphire's house, less than twenty-four hours after they had broken into the place.

As before, Candy parked a block away and they snuck around to the back of the house. It wasn't fully dark yet, but the thick clouds that had been building throughout the afternoon and early evening had darkened and lowered, threatening rain, and a strong wind was kicking up out of the northwest. Sapphire's house looked eerie in the odd slanted dusk light and gathering gloom, like a dark sentinel guarding a long-held secret.

But there were no more secrets to be revealed this night. The back door was locked, and the key was in the exact place

Candy had left it the night before, on a ledge above one of the back windows. It hadn't been moved since she had put it there, as far as she could tell, so unless Cameron had his own key, he wasn't here.

They hovered around the back of the house for a few minutes, debating whether to enter again. In the end, they decided against it. "They're not here," Candy said, the disappointment strong in her voice as she glanced at the upper windows, which showed no signs of life inside. "If they were, we'd know it. We'd see their car or footprints, or hear them talking inside. They're teenagers, after all."

"Where *are* they then?" Maggie asked again, looking as though she was about to burst with anger and worry. She had bitten her lip raw, and her eyes were red and tired. "I just want to find them," she pleaded, to the sky as much as to Candy. "I just want to make sure they're safe."

"I know. Me too." Candy lowered her head and for the first time felt ashamed she had ever thought Cameron could have had anything to do with Sapphire's death. Something was bothering him, yes — something that tore at him, that much was obvious. Whatever it was, it had him running scared, taking Amanda with him. He wasn't a killer — she realized that now — but he still could be in trouble. Candy and Maggie had to find him before he did something they'd all regret . . .

She looked up at Maggie, who stood with arms crossed as the wind tore at her clothes. "Is there anyplace else they could have gone? Anywhere? Maybe Cam has a friend who lives out of town . . . or Amanda? Up in Bangor, maybe?"

Maggie thought a moment, then shook her head. "I've called everyone I can think of."

"Some place, then — where they might hang out, go for walks, hiking, anything like that?"

Maggie tilted her head as her mouth tightened. She closed her eyes and rubbed at her face with her hands. "Think, think!" she commanded herself. "Come on, there must be something I'm missing . . . some . . . ." She stopped, her hands flying away from her face, her eyes wide. "The camp!"

"The camp?"

"Yes!" She jabbed a finger excitedly at Candy. "That's it! The Zimmermans have a camp up north, about two hours away. Cameron and his dad go up there every summer to hunt and fish. It's the perfect place for them to hide out!"

Candy checked her watch. Nearly seven-thirty. A two-hour trip would put them at the cabin well after dark, which came early even in the summer at this far-eastern end of the time zone. "I don't suppose there's a phone up there?"

Maggie shook her head. "I don't suppose there is."

"Where's this place at?"

"East Musquash Lake, up by Topsfield. Do you think that's where they went?"

"There's only one way to find out. I'll have to stop for gas on the way."

For a moment Maggie was silent, but then she rushed forward and gave Candy a big hug. "I'm so glad you're with me. You're the best friend a gal could have."

"You'd do the same for me, right?"

"You know it."

"I wasn't doing anything special this evening anyway," Candy said as they started back to the Jeep. "A night drive might be nice."

"You're just saying that."

"No, really. It'll give us a chance to talk a little."

"That's right. We can talk. You had something you were going to tell me, didn't you?"

"About what?"

"Something you said on the phone — Cameron took something?"

"Oh, that's right!" Candy clutched Maggie's shoulder as she remembered. "I forgot about that! And I have more to tell you — about Herr Georg, and Ray's tree fort."

"All that? Sounds like we have a lot of catching up to do. I guess this *is* a good time for a long drive."

So as the impending storm squeezed the last light from the sky and the night deepened prematurely, they drove out of Cape Willington to Route 1 and from there turned eastward toward the small, quiet Downeast towns of Cherryfield, Columbia Falls, and Jonesboro. Along the way, Candy explained about the break-in at the house, her harrowing search with the shotgun, and her discovery that the files were missing. "I think Cameron took them for some reason," Candy explained, still trying to sort it all out in her head. "He saw us up in Sapphire's attic last night. He must have guessed we took those files."

"But why would he want them? What was in those files anyway?"

"I didn't get through all of them — but I did get a chance to look through Herr Georg's file." As the first raindrops splattered like giant bugs on the windshield,

Candy told her about the e-mails between Sapphire and the German baker, and her talk with him that afternoon, though she kept back some of the details about his past, out of respect for his privacy.

"This is not for public knowledge, of course," Candy finished, "but you've been involved with this from the beginning, so I thought you should know."

"And Sapphire was blackmailing him?" Maggie asked in disbelief. "I knew she was evil, but I had no idea she was *that* evil."

"There's more," Candy said. "I found Ray's hammer." She paused as Maggie gasped, and was just launching into the story of her discovery of Ray's tree fort when Maggie's cell phone rang.

"I can't believe it!" Maggie said in a surprised tone as she dug into her purse. "Wouldn't you know, it hasn't worked all day, and just when we're getting to the bottom of this story, now it suddenly works. Must be something to do with the storm." She glanced at the phone's display, then let out a shriek that nearly split Candy's ears open. "Oh my God! It's Amanda!"

"Amanda? Well answer the dumb thing."

"Right." Maggie thumbed the call button. "Amanda, where are you? I've been scared to death." She listened then, the silence lengthening as they drove east, her stillness speaking more than words.

When she finally lowered the phone to her lap, Candy didn't have to look at her to know her friend was stunned. "Is everything alright? Are the kids okay?"

It took Maggie a moment to answer. "Turn around. We're headed in the wrong direction."

"Why? Where are they?"

"You won't believe me if I tell you."

"I'll believe you. Just tell me."

"They're at Quinn's cabin."

"Quinn? As in Sebastian J.? I don't believe it."

"It gets worse. Cameron's holding a gun on Quinn. He thinks Quinn's the one who killed Sapphire."

Now it was Candy's turn to look stunned. She blinked several times, shook her head, and slowed the Jeep to a crawl, then cranked the steering wheel as she expertly made a three-point turn in the middle of the road. With the Jeep pointed in the opposite direction, she gunned the gas pedal, and they headed back through the gathering darkness toward Cape Willington.

THIRTY-ONE

The cabin Sebastian J. Quinn had rented for the summer was located at the end of a dirt road, on a high, rocky spur that jutted out into the sea. It was a rugged section of the coast, but a cluster of small wooden summer cabins clung tightly to this piece of land, as they had for decades, standing tough against the frequent onslaughts of sea and storm that could be beyond fierce. On summer days, though, when the sea was calm, the sun bright, and the breezes warm out of the south, when the gulls were impatiently wheeling high overhead and distant sails floated lazily past out on the sharp line of the horizon, when you could sit on this piece of land with your feet up and a book in your hand and forget anything or anyone else existed, you knew there was no place else like it on earth.

Quinn's cabin was isolated and peaceful, though the place could hardly be called luxurious. It was fifty years old if it was a day, and that was probably being kind, but it was charming in a rustic way, even though it lacked any aesthetically pleasing features. It was a simple cape, with a gray clapboard exterior and white-trimmed windows that looked as if they hadn't been washed since Eisenhower's presidency. On the sea side — the front of the house — was a screened porch with weathered rockers, and beyond that, out at the edge of the property, just above the sea, sat a welcoming pair of Adirondack chairs, painted blue and yellow.

Candy could picture the cabin's interior in her mind, though she had never been inside, but she knew such places well enough. It would have a camplike feel, with a linoleum floor in the kitchen and threadbare carpeting in the living area, walls of varnished pine that held the smells of the ages, big comfy chairs and perhaps a few antique lights, and a checkerboard set on a side table, waiting for someone to play. There would be a couple of bedrooms up a narrow stairway, and a single bathroom on the first floor that had been added to one side of the house sometime in the sixties or seventies.

It probably went for about fifteen hundred a week and more than likely was never empty from May through October.

A rented white sedan sat in the parking area behind the house. Next to it was Cameron's truck.

Candy drove up slowly behind the truck, eased the Jeep to a stop, switched off the headlights, and shut off the engine.

They sat for a moment in silence, exchanging wary looks, listening to the roar of the ocean. On days when the sea was calm, you'd never know it was there if you were facing the other direction. But when a storm blew in and the sea rose in fury, it could sound like an approaching train — or perhaps a dozen of them all at once. And if the tide was high, and gray breakers pounded at the rocky coast, driving great sprays of seawater into the air — it was then you understood and respected the power of the sea.

Fortunately, the heaviest rain still held off, except for brief waves of heavy drops that sprayed the coastline. Candy leaned forward and looked up at the dark sky, then turned toward the cabin. "I guess we should go inside."

"I guess so."

A pause. "You go first. I'll be right behind you."

"Spoken like a true friend." Maggie took

a deep breath. "Okay, here I go."

She had just reached for the Jeep's door handle when she heard a shout to her right. Looking over, she saw the cabin's back door swing open. Amanda ran out.

"Amanda!" Maggie cried, jumping out.

"Mom, you're here!"

"Amanda! My baby!"

They ran into each other's arms and hugged.

"What took you so long?" Amanda asked, looking worried.

"We got here as quickly as we could. What in the devil's name is going on?"

Amanda hesitated, casting a glance at Candy, then looking back at her mother. She took Maggie's arm, tugging her toward the cabin. "You'd better come inside."

Maggie let her daughter pull her through the door, and Candy followed. They entered a small mudroom, then turned right into a narrow kitchen.

"Amanda, what . . . ?" Maggie began, but Amanda shushed her, then turned toward a doorway that led to the cabin's living area. "Cam, it's me. We're coming in," Amanda called out.

There was a mumbled response. Amanda led them into the room beyond.

It took Candy a few moments to make

sense of all she saw.

The large, gray-carpeted room doubled as a dining area and living room, with a dining table and chairs in one corner, a big comfy sofa in the middle, and windows all along the side that looked out over the sea — an incredible view during the daytime, Candy guessed. Bookshelves lined the back wall, and a stone fireplace occupied the interior wall to her left. It was a cozy, inviting place — though tonight it looked storm tossed, as if a great wind had somehow broken into the place and swept incautiously through.

Near the center of the room, sitting in a straight-backed chair, was Sebastian J. Quinn, wearing khakis, a baggy, faded blue sweatshirt, and old-man's slippers. His hands appeared to be tied behind his back, held in place with repeated wrappings of steel gray duct tape. A gag had been tied around his mouth. Candy shuddered when he looked at her with hateful eyes, then followed his gaze as it shifted across the room.

Candy saw him then, Cameron, the same tall, scrawny kid, standing in a darkened corner. His lopsided grin was gone, though, his shaggy hair even more disheveled, and his green eyes were narrow and intense. A hunting rifle was tucked into his shoulder. His finger rested uneasily near the trigger, the muzzle pointed straight at Sebastian J. Quinn's chest.

Candy couldn't help but gasp.

She noticed how stiff Cameron stood, how stoic his face had become. All the joy had gone out of him. He looked not unlike a caged animal.

"Cameron," she said softly, her voice shaking, "what are you doing?"

Almost simultaneously, Maggie let out a shriek. "Cameron! Put that thing down before you hurt someone!" she demanded sharply.

But he barely acknowledged their presence. Sebastian J. Quinn grunted something, drawing Candy's attention. "Why is he tied up like that?" she asked, the confusion evident in her voice. She started toward him, not sure what she planned to do, although she supposed she should free him. But she was stopped by a shout.

"Don't move!"

"What?" Candy turned to Cameron, her brows falling, her head tilting. "Cameron, I don't understand what's happening. We can't leave him like that. We have to untie him — right now."

"No."

"What do you mean, 'no'? This is crazy. What are you doing?"

Cameron's face shifted just slightly at Candy's questions, as if he were being scolded by a parent. In response, he pointed with his eyes and a tilt of his head. "It's over there."

Both Maggie and Candy turned — and that's when Candy saw the files.

They were piled on the table. One of them lay open, its papers strewn about.

In an instant Candy's confusion was pushed aside as her anger rose. "You *did* take them!" she shouted, looking back at him, her gaze narrowing. "You broke into our house!"

"I had to," he said, his voice deep and husky. "I had to know what was in them."

"But Cameron —"

"It's all there," he interrupted. "Didn't you look at them?"

"Of course I looked at some of them but —"

"I called him," Cameron went on, the words tumbling out of him now as Candy glanced at Sebastian J. Quinn, then moved curiously toward the table. "I called him and told him I knew what he had done. I thought he was coming after us."

"Called him? Who's coming after you?" Maggie asked, a touch of fear creeping into her voice.

Cameron pointed, his eyes darkening eerily. "Him. He did it. He murdered my mother."

"He . . . he *what?*" Maggie gasped.

"He did it, Mom," Amanda piped in from where she stood near the doorway. "It's true."

"I don't understand." Maggie looked hard at Cameron. "What are you talking about? Your mother's not dead. She's still alive. I talked to her just last week. How could he have killed her?"

"Not that mother," was Cameron's answer.

Maggie turned to her daughter, shaking her head, still not understanding. "Amanda? What the hell is going on?"

Candy had reached the table now, and as her gaze swept across the papers on the table she suddenly realized what Cameron was saying. It all came rushing in, engulfing her like a wave, overpowering her, hitting her so hard and fast it almost hurt — all the missed clues, all the puzzle pieces that didn't seem to fit, all the facts that had seemed so confusing but now became so clear.

She spun toward Cameron, her eyes wide, her mouth falling open.

She saw it now — the hair, the eyes, the

posture — so like those of the man in the photo that rested on Sapphire's piano, the man who stood beside the young Susan Jane Vincent, smiling easily, wearing a USM sweatshirt.

Candy raised a trembling finger, pointing it at Cameron, shaking it a little as the words spilled out of her. "Oh my God! You're Sapphire's son!"

THIRTY-TWO

"What are you talking about?" Maggie looked at Candy as if her friend had gone daft.

"That's it! Don't you see!" She jerked her finger wildly. *"Sapphire Vine is his real mother."*

"Whose real mother?"

"Cameron's! He's her son . . . *Susan Jane Vincent's* son . . . aren't you?"

She had turned back to face the teenager, her finger still held out toward him, though after a moment she forced herself to lower it.

In the stunned silence that followed, all eyes turned toward Cameron, who backed farther into the corner, seeking shadow, wary of the attention. Only his eyes shown out, bright and glistening in the muted light, mirroring his uneasiness.

Maggie tilted her head as she looked at him, her face a cloud of confusion that slowly, inexorably gave way to realization. Her mouth fell open, and for a rare moment she was totally, utterly speechless.

Even Sebastian appeared to be stunned. He sat stone still in the chair to which he was tied, studying the teenage boy with disbelieving eyes. Only Amanda seemed unfazed by the revelation, though she stood anxiously with her arms folded across her chest as she watched the others watch her boyfriend.

For a moment all were still. The only sounds were the crashing of the waves and the howls of the building storm outside the walls. Then Maggie's voice, trembling and uncertain, broke into the silence. "It can't be. It's not possible."

"It is, Mom. It's true." Amanda clutched her mother's arm. "I didn't believe it at first either, but Cameron told me all about it. Sapphire was his real mother."

"But how can that be?" Maggie looked as if she were about to collapse as her eyes found Cameron's. "You're so handsome and so smart and so nice! And —"

She clamped a hand over her mouth when she saw the look on Cameron's face. She instantly regretted her words. "Oh, Cameron, I didn't mean that the way it sounded. It's just that —"

"I know what you meant, and you're right." He wavered a moment, as if he were about to tip over, then lowered the gun and let out a long breath. "I know what you're thinking. I understand how you feel. I was shocked myself when I found out. But it's the truth. I've seen the proof."

"But . . . how long have you known?"

He shrugged, as Maggie had seen him do so many times before, and for a moment he was the old Cameron she had known since he was a child.

"A few months now. She told me right after my eighteenth birthday."

As Maggie questioned Cameron, Candy was barely listening, for her mind was racing back through all that had happened over the past few days. She finally spoke up. "It all makes sense, in some strange way," she said thoughtfully. "That's why you were so upset at Gumm's that day, isn't it? That was the first time you heard of Sapphire's death. Of course you were shocked." She paused, still thinking. "And that's why you were staying up in Sapphire's attic."

Cameron cleared his throat, still shifting uneasily. "Yeah, I, um, stayed up there a few times. She liked to have me around. She said it made her happy, after being separated from me for so long. But I wasn't crazy about it. I did it mostly for her."

"And that young man we saw in the photo on Sapphire's piano, and in her photo album — that was your father, right?"

"His name was David — David Squires," Amanda explained. "He and Cameron's mother were students together at USM."

"USM!" Candy slapped her forehead with the flat of her hand. "I should have seen the connection!"

"What connection?" Maggie asked.

"Don't you remember?"

"Remember what?" Maggie looked more confused than ever.

"The night of the pageant. When Bertha Grayfire introduced the judges, she said that one of them had taught at USM — the University of Southern Maine."

"But that was . . ." Maggie's voice trailed off as she thought it through. After a moment her gaze was drawn to the figure tied to a chair at the center of the room. "You don't mean . . . ?"

Cameron nodded, his face pale. "That's why I'm here . . . with this." He nodded down toward the rifle. "And that's why he's tied up there. He killed her."

Candy shook her head. Much of what was going on was still so unclear. "But why? Why would he have killed her?"

Cameron stared hard at Sebastian J. Quinn, who was slowly shaking his head, his eyes hard again, unemotional. "They were all there together, on the campus nineteen years ago," Cameron said, the tension deep in his voice. "My father was getting his master's degree in English lit with a specialty in poetry. Apparently he was a pretty good poet. And that man" — he nodded with his chin toward Sebastian J. Quinn — "was his faculty advisor."

Candy let out a breath of frustration. "And to think I never even opened his file! I was so distracted by what I had found out about Herr Georg that I barely checked up on anyone else."

"It's all there." Cameron indicated the file that lay open on the table. "I went through it over and over again this afternoon. I didn't even know it existed until you found it in that filing cabinet last night. I stayed up in that attic a few times, but I never snooped around. I never knew what she had up there. But when you started digging around and found all those files I had to know what was in them." Cameron's gaze shifted back to Sebastian. "When I reached his file, I finally knew what had happened. My mom collected all sorts of information about him."

"What kind of information?" Maggie asked quietly. "What did he do?"

Cameron's face was a mask of uncertainty, as if he didn't know where to begin — or didn't know how to explain all that he knew. After a moment he nodded toward Sebastian. "Why don't you ask *him?*"

Candy's eyes widened just a bit. On an impulse she crossed the room and removed Sebastian's gag. "What did she have on you?" she asked him point blank.

Sebastian let out a sputter of air as he strained at his bonds, attempting to rise to his feet. But Candy pushed him back down as everyone erupted at once, Cameron, Amanda, and Maggie all shouting warnings. "Just stay right where you are 'til we sort this out," Candy told him forcefully, crossing her arms and staring down at Sebastian. "I want the truth. Was she blackmailing you?"

The words came out of Sebastian in a growl. "Of course she was blackmailing me — she has been for years. She was a witch — a cruel, totally heartless witch who stalked me for years and tried to squeeze every last dime out of me. I gave her everything I had, but that still wasn't enough — she wanted more. She could never get enough. No matter what I did, she wouldn't stop. She was crazy. And I'm glad —" He caught himself then, clamping his mouth shut as he cast a wary glance at Cameron, who stood motionless in the corner. "I . . . I'm sorry you had to hear that, kid, but it's true," Sebastian told him. "You can't believe anything you saw in that file. Yes, I knew your father — and obviously your mother too. But no matter what you might think, I didn't kill her. That's the truth."

"Yes you did, you murderer!" Cameron shouted as his face contorted in sudden rage. Trembling, he raised the rifle as he came forward toward Sebastian, who stiffened in fear and shrieked, "No, don't shoot, don't shoot! I didn't kill her! I swear!"

Cameron brandished the weapon, but before he could do anything foolish, Candy and Maggie both intervened, hands out. "Cameron, calm down!" Candy shouted, positioning herself between Sebastian and the teen.

"Put that rifle down!" Maggie insisted, her fury sharpening as she marched straight toward Cameron and jerked the weapon from his hands. "We'll have no more of this, mister!" She turned abruptly and walked to Amanda, handing the rifle over to her. "Take this out to Candy's car and lock it inside," she instructed, and when Amanda started to protest, she added sharply, "Now!"

Amanda complied. With the weapon gone and the situation neutralized, Maggie turned to Sebastian. "Now we're going to call the police, and then we're going to get to the bottom of this."

She turned and walked to the phone, but before she could pick up the receiver, Sebastian called out. "Wait! Wait!" He struggled against his bonds again, his frustration evident. "I can explain everything . . . just . . . no police."

Candy wheeled on him. "Why not? Talk fast, Sebastian, or I swear, I'll get that rifle again and shoot you myself."

"Okay, okay, okay." Properly chastised, Sebastian settled back in the chair, his fear gone and a strange grin coming to his face. "I'll tell you anything you want to know."

"You'd better. This is your last chance. Now, why was Sapphire blackmailing you? What did she have on you?"

"I'll tell you," Sebastian said, "but you have to understand . . . Susan, um, Sapphire, and I had a long history together . . . we go way back . . . and yes, I hated her . . . and I suppose she hated me too . . . but despite all that, I didn't kill her. You must believe that."

"We don't know what to believe until you tell us what happened," Maggie said testily, still standing near the phone, "and our patience has run out. Talk."

Sebastian settled back into his chair, apparently resigned to his fate. He sighed, turned his head first one direction, then the other, as if considering how to proceed. Finally he closed his eyes and leaned back his head, and then, almost imperceptively, he nodded. "All right. I'll talk."

THIRTY-THREE

"This whole thing goes back about eighteen years," Sebastian began, "when we all were at the University of Southern Maine — myself and Sapphire — er, Susan — and David, Susan's boyfriend . . . his father." Sebastian nodded toward Cameron. "Susan and David were students in one of my English classes — I suppose that's where they might have met, for I seem to recall they started the class as strangers, or at least as only casual acquaintances. I didn't notice Susan much at first, but I certainly noticed David, almost immediately. He was a fairly decent poet — quite creative and passionate, though at times he could become too sentimental for my tastes. His writing was raw and undisciplined. Still, he showed incredible promise . . ."

"Until you killed him," Cameron cut in.

"That's nonsense!" Sebastian replied firmly, his heavy brows falling together. "Utter nonsense. I don't know where you heard that, but it's just not true."

"You killed him for his poetry," Cameron continued.

"I did no such thing."

"You killed him and stole his poetry!"

Sebastian gave a sarcastic laugh. "You don't know what you're talking about. You weren't there. How could you know anything about what happened back then?"

Cameron pointed toward the file on the desk. "It's all in there. I've read it all. Do you want me to tell you what really happened?"

Sebastian's face hardened. "Very well. You have the floor, young man. Illuminate us."

"Okay. Okay, I will." Cameron looked over for a moment as Amanda reentered the room. Outside, fierce gusts of wind were whipping the sea into a frenzied roar. Cameron glanced out at the darkness beyond the windows, gathering his thoughts, then turned his gaze back to Sebastian. "My mother and father met at USM, just like you said, though not in your class. They knew each other before that. They met at a freshman dance. He was a poor kid from Presque Isle, she was the daughter of a boat-builder from Bath. They were inseparable from the start — and from what I can tell, by the time they started your class, she was already pregnant — with me."

"Oh my God," Maggie cut in. "That's why Sapphire looked so happy in that photo! And so *heavy*. She wasn't overweight. She was *pregnant!*"

Cameron nodded sadly. "Yeah, she showed that photo to me. It was taken right before my father died."

"What happened to him?" Maggie asked softly.

"I . . . I don't know. She never told me — and there's nothing in the file . . ."

Maggie gasped, her hand flying to her mouth. Candy only had to glance at her to know instantly what she was thinking, for the same realization had just come to her. "The obituary . . . the one we found in the book last night in Sapphire's attic?"

Maggie nodded, unable to speak.

"What obituary?" Cameron asked.

Briefly Candy explained, and Sebastian confirmed the story. "Your father died in a car accident. Drunk driver. I remember it well. A tragic affair." He shook his head, then looked over at Candy. "You've seen the clipping?"

"I have." She glanced at Maggie. "We both have. Sapphire kept a copy of it stashed away."

"Then you know I'm telling the truth, right?"

Candy said nothing, but after a moment she gave a faint nod. Sebastian let out a breath of air, while Cameron took this news with his lips pursed tight, his eyes glassy with emotion. Sebastian thought he still saw disbelief in those eyes. "I didn't kill your father, kid," he said again for emphasis. "It's the truth, I tell you."

Cameron's faced hardened again. "If you didn't kill him, then why did you steal his poetry?"

It took a long time for Sebastian to work around to answering that question. His jaws tightened and his brow furrowed as he weighed his options. But something inside him must have made him realize that it was time for the truth — all of it. "There was nothing calculated about it, if that's what you're thinking," he began. "It just . . . happened. After your father died, your mother went into a deep depression. I watched it happen from a distance and even tried to intervene. But nothing could be done. She dropped out of school and I lost touch with her."

Cameron let out a breath and lowered his head. After a moment, he said, "She wound up in an institution in Portland and stayed there for six months. That's where I was born, but she gave me up for adoption. That's how I wound up with the Zimmermans."

"And what happened to your mother after that?" Candy asked.

"I'm not really sure about everything that happened back then," Cameron answered quietly, "but some time in the years after she left that place, she changed her name, started a new life, and tried to find out what happened to me. It took her a few years, but she finally traced me here, to Cape Willington and the Zimmermans. That's why she moved up here five years ago — so she could keep an eye on me, she said. The Zimmermans told me I was adopted but they never told me who my birth parents were. Now I know. She waited until my eighteenth birthday to tell me who she really was."

Cameron paused, looking back at Sebastian. "She also told me what you did."

"And what is that?" Sebastian asked defiantly.

"Don't pretend you don't know. She told me all about it — how one day, years ago, she was browsing through a library in Portland and found a book of poetry with your name on it — Sebastian J. Quinn. She remembered you from USM, so she checked it out and read it that night. She was shocked. She knew almost immediately that the poems weren't written by you, were they? They were all written by my father! You stole his poetry and published it under your own name!"

At this accusation, Sebastian blubbered and shook his head in denial, his face growing red, while Candy and Maggie gasped in shock and Amanda nodded vigorously, as if to give affirmation to Cameron's words. "It's true," she said, glaring at Sebastian. "He's a thief."

"I am *not* a thief," Sebastian said indignantly. "As I told you . . . it was not a calculated move. Somehow his papers got mixed up with mine. When I first came across them, I couldn't remember writing them, so I set them aside. Later, when I was assembling a book of poetry, I discovered them again and spent some time reworking them. It was only later that I realized what had happened. By then it was too late. But I never regretted what happened. I know they were David's poems, but without me they would have been lost forever. I gave them a voice and shared them with the world."

"Under your name," Amanda pointed out.

"That's very true, Miss Tremont. But at

the time I felt those poems were too good to go unpublished, and as far as I knew there was no one else in the world who cared about them. I tried but I could never locate David's parents. Apparently after his death they had moved on. Susan — well, Susan was out of the picture by then. So I proceeded in the only way I thought possible. I spent a lot of time perfecting those poems, polishing them, assembling them in a book, promoting them. And yes, there were times I felt guilty about it. But after awhile the guilt faded. History is easily buried. Your father was dead, long forgotten, and your mother was . . . well . . ." His voice trailed off.

"How could you have done such a thing?" Maggie asked.

"It's despicable," Candy added. "I bet Sapphire was freaked when she found out. Is that when she started blackmailing you?"

Sebastian sat with lips pursed, obviously uncomfortable, frustrated, and humiliated by his current position. For a moment it seemed as if he had clammed up, but finally he cleared his throat and tried his best to hold on to what small bit of dignity he had left. "No. She did write to me, threaten me, but it was only later, after I started to gain some national recognition as a poet, that she started getting nasty. She smelled money, I suppose. It brought out the worst in her. She threatened to go public, to tell the newspapers what had happened. I had no choice. I offered to pay her to keep her silent. She's been bleeding me dry ever since." He paused, thinking. "I suppose that's how she paid for that house of hers. She could never have paid for that on her salary as a part-time columnist, could she?"

"How long has this been going on?" Candy asked.

Sebastian shrugged. "Ten years? Twelve? I've lost count — and lost track of how much I've paid her." His head dropped. "It's been torment."

Cameron let out a snort of derision. "Torment? You don't know the meaning of the word. No matter what you've experienced, it's nothing compared to what my mother's been through" — he stopped abruptly, and corrected himself — "what she *went* through." Struck by the sudden realization that his mother was really, truly gone, he shuddered, closed his eyes, and swayed perceptibly. For a moment he appeared overwhelmed, and any anger he had left went out of him then, gone forever.

Everyone in the room felt his grief. Amanda went to him in a rush, her hair flying out behind her, and gave him a hug, a tear falling down her cheek. Candy felt her emotions well up in her as well, and even Maggie wiped at her eyes. "Look at me," she said with a soft, disbelieving laugh. "I'm crying for Sapphire."

Candy put a hand on her friend's shoulder. "So you're human."

Maggie gave her a teary smile. "Yeah, I guess so. Who'da thunk it, huh?" She paused. "You know, it's funny . . ."

Candy looked at her inquisitively. "What?"

"Well . . . this might sound strange, but I think I finally understand Sapphire. She was a woman who lost the love of her life — both loves of her life, first David, then her child — when she was still a young girl. It must have nearly destroyed her. I'm sure it changed her mentally and emotionally. She must have never been the same after that. That's why she changed her name. After David was killed and her baby was taken away from her, the girl known as Susan Jane Vincent must have died in some way, and the only way she could go on living was to change her name, her whole persona — to become someone else. Sapphire Vine was no Susan Jane Vincent. She was one tough cookie. She wasn't about to let this world get the better of her. She decided to fight back — and she did until the very end."

Sebastian cleared his throat. "I can certainly vouch for that," he said, looking visibly moved. "She made sure she got what she wanted, right up until the end. It wasn't a fluke I showed up here this summer, you know. That was her idea. She called me a few months ago and told me that if I did one last 'favor' for her she would leave me alone and wouldn't contact me again. Naturally I agreed. She arranged for this 'vacation' and found this nice cottage for me. And then she made sure I conveniently got a spot as a judge for the pageant. I'm not sure how she pulled that off, but she was a very resourceful woman, as you by now have no doubt guessed. She set the whole thing up magnificently. Of course, it was all part of her plan to win the competition. She pretended she didn't know me, treated me like a stranger in town. But she knew what she was doing. She had it all planned out."

"So you threw your votes her way?" Candy asked.

"Of course. Isn't that obvious?"

Candy nodded. Indeed it was. Herr Georg had told her that even though he voted for Sapphire, he didn't think the votes of a single judge could decide the contest. But the votes of *two* judges . . .

"Did you see her after the pageant?" Candy asked suddenly.

Again, Sebastian's lips clamped tight, and Candy was about to threaten him, but finally he relented and nodded. "Once."

"When?"

"The day before she died."

"You're lying," Cameron shot out.

Sebastian shook his head resignedly. " 'Fraid not, kid. Yeah, I saw her — Sunday night, the day after the pageant. She called me after everything was over and insisted I stop by her place. I didn't know what to expect, but mostly I was just hoping the whole thing was over, once and for all. But it wasn't. Oh, she was thrilled to win the crown, of course. But when I showed up at her house, she told me she needed *more* money. Can you believe it? She was the Blueberry Queen now, she said. She had newfound status. She needed a whole new wardrobe so she could look good around town. And she wanted another five thousand dollars from me. Five thousand!"

He shook his head in disbelief. "I told her I wasn't giving her any more money, that we had made an agreement. But she just laughed at me. She called me a fool. She threatened to tell everyone I was a fraud, that my Pulitzer Prize–winning book had been written by her long-dead boyfriend."

"Is that when you decided to kill her?" Cameron asked, his voice simmering.

Sebastian sighed. "For the thousandth time — I *didn't* kill her. I wasn't even in town the night she was killed."

That caught Candy by surprise. "What do you mean?"

"Just what I said — I wasn't even around this nutty town. I was in Bangor."

"I don't believe you," Cameron said.

"You have to, because it's the truth. I can prove it."

"What were you doing in Bangor?" Maggie asked.

Sebastian gave her a tired smile. "Untie me and I'll show you."

Maggie shook her head. "No way, mister. That ain't happening until you tell us everything."

"I've already told you everything," Sebastian said with a deep sigh. "Sapphire was blackmailing me, yes. But I had nothing to do with her death. Look, this is all a huge misunderstanding. Untie me now and I won't press charges — we'll just let the whole thing go."

"What were you doing up in Bangor?" Maggie repeated.

Finally Sebastian relented. "If you must know, I was seeing a lady friend — an admirer of mine. And before you say you don't believe me again, check the dresser in the bedroom." He nodded up the stairs. "On the top of the dresser you'll find all the receipts, for everything."

Maggie shot Candy a look, and Candy nodded. She moved quickly, across the room and up the narrow stairs to the second floor. She was gone for a few moments, as everyone waited anxiously. Finally she bounded back down the stairs, holding several small receipts in her hand. "Let him go," she said softly. "He's telling the truth."

THIRTY-FOUR

Bones cracked in protest as Sebastian J. Quinn rose uneasily, rubbing at his sore arms and shoulders and knees, which had stiffened during the time he had been kept prisoner in the chair. Candy had found a knife in a kitchen drawer and cut him loose, causing not a small amount of pain and discomfort as she and Maggie had pulled the duct tape off him. But he sat patiently during the process, wincing only occasionally, and now remained standing near the chair as Candy moved to the dining room table, where she had laid out all the receipts in a neat line.

"This is the hotel receipt — and here's the date."

"Monday," Maggie noticed, with a glance at Sebastian, "just like he said."

"He could have checked in and then driven back to my mom's house," Cameron observed.

Candy nodded. "He could have — it's not that long of a drive — but he didn't." She pointed to the next receipt. "This one's for dinner, that same night. Check the time on the receipt — nine forty-five. You figure an hour or so for dinner — that means they sat down at around eight thirty."

"We had an eight-fifteen reservation," Sebastian confirmed, "and drinks at the bar before that."

Maggie's eyes widened when she noticed the total amount of the check. She whistled. "Three hundred thirty-five dollars. Must have been some dinner."

"Two bottles of wine — and expensive wine at that," Candy said, pointing to the receipt with her pinky.

"It was a special occasion," Sebastian explained, sounding annoyed at the scrutiny.

Maggie studied him with newfound interest. "She must be one lucky lady. Anyone I know?"

Sebastian squared his shoulders and clasped his hands behind him. "An old admirer, as I said. I cannot reveal her name, of course. I've given her my assurances of complete discretion."

"She's probably married," Maggie muttered under her breath to Candy.

"Looks like they hit a club after that,"

Candy said, pointing to a third receipt.

"Kicking up the light fantastic?" Maggie asked of Sebastian.

"Something like that."

"And he's got an alibi for later that night too," Candy continued, pointing to the hotel receipt again. "See here — they ordered room service at twelve thirty. Expensive too."

"Champagne, if you must know." Sebastian sniffed.

"Wined and dined her, huh?" Maggie said with a sly smile.

"And they ordered room service again, for breakfast at eight A.M.," Candy pointed out. "Looks like they spent the night together."

Sebastian cleared his throat, trying his hardest to maintain his dignity. "As I've said, I have promised the utmost in discretion, and I hope I can count on the same from you. I've shown these receipts to you only as a last resort, as evidence that I wasn't in town on the night Ms. Vine was killed. But they are not for public knowledge. Besides yourselves, no one else knows of this . . . rendezvous . . . other than the police, of course."

"The police have questioned you?" Candy asked in surprise.

"Naturally. I believe they questioned

everyone connected with the pageant. They assured me it was just a part of a routine investigation. They were completely satisfied as to my innocence in this unfortunate matter. I hope you are the same." He paused, looking at each of them in turn. "I believe I've kept to my word and proved that what I've said is true. I may be a scoundrel . . . perhaps even a thief. But I am not a murderer." He rubbed at his wrists. "That should put an end to this matter, once and for all. Now . . . will you be requiring anything else of me, or may I enjoy what remains of this unmemorable evening in some sort of relative peace, with what small bit of honor and dignity is left to me?"

Cameron glowered at him, some part of him still refusing to believe, but Candy knew they had pushed their luck — and Sebastian's patience — as far as they dared. She gathered the receipts together and handed them back to Sebastian. "I think we've taken enough of your time."

"Indeed you have. It has been . . . interesting, to be sure. At least you came to the right decision," Sebastian said, taking the receipts. "So we have an agreement?"

Candy glanced at Maggie and Cameron, then nodded. "We'll keep quiet about all this, if you agree not to press charges against Cameron."

"You have my word as a gentleman," Sebastian said with a slight bow.

But Cameron shook his head. "This isn't right. What about my dad's poetry? None of this changes the fact that you stole his writings and published them as your own."

Candy and Maggie looked warily at Sebastian, who pursed his lips together. "Hmm. You're right. But my guess is that everything will work itself out in your favor soon enough, young man. You'll be getting an inheritance, you know."

That caught Cameron unaware. He was silent a moment as confusion edged into his anger. "What?"

"Your mother's house, of course. She'll have left it to you, since you're her only kin. You should have heard from her attorney by now. Have you been contacted by a lawyer?"

"He's right!" Maggie said excitedly, turning to Cameron. "Have you received any phone calls this week? Or letters?"

Cameron's face twisted in thought as he shook his head. "I . . . I don't know. I haven't been home much. I guess I haven't paid much attention to that sort of thing."

"Of course not," Sebastian said knowingly.

"You've had a lot on your mind. But my guess is there's a letter waiting for you, or a phone message, if you check when you get home. The reading of the will should take place any day now."

"The will?"

"Oh yes, I'm certain your mother had a will. And if I know her, she's left you not only the house but a sizeable bank account. Rest assured, most of that is your father's money. What your mother took from me, from residuals from your father's work, she put into the house, and probably socked the rest of it away. So you see, it's all coming back to you after all."

Cameron's expression brightened. "It is?"

"Oh yes." Sebastian raised a finger in sudden realization. "Oh, and I have something else for you." He turned and disappeared up the stairs, returning a few moments later with a large manila envelope, stuffed full. He walked to Cameron and held it out to the teenager.

Cameron eyed the package suspiciously. "What's that?"

"Take a look. I think you might be pleasantly surprised."

Cameron hesitated, but upon playful prodding and a whisper of encouragement from Amanda, he took the envelope. He studied it in his hands, then looked up at Sebastian with questioning eyes. For a moment Candy thought he might hand the envelope back to the poet, but his curiosity finally got the best of him. He tugged at the envelope's end flap and peered inside.

He seemed to sense then what the envelope held, and reached inside cautiously with thumb and forefinger, withdrawing a sheet of paper, one among many. He unfolded it carefully, wincing slightly as it crackled with age, and gazed at the page, his eyes shifting back and forth as he puzzled over the tight handwriting he found on the sheet. His brows came together. "Is this what I think it is?"

"It's what's left of your father's poetry," Sebastian said. "I brought it up here with me, intending to hand it back to your mother once this whole business with her — the blackmailing, that is — was finished. But when she went back on her deal, I decided to keep it a while longer. Your father passed that envelope to me nearly twenty years ago. He valued my opinion back then, I suppose. I meant to read it and pass it back to him, but, well, I never had the chance. Some of it has been published — in my first book — but much of it remains unpublished. You see, I'm not a complete thief — I didn't steal everything of his. I'm not sure what I planned to do with it, but that doesn't matter now. It's yours."

Cameron read the words on the page again, then carefully folded the sheet and placed it back into the envelope, which he now held tightly, close to his chest, as if it were a great treasure, and in truth, for him at that moment, no treasure could have held more value. He opened his mouth to speak but shut it quickly, as if uncertain what to say. Finally he said the only thing he could think of.

"Thanks."

"You know," Sebastian continued, "I'm sure there's more than one agent who would be thrilled to get his or her hands on what you've got in that envelope there. If you were so inclined, you could gather your father's poetry together and publish a new book — posthumously, under his name this time." He paused. "Should you require assistance, I would be glad to provide what expertise I could — completely free of charge, of course." He smiled, then added sincerely, "Your father was a good poet, Cameron. The world should be able to read the rest of his work."

For the first time that night — for the first time in several days, perhaps even weeks —

Cameron looked hopeful. "You really think I could get these published?"

"I'm sure of it."

"Well, then, yeah, I'd like to do that."

"Excellent!" Sebastian said. "Before I leave town next week, you and I can sit down and we'll get started."

"Well, I guess that settles it then," Maggie said with a wide smile, clapping her hands together.

But Candy had a difficult time sharing her friend's enthusiasm. "Not quite. Don't forget about Ray. He's still in jail."

Maggie's smile faltered. "Oh yeah. I guess it slipped my mind."

"And there's one big question that still hasn't been answered — who killed Sapphire Vine?"

"Yes. Yes, I see, you're right," Sebastian said thoughtfully, his fingers stroking his beard. He looked up quickly then, around at the others. "Well, obviously, it wasn't me, was it?" he reiterated, just in case anyone had forgotten. "But who else could it have been then?" He considered the problem for a moment, then an eyebrow rose as a thought struck him. "Perhaps one of the other judges?"

"What?" Candy's ears perked up. "What makes you say that?"

Sebastian tilted his head and his gaze narrowed. "Well, it makes sense, doesn't it? Consider the facts: Sapphire blackmailed me into voting for her, but my votes alone probably were not enough to throw the pageant her way. Perhaps she was blackmailing another."

"Perhaps," Candy agreed, still unwilling to tell him of Herr Georg's part in Sapphire's pageant scheme.

But what if there had been a third judge involved? Candy mused.

"Furthermore," Sebastian continued, "she was killed just two days after the pageant. Very suspicious, I would say — it suggests there must have been some connection. And then, of course, there's the matter of Jock Larson."

"Jock?" Candy said, surprised.

"Jock?" Maggie echoed, sounding equally surprised.

"Yes, Jock. His death and the death of Ms. Vine were both suspicious, were they not? Granted, there's no proof that Jock Larson was murdered — but what if he had been? What if there's some connection between the two?"

"What if . . . ?" Candy said softly, her mind working.

"Well," Sebastian said, throwing up a

hand, "I doubt we'll solve the problem tonight. Perhaps it would be best to let the police handle this matter from here on."

Candy nodded, deep in thought. "Perhaps you're right."

"Well," Maggie cut in, "I think that's our cue to leave." She gathered up Cameron and Amanda and steered them toward the door. "Time to go home, kids." As she made her way outside, she waved back at Sebastian. "It's been fun. Really. Let's do it again sometime. Candy, you coming?"

Outside, the storm had eased a bit. The sea was still in a fury, but the driving rain had let up. The lane that led back to the main road was a soggy, puddle-laden mess but proved no problem for Cameron's truck and Candy's Jeep. Maggie sat in silence as they drove through the darkness back toward home, following Cameron's taillights. Candy was silent also, deep in thought. She had the radio on, and the announcer was talking about a severe weather watch and possible flooding throughout the region, but even that barely registered. She felt a buzzing in her chest, the rattling of an idea that was building inside her, layering outward, forming itself into a full-fledged thought that still needed a few moments to mature. But she pushed it forward anxiously, until it threatened to burst from her.

"The judges," she said finally, cutting into the silence, after they had driven a few miles.

"I'm sorry? What?"

Up ahead, Cameron turned off toward Fowler's Corner, but on an impulse, Candy gunned the Jeep and continued on, straight ahead.

Maggie watched Cameron's taillights trailing off to their right, then looked curiously at her friend. "We're not going home?"

"Not yet, no."

"You've got something else in mind tonight?"

Candy looked over at her. "I do."

"And what, pray tell, might that be?"

"I don't think you're going to like this, but we're going to break into Town Hall."

THIRTY-FIVE

"It's unlocked."

"How can that be? They don't leave this place open at night, do they?"

"Who knows? But it's a bit of good luck for us. Now we don't have to break anything — we can just walk right in. Come on." Candy pushed open the back basement door of the Pruitt Opera House and peered at the darkness inside. "Good thing I still had that gear from last night in the Jeep." She flicked on a flashlight and shined the beam into a long dark hallway. Behind her, Maggie folded up her umbrella and noisily shook it out, letting loose a spray of raindrops.

Candy jumped. "Hey, watch where you're shaking that thing," she hissed, obviously spooked. "And try to keep it down, will ya?"

"I am keeping it down," Maggie retorted. "Just taking care of my umbrella."

"Did you have to bring that thing along?"

"I wouldn't have if you hadn't parked so far away."

"I had to park far away. We're breaking in, remember? I don't want someone to see the Jeep parked out front."

"Who's gonna see it on a night like this?"

"It's just a precaution."

"Well, bringing the umbrella along was a precaution also. What if it starts raining heavy again?"

Candy let out a sigh of resignation and took a few steps over the threshold and into the basement hallway. "Let's just get what we came for and get out of here."

"What'd we come for again?"

"The judges ballots, remember? We've got to find out if anyone else threw their votes to Sapphire. It might tip us off to the murderer."

"Oh yeah, that's right. Well, lead on then, Macduff."

"Just try not to leave a bunch of puddles behind with that dripping umbrella," Candy said over her shoulder as she started down the dark hallway.

"Um, I think somebody else beat us to that."

"What?" Candy stopped and looked back at her friend.

Maggie pointed ahead of them, along the

hallway. "See there? On the floor."

Candy gave Maggie a quizzical look, then turned and shined her flashlight downward, then out in front of her.

A trail of wet footprints led down the hall, away from them.

"Where'd those come from?" Candy asked.

They exchanged a look.

"Someone else must be in here," Maggie said, dropping her voice into a worried whisper.

Candy shook her head as she studied the footprints. "Not necessarily. Someone could have come and left. It's been raining for a while. How long does it take wet footprints to dry?"

"At least an hour or so, wouldn't it?" Maggie asked hopefully.

Candy shrugged. "I'm not sure."

"Maybe we should leave," Maggie suggested, hope in her voice.

"No, we have to do this. I think we'll be okay if we're cautious. Come on."

Further on, the hall ended at a cross corridor. Turning right, Candy saw a stairway at the end of another long hallway.

"The town council's office is down there somewhere," Maggie said, looking over Candy's shoulder.

Candy nodded resolutely. "Okay. That's probably where we'll find the ballots."

"Do you think they'll have them locked up? In a safe, maybe?"

Candy didn't reply. She had wondered that herself, thinking this could all be a complete waste of time. But they had to try, she reminded herself. She moved on, holding the flashlight close to her body, so it was half-hidden, its light muted. "I think there's a light on up there."

"Where?"

"In one of the offices. It's real faint, though."

"Maybe they leave a night light on."

"Maybe." Candy found that it took all the courage she had to take the next few steps. The old building creaked as the wind outside drove at it, creating odd moans and echoes that sounded from the dark, distant corners of the basement. Refusing to be spooked, Candy continued on, with Maggie close behind.

Doors passed by on the left and right, all closed, until they came to one that was open, on their left at the far end of the hall. The faint light Candy had seen from a distance turned out to be a desk lamp, its shade pulled down and angled so the light was directed against the back wall. Candy checked the nameplate on the door: TOWN COUNCIL.

"This is it," Candy whispered.

It was a windowless office with three desks and long shelves for books against the back wall. Two of the desks were pushed up against the front and side walls, looking relatively unused. The third occupied a space about halfway into the room, and was positioned so it faced the door. Papers and files were stacked neatly on its desktop, and containers for pens, paper clips, and push-pins were arranged in a neat row to one side. A nameplate on the front of the desk identified its owner as Bertha Grayfire, the chairwoman of the town council.

Candy walked to the desk and scanned the papers, then looked back at Maggie. "Why don't you keep a lookout, just in case anyone's still hanging around. I'll see what I can find."

Maggie nodded from the doorway. "Okay, chief," she whispered loudly. "Just make it quick. This place gives me the creeps."

"You're not the only one." Candy walked around to the back side of the desk, took a moment to assess the layout in front of her, then carefully started paging through the files and papers on the desktop. She found nothing useful, so she stooped and started opening drawers. The top middle drawer was locked. In the ones that were open she found typical items: more pens, pencils, and other office supplies; a box of envelopes; a discarded address book; a box of tissues; a well-thumbed dictionary and an old, battered hardcover copy of *Robert's Rules of Order.*

She paused for a moment as a notation at the bottom of the book's spine caught her attention. She half lifted the book with her finger, tilting her head slightly as she studied it. Hand-printed in white block letters on the spine were the initials *C. W.*

That brought back some memory. What had it been? It took her a moment, but she finally figured it out. It was something Doc had told her a few days ago, about the flashlight that had been found at the bottom of the cliff where Jock Larson had died. The flashlight, he had told her, had the initials *C. W.* on it.

Candy let out a breath and rolled her eyes. Of course! She had thought the initials belonged to a person, and had wracked her brain to try to figure out who it might be. But the flashlight hadn't belonged to an individual. It had belonged to the town! *C. W.* stood for *Cape Willington!*

For a moment she was elated, but quickly

she realized it didn't answer anything. In fact, it only made for more questions. Why had a town flashlight been up on that cliff in the middle of the night? Who had left it there? She pondered those questions as she continued her search.

At the bottom of the desk was a file drawer. Candy dropped to one knee, pulled it open, and had just started exploring the folders inside when Maggie spoke up. "Oh look!"

Candy's head popped up over the desktop. "What is it? Is someone here?"

"No. Look. Pictures."

She pointed, and on an impulse crossed the room to the far wall, where a series of framed photos had been neatly hung. Maggie studied them as if she were in an art gallery, nodding and smiling as she viewed one after the other. Candy went back to the file drawer but was distracted again by Maggie, whose voice suddenly took on a serious tone. "Candy, you'd better see this."

Candy looked up again, her face scrunched in momentary annoyance. "What?"

"This photo." Maggie tapped a picture frame.

"I'm kinda busy at the moment."

"This is more interesting."

Candy squinted, studying the photo from a distance. "What is it?"

"Come and have a look."

Curiosity finally overcoming her reluctance, Candy rose and crossed the room. "So what's so important?" she asked as she gently laid a hand on her friend's shoulder.

Maggie pointed. "I've never seen it before. Have you?"

Candy turned to the photo Maggie indicated, focusing in on the image.

It took her a few moments to register what she was seeing. It was Bertha, she realized, although she hadn't recognized her at first. Instead of being dressed in a business suit or street clothes, Bertha was wearing her Dolly Parton outfit — the one she wore every Halloween when she handed out candy at her home, and for costume parties. It had become a sort of trademark of hers over the years, and she milked it for all it was worth. It was a tight outfit, padded in all the right places, especially in the ample bosom and hips. She wore a pale blonde, almost white-haired wig, piled on top of her head in a beehive style.

Beside her stood Jock Larson, his hand tight around her waist, holding her close.

Jock Larson . . .

"Have you seen that picture before?" Maggie repeated, standing close to Candy.

"No, I . . ."

She stopped suddenly as something clicked inside her, and in a single, stunning moment, everything fell into place for her, and she saw the events of the past week laid out with incredible clarity, as if someone had quite abruptly, with the touch of a cosmic finger, aligned the planets across the starry sky.

"On my God!" A shudder raced through her as she turned to Maggie with the light of new understanding in her eyes. "That's it! I'll be damned," she breathed, her hand instinctively clapping to her mouth as the realization spread through her. "It was her all along, wasn't it? She's the one who . . ."

"What are you doing here?" a harsh voice cut in.

Caught off guard, Candy and Maggie twirled clumsily — and found themselves face-to-face with Bertha Grayfire.

The chairwoman of the town council stood in the doorway, half in shadow, dressed much like Maggie had been the night before. Bertha wore black sweatpants, a dark gray sweatshirt under a dark blue Windbreaker, and black gloves. Her graying hair, usually neatly coiffed, was in disarray, as if she had just walked through a hurricane. In one hand she carried a flashlight; with the other she held tightly to a paper grocery bag.

Her gaze narrowed on the two women as she waited for an answer, but all she got at first were assorted babbles, stammers, and mumbles as Candy pulled Maggie away from the photos. Candy cast about for an excuse, her mind racing frantically, and finally blurted out the first sentence she could think of.

"We were . . . we're, um, here to pay our property taxes!"

"Property taxes?" Maggie scrunched up her face and gave Candy an odd look, until Candy nudged her with an elbow, and Maggie finally got the point. "Oh, um, yeah, that's right." She forced a laugh, trying and failing to sound lighthearted. "You see, we were just wondering who to make our checks out to. I always get confused about that." She looked at Bertha innocently, batting her eyes in expectation.

The silence that followed stretched dangerously long. Though she tried to maintain a calm appearance, Candy swallowed hard. She could hear her heart thumping in her ears and was sure she could hear Maggie's heart pounding as well.

Finally Bertha spoke, in a tone that was

low and harsh. "Property taxes were due three weeks ago. But I don't think that's why you're here." Her gaze shifted back and forth quickly, from Candy to Maggie, then to the photo on the wall. Her jaw tightened and her gaze grew hard as she turned back to Candy. "You were looking for these, weren't you?" She nodded down toward the grocery bag she carried.

Candy was genuinely mystified at the question. "What?"

"The ballots," Bertha said, her voice turning chillingly cold. "That's why you came here, isn't it? You've been running all over town the past few days, trying to help Ray. I've heard all about it. I know what you were looking for. And I knew you'd come here sooner or later — for the ballots. That's why I shredded them."

In an abrupt move, she tossed the grocery bag across the room, so that it landed with a plop at Candy's feet. "Go ahead, get a close look."

Candy didn't need to look too closely. She could see from where she stood that inside the bag were the remnants of shredded documents, a confetti mix of green, white, and gray paper now ripped apart and undecipherable.

She looked up at Bertha, her expression

changing. No sense in pretending any longer, of clinging to some semblance of innocence. They both knew where the truth lay. "Those were your white hairs, weren't they? The ones I found in the folder in Sapphire's home office?" She tilted her head toward the photo. "They were from the wig."

Bertha seemed surprised for a moment, but then surprise gave way to a chuckle, though there was no joy in her voice. "So that's where she put them. I've been looking for those damned strands of hair all week. I'm sorry you found it before I did."

"Where did she get it?"

Bertha scoffed at the question. "You're supposed to be the sleuth. Why don't you figure it out?"

Candy already had her suspicions, which had gone unspoken until now. "My guess? In Jock's bed."

Another silence, as Bertha's expression darkened. "You're smarter than you look."

"You wore the outfit for him, didn't you?"

Bertha's mouth worked, her anger obvious, but she apparently decided to play the game, at least for the moment. "Yes, if you must know. He had a fixation on the Dolly Parton thing. It was his idea in the first place. He liked me to dress up sometimes, give him a show. He was a little strange that way."

Maggie gasped in sudden realization. "So you two were . . . an item?"

Bertha blew out a breath of air. "Oh, come on, Maggie. Try to keep up."

"And Sapphire too," Candy continued. "They were seeing each other?"

"Apparently. I only found out about that later. Jock was a busy boy, as you've no doubt heard."

"That's where she found the strands of hair . . . when she was in Jock's bed."

Bertha shrugged. "I suppose. She was an industrious woman — I'm sure you've heard that too."

"And she used the evidence to blackmail you? So you'd let her win the pageant?"

At that, Bertha actually laughed. "You still haven't figured it all out, have you? Here, I've got something to show you."

Moving quickly, the town councilwoman crossed the room to the desk, took a set of keys from a pocket and opened the top middle drawer. She reached inside, her back to Candy and Maggie, blocking their view.

When she turned back around, she held a gun in her hand. "You want to know the truth?" she seethed, her face a twisted mask. "All right, I'll tell you. Yes, Jock and I were having an affair — but it was much more than that. For six years I gave him anything he wanted. I kept quiet about us, just like he wanted. I was there whenever he needed me. I put up with his constant philandering. He told me he would marry me . . . so I waited and waited for him. But it never happened. Finally I realized he was playing me, just like he played with everyone else in this town. He used me, like he used everyone else. I threatened to leave him, to break it off for good, but he told me he just needed more time, that he would change." She shook her head as she let out a low, sad sound. "But I knew Jock wouldn't change. When I told him it was over, he begged me to meet him at our secret spot — up on Mount Desert Island . . ."

Maggie gasped, and Candy felt a chill go up her spine. They both knew what was coming next.

"I don't know for sure what happened that night," Bertha continued, her voice flat and unemotional. "I thought he might propose to me . . . that's really what I thought . . . but I was as foolish as ever. He had no such thing in mind. He just wanted to make sure I kept my mouth shut about the two of us, once he broke it off. I was furious. I lashed out at him. He was standing too close to

425

the edge when . . ."

Her voice trailed off.

Candy finished the sentence for her. "You pushed him too hard."

Bertha's gaze had grown distant, as if remembering the terror of that night. "He lost his footing, and then . . . he was gone." She shook her head in disbelief. But she gathered herself quickly. Her gaze narrowed on Candy and Maggie. "So now you know. I killed Jock Larson." She paused, raising the gun and pointing it right at them. "And now I'm going to kill you."

THIRTY-SIX

"Bertha, you don't have to do this. Jock's death was an accident." Staring down the barrel of the gun, Candy found herself strangely calm, though her mouth was suddenly dry. Carefully, moving slowly, she held out her hands and tried to sound as friendly as possible, as if talking down someone about to jump off a rooftop. "We can get you help. We'll sort this out. Don't make it worse."

"She's right!" Maggie managed to squeak. She pointed frantically at Candy. "Listen to her. She knows what she's talking about. She's smart!"

"Too smart. You know too much," Bertha growled, brandishing the gun.

Maggie's eyes grew wide. "You know what? Not a problem. We'll just forget everything we said here. We won't tell a soul. Will we, Candy?"

"It's too late," Bertha said. "It's too late.

Don't you think I would end this if I could, if there was any other way? But there isn't." She glanced down at the bag of shredded documents, and suddenly Candy knew what Bertha was talking about. She felt cold in the pit of her stomach.

"You killed Sapphire too."

"She forced me into it," Bertha said, sounding more hysterical with every word. "She was a wicked woman . . . a *wicked* woman!"

"She used the hairs from the wig to blackmail you, is that it? To make sure she was chosen as the Blueberry Queen?"

"Oh no, not that. She knew how to play her cards at the right time. No, she didn't blackmail me. She just went after the judges. I didn't even know until I saw the ballots the night of the pageant. I knew instantly what she was doing, but I couldn't say anything then. There were too many people around. I had no choice but to declare her the winner."

"How many of the judges did she black-mail?" Maggie asked curiously.

"How many?" Bertha gave a mad cackle. "All of them!"

"All of them?" Candy shook her head in disbelief. She couldn't help but, in some strange way, admire Sapphire's scheme. And she saw the last pieces of the puzzle coming together. "So you went to her house that night, two days after the pageant, to confront her — to tell her you knew what she had done."

"I wanted her to resign her crown," Bertha explained. "I demanded that she do so! But you know what she did?" She paused as if waiting for a response, then answered the question herself. "She laughed at me. She *mocked* me."

"And that's when she told you about the hairs she'd found."

Bertha nodded. "She told me all about her and Jock. She told me he loved her. Can you believe that? Jock, loving *her?* That horrid woman! She said she knew Jock and I were having an affair. And that she knew we went to that cliff together, that it was our secret rendezvous. She must have followed us one night — or Jock told her. Maybe he even took her up to that same spot — maybe he took all his girlfriends there. It doesn't matter now. She put two and two together . . . and told me that if I kept her secret, she'd keep mine. But I couldn't do it! I couldn't trust her!"

"So you killed her," Candy prompted.

"Oh, that wasn't my plan, of course," Bertha said, licking her lips. "I tried to reason with her, to explain what had happened, that it was just an accident . . . and that's when Ray showed up. Sapphire made me hide in a back room while she talked to him. She had his hammer in her purse. She said she had found it and wanted to return it to him. She wanted more from him, I could tell, though what I don't know. Perhaps she wanted to use him as a spy, something like that. But he wouldn't play her game. He took the hammer and studied it, turned it over and over, then handed it back to her. When he said the hammer wasn't his, she got furious. She went nuts! She threw the hammer aside, called him all sorts of terrible names. She was like a mad cat. She chased him out of the place."

"And so you picked up the hammer," Candy said.

"It practically landed at my feet. Ray's fingerprints were all over it." Bertha looked at Candy, staring hard into her eyes, and just for an instant Candy saw the desperation that Bertha harbored deep inside, the panic . . . and the madness.

"It was my chance. I had to take it. It was the only way out." Her face suddenly hardened. "Just like now." She motioned with the gun toward the door. "That way . . . and don't make any sudden moves."

Maggie squeaked again in terror, but Candy decided the best way to handle the situation was to do what Bertha asked. Still, she had to try one more time. "Bertha, you can't do this. How will you explain it?"

Bertha shrugged. "Simple. It's Sebastian's gun."

"What?"

"I took it from his place two nights ago when I was over there. He really shouldn't have left it lying around. He's made this much too easy."

"But . . ."

"Shut up and get moving."

"Where are we going?" Maggie asked.

"Up to the auditorium. I figure if I leave your bodies backstage it will be awhile before they're found. Once they find the gun nearby, they'll arrest Sebastian. He's the perfect fall guy."

"But he has an alibi," Candy told her. "We checked."

"It doesn't matter. I'll let the police figure it out. At least I'll be out of it. And with the ballots destroyed, the last piece of evidence is gone. Now move."

They backed into the darkened hallway, Candy in front, followed closely by Maggie, with Bertha right behind them. Candy's mind was in turmoil. What should they do?

As she turned and started down the hallway, she thought of running, trying to escape into the dark building, but she was afraid Bertha would fire. She wasn't too concerned about herself, but she was worried Maggie would get hit. She couldn't take that chance.

So she chewed at her lip, fighting down the fear, trying to think of some way out. She had taken only a few steps when she heard Maggie say to Bertha, "Oh, by the way, there's one thing you forgot."

Maggie stopped, and Candy paused also, turning back to look over her shoulder at her friend.

"What?" Bertha demanded, glowering at them over the pistol.

"This!" In a sudden, fluid movement, Maggie brought up her hand and flicked the button on her umbrella, which she still carried with her. It popped open, spreading out like a shield, tossing off drops of water. She thrust the opened umbrella right up into the surprised face of Bertha, who stumbled backward with a grunt as the gun went off. But her aim was high, and the bullet went harmlessly into the ceiling above Candy's and Maggie's heads.

Maggie screamed, threw the umbrella back toward Bertha, then dashed toward Candy. "Run!"

Pulling each other along, barely containing their panic, they ran forward to the end of the hallway, paused briefly to look down another long hallway to their right, then turned left, pushed through a door, and started up a darkened staircase. Somewhere behind them, Bertha bellowed in anger.

"Smart move!" Candy shouted as they took the stairs two at a time.

"Let's just hope it doesn't get us killed."

Halfway up they reached a landing, turned left, and ran up more stairs. They pushed through another set of doors at the top — and found themselves in a side hallway that fed into the auditorium through a set of double doors. A narrow stream of faded red carpeting sloped downward toward the rear of the building, toward the backstage area. Candy saw an exit sign farther down the hallway but hesitated to go that far. She could hear Bertha coming up the stairs behind them.

"Which way?" Maggie asked.

Candy pointed to a door in front of them, directly across the hall. "That way."

"Into the auditorium?"

"Maybe we can lose her in there." Her decision made, she crossed the hall and pushed through a door into the space beyond . . . and they found themselves in the opera house's auditorium. They had been in here less than a week earlier, the night of the pageant, when the place had been well lighted and full of people. But now it looked completely different, a vast, dark, hollow space, smelling of old wood, old fabrics, and ancient dust. A horseshoe-shaped balcony was directly above their heads; the stage was downward to their right, decorated with scenery for the upcoming performances of *Oklahoma!*

"Is this where we wanted to be?" Maggie asked, close by Candy's elbow.

Candy leaned into the door behind them, pushing it shut and looking for a lock. But she found none. She glanced around. "Which way?" she asked, uncertain.

Maggie pointed frantically. "There! Back-stage!"

"But isn't that where Bertha was taking us?"

"Just get going!" Maggie pushed Candy in the back, and together they ran through the seats toward the center aisle. When they reached it, they angled forward toward the stage, then dashed back into the rows of seats on the far side of the auditorium, trying to put as much distance as possible between themselves and the door through which they had entered.

As she ran, Candy kept looking back over her shoulder, expecting Bertha to burst through the door at any moment. But Bertha fooled them. A creaking sound from another direction drew Candy's attention. She slowed, turned to look, and through a door behind them but closer to the front of the stage came Bertha.

"She's trying to cut us off!" Candy yelled, just as a shot rang out. Yelping in terror, Maggie dropped to her knees between the rows of seats. Candy crouched down beside her.

"You can't escape!" Bertha called out. "Give it up!"

"What should we do?" Maggie asked, near tears.

Candy looked around hurriedly. They weren't trapped yet, but their options were narrowing. "Back that way." She pointed up the aisle on the far side of the auditorium. "Stay low. Try to get back to the lobby, and we'll get outside from there."

Maggie nodded, her eyes wild, but keeping her fear tamped down, she crept to the end of the row, then started up the far aisle as Bertha closed in on them.

"Move! Quicker!" Candy encouraged in a low, urgent voice.

As she ran, she glanced back over her

shoulder. Bertha was running parallel to them, up the center aisle. She was moving sideways like a crab, her eyes holding tight to them, holding the gun low.

She's herding us, Candy thought with a chill as she shifted her gaze forward again. She came to a quick conclusion. "She wants us to go in this direction," she said to Maggie as she rested a hand on her friend's shoulder, slowing her. She knew they had to find another way out.

Maggie looked around, falling to her hands and knees, her gaze pleading. "What should we do?"

Candy urged her friend up and forward again as she tried to figure out their next move. Her gaze swept the auditorium, searching. And then she saw it, almost right in front of them — an alcove to their right, opening off the side aisle, with a narrow carpeted stairway going upward.

Candy's gaze followed it up, her eyes rising . . . to the balcony.

"In here!" She dashed into the alcove, pulling Maggie with her as she heard Bertha shout in frustration.

Up the staircase they thundered, panting now, knowing they were running for their lives. At the top they turned left, into the balcony itself, then right, running up a set of shallow stairs that ran along the rows of seats, heading toward the back row where they saw another set of doors. "We can go through there," Candy said, pointing. "It should take us back down to the lobby."

"Think we can make it in time?"

"We'll have to, won't we?" Candy pushed through the door. They emerged on a long landing with wide curving stairways on either side that lead down to the lobby below. Candy angled right, grabbed the railing, and started quickly down the stairs, but stopped midway when she heard footsteps below. Candy and Maggie both pressed back against the wall as a shadow emerged below them, turned, and looked up in their direction.

"You didn't think you were going to get past me, did you?" Bertha said in a low, menacing tone. She waved the gun at them in a threatening manner. "Now get down here."

Candy cursed. Maggie grabbed her arm. "What should we do?"

Instinctively, Candy pushed her back up the stairs. "We're not giving up yet. Back the way we came. And stay down!"

They both fell into a crouch, the better to avoid Bertha's line of sight, and retraced their steps, heading back up the staircase and through the doors into the balcony. "We're trapped!" Maggie said hysterically as they closed and leaned against the door behind them. Candy turned left, then right, trying to figure out what to do next, when she spotted another narrow staircase, heading up. "Not yet," she said. "There must be another floor. Maybe we can get up to the roof and find a way down from there."

"The roof?" The words practically exploded from Maggie. "Oh my God! I wish I still had my umbrella!"

The stairs led up to the control booth, a small, dingy workspace with sliding windows along the entire interior wall, overlooking the auditorium and stage below. A trio of ancient arc spotlights, sitting atop their three-legged stands, were spaced evenly across the room. Centered in front of the window were light and sound boards, and sitting on a table nearby was a fairly new laptop computer. Folding chairs, empty coffee cups and soda cans, abandoned jackets, and even a moldy old pair of sneakers were scattered about the room. A bank of lockers had been pushed up against one wall, and narrow shelves, overloaded with assorted equipment, hung from another.

Candy looked up. In the ceiling she saw a hatch, and leading up to it, a black-runged steel ladder, set into the back wall. "That's where we're going," Candy said, dashing to the rungs and taking them quickly.

Maggie stood in the center of the room with a confused look on her face. "Where?"

"The widow's walk."

"But . . ."

Candy gave her a fierce look. "No buts. Bertha will be here any minute. Now come on!"

So Maggie went. It took Candy a few moments to figure out how to unlatch the hatch, but finally she threw it open, letting in wind and rain. Tilting her head down and squinting her eyes against the storm, she pushed up through the opening.

THIRTY-SEVEN

The widow's walk of the Pruitt Opera House was a small, octagonal space, about six or eight feet across. Candy emerged into the middle of it and was immediately assailed by the raging wind, which carried with it the remnants of the storm that, for the most part, had passed over them. Though the dome over their heads sheltered them from the worst of the rain, the raw wind tore at her as she bent to help up Maggie, who complained the entire time. "I can't believe you brought us up here," she huffed as she planted her feet beneath her and stood unsteadily. "When I said I wanted to escape, this wasn't what I had in mind."

Candy barely heard her. She turned completely around, looking down over the waist-high stone walls of the widow's walk, down at the sloping slate roof, slick with rain, and down over the side of the building to the ground far below. "Whoa. I didn't realize we'd be up so high."

"How are we going to get down?" Maggie whined, looking out over the roof. "I don't see a ladder or anything."

Candy felt her stomach tighten. "I don't know but . . ."

That's when she caught movement out of the corner of her eye . . . and turned to see Bertha emerging from the hatch behind them.

In one hand Bertha held the gun, wielding it like a spatula at a church social dinner. With the other hand she pulled herself up into the widow's walk, grunting just a bit, all the while keeping a wary eye on Candy and Maggie.

For one wild moment Candy was tempted to dash forward to try to kick the gun from Bertha's hand, as she had seen done so often in the movies and on TV. But this wasn't a movie, she quickly reminded herself, and she knew she couldn't move faster than a bullet. So she and Maggie backed away, to the far side of the widow's walk, as Bertha stood on shaky legs.

She was huffing heavily. It was clear the chase through the opera house had winded her. But she looked no less angry. If anything, she looked more furious than before. She was seething, literally shaking with fury.

"That was a stupid, *stupid* thing to do," she spat as she backed to the opposite side of the widow's walk, keeping the gun pointed steadily at Candy and Maggie. "I've got better things to do than chase you two through a building. I should have shot you in the basement when I had the chance. But you won't get away again. It's time to end this . . . now."

Candy and Maggie both yelped and shut their eyes as Bertha pushed the gun toward them, about to fire, but she was distracted by a shout.

"Hey! You there, up on the roof!"

The words were carried oddly by the wind, and for a moment none of them knew from which direction the shout had come. Candy opened her eyes and looked around desperately. It took her a few moments, but she finally spotted a figure on the street below. It was a man, dressed in black, standing under a street lamp. He was waving his hands frantically, as if to catch their attention, and shouted again. "What's going on up there? Is everyone okay?"

Candy knew instantly who it was — Judicious F. P. Bosworth, the town's sometimes-invisible mystic, who obviously was being seen on this stormy night. She waved back at him, leaning into the side railing and shouting at the top her lungs: "Judicious! Help us!"

"Shut up!" Bertha yelled, turning the gun first toward Judicious, then back to Candy and Maggie. "Shut up!"

"Are you all right?" Judicious called up to them.

Candy jumped up and down frantically. "No! Get help!"

Caught out in the open, and apparently thinking it would be better to get rid of any witnesses first, Bertha swerved, took aim at Judicious, and fired once, twice, just as a car came up Ocean Avenue, its headlights cutting into the darkness. Just before the car reached Judicious, it swerved and bounded up on the sidewalk, its horn blaring . . . and that's when Candy saw something she would never forget for the rest of her life.

Maggie, crouched over like a football player, lunged forward with her shoulders lowered. She covered the space between them and Bertha in an instant, tackling Bertha around the waist. They slammed back against the railing on the far side, both of them grunting. The impact knocked the gun from Bertha's hand. It flew over the side of the widow's walk and clattered down the roof, falling over the edge into darkness.

Bertha was stunned momentarily but quickly regained her senses. She wrapped her arms around Maggie's head and squeezed tight. The two of them fell to the floor in a tangle of arms and legs, kicking and punching.

For a moment Candy was stunned. Maggie? Tackling Bertha? She was sure that hadn't just happened. She turned to look back down at the street. Judicious had disappeared, but the car door opened and Ben spilled out, looking up at her on the widow's walk. She waved to him, screamed for help, then looked back at Maggie and Bertha.

They were still fighting, and she realized with a jolt that her friend needed her. She crossed the space in a near dive, landed on her knees beside Bertha, and wrapped her hands around the chairwoman's thick arms. But rather than being big and flabby, they were strong and muscular. She hadn't known Bertha had been working out, and was impressed as well as surprised. It was like wrestling with a python, she thought vaguely as she tried to pull Bertha off her friend.

They struggled for a few moments until, temporarily able to free herself, Maggie pulled away. Her hair was a terrible fright, her face red and distorted. Bertha kicked out at her while pushing herself back against Candy, and twisting, she turned her attention from one of her attackers to the other. Her eyes were red with fury as she reached out with thick fingers, wrapping them around Candy's throat. She hooked her legs around Candy's, then pushed her back and rolled onto her, pinning her to the floor.

Candy felt the panic rise inside her as Bertha leaned close, breathing into her face. "I waited too long to do this," she snarled, tightening her fingers. "You've meddled in my life for the last time."

Candy clawed at Bertha's fingers, trying to break their grasp on her neck, but it seemed an impossible task. She saw spots in her eyes, felt rain pelting her face and fire in her lungs. Panicking, she tried to kick up with her knees, to push Bertha off, but it was like trying to free herself from the grasp of a bear. She felt her air being cut off and let out a raspy breath, her eyes rolling back into her head.

And then she saw another arm move across her face and tighten around Bertha's neck. Suddenly Bertha was pulled back, off her. Candy sucked in a deep breath. She rolled to her side, rubbing at her throat, trying to get her wind back.

She took several more gulps of air before

she looked to see where Bertha had gone. It was Maggie who had saved her, pulling the chairwoman off her. They were involved in a life-and-death struggle now, and Bertha was winning. She was like a cornered creature, inhuman, fighting for its life, trying to lash out at all costs, inflicting what damage it could. The chairwoman punched out with clenched fists, striking Maggie about the face and shoulders, and Maggie, trying to protect herself, could only cover her face with her hands as she curled in on herself and backed up against the wall.

Knowing she had the upper hand, feeling victorious, Bertha rose unsteadily to her feet. She stood glaring down at the two of them. "You're both pathetic," she snarled between gasps of breath, her face twisted so that she was nearly unrecognizable. "To think I was worried about you. You have to put up a better fight than that if you want to beat me."

She looked around for her weapon, apparently unaware that it had gone over the side. When she found it nowhere, she pushed the wet hair back from her forehead, then rubbed her hands together. "Okay, I guess we'll have to do this the hard way." She looked from one to the other, then settled on Maggie. "You're first."

She stepped quickly to Maggie and lifted her, apparently in an effort to throw her over the side of the building. But Maggie would not go easily. She kicked out at Bertha and flailed at her with her arms, landing a few good punches, which forced Bertha back for a moment. But Bertha would not be denied. She backed away a few steps, then charged at Maggie in an effort to overwhelm her with power and fury.

As Bertha came at her again, Maggie screamed and ducked, her right leg going wide. Bertha stepped on it and lost her balance, just as Maggie came up, trying to throw Bertha off her. Bertha tumbled in the air, her momentum sending her up and over . . .

Her legs went over the far side of the railing first in an arc as her body dropped heavily. But her arm swung out and she managed to hook the top of the railing with her armpit. She pulled herself back in toward the widow's walk and bounced, her chin slamming into the railing's hard stone surface. She almost lost control then and fell back, but her hands flailed about, grabbing two of the rails. She dropped further down as she struggled to hold on. But her fingers were too raw, too cold, and gravity pulled at her. She acted instinctively, self-

447

preservation driving her as she flailed about with one of her hands, reaching through the rails to grab hold of Maggie. She kicked frantically, trying to find a foothold on the slippery roof below her. But the weight of her body was too much for her. Her grip loosened.

Eyes wide and mouth open, she slipped soundlessly over the side. Candy and Maggie heard the thump as her upper body hit the rain-slicked slate roof, then a scraping sound as she slid downward and finally over the edge into the wet, dark night.

THIRTY-EIGHT

The storm blew northeastward overnight, spiraling into the Canadian Maritimes. By ten o'clock Friday morning, when Sapphire Vine was scheduled to be buried at Stone Hill Cemetery, the sun was beginning to break through thin, ragged clouds that reminded Candy of drawn-out balls of raw cotton   all that remained of the fierce storm of the night before.

The ground was still damp, though, squelching under the feet of those who had gathered in this place to pay their last respects. Glassy, shallow puddles that lay scattered across the uneven landscape had to be assiduously avoided unless one wanted well-soaked shoes. More annoying were the few stray drops of cold rainwater that fell without warning on uncovered heads from the glistening summer leaves of maples, elms, and red oaks that inhabited the cemetery grounds.

Standing beside Maggie toward the rear of the crowd, Candy wore a short-sleeve black knit dress and dark gray Birkenstock clogs, which she had thought might be too casual for the occasion but then decided were better than sneakers or her muddy rubber boots. She also had brought along a navy blue raincoat, which she held draped over her folded arms. The day was warming and the worst of the weather was over, so she had decided against wearing it.

Trying not to seem too obvious about it, she glanced first in one direction, then the other, scanning the crowd huddled solemnly at the graveside.

It's a pretty good turnout, she thought as the Reverend James P. Daisy delivered a last few words, and Cameron Zimmerman, looking thin and bone weary in an ill-fitting dark brown suit, threw a balsam garland laced with ribbons and blueberries onto the descending black coffin.

So ends the shortest and strangest reign of a Blueberry Queen in all of Cape Willington's history, Candy reflected with a mixture of melancholy and resignation. *Still, Sapphire would be proud. She's had a good sending-off.*

Maggie must have sensed her thoughts. "The Queen is dead," she murmured, looking uncharacteristically tearful. "Long live the Queen."

"Here, here."

Maggie dabbed at her eyes with a lace handkerchief. "Oh, Sapphire, Sapphire, we hardly knew ye! Why, oh why, did you have to be such an obnoxious flake? We could have been such good friends, you and I, if only you had been just a little bit normal!"

"Normality is in short supply around this place, in case you hadn't noticed," Candy mused with another furtive glance around at the crowd. "Besides, it's like you said — her strange behavior wasn't really her fault. She never fully recovered from the shock of losing both David and Cameron in such a short period of time. She'd been living in some sort of dreamworld of her own making ever since. I guess she really was crazy."

"Done in by someone who was even crazier than she was." Maggie shook her head. "It's so sad. Just so damn sad." Her voice trembled a bit as she spoke.

Candy took Maggie's elbow empathetically. "Well, at least Sapphire's left behind something good — a wonderful legacy, of which she had every reason to be proud." She nodded toward Cameron and Amanda, who were approaching them.

In a blubber of tears and sobs, Maggie

ran forward and hugged Cameron tightly. He looked uncomfortable for a moment, then leaned into her, put his arms around her, and hugged her back.

"It's done," he said softly. "She's finally at peace. Now she and my father can be together."

"Oh, Cameron," Maggie said tearfully.

With the appropriate words spoken, the ceremony ended. Reverend Daisy came over to shake their hands and offer some words of condolence before he turned away to talk to others.

As the crowd began to disperse, starting off toward a line of cars nearby, Cameron, Amanda, Maggie, and Candy stood arm in arm, heads bowed, paying their final, silent respects to the former Susan Jane Vincent, alias Sapphire Vine.

"Rest in peace," Candy said softly.

Maggie squeezed her hand. "She can, thanks to you. You're the one who solved this murder case. If it wasn't for you . . . well, a terrible injustice would have remained, um, unjustified."

Candy smiled. "I had help — the best partner anyone could ask for."

"We *are* a good team, aren't we?" Maggie asked, brightening a little.

"You never did tell us everything that happened last night," Amanda said, looking over at the two of them. "When are we going to get the full story?"

Candy pondered that for a moment. She had just come from the police station, where she had spent an hour recounting the events of the night before. After that, she had received a stern warning from Chief Durr, who told her, once again, to never, ever do this again. But then he grudgingly shook her hand. "If you ever need a job," he told her sincerely, "I might be able to find a spot for you in the Department."

"It was nothing really," Candy finally said to Amanda. "Just a little scuffle with Bertha Grayfire."

"A little scuffle?" Maggie said, aghast. "We were fighting for our lives! We're lucky to be here!"

"How'd you beat her?" Cameron asked, intrigued. "I heard she had a gun."

Candy took Maggie's arm. "This is the real hero," she told Amanda. "Your mother was amazing last night. She saved us both."

Maggie glowed in the praise but was quick to return it. "And what about you? I watched you all week. You were like Sherlock Holmes on the trail of Professor Moriarty. You knew Ray was innocent, so you flushed out the real killer. It was genius, pure genius!"

Candy snorted. "I got lucky, that's all. Heck, I almost got us both killed. I wouldn't call that genius."

"No, Maggie's right," Cameron said to Candy. "You're the only one who was smart enough to start snooping around. If it wasn't for you, who knows what would have happened? You deserve a medal or something."

Candy's eyes flashed with sudden humor. "I'd settle for someone to help me fix that broken window in my back door."

Suddenly put on the spot, Cameron stammered a bit, uncertain how to reply, but Maggie and Amanda laughed. "Oh, I'm sure Ray will be over first thing in the morning to help you with that," Maggie said, coming to his rescue. "Maybe Cameron can come up with a better reward for you, once he comes into his inheritance."

"Um, yeah, I'll think of something," the teenager mumbled.

Candy laid a hand on his shoulder. "Don't be silly, Cam. You don't owe me a thing. I'm just glad we're all safe, and that Bertha Grayfire is in custody, where she belongs."

"Is she going to live?" Cameron asked.

Candy nodded. "I think so. The police told me this morning that she has a broken collarbone, a broken hip, and two broken legs. But she's going to survive to stand trial." As she spoke, her gaze shifted toward a figure walking from the graveside. "Excuse me a moment. I'll be right back."

Leaving her friends, she hurried down the slope at an angle, so she could intercept the lone figure as he headed toward his car. "Herr Georg!" she called after him.

Hearing his name, the baker paused and looked back. His expression brightened as he gave her a muted wave. "Hello, Candy."

She smiled and waved back. When she caught up with him, he continued, "It was a lovely ceremony, yes?"

She took his arm as they continued down the slope toward the cars. "It was lovely, yes. Sapphire would have been very pleased." She paused a moment before she continued, her tone becoming more serious. "Herr Georg, there's something I must say to you."

He turned to look at her expectantly. "Yes?"

"Well, I . . . I wanted to apologize to you for what happened yesterday — about our conversation in the park. I didn't mean to pry into your private affairs like that, and I hope you didn't think I was accusing you of having anything to do with Sapphire's death. I know I probably jumped to conclusions, but I should have realized you were . . ."

She broke off as Herr Georg waggled his finger in the air. "Candy, Candy, *meine liebchen.* You of all people owe me no apologies. You have been a better friend than I could have ever asked for. It is I who should apologize to you, for not being truthful with you from the start. If I hadn't been so protective of my past, all of this might have turned out differently."

Candy squeezed his arm. "You shouldn't blame yourself about anything that happened at the pageant. You weren't the only one being blackmailed, you know — and you weren't the only one who adjusted those scores."

"I wasn't?" This took Herr Georg by surprise. His eyes grew wide. "But who else could have . . . ?" But he stopped himself and smiled again. "Ah, but that is in the past, isn't it? And it is over."

Candy nodded emphatically. "It's over."

He patted her hand, noticeably relieved. "Well, that is good to know."

She took him by the hand then. "Come, I have something for you."

She led him to her Jeep, which was parked not too far away. Opening the passenger-side door, she withdrew a thick manila envelope, stuffed with papers, photos, and documents.

"These are yours," she said, passing the envelope to him. "It's the rest of the documents Sapphire collected about you. I'll let you decide what to do with it, though I'd recommend having a nice bonfire in your backyard some night very soon."

Herr Georg took the envelope appreciatively, his expression solemn. "Candy, I don't know what to say."

"You don't have to say anything. As far as I'm concerned, this whole issue is closed."

She leaned forward and kissed him lightly on the cheek. He blushed deeply, making his hair and handlebar moustache seem all the whiter.

At that moment a voice cleared behind them, and someone else spoke. "Miss Holliday?"

Candy turned.

Helen Ross Pruitt stood behind her, looking quite sophisticated in a stylish black suit, a lavender silk scarf that added a bit of color, and a wide-brimmed black hat with a matching lavender band. Candy's gaze flicked to the right. Standing just there, off to one side, hands folded formally in front of him as he waited patiently, was Hobbins the butler.

With the height of dignity and compassion, Mrs. Pruitt extended a thin-boned hand to Candy. "I have spoken to Cameron and the others," she said, "but I wanted to express my utmost condolences to you personally on the passing of your friend. I can't say I knew Ms. Vine well, but I do know that she had a wonderful spirit and energy. She certainly will be missed in this town."

Candy shook hands with her. "Thank you for your kind words."

Mrs. Pruitt then turned her gaze to Herr Georg. "Might I borrow Ms. Holliday for a moment," she asked politely, "so we could have a private word?"

Expertly taking his cue, Herr Georg first kissed Candy's hand, then bowed deeply to them both. "Of course. I must get back to work. Candy, I will have a little surprise for you early next week. Something special I'm baking. I'll bring it by the farm."

She smiled at him warmly. "I can't wait."

He nodded to Candy, then to Mrs. Pruitt. "Ladies," he said gallantly and took his leave.

Candy turned back to Mrs. Pruitt. She noticed that Hobbins the butler had stepped away to a discreet distance, far enough so he was out of earshot, yet not too far away should Mrs. Pruitt have need of him.

It was just the two of them now, standing beside the Jeep, under the clearing sky.

"I would simply like to tell you," Mrs. Pruitt began, leaning in toward Candy and speaking in low tones, "that I am aware of what you have been up to this week. I wanted you to know that I am greatly impressed by your valiant efforts and congratulate you on your success. I'm not sure you're aware of it, but the whole town is talking about your sleuthing skills."

Candy tried not to appear as surprised as she felt. "I . . . wasn't aware I had those skills. But thank you very much anyway, Mrs. Pruitt. That's very kind of you to say so."

"Risking your own safety as you did, and capturing that horrid woman. It's quite amazing, really."

"I had help," Candy said magnanimously.

"So I understand. But you were the catalyst. Your conviction and tenacity were admirable."

"Thank you," Candy repeated awkwardly.

"As you know," Mrs. Pruitt went on, "Haley is scheduled to be crowned as the new Blueberry Queen on Sunday afternoon."

"Oh, yes!" Candy looked around. "Where is Haley?"

"She's waiting in the Bentley. I've asked her to give us a few moments to talk alone. Well, to come to my point: we would be honored if you would join us at Town Hall on Sunday for the ceremony and for a brief reception afterward."

"Of course. It would be my pleasure."

Mrs. Pruitt nodded in acknowledgment. "Excellent, excellent. We shall look forward to seeing you there. Two o'clock sharp." She started away, then stopped and turned back. "Oh, and Candy dear — perhaps you would like to come to Pruitt Manor for tea some day next week? We could tour the gardens afterward. I know how much you love them."

Candy was almost at a loss for words. "That sounds wonderful. Yes, I'd love to."

"Good! I'll have Hobbins arrange it. And do you think your friend Ms. Tremont would like to join us?"

"I'm sure she would, yes."

"Very well. Please extend my invitation to her also. She's such a nice woman. Delightful sense of humor."

Candy had to hold back a chuckle. "She certainly has that."

Mrs. Pruitt gave her a pleasant smile and

started away again, but a thought suddenly popped into Candy's mind. She couldn't help blurting out, "Oh! Mrs. Pruitt!"

"Yes?" Helen Ross Pruitt looked back expectantly.

"I — I have just one more question for you."

"Yes?"

"Well, I was wondering — why did you hire that lawyer for Ray?"

Mrs. Pruitt gave her a long look that seemed to tell her the answer was obvious. Still, she answered as pleasantly as she could. "Just like you, Ms. Holliday, I, too, knew Ray Hutchins had not killed that girl. He has been doing good work for us at Pruitt Manor for many years, and I am quite a good judge of character. Ray's innocence should have been clear to anyone with a bit of common sense, but it seems you and I were the only ones who knew the accusation against him was a grievous error. Regardless, I wanted to do something to help him, and since I knew he did not have the financial capabilities to hire a good attorney himself, I thought it was the least I could do, to help out a fellow Caper. Wouldn't you have done the same had you been in my place?"

"Of course."

"And I did set you onto the right trail, didn't I, when you visited me Wednesday morning?"

Candy had to think about that a bit, recalling the conversation they had had at Pruitt Manor that day. Yes, now that she thought about it, Mrs. Pruitt *had* brought up the subject of bribery, which had fueled Candy's curiosity, driving her to dig deeper.

"You did," Candy acknowledged.

Mrs. Pruitt nodded emphatically. "Well. There you are. 'Til Sunday then."

And taking the arm of Hobbins the butler, Mrs. Helen Ross Pruitt walked regally toward her waiting Bentley, her chin held aristocratically high.

"She's a piece of work, isn't she?"

Candy looked around. Maggie had come up behind her.

"She's a pistol all right. Definitely someone who marches to the beat of her own drummer."

"Have you noticed that we seem to have a lot of those kind of people in this little town?"

"I've noticed."

Maggie sighed dramatically. "I guess every town has its own burdens." She tilted her head toward the departing Mrs. Pruitt. "So what did she have to say?"

"Well, for one thing, she's invited us to Pruitt Manor next week for tea."

"Ooh! Did I hear you say *us?* Does that mean me too?"

"It means you too. But we'll have to do it later in the week. I've got some busy days ahead of me."

"The farm?" Maggie queried.

"Oh, yeah, that too. I almost forgot — it's berry-picking time, isn't it? Thank goodness we're ready for it. Doc's got the winnower and rakes all set to go, and we've a truckload of crates from the plant. But that's just part of it. I've also got to find some time to write a column for the newspaper and bake pies for Melody."

"That's right! The café! I forgot about that."

"I almost did too, until Melody called me this morning to make sure the pies were coming on Monday. She says she's counting on me. So is Ben, with the column." She paused, her eyes darting. "Speaking of Ben."

She nodded as he joined them. "Good morning, Maggie, Candy," he said, nodding to each of them in turn. "You look like you've recovered well from last night's excitement."

Maggie rubbed at her shoulder. "Just a

few bruises. Right, Candy?"

Absently Candy's hand went to her throat. She could still feel Bertha's hands wrapped around it, and that morning she had indeed noticed some bruising on her neck. But she nodded. "Right . . . just a few scrapes. But it would have been a lot worse if you hadn't showed up," she told Ben.

He smiled. "I'm just sorry I arrived too late to get in on all the fun."

Candy knew that though they were all speaking of it lightly, those had been some harrowing moments up on the widow's walk of the opera house. Ben was the one who had been driving the car, the one that had swerved and gone up on the sidewalk. Right after Bertha had gone over the side of the building, he had burst through the hatch door, scaring Maggie and Candy half to death. He called the police and an ambulance. The police found Bertha severely wounded from the fall off the roof, and rushed her to the hospital.

"It's just a good thing you showed up when you did," Candy said. "When you swerved and missed Judicious, it was just enough to distract Bertha."

Ben looked at her oddly. "Judicious?"

Candy nodded. "He was standing there under the light, halfway out into the street.

You must have seen him. Isn't that why you swerved the car?"

Ben shook his head. "I heard gunshots. I thought someone was shooting at me."

"You didn't see Judicious?"

Ben gave her an indulgent look. "I'm afraid not. I was alone down there."

"But . . ." Candy looked over at Maggie. "You saw Judicious, right?"

When Maggie didn't respond, Candy pressed her friend. "You saw him, right? You heard him shouting?"

Maggie shrugged. "I might have heard something. I thought you were trying to distract Bertha."

"I was, but . . ."

She saw him then, standing about fifty feet away under a tree, dressed in a black suit with a white shirt and black tie. Judicious F. P. Bosworth. He smiled faintly, gave her a nod. Surprised, she glanced at Maggie, then at Ben. They were both looking at her strangely. "But . . ."

When she looked back at Judicious, he was gone.

She let out a disbelieving laugh. "Well I'll be. Maybe he really can make himself invisible."

Looking concerned, Maggie put a hand to her friend's forehead, as if checking for a fever. "Are you sure you're feeling alright? Maybe you got a bad bump on the head last night."

Candy let out a sigh. "Perhaps you're right."

Just then they heard a horn beep. They turned to see Doc drive up in his old pickup truck, waving through the windshield. As he pulled up beside them, he called out, "Look who's with me!"

It was Ray. He had been formally released from the county jail earlier that morning. Doc had driven up to Machias to give him a ride home.

Ray was overwhelmed with joy as he climbed out of the cab. He immediately dashed to Candy and embraced her. "Doc told me what you did," he said, barely able to contain his emotions. "I can't thank you enough, Miss Candy."

"You don't have to thank me, Ray. That's what friends are for."

"You're the best friend I ever had, Miss Candy."

"Thanks, Ray. That's very sweet."

He glanced up the slope, where Sapphire's grave was being filled in. "I'm sorry I missed it," he said quietly. "I'm sorry she's gone."

"We all are," Candy agreed.

"I'm taking Ray home," Doc said from

the driver's seat. "I just thought we'd stop by and say hello. What do you say, Ray? Ready to see the old place and get back to normal?"

Ray smiled tentatively and bobbed his head. "That sounds good."

He climbed back into the cab, and Maggie glanced at her watch. "I've got to get back to work," she said. "I've got some folks coming in for a meeting in twenty minutes."

They began to disperse then, Ray and Doc driving off, Cameron and Amanda heading to Gumm's, Maggie heading to her office. Soon only Ben and Candy were left standing by their cars.

"Well," he said, "I guess I should get back to work as well." He looked over at her. "How about you? What have you got planned for today?"

Candy shook her head. There was so much to do. But she knew what was at the top of her list. "Well, for one thing, I've got a column to write."

"Oh?" Ben gave her a curious look. "So what are you going to write about?"

Candy stood for a moment, looking back up the hill, then at the departing cars, then back to the tree, where she had seen Judicious standing a few minutes before.

And it struck her then, something Doc

had said to her the day before at the kitchen table. *What do you want to do with your life?* he had asked her.

She hadn't known then, but she knew now. She wanted to stay here, in Cape Willington, with these people. She wanted to run a farm and raise blueberries. She wanted to hang out with Maggie and Cameron and Amanda. She wanted to bake pies and work in Herr Georg's shop.

And she wanted to write columns for Ben.

Tall, handsome, smart, employed Ben.

She looked over at him, batted her eyes, and smiled sweetly. "Oh, I'm sure I'll think of something."

RECIPES

CANDY HOLLIDAY'S BLUEBERRY WHIPPED CREAM

2 cups whipping cream
1/4 cup sugar
2 teaspoons vanilla extract
3/4 cup Maine wild blueberries, mashed

Mix together all ingredients in a deep bowl (it spatters).

Whip with a mixer for 8 to 10 minutes or until it is a nice whipped-cream consistency.

It will be a beautiful shade of lavender.

Candy loves this on fruit, blueberry gingerbread, or any pie.

Refrigerate if you have any leftovers.

HERR GEORG'S BAVARIAN BLUEBERRY PRETZELS

1 package of yeast
1 1/2 cups warm water
1 teaspoon salt

1 tablespoon sugar
1 tablespoon oil
4 cups white or white whole wheat flour
1 cup dried Maine wild blueberries
1 egg
1 teaspoon water
Kosher salt

Preheat oven to 425 degrees.

Dissolve the yeast in the warm water; let sit for 5 minutes.

Add oil to the yeast mixture.

Sift the dry ingredients (salt, sugar, and flour) together and add the sifted ingredients to the yeast mixture.

Add the dried blueberries to the mixture.

Mix together until dough forms.

Put dough on a floured surface and knead until smooth, about 7 minutes.

Divide into 16 sections; roll each into an 8- to 10-inch strip.

Twist the strips into pretzel shapes and place on an ungreased baking sheet.

Mix the egg and 1 teaspoon water.

Brush the pretzels with the egg mixture.

Sprinkle with Kosher salt.

Bake for 12 minutes or until a golden brown.

Makes 16 *wunderbar* pretzels.

BLUEBERRY LEMON SHORTBREAD

2 cups white or white whole wheat flour
1/8 teaspoon salt
1/2 cup dark brown sugar
1/2 tablespoon grated lemon peel
3/4 cup dried Maine wild blueberries
1 cup butter

Preheat oven to 350 degrees.

Mix the flour, salt, sugar, lemon peel, and dried blueberries.

Cut in the butter and mix until crumbly.

Continue mixing until a smooth dough forms.

Chill for 30 minutes.

Roll out the cold dough to 1/2-inch thickness between two sheets of wax paper. Cut out with cookie cutters or score and cut into squares.

Place 1 inch apart on an ungreased cookie sheet.

Bake for 15 to 18 minutes or until lightly browned.

Yield: about two dozen.

BLUEBERRY GINGERBREAD
Soon to be sold at Melody's Café!
1/2 cup butter
1/2 cup dark brown sugar

1 cup molasses
1 egg
2 1/2 cups white or white whole wheat flour
1 teaspoon baking powder
1 teaspoon ginger
1 teaspoon cinnamon
1/2 teaspoon salt
1 1/2 cups Maine wild blueberries (fresh or
   dried blueberries only)
1 cup hot water

Preheat oven to 350 degrees.

In a large bowl, cream together the butter and sugar.

Mix in the molasses.

Stir in the egg.

In a separate bowl, combine the dry ingredients.

Take out 1 1/2 tablespoons of the dry ingredient mixture and add to the blueberries in a measuring cup or small bowl; set aside.

Add the dry ingredients and the hot water alternately to the butter mixture, beating after each addition. Continue beating until mixture is smooth.

Fold in the blueberries.

Pour batter into a greased 8-inch square pan.

Bake for 35 minutes or until a toothpick inserted in the center comes out clean.

The employees of Thorndike Press hope you have enjoyed this Large Print book. All our Thorndike, Wheeler, and Kennebec Large Print titles are designed for easy reading, and all our books are made to last. Other Thorndike Press Large Print books are available at your library, through selected bookstores, or directly from us.

For information about titles, please call:
  (800) 223-1244

or visit our Web site at:
  http://gale.cengage.com/thorndike

To share your comments, please write:
  Publisher
  Thorndike Press
  295 Kennedy Memorial Drive
  Waterville, ME 04901